The Albion Conspiracy

Publisher's Note:
The Albion Conspiracy is a work of fiction. Any resemblance to actual persons, alive or dead, is entirely coincidental.

For
'Mum and Dad'

MICHAEL HEATH

THE ALBION CONSPIRACY

All good wishes

Michael Heath

DESERT ISLAND BOOKS

First published in 2006
by
DESERT ISLAND BOOKS LIMITED
7 Clarence Road, Southend on Sea, Essex SS1 1AN
United Kingdom
www.desertislandbooks.com

© 2006 Michael Heath

The right of Michael Heath to be identified as author of this work has been asserted under The Copyright Designs and Patents Act 1988

British Library Cataloguing-in-Publication Data
A catalogue record for this book is available from the British Library

ISBN 1-905328-19-2

All rights reserved. No part of this book may be reproduced or utilised in any form or by any means, electronic or mechanical, including photocopying, recording or by any information storage and retrieval system, without prior permission in writing from the Publisher

Printed in Great Britain
by
Biddles Ltd, King's Lynn

Prologue

Switzerland

Gavin Bentley smiled with quiet satisfaction. He always found the high Alpine air fresh and invigorating but on such a day as this, when the dazzling early morning sunshine cut through the chill and glinted on the newly fallen snow that painted the peaks for miles around, there was a cleanliness and purity, a sense of everything being new-born and untouched. It was a world of potential; of nascent possibilities; and it seemed to validate his own hopes and vaulted ambition.

He holidayed in Switzerland at least once every season; twice if he could manage it; always staying in the most expensive resorts. His profession, or rather the people who required his services, had accustomed him to limousines, first class hotels and restaurants and the general excesses that accompany status and privilege. It was a life-style he strove to maintain out of working hours and, to the considerable annoyance of his bank manager, took him frequently beyond the limits of his income; but he had never been overly prudent or cautious with money and here in this chic mountain resort, socialising with the wealthy, nothing was further from his mind than the substantial overdraft that awaited his return. His vantage point at the top of the slope afforded a panoramic view and his only thoughts were of the magnificent landscape that stretched to the horizon on all sides and the thrill he felt just being there.

It was a far cry from the family package-holidays of his childhood but he had been bright and his exceptional ability with languages had brought a university scholarship, a first class degree and the upper echelons of the civil service with all the connections that illustrious "club" provides. He was tall and slim with quiet good looks and an acquired self-assurance that enabled him to move with ease amongst the rich and famous. Having watched, and assiduously studied at close proximity, the heads of state, politicians and various dignitaries he continually met, he had not only learned from them but had come to appreciate them for what they really were. He could separate the wheat from the chaff, the real thing from the self-made. Perhaps it was simply a recognition of his own kind when he saw it that exposed the imitations from the genuine article but, more than anything else, it was all about style. He had discovered that people born to money or rank emanate a certain air. They possess a natural confidence and ease that, in itself, opens doors and establishes connections for them wherever they go. Even when he'd seen their money run out or watched them fall from grace, they still managed to survive, calmly riding out one tragedy or scandal after another. They simply behaved as if nothing had changed and, to his amazement, people treated them as though it were true. He envied such arrogant self-confidence but knew it was somehow in-bred and not to be attained by outsiders. It wasn't something one could fake and, after several years of keen observation, he prided himself that he could spot a phoney at fifty paces. That was what made her so intriguing.

He had met her only four days previously but already had to admit that he was enjoying this holiday more than any he had for some time. She had quite literally bumped into him during "happy hour" in the hotel bar and had tipped one of her two cocktails down the front of her dress, where a stream of Pina Colada turned the expensive Gucci green to a rather unpleasant cream. Having apologised profusely for what had clearly not been his fault, he had compensated for the accident by insisting on buying her dinner when she returned from changing her ruined garment. Despite its inauspicious beginning, the evening had been extremely pleasant. Her dark, latin looks and her natural effervescence made her a more than charming dinner companion and she had spoken freely as though he were an old friend rather than a stranger. He had listened with growing interest as she candidly told him her story.

She was French and, so she claimed, of Italian aristocratic descent. Her great grandfather had been a count and made a fortune from engineering. As she blithely put it: "… darling, arms manufacturers are the only people guaranteed to gain from warfare, no matter who wins!" He had survived the end of the second world war with most of his wealth intact and settled in France. As a result, she was now apparently heiress to a considerable fortune. To a man of his strained means it was a most alluring prospect. She was attractive, wealthy and single. It was almost too good to be true; and it probably was, because he didn't believe a word of it.

Her family antecedents may well have been from Italy. The occasional words of Italian she had used in telling her story had been, to his professional ear, genuine in a way that non-native speakers seldom acquire; but there was something missing. For him, that style and ease he had come to understand so well was lacking and not recognisable as the mark of aristocratic breeding. None the less, he found her irresistible. In addition to her physical charms she was intelligent and fun and when, two nights later, she had taken him to her bed, she had proved a willing and enthusiastic lover.

What did it matter if she was feigning some romantic nonsense of wealth and gentry? Wasn't he also guilty of pretence, always studiously avoiding mention of his own background and humble beginnings? Whatever the truth of her might be, he simply didn't care.

She waved to him from her position some hundred metres down the slope to let him know she was ready. She had insisted on a race with the loser paying for dinner that evening, complete with champagne. He was an excellent and experienced skier so, in deference to her lesser abilities, they had agreed a handicap start. He checked the clamps that held his boots to his skis, took a deep breath of the air that he loved so well and waved his arm above his head to signal her to begin. As she energetically took off, he pulled his goggles down firmly over his eyes and set his arms in readiness.

"The champagne is on you, chérie!" he declared with a laugh and, pushing down into the crisp snow, sped after her.

She was quite an adept skier but had none of the grace and technique he had learned over the years. He decided to let her keep ahead for most of the distance and then to make his move on the last part of the run. He knew exactly where the slope would allow him to pick up extra speed and it would be no problem to overtake her just a few metres from the finish. He had at first considered letting her win, but a champagne dinner, particularly in this part of the world, was an extremely expensive prize so he had decided on a close finish with her picking up the wooden spoon and the bill for the meal. He grinned as he crouched lower to accelerate, enjoying the cool wind-rush across his face and comfortably and easily following her every manoeuvre as she carved her way down the piste.

About a third of the way down the slope there were some shrubs and a clump of small conifers on the inside of the curve as the main track weaved into a left-hand bend. She steered herself confidently across and sped between the trees and the bushes, looking playfully over her shoulder to him as she re-joined the main track.

"Racing lines through the corners!", he said to himself. "You are improving, chérie!" and he pushed harder into the snow and gained speed to follow her path.

Even at forty to fifty miles an hour, a good skier's vision is accurate and his reactions are fast but his concentration is geared to the run and not to the surroundings. He was only vaguely aware of a slight movement from somewhere within the conifers and he never saw the hands that gently lifted the steel wire, as it rose from just under the surface of the snow, and fastened it taught some ten inches above the ground between one of the firs and the largest of the green shrubs. For the smallest fraction of a second, as his skis went under it and the wire cut cruelly into his legs, he was aware of the sudden hurtling forward and the loss of control but all quickly became oblivion as his body twisted viciously and bounced, breaking his neck on the first impact.

One

England

"Taniel, have you seen my briefcase?" Alan Russell called impatiently to his wife as he rummaged around the living room.

She appeared at the doorway, calmly holding up the missing briefcase. "It's here. And your notes and itinerary are inside".

He grinned at her. "What would I do without you?"

"You'd manage; but you'd be very disorganised" she said as an affectionate smile broke impishly across her face.

He grabbed the briefcase and, with one arm through his coat and the other struggling to find the remaining sleeve, lowered his head and stole a quick kiss as they hurried into the hallway. Her brown eyes sparkled at him as she held open the front door.

"Drive carefully" she commanded, just as she always did.

"I will" came his standard reply and he stepped outside and crossed the drive to his Mondeo.

As he turned the key in the ignition he glanced back at her, her petite body leaning against the doorframe. Moroccan by birth, she had jet black hair that she often wore pulled up but that now hung lose around her shoulders and delicately framed her olive-skinned face. He still found her as attractive as he had when they'd first met and genuinely missed her company when his work took him away for any extended period. He smiled and blew her another kiss as he put the car into gear and pulled out of the drive and onto the road.

Luciano Pavarotti effortlessly finished the final cadenza of *Una Furtiva Lagrima* as, ninety minutes later, Russell dropped the Mondeo into second gear and accelerated onto the M11. His CD collection showed an eclectic taste in music but he found operatic arias relaxing for motorway driving and aimlessly hummed along as the Italian virtuoso began *La Donna è Mobile*.

The weekend in prospect had come as something of a surprise but was none the less a welcome change from the meeting he had been due to attend at the Ministry of Agriculture. He found it hard to disguise his boredom with the endless wrangling that was always part of discussions on E.U. quotas and subsidies and a pleasant weekend in Cambridge was a far more enjoyable proposition. It was also a form of promotion.

Now thirty-eight, Russell had been with the department just over twelve years. An amiable, easy-going man, he was good at his job and popular with his colleagues. His progress had been steady, if unspectacular, and he was content with his lot. It was typical of his approach to life in general. He was nobody's fool but would never be one of life's movers and shakers; he had his own beliefs and convictions, and could not easily be swayed by the tide of opinion, but would never be leading the cavalry charge. He was a confirmed moderate; a fully paid-up member of the middle ground.

His natural linguistic ability had been the saving grace of what would otherwise have been an average academic career and it was a short step across town from London University to Whitehall. He had toyed with the idea of the Diplomatic Corps but, whilst the travel possibilities appealed, he found politics to be generally devious, frequently unjust and often demanding of a ruthless ambition that he simply didn't possess. So he had opted for the Civil Service and the department of interpreters and linguists.

The section was large but always had more applicants than vacancies so the competition was keen and only the best were accepted. Even so, one spent the first few years translating everything from obscure government pamphlets on how visiting tourists should reclaim their v.a.t. to instruction manuals for generators en route to the third world. Eventually one progressed from "scribing" to "vocals", as they were known in the trade, and began attending meetings, functions and foreign visits as an on-the-spot interpreter. There was still a pecking order of course and the plum jobs, the high security assignments to attend heads of state and royalty, were reserved for those of senior rank but Russell was more than satisfied. He enjoyed his work, it was well paid, he met interesting people and another couple of years would see him established amongst the higher grades and the top jobs. This unexpected trip to Cambridge was a bonus; one of the occasional prestige duties that he'd been getting more often of late and, as the motorway stretched before him under the grey November sky, he eased the car into top gear and contentedly drummed his fingers on the steering wheel in time with

Verdi's jaunty theme.

He'd been summoned early that morning by Ramsey, his immediate superior, whose tone, as ever, had been archetypal Civil Service. "Ah, Alan dear boy. You'll be pleased to hear that you can forget the Min. of Ag. meeting about the contretemps with our French cousins. We'd like you to proceed A.S.A.P. to Cambridge where, due to the indisposition of the present incumbent, you are to take over at an international conference." Ramsey had an annoying habit of issuing instructions like an office memo. He continued: "Hotel's booked for tonight; press call tomorrow; conference ends Monday. Any problems?"

Russell had barely had time to return home and pack a bag. That was one of the problems of living out of town but he and Taniel had decided it was worth it. It was one of the many changes they had made in the last eighteen months since, to the surprise of all their friends, she had finally ended his confirmed bachelorhood and they had married.

Few women would have described him as particularly handsome or especially attractive but his fair hair, purposeful face and warm blue eyes had never left him long without the attention of the opposite sex and he'd had more than his fair share of girlfriends before Taniel arrived on the scene. But she had been different; it wasn't just her nationality and culture, it was the whole relationship that was like nothing he had known before. Everything had simply felt right; exactly as it should be; and he'd easily settled into becoming a couple like slipping into comfortable, familiar shoes – it was just a perfect fit. Soon it had seemed tacitly understood that this was going to be a permanent relationship and, to his own amazement, it was something he wanted. Formalising it by marriage had just been the next natural step along the way.

The move from London had been a tougher decision but Russell had no regrets. The peace and quiet of the countryside was worth the occasional frantic journey and, in any case, the unpredictable nature of his work and the changes it brought to his routine was one of the main reasons it appealed to him so much. He enjoyed the variety. As the car sped past the bank of England printing works at Debden, he slowed to a steady seventy and, turning down the volume on Pavarotti, settled back in his seat to once again turn his mind to the details of Ramsey's brief.

The World Health Organisation was deeply concerned about the relentless spread of the A.I.D.S. virus in Africa. Whilst it was still a major problem in other areas of the world, the developed nations had at least managed to organise and co-ordinate their services to confront the disease but in Africa it was outrunning all attempts to contain it. The W.H.O. had drawn up plans for a united defence against the epidemic and the European Union had agreed to fund both new research and additional on-the-ground support, organised jointly by the British Red Cross and the International Médecins Sans Frontières. The campaign would be launched in three stages with an opening conference at the M.S.F. headquarters in Geneva to discuss logistics and delivery of front-line care, one in England to set up and co-ordinate the research programme, and then a much larger event in Paris where the finalised plans would be announced and discussed with the affected African nations. The Geneva seminar had taken place in October and now, one month later, Cambridge was to be the venue for the British gathering. The big coup that the W.H.O. had achieved was the participation of Professor Max Litvinov. The elderly Russian scientist was generally acknowledged to be the world's leading virologist and it was hoped he would direct and lead the main thrust of the research.

To ensure accuracy at such meetings, each party always brought its own linguist. Russell was to act as personal interpreter to Sir Peter Mayer, the leader of the British team. The format at international conferences was always the same; he would translate what was said by his delegate and then listen to check that the reply was accurately repeated by his opposite number across the table. These particular discussions would be hard work because, being tri-partite, he'd have to work in both French and Russian and, above all, they'd be full of medical terminology and jargon. Ramsey's information sheets would set out the main areas of discussion and hopefully prepare him for the more obscure details he was liable to encounter.

The journey was uneventful and he made good time. The console clock read exactly four-thirty as the car approached junction fourteen. From there it was only a couple of miles along the A45 to Impington where he would find the Posthouse hotel.

Russell indicated left, entered the slip road and slowed the Mondeo as it climbed the long slope to the interchange. The early November dusk was beginning to settle as he brought the vehicle to a halt at the large roundabout junction and waited for an oncoming van to pass. He was thinking he would make a hot shower and a shave his first priority after checking-in when the quiet of the moment was shattered by the deafening resonance of steel against steel and he was suddenly unceremoniously jerked forward against the restraint of his seat-belt.

The initial shock lasted only for an instant as the immediate realisation of what had happened angrily replaced the surprise. Cursing loudly, Russell released his seat-belt and opened the car door. He stepped out to find a beige-coloured Ford Focus driven hard into the rear of his vehicle and a young woman sitting behind the wheel. The expression on her face was a strange mixture of surprise and helplessness.

He stood in silence and looked at the damage. He was amazed to find that such a loud impact had resulted in only minor injury to his car. The number plate was cracked and the bumper dented but there appeared to be little else to show for the collision. The Focus, however, was a different story. Russell's Mondeo had a tow-bar affixed to the rear that protruded in a small V shape and terminated in a large steel ball. The other car's radiator was impaled upon it and the small river of rusty, dark-green coolant that was leisurely flowing back towards the motorway showed it had penetrated deeply.

Russell went to the now open window of the offending car to confront the apologetic face of its occupant.

"I'm very sorry" she said at once. "I didn't see you. It's my fault. I'm so sorry." She spoke with a slight Russian accent.

Had she been a man, he later wondered, would he have acted differently? Would he have angrily demanded "What do you mean, you didn't see me? Were you driving with your eyes closed? How the hell can you not see what's directly in front of you?" But she was a woman and clearly shaken and embarrassed. Some fundamental, protective male instinct arose within him and, his anger somewhat appeased by the apparent lack of serious damage to his vehicle, he found himself merely nodding resignedly and calmly asked her:

"Are you hurt?"

"No, no, I'm fine. I'm just cross with myself for being so stupid! It's driving on the other side that does it. You'd think I'd be used to it by now but I still hate roundabouts. I was so busy remembering to look to the right that I didn't see you stop. I do apologise."

She opened the door and got out to inspect the results of her handiwork. Russell estimated her to be around twenty-eight or twenty-nine years of age. Her face was very appealing. She had large, bright hazel eyes and auburn hair that fell in soft layers to her shoulders. Her cheek bones were high and framed a gentle mouth that distorted into a grimace as she saw the damage.

"Oh dear. It seems to have been quite a bang, doesn't it?"

Russell bent down for a closer look.

"Well my car's not too bad but your radiator is a bit of a mess."

"Yes, I can see. And it isn't even mine; it's a hire car. I hope there won't be too much trouble."

She was wearing a large grey anorak that she hugged about her against the cold. Russell was beginning to feel a little sympathy.

"I'm sorry but I'll have to ask you to exchange details, I'm afraid."

"Yes, of course. All the documents are in the glove compartment." She went back into the vehicle to retrieve them as she spoke. "Do you think we could patch it up? Just to do a couple of miles? I don't have far to go."

He shook his head. In the first place he was not dressed for roadside repairs and had no intention of delving through oil and dirt to find the true extent of the damage. In the second place, the ever increasing flood of coolant told him that the leak was substantial and the radiator would soon be empty.

"I'm afraid not. If you attempt to drive it in this condition you'll write off the whole engine."

She shrugged in reluctant acceptance. "I thought you'd say that."

She looked tentatively at him as though she were trying to find the right words to use.

"Look, I know I shouldn't ask this, especially as it's all my fault, but it's getting dark and ..." tilting her head slightly, she smiled in open acknowledgement that he knew what was coming next. "Do you think I cold impose on you for a lift?" Then she swiftly added "I'm not going far; just to my hotel. It's fairly close."

Her breath misted in front of her as she spoke and standing there in the fading light, alongside her stricken car with her shoulders hunched against the cold, Russell's compassion for her obvious plight finally dismissed all traces of his annoyance.

He grinned. "Well I can hardly leave you stranded here, can I?"

Her smile broadened with gratitude and relief.

"Thank you. You're a knight in shining armour!"

"Well my charger's a little bruised and battered but it seems to have survived your attack. So climb aboard."

Thanking him profusely, she gathered her bags and transferred them to his car.

Seating himself behind the wheel of the Focus, Russell eased off the handbrake and allowed the incline and the weight of the vehicle to gradually roll it backwards and disentangle itself from his own. He then steered it as high onto the grass verge as the momentum of the freewheeling would allow and, his Good Samaritan act complete, left it to its fate.

"This is very kind of you," she said gratefully as he sat next to her and fastened his seat-belt. "Especially after I damaged your car."

"Please don't keep apologising; what's done is done".

"My name is Nina, by the way," she offered.

"Alan. Alan Russell."

"Pleased to meet you Alan Russell." She smiled at him. "And I'm sorry it was not under better circumstances."

Russell returned the smile and steered the Mondeo onto the Cambridge road and into the dark grey shades of the fading day,.

"Where exactly are you heading?" he asked.

"The Posthouse. Do you know it?"

"I'm going there myself."

Her eyes widened in surprise. "That's perfect! Then I haven't put you out too much."

Russell laughed. "No, you haven't put me out at all. Not if you discount denting the back of my car."

"Oh I'm sorry, I didn't mean ..."

"It's alright," he interrupted her. "I'm only teasing and no, you are not taking me out of my way. Are you here for the Cambridge conference?"

"Yes" she said, a little taken aback. How did you know that?"

"Well, your accent and the hotel made it a fair bet."

"Of course. One never thinks of oneself having an accent but it must be the first thing people notice. Yes, I'm here for the conference. I'm covering it for my magazine; I'm a journalist. Are you involved at all?"

"I'm with the British group".

"Really? I'm sorry, I don't remember you from Geneva."

"That's because I wasn't there. One of them went sick and I'm the replacement. In fact I only knew about it myself this morning. It's very much a last-minute affair."

"So you are a medical man?"

"No. I'm a linguist. I'm here to interpret."

Once again her face broke into a smile of surprise. "No! Viy Gavareetye pa Ruske?" she asked him.

"Da, kanyeshna; and also French and German but Russian is my main work."

"Wonderful! I couldn't have found a better victim for my driving if I'd tried."

They both laughed. Russell looked across at her sparkling eyes and it was only at that moment that he was struck by just how attractive she was.

The Posthouse was only a short distance from their impromptu meeting and it seemed like no time at all before Russell was driving through the hotel's gateway. They had made small talk and the occasional reference to the coming weekend's business but he really knew nothing more than that she worked for a monthly Moscow magazine called *The Russia Journal*, had covered the Geneva conference and would be in Paris in January.

He followed the long drive that wound its way around the hotel and into the parking area where he brought the car to a final halt. As he switched off the engine she turned to him.

"Alan, I can't tell you how grateful I am. As soon as we've registered I'm going to buy you a drink."

"I'll hold you to that" he said with a smile and gathered their luggage from the rear of the vehicle.

The obviously busy receptionist greeted them with a polite "Good evening", that was more efficient than well meant, as Russell put down his bags.

"Hello. I have a reservation. My name is Russell and this is Miss ..." he paused and waited for her to provide the surname he realised he had not yet learned.

"Petrova. Nina Petrova. I also have a reservation."

They had been allocated rooms on opposite sides of the hotel so, having completed their registration, Russell asked for a porter to carry Nina's luggage. As he bent to pick up his own bags she held up a restaurant menu that was lying on the counter.

"Look, they serve dinner from seven-thirty. Why don't we freshen up and settle in and then meet in the bar around seven? We can have that drink I promised and then I can buy you dinner."

"That sounds very pleasant but I haven't even looked at my notes yet."

"But you have to eat!"

"I was going to have something sent to my room so I could work and ..."

She spoke before he could finish.

"I promise not to keep you too late. And, after all that's happened, it would make me feel *much* better."

Her eyes widened and she titled her head slightly as she tentatively added "please?" It was genuine charm rather than flirting and Russell couldn't help the grin that broke across his face.

"How can I refuse?"

"Wonderful. See you in the bar". She turned and followed the porter across the lobby. As Russell made his way to his own room, he found he was humming to himself.

Sitting in the corner of the reception lounge, a dark-haired man in a navy blue blazer lowered his copy of *The Times* and followed Nina with his eyes as the porter held open the door for her and they disappeared into the corridor. Running the crease of the folded paper deliberately between his finger and thumb, he dropped it casually onto the coffee table beside him. He reached into his pocket, took out his cell phone and tapped in a number, looking around him to check that no one was within earshot as he waited for the call to connect.

"Yes?" enquired the voice in his ear curtly.

"He's here. Just checked in".

"And her?"

"Yes. They arrived together."

"Huh, doesn't waste time, does she?" enquired the voice in an almost complimentary tone. "Very well, I'll leave tomorrow morning. Organise lunch, will you? Around one'ish."

The line clicked off abruptly.

"Certainly, sir" said the dark-haired man with mock subservience and quietly flipped closed his cell phone before picking up *The Times* and returning to his half-completed crossword.

Two

Germany

The outside temperature at Berlin Tegel had dropped to a chilling minus four by the time the disembodied voice of the airport public address system gave the final call for Air Berlin's flight AB8294 to London Stansted. As the last of the embarking passengers disappeared from sight, a small party exited the VIP suite and crossed to the departure gate. The large digital clock on the far wall read exactly seventeen-fifteen.

The security guard who stood at the exit doorway quietly nodded to the tall man leading the group to indicate that all other passengers were now on the aircraft. Returning the guard's nod, the tall man handed five boarding passes to the smiling stewardess and ushered his party through the gate and into the walkway that led to the waiting Fokker 100 jet. As the young girl who welcomed them aboard led his four companions along the aisle to their seats, the tall man paused at the doorway.

His physical appearance was something of an enigma. Despite his height and lean frame, he had long ago learned the art of merging with the crowd, inconspicuous and unnoticed. Yet, when the need arose, his decisive manner and the piercing stare that could flash menacingly from behind his square-rimmed glasses gave him a commanding and almost sinister presence that no one could ignore. Those same eyes were now cast quickly around the aircraft's one hundred seats and their occupants, registering every detail and missing nothing. In principle, scheduled flights were always a high risk but at least a small-scale operation like this was preferable to large jets and passing through airports like Heathrow. He had broken their journey from Moscow and changed planes at Berlin specifically to avoid London's major airport and travel in this smaller aircraft to land at Stansted. He'd had the passenger list checked as a matter of course and had also received a run-down of the crew. His face, as always, registered nothing and his impassive expression didn't alter as he noted the passenger who sat reading in the last aisle-seat on the right-hand side.

He followed the others through the cabin to where the stewardess turned to face him and indicated his seat with a polite "Mr. Gurevich".

Dimitri Gurevich was forty-six years old and had been in the security service for over twenty of those years. His parents had been staunch party members and enrolled him into the youth section at the age of twelve. He had become a police cadet as soon as he reached the minimum entry age, and his progress in the Party had been mirrored in his career. His quick wits, natural resilience and devotion to the cause not only earned him promotion but brought him to the attention of a particular kind of talent scout; by the time he was twenty-four he'd been channelled into the intelligence services and found himself training at Loubianka in Moscow, where the old Russian Insurance Company building then housed the headquarters of the K.G.B.

The coming of Gorbachev had heralded a new and, to the faithful, uncomfortable era. The so-called openness of Glasnost and Perestroika had threatened to destabilise and divide the organisation; but those who hold the secret keys to the store know how to protect and preserve the family business. They had survived. They lived through Yeltsin and then the struggles to oust him and, once the dust had settled, quietly regrouped. The names and places were different of course – the organisation was now called the Federal Security Service and was known as the F.S.B. – but the captains of old were still at the helm. The regime of Putin, himself an ex K.G.B. officer, was slowly bringing back the discipline and the hard line of earlier times and those like Gurevich, who had remained stalwart throughout, were now part of the elite and among the favoured few.

His field duty in both London and Berlin had proved him to be one of the service's most successful operatives and four years previously, after an abnormally long and successful "active" period, he had been recalled to Moscow where he now held the rank of Colonel. These days his work was all done from behind a desk but, on occasion, he would receive a request from above to handle something personally, and so it was that he found himself on a plane bound once again for England.

Above all else, Gurevich was a professional. In prolonged active service he'd developed instincts and an insight that were virtually infallible. His life had depended on such perceptions and he couldn't afford to be wrong. It was those very instincts that made him slightly uneasy as the

Fokker's powerful twin Rolls Royce Tay engines lifted the plane off the runway.

To all intents and purposes it was a straightforward assignment. He had been instructed to escort the ageing scientist who sat next to him to three A.I.D.S. conferences in Geneva, Cambridge and Paris. Outwardly it was to be a low-key affair; just the professor and his assistant, an interpreter and one of Gurevich's own men to accompany him; but such everyday security was the routine work of the service and was never allotted to one of Gurevich's rank and experience. No explanation had been offered, just the insistence that it must appear a small affair, involving no more than the specified personnel and, above all, the order to handle it personally. This inoffensive little scientist was clearly of extreme importance to them. What wasn't clear was *why*?

Gurevich knew better than to question such requests from higher up but, at his briefing session, had tried to gather more information. It had been a waste of time. They were disclosing nothing.

He had continued to make discrete enquiries but had gleaned only very little. When A.I.D.S. had first manifested as a major international threat, the old Soviet Union had publicly denied it was a problem. It had been designated a disease of the decadent West, spread by homosexuals, drug addicts and prostitutes and, as these were not officially tolerated under the old regime, it could not be admitted as relevant. By 1986, when European nations were in the midst of major, country-wide advertising campaigns to promote awareness, only twelve cases had been officially acknowledged within the old U.S.S.R. The problem was compounded because a government can hardly issue advice to needle-sharing addicts, whores and promiscuous gay men when it denies their very existence. Unofficially it had been a different story and research had continued apace. It had centred, principally, around the man now sitting next to Gurevich, Professor Max Litvinov. Now that the new Russia was able to acknowledge his work, the old man had become a major figure in the world's scientific community.

The stewardess appeared at his seat and politely asked what he would like to drink. Gurevich ordered a gin and tonic for himself and a glass of orange juice for his companion.

He looked at the small, benign-looking man with the sparse, unruly white hair who had quietly nodded off to sleep. The one thing he knew for certain was that Litvinov was very important to his masters. So, ever cautious, Gurevich had decided on a little extra insurance and the passenger at the rear of the plane, innocuously browsing the in-flight magazine, was one of his own men. In addition, ahead of them in England, he had two operatives who had been checking people and places for the last month and who would be close at hand throughout the next three days.

It was a clear contradiction of his orders and, a few years ago, would have been unthinkable to him; but Dimitri Gurevich had changed. The motivation of his youth had given way to a fair degree of cynicism and he saw himself now as simply a man with a job to do. This particular job was not to his liking but, so far, had provided no upsets. The Geneva conference had gone smoothly and he had no reason to suppose this trip to England would be any more of a problem. He had been his usual thorough self and his team, as always, was working well. His masters had given him a high-security assignment with inadequate information and a low-security profile. Such a situation went against his instincts and he'd gamble on his instincts every time against directives from above. If there were repercussions, he'd face them when they arrived. In the meantime his priority was the job in hand.

The stewardess arrived with their drinks. He sipped his gin and tonic and left the orange juice on the pull-down tray in front of the Professor, deciding not to wake his sleeping companion. In seventy-two hours they'd be on their way home and his mission would be accomplished.

* * * * *

France

The bomb went off at exactly 6.03pm. The dull thud of the distant blast had been heard as far away as the Pont de la Concorde in the south and the Rue Fontaine to the north. It had been strapped underneath a Fiat Uno that was parked outside a subsidiary office of American Airlines and the blast from the ninety pounds of explosive had wrought its intended havoc with devastating effect. The whole of the front of the building's ground floor had been blown out. Another device had been similarly planted some distance away outside the American Express bureau but somewhere in the great cosmos of religious ideologies, where various Deities are beseeched to lend their name to acts of fanaticism, one of them chose to smile on Paris that cold evening and the second bomb failed to go off.

Henri LeBec wasn't so sure he believed in any God. He sat uneasily in the back of the Peugeot and stared intently at the city that flashed past him as the car, its siren wailing as if keening for the atrocity that had been unleashed, sped through the busy streets of the French capital.

It could have been any one of them he thought; any shop or office-building; a metro station or a crowded restaurant or bar. How could the bastards be so indiscriminate? If there was a God, how He could create monsters capable of perpetrating such outrages was beyond the reasoning of this particular French detective.

LeBec was a career policeman. Although of only average build, he was a strong character with a square, determined jaw and his face, bearing the world-weary lines of a first-hand knowledge and experience of violence, gave him a concentrated and stern expression with which few chose to quarrel. His blue, compassionate eyes could turn instantly to steel and many an adversary had thought twice before risking the wrath that they suddenly promised. If LeBec was unsure of the existence of a deity, he had a very genuine belief in law and order. He'd sought to make what he saw as his contribution with a dedication to the job that had earned the respect of his peers and promotion through the ranks of the Police Judiciare to Chief Inspector.

Several years in the serious crimes squad had, he thought, hardened him to most of the atrocities of which the human race, or at least its lowest members, were capable; but now, at forty-nine years old, he was assistant head of the anti-terrorist unit and discovering a whole new world of horrors within the capacity of man. He was mentally preparing himself for just such a sight as the car tore out of the Rue Daunou and across the Boulevard des Capucines where the early evening drinkers sat calmly in cafés with their wines and aperitifs, blissfully unaware that death had passed within a whisker of their warm seclusion. The Peugeot swerved into the Rue Scribe and LeBec glanced at his watch. It was

6.24pm.

There were five ambulances parked in the street, their flashing lights strangely illuminating the dark of the cold night. The eerie shades of blue flickered callously over the gruesome scene and the faces of the bustling mêlée that confronted the car as it screeched to a halt. Sergeant Nicot, a squat, overweight man in a grey raincoat, hurried towards the Peugeot as LeBec climbed out of the vehicle.

"How bad is it Paul?" he asked the approaching sergeant.

"Could be a lot worse. Only one outright fatality; two very serious and one that will probably be D.O.A. by the time they reach hospital. The rest are nearly all flying-glass injuries. Some are quite nasty, but they'll live."

They walked briskly towards the waiting scene of carnage as LeBec continued to question his harassed sergeant, their footsteps accompanied by an ominous chorus of crunching glass as they walked through the millions of fragments that were all that remained of the office's glazed frontage and the windows of surrounding buildings.

"How many were inside when it went off?"

"Fortunately only three. The other two regular staff had already left."

"Find them. Straight away. I want them brought in for questioning immediately. They may have seen someone parking the car and I want them while it's still fresh in their minds."

The plump man nodded. "There's not much left of the place itself. Thank God it wasn't a couple of hours earlier; we'd have had far more casualties."

"I don't think they'd have risked it earlier. Illegally parking in a crowded street can attract too much attention. My guess is that it was left no more than fifteen or twenty minutes before the explosion. If I'm right, there's a good chance the staff may remember something."

A large crowd had gathered and was being held back by several gendarmes while the medical teams tended to the many wounded. A child was crying loudly and being comforted by its mother. Somehow the little girl had escaped unhurt but the mother's left eye was being heavily bandaged against the large flow of blood that ran across her cheek, down her neck and ballooned across the top of her raincoat in a dark, grim stain.

LeBec stopped and bent down to where a standard-issue grey blanket lay unceremoniously over a body. He pulled back the covering and looked at the face. It couldn't have been more than twenty-two or twenty-three years old. The detective wondered where the young man had come from; whether there was still someone waiting for him at home, still unaware that he was no longer part of this world and that he would never be returning home again; that there would be no chance to say a goodbye; no fond farewells or good wishes; no chance to acknowledge feelings or the good times that had been; at one swift and irrevocable stroke, all had been extinguished.

Lying a little way from the body was a glasses case. It was twisted and bent yet close beside it the glasses themselves lay completely unscathed; not even a scratch to the lenses. Although he'd seen similar things before, LeBec shook his head in mute surprise. Blast was a strange phenomenon. He'd known people killed some thirty metres from an explosion whilst others, standing almost on top of it, had survived with virtually no injury. It was this haphazard, indiscriminate nature of the killing that angered him more than the suffering itself.

This was the first incident for four months. The summer had seen one small-scale explosion outside the warehouse of an American-owned freight company, which had damaged the building but hurt no one, and a letter bomb sent to the American embassy which had been detected by their screening process and rendered harmless. They were clearly the amateurish efforts of a small group and LeBec's department had found and arrested two of them within less than a fortnight. This was different. It was of a much bigger order and the slight knot in his stomach told him there was a good deal more to come.

The supposed logic of it evaded him. France had been against the invasion of Iraq, for God's sake. Hadn't Chirac stood up and said so? Hadn't he condemned the Americans and the Brits and refused them his support? So why a campaign against them on French soil, killing innocent Parisians in the process? What worried LeBec even more was that this had the hallmarks of a cold detachment. This was not a suicide bombing; not some fanatic, with his package of death strapped to his waist, walking into an "infidel" crowd and blowing them to hell while he claimed his right to paradise with seven virgins to wait upon his pleasure. This bomber intended to survive; intended to return to fight another day. This was a planner; a thinker who undertook his perverted sense of justice with a clinical precision. To find them this time was going to be no easy task.

"Have they claimed responsibility yet?" asked the sergeant as his chief carefully replaced the blanket over the dead man and slowly rose to his feet.

LeBec shook his head. "Not yet. But they will."

Their attention was taken by a sudden shout of "Henri! Henri!" They looked across the road to the crowd that had ghoulishly gathered to watch the scene and saw a young man waving at them from behind the outstretched arms of a burly gendarme. LeBec nodded his assent and the constable allowed the man through the cordon.

"Doesn't take the vultures long to arrive, does it?" said Nicot sardonically.

"Thanks, Henri" the young man offered gratefully as he reached the two policemen. "Is it as bad as it looks?"

Bernard Gillet was a freelance reporter whose principle field was crime. Bright, intuitive and with a natural chutzpah that would not have shamed a market barrow-boy, he moved easily between the haunts and watering holes of the more dubious members of society and the forces of law that were frequently pursuing them. Back in his days with the serious crime squad, LeBec had periodically found him a useful alternative when his conventional sources of information dried up. In return, Gillet had been allowed the odd exclusive story or the occasional tip in advance of an official press release. It was an arrangement that, despite a healthy caution, had established a trusting relationship between the two. Even as his right hand took LeBec's in handshake, his left lifted the Minolta from around his neck and he began snapping freely at the tragic scene of destruction; his eye concerned with the framing and editorial value of his subject, his mind well practised at ignoring the pain and suffering it represented.

"You didn't waste much time in getting here, Bernard."

"Just lucky. I was in the Rue La Fayette when the ambulances went screaming by." He continued shooting as he spoke, anxious to capture as much as he could before the injured were taken away. "I knew it must be big if it needed five."

He paused for a moment and looked at the detective.

"I suppose it *is* The Lions of God?"

"Yes. Not official yet; but it's them alright. They planted another one up the road at the Amex office but it didn't go off. Our boys dismantled it."

The two men entered what was left of the office. The twisted structure of what had been the frontage outlined the scene like some macabre picture frame, a grotesque border to the black and hollow interior that had been so bright and alive just a short while before.

"So it's starting up again" said Gillet soberly. Is it a new cell?"

"Looks like it".

"Can you survive that?" I mean, if it's kicking off again, especially with Christmas coming, people are going to be asking questions. Where was our intelligence? Why didn't we see it coming?"

"I'm a policeman, not a psychic. I got them before and I'll get them again. It's just a question of time."

Gillet wasn't really listening to the answer. He had long ago learned that it was not what people said that counted but rather how they said it. His reporter's instinct was checking for signs; something in the detective's manner that might reveal his true feelings; how confident or concerned he really was. He pressed the point.

"That's all very well for you to say. You're not slipping in the popularity polls like our illustrious President. Are you getting pressure from above? Will there be a new approach; more money; more men?"

It was just another couple of moves in their eternal chess game; the probing, the parrying, the thought behind the move behind the real intention that would later follow. LeBec smiled knowingly at the young reporter.

"My dear Bernard, I am not concerned with presidential popularity. If Monsieur Chirac wants to earn a few more votes by showering me with money and men, that's fine. But with or without them, I am going to nail these bastards. And when I do, you will be among the first to know."

Gillet's customary impish grin returned to his face. "Can I quote you on that?"

Before LeBec could respond to the redundant question they were interrupted by the return of sergeant Nicot.

"A bit of luck Chief Inspector. We've found both the staff that left early. They're being brought in now."

"Good" said LeBec, turning away from Gillet who, knowing his privileged presence was shortly to end, immediately returned the view finder to his eye and locked the tragic scene into digits that would soon be winging their way around the internet to the world's waiting picture editors.

"I'll head back right away and question them myself. Make sure we have enough men down at the hospital to get statements from everybody; and I mean everybody. I want nothing missed. Let me know as soon as you have anything from the forensic boys here and tell them that the first thing I need is a make on the car, or rather what's left of it."

"And him?" asked his sergeant, with a just detectable trace of disdain in his voice.

"Good night, Bernard" said LeBec in a tone that was all command and no farewell. "Time to make yourself scarce."

"Good night, Henri. And thanks! I owe you one."

"You can bet on it" the detective called over his shoulder, as he walked out of the remains of the building and turned pensively towards his car.

Most of the injured had been taken to hospital and there was now only one ambulance in the street, its team still ministering to the many people with minor cuts and bruises. A television crew had arrived and was frantically setting-up on the other side of the road, desperate to record as much of the grizzly scene as it could before its unfortunate victims were all removed.

LeBec was hoping against hope that the long night's interviews would throw up that one vital clue; the one tiny piece of information that would set him on the right path. As he approached the waiting Peugeot he caught sight of something out of the corner of his eye and stopped. He bent down for a closer look and there, lying in the gutter in a pool of blood, was a small terrier dog. A large shard of glass had penetrated the terrified animal's neck and protruded like some crystal collar. The animal must have been lying there almost half an hour, unnoticed in the chaos that had erupted all around it and that was oblivious to its slowly ebbing life. The dog whimpered weakly in a forlorn plea as LeBec knelt next to it and gently touched its reddened head.

"Steady, fella. Take it easy" he murmured softly.

Somehow, although he didn't know why, it seemed even more pathetic than the injured humans. There was something about a dying dog, that didn't know a terrorist from a tin can, that never knew what defined a country or the borders and boundaries over which mankind waged incessant war and slaughtered itself so enthusiastically, that saddened the hardened policeman more than he could understand. This dumb, whimpering animal spoke more eloquently of the madness and futility of it all than any words he could have found. Gently whispering to it all the while, he picked up the creature and slowly stood, cradling its blood-soaked body in his arms. As he did so there was a bright flash and he turned, startled, to see Bernard Gillet with his camera.

That was the picture that featured in every magazine in Europe.

* * * * *

England

By the time LeBec was walking back through the door of his office to begin the night's work, the traffic controller at Stansted, some two hundred miles to the north, was completing the landing procedure for flight AB8294 from Berlin Tegel. Professor Litvinov had slept throughout the journey and Gurevich had gently woken him when the *fasten seat-belts* sign had illuminated to signal the end of the flight.

The pre-arranged procedure was similar to the boarding arrangements. Gurevich and his four companions would wait until all other passengers disembarked before leaving the aircraft. His incognito man from the rear of the plane, Andrei Melekhin, would make his way through customs and immigration as swiftly as possible and be waiting in the arrivals lounge to cover the party's exit. He would then be met by a contact and together, at a discrete distance, they would tail the official cars into Cambridge. Dimitri Gurevich had no reason to suppose there would be any problems. His meticulous planning would, as ever, be carried out like clockwork; but that didn't stop his field operative's instincts locking smoothly into gear. He sensed the familiar tension imperceptively stiffen his lean frame; the alertness heightened his hearing; his vision seemed to widen a few degrees; even his sense of smell appeared more sensitive and he noted the lilac-scented perfume of the stewardess, bidding them an obligatory farewell, before he was within three metres of her.

The formalities of arrival completed, he led his party through the exit doors and into Stansted's main hall where a small bespectacled man and his somewhat taller lady companion immediately rose from their seats and approached. The diminutive figure spoke loudly and enthusiastically as he hurried across to meet the new arrivals.

"Professor, welcome, welcome! Welcome to England." His musical Welsh tones rose and fell in energetic cadence as he reached out and enthusiastically shook the hand of the elderly scientist who, still slightly sleepy, peered a little indignantly over his glasses at the stranger who was so delighted to see him. "My name is Thomas, David Thomas; and this is Miss Heston whom of course you know."

Gurevich immediately recognised the woman as one of the W.H.O. officials that had been present in Geneva. She welcomed the professor in carefully practised but none the less passable Russian and then, her obligatory attempt at foreign greeting complete, reverted to English as she turned to the taller man.

"Mr Gurevich, how nice to see you again. I hope you all had a good journey?"

He politely took her proffered hand and replied that the flight had been very pleasant but, whilst appearing to direct his gaze towards her, his practised eye was actually taking in the background behind her. Melekhin was seated a few metres away quietly reading a newspaper. The rest of the hall was none too busy; just the normal bustle of an airport. Satisfied that nothing was untoward, he turned his concentration momentarily back to the woman in front of him.

Unlike the animated Welshman who stood smiling incessantly at her side, Barbara Heston had the seasoned air of one who is well used to such encounters and there was a calm authority in her voice as she turned to address the party of newcomers.

"Gentlemen, may I introduce Mr David Thomas, the conference organiser and your host for the next three days."

One by one they were each introduced: the Professor, his colleague Dr Piotr Radischev, Pavel Golombek the interpreter, Gurevich and his assistant Ivan Zhukov. Gurevich and Zhukov were described by the efficient Miss Heston as officials of the Russian health ministry and indeed, despite her many years with the W.H.O., she fully believed they were.

David Thomas led his guests outside to the two waiting Rover cars and their attendant chauffeurs, who were holding open the doors of their vehicles in polite anticipation. Thomas was clutching the professor by the arm and firing-off every word in his extremely limited Russian vocabulary to convey his personal delight at the old man's presence. Barbara Heston caught Gurevich's eye and allowed herself a confidential smile.

"He's a little too enthusiastic I'm afraid, but he's really a very nice man. And very good at his job" she added as an excusing but encouraging afterthought.

"One can never be too friendly, Miss Heston. It's nice to be made so welcome."

"I'm glad you think so" she said as she gestured to the open door of the first Rover and Gurevich slid onto the back seat next to the professor and the still chattering David Thomas. Zhukov made his way to the front of the vehicle and sat himself next to the driver. Barbara Heston got into the second car with the rest of the party and the two shiny black Rovers, their highly polished coachwork glinting with the refection of the building's neon lights, made their way sedately out of the concourse and headed for the motorway.

Less than a minute later, the door of a parked red Vauxhall was opened from the outside and Andrei Melekhin quickly threw his hold-all onto the back seat and climbed inside.

"Let's go" he snapped at the driver and the car pulled away in pursuit of the other two vehicles. "Did you bring it?" he asked as he settled himself down into the vinyl seat.

The driver, a lanky Englishman named Philips whom Gurevich had first recruited in London some twelve years earlier, nodded his head towards the glove compartment.

"What did you do with your own?" he enquired of his new companion.

"It went back on the plane. We both had one hidden under the seat by the life-jacket. We put a man into the ground crew three weeks ago to set it up. We couldn't risk walking through with them. There's no diplomatic cover on this one; it's all unofficial."

As Melekhin spoke he leaned forward and flicked open the glove compartment in front of him. He took out a shoulder-holster, that held a Walther automatic pistol, together with three magazine clips. He removed his jacket and fastened the holster in place.

"That's better. I feel dressed again" he said with a smile as he scanned the motorway in front of them. "Careful. Don't let them get too far ahead."

Philips accelerated and the Vauxhall quickened in pursuit of the red tail lights that glimmered a quarter of a mile or so in front of them and reflected on the wet tarmac where the persistent English drizzle had again started to fall.

Melekhin pulled a fresh packet of duty-free cigarettes from his jacket pocket and offered one to the Englishman, who gratefully accepted it. Relieved that his journey would soon be over and the object of their concern safely delivered to his hotel room for the night, he eased himself back into his seat and slowly blew a languid ring of smoke at the roof of the car.

"Anything to report this end?" he lazily enquired.

"Nothing out of the ordinary. Everything looks fine."

"What about the new interpreter on the British team?"

Philips shook his head and exhaled a large puff of smoke of his own. "Seems fine. Enquiries have thrown up nothing at all so far. His name's Russell. Alan Russell. We're still checking but he looks to be ok. The genuine article."

The Russian nodded a satisfied approval. As he did so, he took the Walther from under his left arm, and quietly but very precisely checked it over.

"Good" he said. "That's what we want. No hiccups; no problems. Just a nice quiet English country weekend." He replaced the weapon in its holster and slowly re-buttoned his jacket. "Let's hope that's exactly what we get."

* * * * *

While he was being discussed by her fellow countryman newly arrived from Berlin, Alan Russell was fully occupied with the particular Russian sitting opposite him. Her eyes now bore the subtlest addition of a little make-up and the serviceable but shapeless anorak had been exchanged for a stylish cocktail dress of midnight blue that stressed the line of her breasts and the curve of her trim waist. More than one head had turned as she'd crossed the hotel lobby to the bar and Russell couldn't deny the distinct pleasure he'd felt to know it was to him that she was heading. Their conversation had been relaxed and easy and they'd finished a couple of Martinis before making their way into the hotel's restaurant.

His job had accustomed Russell to meeting strangers. He was very good at small talk and keeping a conversation going but he needed no such devices with this dinner companion. He found her absorbing and interesting and the time flew by unnoticed as he learned more about her. She'd been born in Moscow of an English mother and a Russian father whose minor position in a government department had entitled them to a standard of living that, whilst far from high, was none the less above the meagre existence of the average Russian worker.

"My parents divorced when I was twelve and mother went back to England. It was fairly acrimonious and there was a great deal of wrangling but eventually my father was granted custody." She laughed. "Poor poppa. He did his best, but coping with a head-strong teenage daughter was way beyond him. I think he was quite relieved when my holidays with mother grew longer and longer. I loved England. So much that, during my University course, I tried for and eventually was granted a year at L.S.E. as an exchange student. It was while I was there that I sent a few pieces I'd written back home. "A Russian student's view of London," that sort of thing. It was hardly inspiring stuff but the magazine must have liked it because it was published and they wanted more. Eventually I was spending more time writing than studying and by the time I went home and scraped through my degree there was a job waiting for me."

As she told her story, relaxed, confident and with such vitality shining in her eyes, Russell could well imagine the difficulties her father had in denying her anything.

"Was that with *The Russia Journal?*" he asked.

"No." She smiled and shook her head dismissively. "Far less grand. It was a small arts periodical. I outgrew it rather quickly and went straight into freelancing, although I tend to work mostly for the R.J. My real interest is political coverage but I spend a good deal of time reporting gossip about your Royal family or the latest scandal involving movie stars. I'm afraid journalism is like any other job, it's the bread-and-butter stuff that pays the rent."

She shrugged and raised her eyebrows a little in resignation. A small crease formed in the curve of her chin and Russell wondered why he noticed it.

"Still, I'm not complaining," she continued. "And the occasional bit of jam like this conference is a bonus."

"Are you based in London?"

"Yes. I rent a flat in Chelsea. The cheaper part, of course. It's as easy to cover European cities from London as anywhere else and England is like a second home to me. So here I am!"

"I don't suppose you see much of your father, then?"

"Actually I saw him last week. He's quite elderly now and I don't get to visit as much as I should so it was good to spend a few days with him. In fact I'd only been back twenty-four hours before I set out for here and … " she smiled and feigned a sheepish look "bumped into you. You'd think I'd be well accustomed to driving on the left by now but even after a *short* trip home I'm in trouble!"

They laughed. As he looked at her across the table, relaxed and clearly enjoying their evening together, he realised that he too felt totally at ease in her company and was likewise finding great pleasure in spending time with her. The Russian character had always appealed to him; the undercurrent of melancholy that ran through the art and music, literature and poetry that he'd studied as part of learning the language had always attracted him but it was the indomitable soul that shone through it all that really struck a chord; the sense that, no matter how great the adversity, the human spirit would ultimately triumph. He felt a kinship with it and had always enjoyed his time in the country and being among its people. So it was natural, he told himself, that he should feel equally at home and comfortable with Nina. Yet there was something about her that was different. He wasn't sure what it was and it intrigued him. In her turn, she seemed to find him no less interesting and wanted to know all about him.

He told her of his background, his marriage to Taniel and about his life generally; but it was his work that provided them with the most common ground and that she seemed to find particularly absorbing.

He poured them each another coffee from the cafetière that had been brought to the table. The bottle of Chablis had long since been exhausted and removed. Her elbows resting on the table, Nina held the cup between the fingers of both hands and brought it delicately to rest just below her chin as she looked across at Russell through the slight steam that was rising from the hot liquid.

"If you are covering Cambridge, I don't understand why you weren't in Geneva" she said gently. "I thought consistency of personnel was important."

"It is. My predecessor should have be working on all three conferences but he must have been taken ill or something. I was sent-for first thing this morning and told he was indisposed and that they'd like me to take over immediately. So here I am."

She took a small sip of coffee and raised her eyes to gaze at him over the cup.

"Well, I don't wish the gentleman any harm but I'm glad he couldn't make it."

Unsure how to take the obvious compliment, Russell merely replied "Thank you. So am I" but he was unsettled by the remark. Her tone had been slightly hushed and, whilst not exactly seductive, was none the less loaded and had taken him by surprise. Before he could decide whether or not she was seriously flirting with him, the moment was interrupted by the voice of the waiter who had attended them during their meal.

"Excuse me sir, but will that be all or is there something else I can get you?"

Russell looked up and was amazed to see that all the other tables were empty and they were alone in the restaurant.

"Perhaps you'd like to take a drink in the lounge, sir?" the waiter enquired optimistically, clearly hoping he could finish for the night and go home.

A few minutes later Russell and Nina were in front of the lounge's large open fireplace where two burning logs gave out a warm glow and sent their welcoming flames darting up into the chimney. Russell ordered two brandies and they settled comfortably into the capacious blue velvet armchairs. They talked until just before 2am, when Nina finally paid heed to the lateness of the hour.

"Alan, I could go on chatting all night but we both have a busy day tomorrow and we won't be of much use without sleep so, reluctantly, I must say good night."

They both stood and she stepped close to him, gently placing a hand on his arm.

"It's been a really lovely evening," she said affectionately. "Thank you." She leaned forward and kissed him lightly on the cheek. "Goodnight, Alan. Sleep well."

He watched her walk across the room and leave. There was a feline quality to the slight sway of her hips and the slender curve of her shoulders. He was puzzled by the effect she had on him. In the course of his work he had met attractive women on numerous occasions, often socialising with them, but not since he first met Taniel had he been aware of such a quick attraction. There was something easy and natural about the way they talked, as if they had known each other far longer than the few hours they actually had; her smile and her eyes conveyed an intimacy beyond the so-recent connection they had made and yet it felt quite normal and appropriate. He shook his head and dismissed the whole question as he looked down at his watch, concerned at the lateness of the hour. He walked straight to the reception desk and spoke to the elderly night porter who was quietly reading a book.

"I'd like to change my morning call, please. Breakfast in my room at 7am sharp. Continental, with plenty of coffee. Room 255."

The porter noted down the instructions and Russell made his way upstairs to his room. He set the alarm in his wrist-watch for 6.30am. He reckoned he could just about manage with four and half hours sleep, then, if he showered and shaved quickly, he could read Ramsey's notes over breakfast and still get away by 8am. In the normal course of events he would have spent the evening quietly in his room absorbing Ramsey's precise and always meticulous information and not wining and dining the charming Miss Petrova. But what the hell?, he told himself. Ok, he found her attractive. Who wouldn't? But there was nothing untoward in that and the occasional dinner with an interesting woman was one of the perks of the job. A few hours sleep was a small price to pay for such a pleasant evening.

Three

England

His wrist-watch sounded its piercing alarm tone at exactly 6.30am and brought Alan Russell slowly to his senses. He lay still for a few seconds and then, fighting the heaviness of his eyes, reluctantly swung his legs out of bed and sat upright before reaching to the bed-side table to silence the annoyingly insistent bleeping.

The gentle pounding of the warm shower gradually cleared his drowsiness and by the time his breakfast arrived he was shaved, dressed and feeling reasonably alert and receptive. He pulled back the curtains on what promised, from the just breaking dawn, to be a bright and clear day and set himself to reading his brief. By eight o'clock he'd digested both his breakfast and the background to the day's discussions and was driving out of the hotel grounds and heading for Girton college, the venue for the three days of the conference.

The college was an old building and had a definite atmosphere; a kind of hushed solemnity, as if the very walls knew the long history of learning that had passed within them. It was a pleasant ambience and Russell felt comfortable within it. He still had twenty minutes to spare so he found a quiet corner and took out his cell phone to call Taniel. They made it a rule to speak to each other at least once a day whenever they were apart. I don't mind the separation, she would say, as long as I know you're alright. Wherever you are in the world, there must be at least one moment in the day when you can call me.

Though he would tease her about checking up on him, Russell none the less welcomed the routine. He felt very protective towards his wife, despite her strength of character, and was happy to keep his promise and call for his own peace of mind as well as hers.

They'd first met at a conference on medicine and the availability of health facilities in the poorer countries of the world. She was a student at University College, studying to be a doctor, and he'd been fascinated by her. Many Moroccan girls are condemned to a traditional role of subservience but her father, a successful businessman in Casablanca, had realised she was intelligent and was sufficiently liberal in his views to want to educate her to her full potential. He had sent her to England at the age of nine and now, with a Western education and a Moroccan birthright, her natural femininity had melded with an inner strength and determination to be her own woman. Such a combination in a petite, graceful girl with shining dark eyes and a beautiful smile had drawn Alan Russell like a magnet. They'd spent all the time together that his unusual hours and her studies had allowed and, almost before they knew it, had settled happily into a close personal relationship.

They'd lived together for two years in his Islington flat but when she was offered a junior registrar's post at Tunbridge Wells hospital they decided to actually make the move they'd been threatening for so long and bought a thatched cottage in Ashdown forest, a few miles from Wych Cross. Russell, to the surprise of all who knew him and the astonishment of Taniel herself, completed the picture of domesticity by asking her to marry him.

Falling in love with Russell had been a major upheaval in Taniel's plans, not to mention a disaster to her family, but her heart had ruled her head and, although she still talked about going back some time in the future, for the present she would minister to the sick of Tunbridge Wells rather than Tiznit.

They exchanged a few words but Russell kept the call brief and then made his way to the reception room. The lack of sleep hadn't yet caught up with him and he felt reasonably fresh and in good form as he introduced himself to Sir Peter Mayer and the British contingent.

Mayer was an imposing man, tall and very distinguished in an expensive blue pinstripe and sporting a fresh, budded rose in his lapel. He shook Russell firmly by the hand and greeted him in a slightly plummy but none the less natural and non-affected accent.

"Good morning. Nice to meet you and glad to have you aboard. Do help yourself to coffee and then I'll introduce you to everyone."

Having done as he was bidden, and anxious not to spill the hot coffee, Russell manoeuvred carefully back through the now crowded room to meet Mayer's team. It comprised three men and one woman, all of whom had been working on his A.I.D.S. research programme for over a year. They made Russell welcome and he had just about got through shaking hands with them all when the noise of the communal chatter subsided and the room was called to order.

With everyone assembled there were over forty people in the room but the atmosphere was already good humoured and friendly. Unlike Russell, the majority had all met the previous month in Geneva and were known to each other, so the usual first-morning apprehensiveness was not in evidence.

Russell correctly surmised that the effusive Welshman making the speech of welcome was David Thomas who, to the relief of all present, kept his remarks brief and to the point. As host nation, Sir Peter introduced the British party first and was followed by Dr Maurice Aubernon for the French team. Professor Litvinov, who was older than the others and certainly the most revered man in the room, spoke no English at all and simply smiled a polite *good morning* as he passed the task of introducing the Russians to his interpreter.

Russell thought the elderly professor, in contrast to the suavity of men like Mayer and Aubernon, actually looked like a scientist. Despite the way he smiled warmly across the room, he seemed pre-occupied and slightly detached which, together with his small spectacles and un-combed white hair, made him appear the archetypal great man of science.

Unlike any other medical conference Russell had ever attended, the media interest at the press call was enormous. The proceedings attracted two television crews, a radio unit and some thirty reporters.

It's big, thought Russell as he looked at them, unable to conceal a certain disdain. Other killer diseases can wipe out millions around the world and they don't turn a hair; it hardly warrants a column inch. But a sexually transmitted killer in their own back yard frightens people. It's all too close for comfort – so suddenly it's news.

Nina was seated in the third row and had smiled up at him as he'd entered to take his seat on the rostrum. When the press call finished just after 10am he tried to find her to say a brief hello but she had disappeared along with the rest of the journalists.

The conference finally got underway at 10.30 and Russell found himself well and truly occupied. The most tiring aspect of his work was not the act of interpreting itself but the intense concentration needed to do the job with speed and accuracy. By the time they called a halt to the first session at 1.30, he was well and truly ready for a break and looking forward to a good lunch.

* * * * *

France

Lunch on that November Saturday for Henri LeBec was coffee, a cheese sandwich and a packet of peanuts as he sat behind his desk and stared at the crudely drawn sketch that hung on the opposite wall. It showed the layout of the streets where the previous day's atrocity had occurred and listed the timings of events, as far as they were known, down the left-hand side.

The shadowy lines that emphasised the bags under his eyes bore testimony that, like Alan Russell, LeBec had managed little sleep during the night. He pulled a battery-powered razor from the top-right draw of his desk and, working by feel rather than bother to walk to the men's room to use a mirror, applied it to the stubble on his chin. He looked at the policeman who sat, equally tired, on the other side of the desk.

"Alright, Paul, let's have an update on everything we've got so far. From the top."

The portly sergeant sighed, took out his notebook and began to recite what little information they had pieced together.

"At approximately 5.30pm yesterday afternoon, a small boy, Guillaume Verney, was outside the American Express office in the northern Rue Scribe. He was waiting for his mother who was inside changing some traveller's cheques. He dropped a coin he was flicking and it rolled across the pavement and under a Volkswagen Beetle that was parked in the kerb. A man walking by, a native Parisian named Guy Moncourt, saw the boy drop his coin and stopped to help him. He bent to look under the vehicle to try and retrieve the boy's money and noticed a package that was taped to the underbody. He was puzzled and took a closer look. Fortunately for us he guessed immediately what it was. He was the first one to sound the alarm."

"Thank God he did!" interrupted LeBec. "The average bloke in the street wouldn't have the savvy to think it could be a home-made bomb, let alone the presence of mind to clear the area. Most would have either done nothing or just called the police and sat and waited."

As he spoke he lost concentration on the razor in his hand and caught the edge of his lip.

"Damn!" he exclaimed as a crimson bead of blood appeared at the corner of his mouth. "Sorry, Paul. Do carry on."

The sergeant pulled a small packet of tissues from his pocket and, without taking his eyes from his notebook, passed one across the desk as he continued to read.

"The bomb squad arrived by 5.50pm and finally diffused it by 5.58. The phone inside showed a call had been received at 5.56 but it had somehow failed to go off. Had it done so it would have exploded while they were working on it."

"Poor sods!" said the chief inspector. "What a way to earn a living. I couldn't handle that kind of pressure."

The sergeant smiled. "At the moment you can't even handle shaving."

"Very droll" replied LeBec, whose lip was still trickling blood. Nicot chuckled and passed him a second tissue as he continued his summary.

"At 6.03 exactly the second device went off at the American Airlines sub-office in the Southern Rue Scribe. This time the car was a Fiat Punto. Both cars had false plates of course and both had been reported stolen; the Beetle from a station car park in Dijon six weeks previously and the Fiat from Chaumont a month ago. Forensic says both bombs were Semtex, both triggered by a cell phone, and had identical mechanisms: the wires taken up through the floor to the glove compartment so it can be activated once the car is parked and there's no risk of it going off while being driven to the target."

LeBec nodded. "Cautious bastards aren't they?"

He opened the left drawer of his desk and took out a half-bottle of Cognac. Emptying a small measure into his coffee, he stirred it vigorously and screwed the cap of the bottle back in place. The sergeant gave an obvious exaggeration of a polite cough and held out his own coffee mug.

"Oh sorry, Paul. Just trying to save you calories," said LeBec.

Ignoring the comment, as he did with all his boss's jibes about his weight, Nicot carried on while the chief inspector unscrewed the bottle again and added to his sergeant's coffee.

"Reports from the area traffic wardens show that the Beetle wasn't in place at 5pm and the Fiat couldn't have been parked before 5.25. All potential witnesses have been questioned, including the staff that left the A.A. office before the event and, so far, nobody remembers anything significant. As to the effects of the explosion, the damage you saw for yourself and the injuries report, although not yet complete, shows two fatalities, seven major injuries and countless minor ones."

The sergeant snapped shut his notebook and looked across at his chief.

"So where do we begin?"

LeBec sat back and stared at the sketch on the wall, gently sipping his fortified coffee and enjoying the warm sensation it brought as it trickled down his throat.

"The Airlines office and the Amex bureau are both big American concerns, so we can safely assume they were targeted. Now put yourself in the place of the driver of the car. You need to get in and out as soon as possible but you must be on target. That's no easy task. This is Paris for God's sake; it's practically impossible to park anywhere. You are trying to leave a vehicle in a restricted area and at the same time you must not draw attention to yourself or the car. So what do you do?"

He looked across the desk as he asked the question but didn't wait for a reply.

"You drive around until you see the warden has definitely left the street and moved on, that's what you do. Then you know that, with luck, the car will be o.k. for the next half-hour or so, maybe more. That gives you time to activate the bomb and be well away before you make the phone call and set it off."

The sergeant nodded and took a long swig of the comforting coffee. LeBec crossed to the sketch map to continue with his scenario. He drew a line along an imaginary route.

"Allowing for the traffic flow, which is particularly heavy at that time of night, I would guess the Beetle drove around this way and that the Fiat circled like this, avoiding the Rue Auber." He drew a second line across the sketch and stood back to view his artistry. "That's a relatively small area, Paul. We know when they were there, what they were driving and we know they're Arabs. Surely to God, someone in that area must have noticed something?"

The sergeant shrugged. "So far we've drawn a blank. But I'll tell the boys on the street to go back to those particular routes. Also, the papers came out this morning with full reports and a photo of the Volkswagen; that'll help. Maybe we'll get lucky?"

LeBec shook his head. "I don't believe in too much good fortune. I reckon one lucky break in a case is as much as any of us can hope for and this has already thrown up two. The Amex bomb was not only found but it failed to go off when they rang the number. Nobody can reasonably hope to get luckier than that."

* * * * *

England

Alan Russell gingerly put his fork into the leg of fried chicken and sliced it with his knife to ensure it was cooked all the way through. He'd always enjoyed chicken but had felt dubious about it ever since Taniel, who was virtually vegetarian, had returned home triumphantly waving a copy of some medical report. It claimed that ninety percent of chickens consumed in Britain were subject to Salmonella and it could only be neutralised by thorough cooking. So he now found himself going through this ritual whenever chicken appeared on the menu. He folded his copy of the *Independent* and placed it next to his plate and, satisfied his meal was well-cooked, was about to begin eating when he heard his name tentatively spoken.

"Mr. Russell?"

He looked up to see a tall man standing at his table, carrying a tray bearing a meal.

"Excuse me but it is Mr. Russell, isn't it?"

"Yes, it is." Russell recognised him at once.

"Gurevich. Dimitri Gurevich," said the man extending his hand. "I am with the Russian party. May I join you?"

Russell had deliberately chosen to sit alone at a corner table because he preferred a quiet break to talking shop all through lunch but there was no polite option other than to invite the overseas visitor to join him. He managed a smile and said "Please do" as he gestured to the place opposite him. Gurevich eased his tall frame into the chair and settled his tray onto the table.

"Thank you. I saw you sitting alone and thought I would come over and speak. We get so little time for socialising once work has begun."

"No, indeed" said Russell, managing an unforced smile. He moved his paper to make room for his new companion.

"Ah. You read the *Independent*. This is my favourite of your British press. I find it ... what is the word ... balanced. Although it only gave a small mention to the conference; just a couple of paragraphs. In Geneva it was very big news."

"Oh that's just the announcement. It was a big press call this morning and there will be a good deal of coverage over the next few days."

The Russian smiled. "Yes, I expect so. You were not with us in Geneva, were you?"

"No. This was a last-minute assignment for me. I only knew about it twenty-four hours ago."

"Really? Do you often work at such short notice? Life must be quite exciting."

"I'm afraid not. Generally my duties are quite mundane."

"Oh I'm sure you are being modest. You must come across many interesting people and places in a job like yours. Anyway, I can promise you it's certain to be more exciting than mine." He laughed. "Nothing could be more mundane than the *State Health Ministry of Russia* I assure you!" He stressed the title in pedantic and sarcastic tones, belittling the bureaucracy of his own organisation."

Russell smiled. "I think working for a government department is pretty much the same everywhere, don't you? More time spent on red tape and paper work than actually doing the job you're paid for."

Gurevich laughed again. "You may be right, but believe me, no organisation in the world knows how to generate red tape like a Russian state department! But please. Tell me more about your work. I find it most interesting to learn how fellow civil servants operate within other countries."

The ice was broken. Gurevich, the seasoned professional, had, as usual, played his role to perfection. He was a dedicated ministry man, a fellow minion in the grand processes and procedures of international conferences; a colleague, a friendly face, an agreeable associate for the next three days. The lunch passed pleasantly and he was a keen listener as Russell talked about his job and his life generally. By the time they were making their way back for the three o'clock afternoon session, they were on christian name terms and chatting freely.

* * * * *

France

As three o'clock struck in his Paris office, Henri LeBec looked up to see the third stroke of luck that fate was dealing him walk briskly into the room in the short, squat shape of the redoubtable Madame Charnier.

"Are you Inspector LeBec, monsieur?" she demanded emphatically, as Paul Nicot hurried into the office behind the rumbustious woman.

"*Chief* Inspector LeBec, yes I am."

"Good. Then you are the man I have to see. Why nobody could tell me that three hours ago instead of keeping me waiting I do not know. People have no manners these days. Even you policemen show no respect. But we haven't time to argue about that now. What are you going to do about compensation?"

Without waiting to be invited, she sat herself in the chair in front of LeBec's desk and firmly folded her arms across her ample bosom, as if to emphasise that she had no intention of moving until she received an answer.

LeBec stared at the old woman opposite him in amazement. She was well into her seventies, perhaps even eighty, and had the kind of complexion that can only come from a life outdoors. There were several broken blood vessels in her wrinkled face, suggesting an over-fondness for drink, and the brown fingerless mittens on her pudgy hands had once, long ago, matched her tatty woollen scarf and the round woollen hat that topped her dishevelled grey hair. She wore a heavy navy-blue topcoat that had long seen better days and was fastened around her substantial middle by an old and cracked black leather belt. She bore a commanding expression, like a once mighty battleship that was now rusting in dry-dock but somehow refused to acknowledge it was no longer at sea and ruling the waves.

The detective looked up enquiringly at his sergeant.

"Well, Paul?"

"Chief Inspector, this is Madame Charnier ..."

She quickly interrupted him. "That's right, C-H-A-R-N-I-E-R." She tapped the desk pointedly with her forefinger as she spelled out the name. "And I'm not leaving here until I get what's due to me."

The sergeant looked apologetically at LeBec as he tried to quieten the old woman.

"Yes, Madame, we understand. Now please let me explain to the Chief Inspector, then you can tell him all about it."

"I've been telling people about it all morning. But nobody does anything!"

Nicot raised his voice to her in exasperation. "Madame, please!"

"Oh very well" she reluctantly conceded, not in the least fazed by his tone. "But mark you get it right. Four thousand five hundred Euros and not a sou less!"

She sat back in her chair and Nicot gratefully turned to LeBec.

"Madame Charnier is a flower seller. She has a street stall in the Rue Scribe opposite the American Airlines office ..."

Again the old woman butted in to the sergeant's flow.

"I do a good trade; especially with the audiences going to the opera; it's only round the corner. Nice class of people. They never grumble about the price. They ..."

She caught the sergeant's glare.

"Oh, sorry."

Nicot continued.

"Madame was injured in the explosion yesterday. Fortunately it wasn't too serious; some cuts to her legs caused by flying glass; but she refused to go to hospital. She went straight home to bandage her legs herself. That's why we didn't know about her."

"I never did like hospitals" she added in a conspiratorial tone. "I can look after myself."

LeBec smiled at her. "I have no doubt of that, Madame. Carry on Paul."

The flower stall itself was badly damaged by the blast and the flowers were all ruined …"

Animatedly, she again cut in.

"Not a single bloom left untouched. Nothing worth selling anyway. Lost the lot, I did. The whole fu***" she stopped herself before she let out the expletive she had begun. "Well, they were all useless and that's the truth!"

The exasperated Nicot struggled on.

"First thing this morning, Madame went to the local police to put in a claim for compensation. The boys at the station were not too sure what to do with her but after a couple of hours one of them realised she hadn't been interviewed by any of our lads because she'd gone straight home. He put in a call here and Lucien went over to take a statement.

Madame Charnier leaned forward across the desk to the Chief Inspector.

"I told him" she said with authority, as if stating an acknowledged truth. "My family have run that stall for generations. The bloody Bosch couldn't shift us – we were there all through the invasion – and no shifty-looking Arab is going to stop me now."

LeBec sat up quickly and looked at his sergeant.

"Exactly!" said Nicot excitedly, as his boss turned back to the old woman, his eyes eager with anticipation.

"Madame, I promise you I will help you with your problem but first you must answer a few questions for me. Now please think very carefully and make certain you understand what I am asking you. Did you watch television last night or hear the radio?"

Charnier looked at him as though he were mad.

"What on earth do you want to know that for?" she asked incredulously.

"Please, Madame" the detective replied firmly, "answer the question."

She sighed, resigning herself to that fact that LeBec had taken leave of his senses but content to play his game if it would get her a solution to her problem.

"No I did not. When I saw what had happened to my flowers I closed up the stall, or rather what was left of it, and went home to tend my legs. Normally I go to Renée's bar, but I thought it best to stay off my legs until the bleeding had stopped. So, I went to bed. Best place really when you're poorly. I had a little drink - to help me get over the shock you understand - and slept like a baby till just after five. I always get up at five. Have done for fifty years."

"And did you read any papers this morning?"

"Phuh!" she blew through her lips in her distaste. "I never read papers. I'm far too busy to waste time on that sort of nonsense."

"What did you do this morning?"

She sighed again heavily and pointed to Nicot.

"As I've told this gentleman here, I got up, washed and dressed myself, went to the café - well, there was no point in going to market was there, not with my stall in ruins and no cash to re-stock it - and after I'd eaten I went to the police commissariat. And I've been waiting for someone to do something ever since!"

LeBec spoke to her calmly and precisely.

"So you have seen no papers or television and heard nothing on the radio about the bomb?"

"No, I keep telling you, don't I?"

"Then why do you mention an Arab, Madame?"

"Because I saw him of course, why d'you think? Little brown bastard. If I see him again he'll know all about it, I can tell you."

LeBec gave silent thanks. Either to the God in whom he wasn't sure he believed or to whatever power might be out there somewhere. It didn't matter. What counted was that somehow he had been delivered of an eye witness. This colourful, formidable old lady, who'd worked her pitch for over fifty years, might prove to be the decisive weapon in his fight to bring the killers to justice. The Paris streets had provided one of their own to strike back at those who had come bringing death and destruction. There was something balanced and fitting about it that appealed to LeBec. Whatever hand of fate, or act of whatever god, may be responsible he didn't care. He was just grateful.

"Please, Madame, tell me very carefully exactly what you saw yesterday."

"Well alright" she reluctantly agreed. "But you promise you'll do something about my compensation if I do?"

"I promise, Madame. Now please; absolutely everything you can remember."

Sergeant Nicot drew up a chair and took out his notebook as the elderly flower-seller settled herself to begin the story that had led her to LeBec's office.

"It had been an average sort of day; business-wise I mean. But there was a performance at the Opera House that evening so I was expecting to do better once the crowds started to appear. I don't normally pay any attention to the traffic. To tell you the truth I don't know one car from another. And I wouldn't have noticed this one if he hadn't come so close to hitting me."

LeBec interrupted her. "How do you mean, Madame, hitting you?"

"What I say, hitting me!" she replied with annoyance. "If you let me finish, I'll explain!"

Nicot grinned at his boss as LeBec received Madame's indignant rebuke for disturbing the flow of her narration.

"Excuse me, Madame" the detective apologised. "Please continue."

Warming to her situation and beginning to enjoy the status conferred on her by their avid interest in her story, the old woman rejoined her tale with added enthusiasm. The battleship was once more at sea and cresting the waves.

"Every Friday evening at five forty-five - you could almost set your watch by it - one of my regulars buys a bunch of flowers for his wife." She laughed raucously. "At least, I presume they're for his wife; it's not my business to ask! But, whoever it is, she's been getting them regular, every Friday, for the last ten years. A nice man he is; a proper gentleman. He's a doctor somewhere in the Rue St. Honoré. His name's Guichard; Doctor Guichard. Anyway, he drives this big car. I don't know what it is but it's long and black and always ever-so clean and shiny; and it's such a busy time of day you can't stop, not even for a minute to buy some flowers."

She paused to give a deep sigh and shake her head.

"If you ask me, that's what's wrong with the world. Everybody's so busy rushing about, there's no time for anything any more. This is what it comes to when they're all running around so fast they can't stop and buy a flower from an old lady. If they can't take the time to do the simple things like that, it's no wonder they're all blowing each other up!"

LeBec was struck by the way her simplistic, homespun wisdom seemed actually to speak volumes about the fanaticism he was fighting.

"Yes, Madame" he said with a wry smile. "You may be more right than you know."

Madame Charnier looked at him in genuine surprise.

"Of course I'm right. Anyway, where was I? Oh yes, well like I said, Doctor Guichard can't stop his car for long so I always take the flowers over to him. He pulls up on the other side of the road and gives two short beeps on the hooter and I take them across. He always gives me a little extra, for a tip. But then, like I said, he's a proper gent and there aren't too many of those left these days."

Nicot leaned towards her. "And this is what you did last night, Madame?"

"Yes. Just like I'm telling you. So I take them across - Chrysanthemums they were, beautiful. I'd been saving them specially. And he pays me and gives me a tip just like always. Then, as I step back, there's a great screech and this little green car pulls up not two centimetres from where I'm standing! I mean, you have to have eyes in the back of your head these days. Driving like that! He could have run me down! So, I stood there and gave him a piece of my mind. Little bugger! If I'd have known then he was going to blow up half the street he'd have got a lot more besides!"

On another occasion the description of Madame Charnier holding up an entire street of Parisian rush-hour traffic while her rage was in full flight would have been worth hearing, but LeBec was far too concerned with the driver of the offending car to let her elaborate any further.

"Did you get a close look at the driver, Madame?" he asked hopefully.

"Well of course! He was no further from me than you are now. I could see him through the ... the glass ... what d'you call it?"

"The windscreen, Madame?" offered Nicot.

"Yes, yes the windscreen. He was holding up his hands and mouthing *pardon, pardon* at me. Anyway, I stepped to one side and he tried to drive off but the traffic was so thick that he only drew level with me. I could see him plain as day and that's what I remember was so odd. Soon as he saw me looking at him he turned his face away, right round so I could only see the back of his head. Well, I just thought he was a bit embarrassed and thought no more of it. I went back to my stall."

"But do you think you saw him clearly enough to recognise him again, Madame?" asked Nicot.

"Well I did see him again, didn't I? That's how I know it was him that did it. He drove off with the traffic but blow me if he didn't turn up again a few minutes later. He must have just driven round the block. Anyway, he stops on the other side of the road right where Doctor Guichard's car had been. I was so surprised."

She chuckled to herself. "I thought perhaps he'd come back to have another go at running me down! He stayed in the car for a couple of minutes and then got out and crossed the street right in front of me."

She shifted a little in her chair and became more animated as she re-enacted the scene, wagging her finger at the imaginary foe.

"Well, well" I said. "If it isn't the speed king of the Rue Scribe! Come back to have another go at me have you? He looked really shocked to see me and just froze on the spot. That's when I noticed it. A big scar. Nasty it was. Right down his cheek. Then he just ran off; towards the Boulevard des Capucines he went. And that's the last I saw of him. 'Course, I thought no more about it and then when that bloody bomb went off, well I didn't know where I was at first. I just found myself on the pavement, all covered in glass and with my legs in such a state. But after a bit someone picked me up and gave me a blanket and a glass of water and sat me down. I came back to my senses and that was when I took it all in. I knew it was a bomb alright, I'd seen enough of the war to know that; I just didn't understand where it had come from. Then someone told me it had been in a green car on the other side of the road. It wasn't until I got home I realised it must have been that bloody Arab. That explains why he ran away of course."

LeBec nodded his satisfaction to his sergeant and sat back in his chair.

"So you are willing to swear, Madame, that you saw this man clearly and saw him park the Fiat outside the American Airlines office?"

The old woman's face screwed up in a puzzled look. "The what?"

"The Fiat. The green car."

"Oh, is that what you call it? Well I don't know what sort of car it was but I saw him leave it there alright, and I saw his face; clear as I'm seeing you now."

The detective banged the desk in delight.

"We've got him, Paul! If we can get a good likeness we'll find him; and if we can find one, we'll get the others."

He turned again to the elderly lady who was now his sole and vital witness.

"Do you think, Madame, if I take you to one of our police artists, you could help him make up a picture of this man so we can put out an identikit photo in the papers?"

The old lady raised her eyebrows and stared at him as though she were peering over spectacles that she didn't wear.

"I could do a lot of things, Monsieur. But first there is the matter of my compensation."

LeBec laughed. "Yes, there certainly is. Sergeant Nicot will take you downstairs and make sure you have a good lunch. Then, while you are helping us put together a picture of this man with the scar, he will organise your compensation."

Nicot looked stunned.

"But Chief Inspector, it takes time. The paperwork alone ... and then approaches to the criminal injuries board. It takes months to process a claim. There's no way it can be done so quickly."

"Find a way" LeBec commanded. "Madame Charnier's testimony is our one and only chance to prevent what might be a whole campaign like last night. If she will co-operate with us then we must do so with her. I don't care how you do it, but get our complaining city fathers off their backsides and find a way of getting this lady her four thousand Euros sometime today or tomorrow. Tell them there are no votes in more bombings and a lot of votes in convicted terrorists. Tell them anything you like, but get Madame her money."

He turned back to the elderly woman, who was clearly enjoying her new found sense of importance.

"Then we will take her to a nice house, with her own police guard, where she will live safe and sound at our expense until all this is over."

The old flower seller leaned forward across the desk to the Chief Inspector and spoke softly, in her politest tone.

"Excuse me, Monsieur. You are very kind but it was four thousand *five hundred* Euros, if you please."

LeBec looked up at his sergeant.

"Four thousand *five hundred*, Paul, if you would be so kind."

Madame Charnier's wrinkled face broke into an enormous smile.

"Well that's what I call service!" she declared and winked coquettishly at the detective.

LeBec roared with laughter and returned the wink.

Four

England

Saturday evening found Alan Russell once again sharing a dinner table with the attractive Miss Petrova. The restaurant was crowded that night, mostly with people whose presence, in one capacity or another, was due to the conference. The air was full of the constant hum of conversation and the continual clink of cutlery against china as the hard-pressed waiters and waitresses hurried busily between the tables.

At least two of the diners that evening were not involved with the Cambridge seminar. The dark-haired individual in the blazer, who had carefully watched Russell's arrival the previous afternoon, was now joined by an older man. His immaculate silver hair, slicked carefully into place, shone either side of a razor-sharp parting and he sported a precisely groomed moustache. The sparse and infrequent conversation that accompanied their meal was not due to any lack of interest in each other, but because their attention was wholly given to the table across the room where Nina Petrova was so attentively listening to her dinner partner.

She had freely admitted that the journalist in her wanted to pick his brains about the day's developments when she suggested they again dine together but had also graciously added that, with or without his inside information, she would enjoy spending another evening with him. Russell had been happy to oblige.

Why not? he asked himself. What was the point in dining alone? She was interesting and stimulating company and they were both in the same hotel. It would be ridiculous if they were eating at separate tables. More to the point, she really wanted information and was more interested in what he had to say than in Russell himself. It was part of his job to socialise and in the natural order of his routine. It was totally harmless so why not enjoy her company?

But as he looked across the table at her, the subdued lighting subtly illuminating the delicate contours of her face and her hazel eyes sparkling as she spoke, no amount of logic or reasoning could deny his awareness of her physical charms. Yes she was attractive; any man could see that. But there was a grace, a femininity that seemed to radiate from the simplest things that she did. The way she held her glass and sipped her wine, the way her head inclined slightly when she smiled; something within the little gestures and movements reached out and touched him and he didn't know why.

"Is there really much free exchange of information between the scientists?" she asked, the doubt evident in her voice. "I mean, whoever finally comes up with the answer is not only assured a place in history but will also be sitting on an enormous fortune. Even in the face of an epidemic like this, I would have thought the competition to get there first would be hard to put to one side."

"Oh I think the element of competition is there alright" said Russell, suddenly aware of the way her hair fell across her shoulders. "It's mainly a case of dividing the research into different areas and each following their allotted path. They're still keen to be the first with the answer but at least no time will be wasted duplicating each other's work."

She leant back in her chair to sip the cool white wine.

"What do you make of old Litvinov?" she enquired casually.

Russell smiled as he called to mind the elderly scientist.

"Well, he's obviously brilliant. Certainly the others seem to have a great deal of respect for him. I must confess I find him a little amusing."

"In what way?"

"In his manner." The recollection made him laugh as he described the Russian Professor. "He's held in such high esteem and spoken of in such reverent tones that you expect him to be some dynamic genius, dispensing pearls of wisdom with every other sentence. Whereas, in reality, you meet this inoffensive little man who can never find his pen or the right set of notes and who gives the distinct impression that his mind is on other things and he'd really rather be somewhere else."

Nina smiled at this portrait of one of the world's leading men of science.

"But does he strike you as ... content? Happy to be here?"

"Yes, I think so. Why do you ask?"

"Oh, I don't know. Russian scientist – servant of the all powerful state whether he likes it or not, that sort of thing. I suppose it's just my journalistic mind. Can't help it; I'm naturally suspicious. I always look for an alternative angle; an ulterior motive."

"Well, if you promise not to accuse *me* of ulterior motives, what about another bottle of Chablis?"

She laughed. "I think that's an excellent idea."

Across the room, the dark-haired man spoke quietly as he watched Russell order the wine.

"A second bottle of vino. This could be a long evening."

"Perhaps. We shall see," replied his companion. "Would you like a brandy? On the firm, of course."

"That's very kind of you, sir. Thank you. Yes."

The silver-haired man immediately caught the eye of the waitress, who hurried across to serve him. It was typical. He never had to wait to be served at a bar or restaurant. Taxi drivers seemed always to be at hand when he needed one. Hotel receptionists always found him the best rooms and porters were extra careful and obliging as they carried his bags. It was nothing he said or did that inspired such service. It was his manner and bearing. The precise grooming of his hair and moustache matched the always impeccable knot in his tie and the perfect crease in his Savile Row suit, from which exactly the right amount of white cuff emerged at the sleeve. Always supremely polite, the quiet self-assurance of his calm and perfectly rounded tones elicited an unwitting compliance and respect in others who seemed naturally to accept that, in the pecking-order of life, here was an authority not to be questioned.

"Two brandies please" he said to the waitress. "The best you have."

"Certainly, sir" replied the girl with overt courtesy. "Shall I serve them here or would you prefer to take them in the lounge?"

"No, we'll take them here. We may move to the lounge later." The waitress nodded politely and turned on her heel as the man lowered his voice and, studiously addressing the coffee cup he was stirring, added sardonically: "It all rather depends on Mr Russell and Miss Petrova".

Thirty minutes later, the two objects of his remarks finished their meal and did indeed retire to the lounge where they chatted intently for the next two hours and failed to notice the two men who had quietly followed them out of the restaurant and seated themselves in the corner of the room.

Not wishing to start Sunday on as little sleep as he had managed the previous evening, Russell decided on a reasonably early night and, as the grandfather clock in the lobby struck a resonant twelve, stood up to take his leave.

"I'm afraid I must say goodnight. Will I see you tomorrow?"

"I'm not sure" said Nina. "I have an exclusive interview tomorrow at the close of the session with Jong-Wook Lee and have no idea how long it will last."

Russell knew the name. Dr Jong-Wook Lee was the current head of the World Health Organisation and would be flying in to address the Sunday session of the conference.

"An exclusive! I'm impressed. How did you manage that?"

"Oh, a little luck and just a teeny bit of feminine wile."

As she spoke she posed coyly and fluttered her eyelids. Despite her play-acting, Russell was sure she was seldom refused much that she wanted if she set her mind to persuading people and turning on the charm.

"Seriously, Alan" she said. "I don't know what time I'll be finished so don't wait for dinner but, if you like, I'll meet you in the bar later on; say, about ten? After all, tomorrow is our last night here. We should at least mark it with a farewell drink."

She rose and stood next to him.

"And thank you once again for a delightful evening. I've really enjoyed it."

Raising her head she leaned forward to kiss him. He was expecting a peck on the cheek as she had done the night before but this time she kissed him on the lips. It wasn't a passionate kiss but it was just long enough to be more than simply a friendly gesture. He was suddenly very aware of the intimacy of her, the smooth softness of her skin, the silky texture of her hair and the delicate scent of the Rive Gauche perfume she was wearing. All of them assailed his senses in an immediate and unexpected closeness that was usually the province of lovers not friends; and certainly not acquaintances. The brief extra moment of contact not only surprised him but also stirred him considerably more than he wanted to admit.

"Goodnight, Alan" she wished him softly.

Her semi-hushed voice was not really a whisper but, none the less, lent an overtone to the simple words. Russell told himself his imagination, fuelled by the Chablis, was reading more into the goodnight kiss than was intended but, as he watched her walk away, he was again conscious of the balance and curves of her body. And he couldn't pretend the touch of her lips on his own hadn't aroused him.

"Oh well" he said under his breath resignedly. "You can't get caught for thinking about it!" and turned in the opposite direction and headed for his room.

The silver-haired man in the corner nodded gently to his companion who carefully put down his glass and rose to follow Russell out of the lounge. He stayed at a discrete distance and, unnoticed by his quarry, followed up the stairs and along the corridor where he stopped and pretended to look for his key while Russell, at the other end of the passage, entered his room and closed the door firmly behind him.

The dark-haired man waited for five minutes to satisfy himself that Russell had no intention of leaving again that night and then made his way back to the lounge. Settling back into the blue velvet of the armchair, he picked up his drink.

"Well?" asked the older man.

"Gone to bye-byes like a good little boy."

"Alone?"

"Yes."

"Hmmm. In that case we may as well do likewise."

The silver-haired man stood and reached into his pocket but emerged with an empty hand.

"Oh, sorry. No change. Leave a little something for the waiter, will you? Goodnight."

"Goodnight, sir."

The younger man watched the other leave and then swiftly swallowed the last remaining sips of his brandy. Pulling some change from his pocket, he reluctantly placed a couple of coins on the saucer of his coffee cup and walked smartly from the room.

* * * * *

With deference to it being Sunday, the next day's session was not due to start until 10.15am so Russell slept until 7.30, quickly showered and shaved and then went down for a long, leisurely breakfast. At home, he and Taniel seldom ate more than a little toast in the mornings but there was always something peculiarly appetising about the smell of bacon wafting from a hotel kitchen and he could rarely resist it. He ordered a full breakfast with all the trimmings and poured himself a large coffee before sitting back to enjoy a quiet hour with the *Sunday Independent*.

The paper devoted a good deal of space to the car-bombing that had taken place in Paris two days previously. There were several small pictures of the destruction and the wounded and, in the centre of the page, a much larger identikit picture of an Arabic-looking man. He appeared to be in his late twenties to early thirties with a gaunt face, lank, untidy hair and bore a two-inch scar along his left cheek.

Russell was struck by the eyes in the photo-fit. Though the likeness was made up of computer generated sections and could only be an approximation of the reality they portrayed, the manufactured eyes were hard and cold and carried a sense of real evil lurking behind them. The picture was entitled *The Man All Paris Wants To Find*.

Russell stared at the face and wondered about the man it represented. He'd always had a revulsion of violence in any form. He was, he liked to think, no coward but violence had always seemed to him to be pointless and ultimately self defeating. Even at school he'd never understood the natural hierarchy that boys evolve, according misplaced respect to those who are the strongest or can hit the hardest; how that insane logic could be twisted further by religious fanatics to somehow justify the indiscriminate killing and maiming of others was totally beyond him and he found it a sobering thought that, in the modern world, no city was free from their threat.

His reverie was interrupted by the arrival of his breakfast and so he closed and folded the paper and turned his thoughts away from the violence of Paris to the Sunday crossword.

* * * * *

Dimitri Gurevich had also breakfasted early that Sunday morning and while Alan Russell was solving crossword clues he was driving a Fiesta through the streets of Cambridge.

On the pretext of taking advantage of the conference's late start to see something of Cambridge itself, he had ordered a cab and asked the driver to drop him in the city centre. He had then walked immediately to the station car park where the Englishman Philips had left the Fiesta with the key taped to the underside of the rear bumper. He had then driven quickly eastwards through the sparse Sunday morning traffic in Newnham Road and onto the A603. A quarter of a mile later he turned right and, slowing down to avoid attention, drove along Grange Road to the University library. There, standing at the roadside and idly browsing a newspaper, stood Andrei Melekhin.

As Gurevich brought the vehicle to a halt, Melekhin quickly got into the passenger seat and the Fiesta glided away again.

"Excellent timing" Melekhin told him. "I'd only been there three minutes."

"Good. We don't have long. This is supposed to be a brief sight-seeing jaunt and I must be back in time to leave for the conference with the others. Now tell me what you have."

"Nothing at all. Everything checks out. The security is all a basic run-of-the-mill job. We can find no one on the ground with even a hint of suspicion about them. If anyone is planning to make a move then it's the most covert operation I've ever seen. It's just like Geneva; clean as a whistle." He shrugged and looked across at his senior officer. "I'm beginning to wonder why we're here at all. Anything on the inside?"

Gurevich slowly shook his head. "It's the same story. Everyone is legitimate."

"What about the new guy, the interpreter, Russell? What do you make of him?"

"He's exactly what Philips said. A genuine last-minute replacement. We're keeping a close eye on him of course but I've spent enough time with him to know."

Melekhin slid a little lower into his seat, grateful that his boss had not brought him any bad news and that there would be nothing serious on his agenda. He pulled a packet of English cigarettes from his top pocket and withdrew one.

"Well then" he said contentedly, "it looks as if we can relax a little. Tomorrow night it will all be over."

"On the contrary" said Gurevich emphatically. "The fact that we've found nothing is all the more reason to be wary."

"Maybe so" replied Melekhin as he flicked his lighter into life and then drew deeply on his Silk Cut and savoured the taste. "But I think this is just a case of being over-cautious. We're playing baby sitter – but nobody's threatening the baby."

Gurevich nodded. "Let's hope your right, Andrei. Let's hope you're right."

But Dimitri Gurevich didn't share the other man's confidence. He knew his superiors were not simply over-cautious but were extremely concerned. Whatever it was that made Litvinov so important to them would, by definition, make him equally important to the opposition. Gurevich would not be happy until the old man was safely back in Moscow.

* * * * *

Alan Russell put down his empty glass and glanced at his watch. It was just after 10.45pm. Presuming that Nina's interview had gone on longer than anticipated, he decided to call it a night and return to his room and watch television. As he made his way across the lobby he heard his name called in a familiar accent.

He turned to see her hurrying from the glass entrance doors towards him. She was carrying a large tote bag over her shoulder and a small recorder in her hand. She was once again wearing her baggy anorak and her head sported a shapeless woollen hat, but her enigmatic smile beamed from beneath it and somehow, despite the ungainly bustle as she struggled against the weight of her burden, she looked as appealing as ever.

"I'm sorry I'm so late" she apologised. "I really couldn't get away."

"That's alright. How did it go?"

"Oh, very well. I had a long interview with Dr. Lee and then he introduced me to some of the people involved with their P.R. and publicity.

They were anxious to co-operate of course because they want the coverage but it made me much later than I anticipated. I hope you understand."

"Of course." He nodded in the direction of the bar. "Would you like a drink, or are you too tired?"

"I'd love one. But first I need to shower and change. It's been a very long day!"

"Ok. I'll wait for you here."

She gave him a sympathetic look.

"Poor Alan. I mustn't keep you waiting any longer. Look, I tell you what; I'd like you to hear some of the interview. I think you'll find it interesting. Let's order a bottle of wine and have it sent to my room. You can listen to the recording while I shower and change. That way I won't have to rush and you won't have to hang around. What do you think?"

Russell thought many things. The pause before he answered cannot have been more than a second; two at the outside; but in that brief space of time a myriad thoughts went racing through his mind. This would be crossing a line. A happily married man does not enter the hotel room of an attractive woman alone. Yesterday's brief goodnight kiss came rushing back to him and he could sense the momentary taste of her again on his lips. If he declined her invitation it would be implying it was loaded; that would be an unacceptable assumption and offensive to her. If he accepted, was he tacitly inviting or agreeing to something more? He didn't know; or did he? An image of Taniel, smiling as she waived him goodbye, flashed in front of his eyes but at the same time he was conscious of the bright, hazel eyes that were smiling up at him from under that completely unfeminine woollen hat. All this in the briefest moment of time until he heard a voice say "Yes. Why not?" and realised it was his own.

"Wonderful!" she said with a simple smile that conveyed no ulterior motive and seemed as innocent as an invitation to a Sunday school picnic. It reassured him and he told himself he was worrying over nothing.

"You order the wine" she continued, "and I'll see you in a minute. Room 147. And make sure you charge it to *my* account. This one's on me."

She leaned sideways against the weight of the tote bag and hurried out through the doors at the end of the hall. Russell went to the bar and instructed room service to take a bottle of the same Chablis they had drunk the previous evening to room 147. Two minutes later he was himself knocking on the door that bore that number. She opened it to him, still wearing her anorak.

"Come in. Make yourself at home. The room's a bit of a mess I'm afraid. It goes with the job."

As with all purpose-built hotels, the room was an exact replica of his own. Even the uninspired décor was identical. But, unlike his own, it held the unmistakeable presence of its occupant's femininity. Where his side table was bare, hers held the lotions and creams she used on her skin and the cotton-wool and tissues she used to apply and remove them. A single stocking lay across the pillow of the unmade bed and on the floor, next to a pile of papers, were the black skirt and slip she had worn the night before, left just as she had stepped out of them.

She removed her anorak and shoes and went into the bathroom, where he heard her turn on the shower.

"The recorder's on the bed" she called out to him. "Have a listen to the Lee interview. It's the first track. I won't be long, I promise."

She closed the bathroom door behind her and he picked up the small digital recorder and turned it over until he found the play control and selected track one.

Five minutes later his listening was interrupted by a loud and rhythmic knocking. He switched-off the recorder and opened the door to find a young waiter of about eighteen or so who had a tray, with two glasses and a bottle in a wine cooler, stylishly balanced on his right palm, which was flattened backwards at shoulder height.

"Wine for 147?"

His voice echoed the confidence of his tray-carrying.

"Yes. Put it on the table please."

The young man breezed past him and did as Russell asked. He then pulled a chit from his pocket and looked at it quizzically.

"It says here, *147 Miss Petrova*. Is that right?"

"Yes, that's correct. I'll sign for it" said Russell taking the slip and the ballpoint pen that was being proffered.

The running shower in the bathroom was clearly audible and, as he signed for the wine, Russell could see the youngster looking at Nina's shoes by the bed and the skirt and slip on the floor. He handed back the bill and at the same time gave the waiter a pound coin.

The young man grinned and looked up at him.

"Thank you, sir."

The smile on his face was a strange mixture of innuendo and envy as he added "Have a good evening" and walked briskly to the door and closed it behind him.

"Cheeky sod" said Russell to the air.

"Was that the wine?" called Nina above the noise of the shower.

He walked to the closed door and spoke loudly. "Yes. I'll pour you a glass."

A knowing laugh rang out from the other side.

"In the movies, this is where I'm supposed to ask you to bring it in to me. But don't worry. I'm almost finished."

A few minutes later the door of the bathroom opened and Nina emerged. She was wearing a white bathrobe and her hair was encased in a turban she had wound from one of the hotel's towels. The sharp fluorescent light from the bathroom cut a shaft into the subtler lamp-light of the bedroom, illuminating the steam from the heat of the shower as it wafted gently through the open doorway like an early morning mist.

"Oh, that's better" she sighed. "I feel human again."

Russell rose and offered her the wine he had poured.

"Lovely. Thanks" she said, gratefully sipping the cool Chablis. "What did you think of the interview?"

She sat herself on the bed and looked up at him. The act of sitting caused her robe to gape slightly at the top and the depth of her cleavage was clearly visible. Russell was suddenly very much aware of her nakedness beneath the white gown.

"Well, I've only heard the first few minutes" he said, trying to sound as casual as he could. "But he seems to know his stuff."

"He does. And he's more concerned with getting the job done than his own standing or whom he might upset in achieving it. That's quite rare these days."

"It certainly is in Whitehall" he said with a laugh; but he was aware that it sounded awkward.

Nina put down her drink and un-knotted the towel around her head, shaking free her brown tresses as she unwound it. Heavy with moisture, her hair shone in the reflection of the lamp-light and fell damp and unruly about her face. She looked positively beautiful. It bothered him and he felt decidedly uncomfortable. His unease was clear to see.

"Is anything wrong, Alan?" she asked him softly.

"No. No, of course not" he lied. "It's just that you're a very attractive woman and …" he tailed off, unable to find the right words.

"And?" she said gently.

He forced a smile but knew that it must have looked as false as it felt.

"And right at this moment I wish I wasn't married to a woman I love. But I am."

"And tomorrow she'll have you back" she whispered.

His pulse was rising and he could feel the tension that was slowly tightening his shoulders. I'm an idiot he told himself. She's attractive, desirable and any man in his right mind would want to be here. For God's sake, you don't have to be Einstein to know what's on offer when a beautiful woman invites you and a bottle of wine to her room while she takes a shower. I knew what I was doing when I said yes, didn't I? So why am I so unsure now?

She rose and stood in front of him and he could smell the delicate, familiar scent of Rive Gauche perfume, a little stronger than usual because she had so recently applied it.

"This is our only night; and I want it to be special" she said quietly as she gently slid the robe from her shoulders.

Linking her arms around his neck, she kissed him hard on the lips and the insistence of her warm mouth, together with the sensation of her naked breasts against his body was too arousing to deny. He began to return the intensity of the kiss. Instinctively his arms went around her waist and pulled her tighter to him but, even as he did so, his very real desire for her was waging war with his conscience and he withdrew them again.

Sensing his hesitancy, she began to kiss the underside of his chin and her lips gradually worked their way down the line of his throat and onto his chest as she slowly lowered herself against his body, kissing him all the while through his clothing until she was kneeling at his feet.

Russell's mind was racing with conflicting thoughts and emotions. He wanted her. He badly wanted her. Perhaps he'd wanted her from the beginning when she'd first stepped out of her car? Maybe he'd spent the last two days subconsciously hoping it would all lead to this moment? He wasn't sure. It didn't matter. What he did know was that right now she was there and she was willing. There was nothing to stop him enjoying her right now; nothing except the guilt that was overwhelming him.

Nuzzling into the hardness that was now straining against the confines of his trousers, Nina reached up and began to undo his belt buckle. An image of Taniel suddenly flashed into his mind. It was a ridiculous picture. She was standing in the kitchen pouring herself a coffee. Why in hell did that spring into his head? He didn't know. But at that moment the battle of his conscious was finally decided and, before he changed his mind, his hands went down to her wet hair and held her head still.

She knew what he was thinking without looking up and she froze.

He had a vague notion of trying to explain why fidelity and not cheating on his wife were important to him but, looking down at her, beautiful, half naked and so desirable, he wasn't sure he could convince himself, let alone her.

"I'm really sorry, Nina" he said. "I ..." he broke off unable to find the words and certain that no explanation was adequate anyway. Acutely embarrassed, and feeling a complete heel for having allowed the circumstance to develop in the first place, all he could offer was another "I'm sorry" and he quietly left the room.

Nina Petrova fell back against the bed and stared unbelievingly at the back of the closed door. She sat silent for a few moments and then gave a fierce sigh of exasperation and angrily yelled "shit!" as she banged her fist against the floor.

* * * * *

France

Earlier that same evening Henri LeBec was seated at his desk studying a newspaper photograph. It was the shot Gillet had taken of him in the

Rue Scribe holding the wounded dog. As he began reading through the accompanying article the door opened and his sergeant entered with a wadge of papers.

"These are the calls we've had since the papers hit the streets this morning" he said wearily.

"Anything?"

"The usual bunch of cranks of course" said Nicot, as he lowered his considerable bulk into a chair. "One woman's convinced the mob we want are living in the flat above her." He handed LeBec a sheet of paper as he continued. "She's not sure if they're Arabs or Italians but she claims they must be terrorists because they speak in a foreign language and they tried to poison her cat."

"Huh" said LeBec wearily as he glanced quickly over the transcript of the call. "Well if they'd tried to blow it up with Semtex we might be interested. Anything else?"

"Only this." His sergeant handed him a second sheet. "It's just come in. A guy in Chelles claims he recognises the Volkswagen."

"Have you detailed someone to follow it up?"

"I think you'll want to check this one out for yourself."

"Why?"

"He says the Volkswagen driver is Syrian."

LeBec was up and out of his chair almost before his sergeant had finished speaking.

"Get your coat, Paul."

* * * * *

England

Russell was still haunted by the previous night's embarrassing scene when the alarm woke him early on Monday morning.

While showering and shaving he could think of nothing else but Nina and how she must have felt after he left. He considered going to see her and again apologise but decided it would only make matters worse. He should never have gone to her room and he knew it, but no expressions of regret would be adequate. So, unable to think of any way of making amends, he elected to do nothing and, in sombre frame of mind, went down to breakfast.

At the foot of the stairs he turned towards the lobby and walked past a small settee where the dark-haired man in the blazer was sitting reading *The Times*. At his approach, the man put down the paper and stood.

"Mr. Russell?" he enquired politely.

"Yes." Russell was a little surprised at hearing his name from a total stranger.

"I'm sorry to bother you so early but I've been waiting for you to come down. I wonder if you'd mind helping us out? I'm from hotel security. It's just a small matter. We've got something we think you can identify for us."

"Identify? I don't understand."

"It will only take a moment and we would be extremely grateful."

Despite the polite manner, the tone was firm and authoritative. Russell checked his watch.

"Oh very well. But I don't have too much time."

"Thank you. I promise it won't take long. Would you follow me, please?"

The man turned and led the way through the double doors opposite the stairs and along the ground-floor corridor until he stopped outside room 131. He gave two short knocks on the door before ushering Russell into the room. Once inside, the man in the blazer closed the door behind them and Russell noticed that he turned the centre-piece of the handle to lock it. He then walked into the room and said simply "Mr. Russell, sir."

The recipient of his introduction, the silver-haired man with whom he had previously been watching Russell and Nina, rose from his seat in the corner.

"Mr. Russell. Good of you to come. Please sit down." He gestured to a chair in the centre of the room.

The bed had been moved back from its usual position and turned flat to the wall so as to make room for the two extra chairs that had been brought in. Russell sat.

"I understand you want me to identify something?" he asked.

"In a manner of speaking, yes. It's a little delicate really. I think it would be best if we simply show you what we have and then take it from there. I think it would be easier than me trying to explain." He nodded to the man in the blazer. "Would you mind?"

The other man drew the curtains across the window and then turned on the television set that had been moved from its usual stand to the centre of the table. Next to it was a small silver box that appeared to be some form of video or disc player. He pressed one of the front-panel controls and the television screen filled with jagged lines that looked like interference before clearing to reveal a picture.

"I'm afraid the image is a little orange" said the silver haired man. "It's due to the low light. But I think it's clear enough."

The image was indeed slightly orange in tone and not very bright but it was none the less recognisable as the interior of a room. As Russell's eyes adjusted to the picture, he saw it was one of the hotel's own rooms.

Suddenly Russell went cold and a knot tightened in his stomach. He watched a man walk into shot and pick up a glass of wine and realised with horror that he was looking at himself. His hands gripped the edge of the chair. The picture instantly became brighter and clearer as Nina appeared on the screen and the light from the bathroom she had just left gave greater illumination to the scene.

Stupefied, Russell turned to look at the other two men in the room. The eyes in their expressionless faces were fixed upon him, ignoring the television pictures and concerned only with his reaction to them. He looked back at the screen and for a few moments stared in utter disbelief, vainly searching for some logical explanation as to what was happening to him. Then, as he watched Nina's half-naked body embracing his own, his anger brought him to his senses and he stood and shouted at them.

"Turn it off! Turn it off!"

The man in the blazer reached forward to the recorder and the screen went black.

Russell rounded furiously on the older man.

"What in the name of God is going on here? Which one of you bastards is responsible for this?"

He turned back to the dark-haired man, his voice still loud and indignant.

"Was it you?" he demanded. "Is this your handiwork? Did you set this up?"

The voice from behind him was calm and unruffled.

"My dear Mr. Russell. *We* didn't film this little epic. *She* did."

Five

France

The rifle barrel came carefully to rest on the parapet of the apartment-block roof and the telescopic sight was brought sharply into focus and trained on the opposite first-floor window of number 17, Rue Bruant. Twenty metres below, within the ground-floor flat, similar beads were drawn on the front door and downstairs window of the house as two other marksmen stared unblinkingly at their magnified targets. The road block had been set up so as not to be visible from within the street itself and, at 6.30am, the silence and lack of activity seemed perfectly normal. Apart from the residents of this particular block and the immediately adjacent buildings, who had been silently evacuated during the night, the Parisian suburb of Chelles was awakening to what appeared to be an ordinary Monday morning.

Henri LeBec's Peugeot pulled to a gentle halt outside number 11 and he picked up the radio handset as Paul Nicot switched off the engine, applied the handbrake and eased himself back into the complaining vinyl of his seat.

"LeBec to all units. Identify and confirm please."

One by one they called in and confirmed their positions. The marksmen in the building opposite, the men in cars at either end of the street, the two officers at the back of the house and the man on the roof of number 17 itself. Last to reply was Clémence. He stood several metres along the road from LeBec's car, dressed in the donkey-jacket and overalls of a street cleaner. He was half-seated on the edge of the hand-cart that completed his disguise and quietly rolling a cigarette. He inclined his head slightly to the left to speak into the small microphone that was attached to his lapel.

"Clémence, guv'nor. In position outside with my little brush and cart. And may I say, guv, this is not quite what I thought they meant when they told me I could help 'clean up' Paris."

There was a general murmur of laughter from around the radio link as Clémence's remark had its intended effect and momentarily broke the tension.

"Cut the crap, Clémence and leave the funnies till we know we've got something to laugh about" said LeBec dourly. But he appreciated his officer's attempts to ease the nervousness of his colleagues. Clémence was a rough diamond of a man with few social graces but he was a dedicated, efficient policeman and very popular with all the ranks. LeBec could think of no one he'd rather have with him if the going got tough. "What are you carrying?" he added.

"The usual" came the reply from the distant figure, discretely tapping the pocket of his jacket. "And a little extra artillery just in case there's a few more in there than we think."

"Where is it?" asked LeBec.

Clémence didn't reply but instead lifted the lid of his cart where, hidden from view, he had an automatic rifle. He spat into the bin and grinned in the direction of the Peugeot as he replaced the lid and settled back to his cigarette.

LeBec muted the handset he was holding. "I'm glad he's not cleaning *my* street" he joked to his sergeant and flicked the button back to transmit.

"All units. Remember – I want no heroics and no risks. Above all we need information, so I want him nice and healthy and talkative. Understood? LeBec out."

His sergeant shifted his bulk in the confines of the seat and turned to his boss.

"What do you think our chances are? Of taking him alive, I mean."

LeBec slowly shook his head.

"Who knows? When you're dealing with fanatics, anything's possible."

The radio speaker suddenly crackled into life.

"Chief Inspector, there's a call for you from H.Q. It's Chief Vollard. They've patched him through."

"Christ" muttered LeBec under his breath. "Alright, I'll take it." The channel clicked again. "LeBec here, sir. Go ahead."

The voice that replied was gruff and unemotional. "What's your situation, Henri?"

"We've got the house staked out from all angles, sir, and the immediate neighbours have been evacuated. The rest of the street's been told to stay indoors and keep away from windows until further notice."

"Do you know for definite who's inside?"

"Well, we're not absolutely sure but we think there's just one man and a girl. We were tipped off by a neighbour. The general description of the suspect was a bit vague but he recognised the Volkswagen from the newspaper report and put two and two together. He'd seen him drive it out of a garage block at the end of the street. He remembered it because he'd had words with the guy a couple of weeks before about double parking a van or something, and he was surprised to see him driving the Beetle and not the van they'd argued over."

"And the girl?" enquired his superior in an uninvolved and detached manner.

"According to our witness she's the girlfriend. French; Caucasian; blonde; middle twenties. She may be part of it or simply a dupe that he's using for cover. She normally leaves for work around 7.15 so we're hoping to nab her as she comes out and get her away, in case he tries to use her as a hostage."

"Alright. Well, keep me posted will you? And good luck."

The line unceremoniously clicked into silence and LeBec looked at his sergeant.

"What does he expect?" he asked despairingly. "A running commentary?"

Nicot smiled. "Well he needs to know what's happening so he can claim the credit for it later, when we've done all the work. That's what being promoted is all about."

"Well if we don't pull something out of the bag from this little jaunt, that's a problem that you and I won't have to contend with."

The tension of simply sitting and waiting is something that even "old hands" dislike. Clémence had swept the same piece of kerb at least six times and Paul Nicot was halfway through his second packet of mints when, at 7.22, the door of number 17 opened and a young blonde woman stepped into the street.

LeBec's voice spoke through the small earphone that was clipped to Clémence's right ear. "Off you go. And gently does it."

Clémence leaned his broom against the cart and turned to the girl as she approached. He politely touched his beret as he stepped towards her.

"Morning Mam'selle. Excuse me, but would you have a light, please?"

"No" replied the young woman without really looking at him. "I'm sorry, I don't."

By the time she drew level with Clémence he was walking in step with her and, in one easy movement that didn't allow her pace to falter, he grabbed her firmly by the elbow and began marching her away as he spoke.

"Then perhaps you would be good enough to accompany me to the end of the street. Don't worry, I'm a police officer."

The look of indignant surprise quickly left her face as she suddenly realised the full import of why Clémence was there. If LeBec had any doubts as to whether she was aware of the darker side of her boyfriend's activities, they were swiftly dispelled as she threw back her head and screamed at the top of her voice "Samir! Samir!"

Clémence immediately clapped a hand to her mouth but she bit savagely into his middle finger and, in the second in which he winced against the pain and his hold on her weakened, she broke free from his grasp and turned back towards the house, still screaming in panic.

LeBec was out of the car and running towards her in a moment but her warning had had its effect and, by the time he reached her, the door of number 17 had opened behind him. The young Syrian man who emerged was slim, olive-skinned and stark naked save for the 9mm Browning pistol that he raised as he ran towards the Chief Inspector and the struggling girl.

LeBec turned in time to see the oncoming man level the gun at him. The barrel was pointing directly at his chest but, almost before he had time to register the fact he was an unmissable target, there were two short, clear reports and the naked man fell heavily to the ground. The echo of the shots bounced menacingly across the street from wall to wall. Then, for a moment, all was stillness.

The eerie silence was suddenly broken by a long drawn-out wail of "No! ..." and the young woman wrenched herself free from LeBec's grasp and ran to the prostrate body that was now oozing blood.

Clémence ran to the doorway, his pistol in hand, and flattened himself against the outside wall. As he did so, Paul Nicot hurried from the

Peugeot and took a similar position on the other side of the opening. With a nod to each other, Clémence yelled "Go!" into his lapel microphone and the two men rushed into the dark of the yawning doorway while, responding to his cue, the officers at the back of the building and the man on the roof simultaneously burst into the house.

LeBec stood over the woman, who was cradling the head of the young Syrian in her blood-soaked arms, sobbing in anguish and repeating his name over and over: "Samir, Samir ..." The presence of the silent policeman made her look up, her anger surging through her grief.

"You fucking pigs!" She spat the words at him in her hatred. "How many of you does it take? You've murdered him!"

LeBec knelt and turned the head of the shot man. There was no scar on either cheek.

"You've murdered him!" she wailed again.

Picking up the arm that lay limp at the side of the naked man and feeling at the wrist for some sign of a pulse, the detective shook his head.

"Not quite, Mam'selle. Not quite."

Paul Nicot stepped back into the street from the door of number 17 and waived an all-clear to the marksmen in the opposite building. Then he ran to where his boss was crouched over the body.

"How is he?" he asked.

"One in the chest, looks like a collapsed lung, and one in the abdomen. It's bad. He's bleeding heavily."

"Will he live?"

"He might. If we get him to hospital in time."

Nicot made to move. "I'll call up the medics. The ambulance is waiting at the roadblock."

"Just a minute, Paul."

LeBec turned to look directly into the distraught face of the weeping blonde.

"Lover boy's in a bad way. He needs help. But then so do I. Now I'm a fair man and if he helps me, I'll help him. So let's wake him up, shall we?"

He leant forward and began tapping the cheeks of the unconscious Syrian, all the while continuing to hold his wrist.

"Come on, sunshine. Wakey, wakey!"

The young woman stared at him in disbelief.

"You bastard! He's dying for Christ's sake! Call the ambulance! Call the fucking ambulance!"

LeBec ignored her and continued to address the unhearing face of her lover.

"Come on, Samir. Who's the man with the scar on his cheek? Wake up, Samir! Who's the man with the scar?"

"Stop it! Stop it!" she screamed at him. "Fetch the ambulance!"

She turned her plea to the sergeant.

"For Christ's sake fetch the ambulance! Please!"

Nicot didn't like what was happening but, right or wrong, callous or not, he had to follow his boss's lead. He remained silent and his impassive face offered the woman no hope.

"Kahlil!" she yelled at LeBec. "Kahlil! The man with the scar is Kahlil!"

"Where is he now?" he demanded.

"I don't know" she wailed. "I don't know!"

The policeman turned back to the blood-soaked Syrian and again began tapping his face.

"Come on, Samir. Where's Kahlil?"

Frantic, the woman shouted at him in desperation.

"We don't know, I tell you! They daren't meet after an operation, not for days. He could be anywhere!"

The damn was breached and LeBec pushed home his advantage, his tone ever more insistent and demanding.

"How do they make contact? Come on woman, he's dying! Answer me!"

She was sobbing in fear and frustration, hating this policeman more than she'd ever hated anyone in her life. But LeBec got what he wanted.

"By post! A card arrives with a time and a phone box. He gets a call with instructions and they meet – but it's never the same place!"

"Then where was his last supply pick-up?"

"Vaugirard. Somewhere near the Quai de Grenelle. That's all I know. I swear it! I swear it!"

Her sobs began to overtake her and she collapsed over the body of Samir.

LeBec looked up at his sergeant. His face was a mixture of grim satisfaction and relief.

"Can I fetch the ambulance?" asked Nicot anxiously.

His boss laid down the lifeless arm and stood.

"Yes" he replied quietly. "But tell them not to panic. He was dead before he hit the ground."

LeBec walked across the street to where Clémence and the rest of the team had gathered. He looked at them one by one. As always they had gone into the operation not knowing what to expect and the relief that there had been no major action and none amongst them had been hurt was apparent in their faces. At the same time, they were all aware they had not been successful and had failed to take their man unharmed.

"He's a gonner" said LeBec impassively.

"Shit!" murmured Clémence, as he finished tying a knot in the handkerchief he had wrapped around his bleeding finger.

"Who got him?" asked the Chief Inspector.

"We did, sir."

He looked at the two men to his left, one of whom had been in the ground floor flat of the apartment building opposite, the other on the roof. The man who had answered him spoke again.

"We tried to wing him, sir. But he was moving very fast and there was precious little time."

LeBec nodded. "Alright. I understand." He turned to Clémence. "You can wrap it up now. Hang on here yourself until forensic arrives and then make sure the local boys know what to do."

"Right, guv'nor" said Clémence. "Come on you lot, let's get moving."

As the group broke up, LeBec called to the two marksmen who had so devastatingly found their target and saved his own life.

"Oh and gentlemen ..."

There were seldom any effusive words between LeBec and his men but the two officers knew the full depth of his gratitude as they turned to face him and he said simply: "Thank you". And then poignantly added "Very much."

*****

Alan Russell fell back against his chair in stunned silence, unable to believe what he had just heard. He turned to the silver-haired man opposite him.

"I don't understand" he told him quietly.

"I'm sure you don't" came the calm reply. "But if you'll allow me to explain I think it will all start to make sense."

The man looked up at his colleague with the air of a benign headmaster.

"I think some tea is in order, don't you? Would you oblige?"

As Russell heard the younger man pick up the telephone and dial room service it struck him that it was a particularly British absurdity to think of ordering tea at such a moment. Then, suddenly, despite his bewilderment, he realised there was more about his two companions than a desire to order tea that held a familiarity for him. The younger man behaved with an almost military deference to the other and at no time had they referred to each other by name. It was a pattern he had seen before.

Russell looked again at the older man. Everything about him was precise and perfectly presented; his suit, his shoes, his collar and tie, all were immaculate; and his hair and moustache looked as if he had just left his barber. Ex Guards, he said to himself. And probably Eton and Sandhurst before that.

"I take it you are not from hotel security?" he ventured.

"You take it correctly."

"And you are not the police, are you?"

"No, we are not the police" said the silver-haired man with a mildly sympathetic smile.

The non-committal reply was enough to let Russell know that his assumption was correct and the shock and confusion of the last few minutes gave way to a cold caution. He still had no idea how or why he was in this situation but he knew that it had something to do with the previous evening and that it was somehow important enough to arouse the interest of the anonymous men who now confronted him. It alarmed him.

"What did you mean, *she* filmed it?" he asked cautiously.

"The camera was probably on the coffee table at the end of the room. Nothing out of the ordinary; a small domestic video camera about the size of a paperback. Shielded by a handbag or hidden under a scarf you wouldn't have known it was there."

"But why? I don't understand. And how did you get hold of it?"

"We borrowed it. Miss Petrova breakfasted early this morning and then left the hotel rather hurriedly but she was in the restaurant long enough for us to search her room. Once we found the camera we simply copied the memory card and replaced it again. It takes no more than a couple of minutes. As to why ... it was insurance; a back-up for future reference."

Russell shook his head in genuine bewilderment.

"I still don't understand."

The other man paused and then lowered his voice a little, like a doctor about to deliver an unpleasant diagnosis to his patient.

"I'm afraid the attentions of the rather alluring Miss Petrova have not been directed towards you for entirely selfish reasons, Mr. Russell. She was following orders."

Russell could only stare blankly, inviting further explanation.

"She was trying to recruit you" said the older man, as though stating the obvious. "She's an agent of the Russian government. Also known as Nina Panova, Galina Zagorinskya and sometimes Yekaterina Belova. We've been aware of her for some time. She works for Gurevich."

"The Health Ministry guy?" asked Russell in amazement.

"He should have been more correctly introduced to you as *Colonel* Gurevich. He's a senior and highly respected officer of the Russian secret service."

He continued calmly, showing no reaction to the disbelief that was registering on Russell's face.

"I've shown you this rather unpleasant recording because I felt, without such proof, you wouldn't believe my accusations towards Miss Petrova. However, should you still doubt me, you will find a current Moscow telephone directory on the table. Please call *The Russia Journal*. You will find they know of no journalist of that name working for them. Her current press accreditation and her working visa are both bogus."

Every word he heard only served to deepen Russell's disorientation. He could find no connection between the reality of the girl he had known during the previous days and the extraordinary scenario that was unfolding. Still searching for some rational explanation he asked:

"But even if what you say is correct, why should she be interested in me? What's the point of it all?"

The silver-haired man sat back and clasped his hands together, interfolding the fingers, and delicately brought them to rest in his lap. He was a strange cross between a judge about to pass sentence and a priest hearing confession.

"That brings us to why we asked to see you this morning. You are aware of course that as a servant of the crown and a signatory to the Official Secrets Act, you are legally bound to honour the confidentiality of what I may tell you. However, I must also inform you that the details of Miss Petrova's intentions and the background to them are highly classified. Such knowledge would place certain further restraints and restrictions upon you."

The conversation was suddenly interrupted by the knocking on the door of the room-service waitress. Having relieved her of her burden, the man in the blazer brought the laden tea-tray into the room and benevolently asked: "Shall I be mother?"

Though still confused and shocked by all that had taken place in the preceding quarter of an hour, Russell's caution was beginning to give way to his anger and he was in no mood to be patronised.

"Now look" he said firmly. "I've been brought here under a false pretext, made to watch a voyeuristic recording of a private room and spun some story about spies and classified information. Now you expect me to sit calmly and drink tea as if we're on some family bloody picnic!" His impatience and his volume rose considerably. "Well, before this charade goes any further, I want to know exactly who you are and just what the hell is going on here!"

The man in the blazer continued to pour the tea, leaving the answer to his superior whose tone was totally unruffled by Russell's indignation.

"Very well, Mr. Russell. I can appreciate how you must feel."

He held out his hand to accept the proffered cup and saucer

as he continued.

"My name is Caswell. Major Caswell. This is Blair." He gestured towards his companion, who nodded his head in Russell's direction. "I run a very small and somewhat specialised department within the Special Intelligence Service."

"You mean MI6?"

"A section within it, yes. But it's not something we like to broadcast as I'm sure you'll understand. Perhaps you now appreciate our desire for caution."

This wasn't a question, it was a statement.

"And I don't suppose those are your real names?" Russell enquired.

Caswell shrugged. "In the words of the bard, Mr. Russell, 'what's in a name'?"

Russell couldn't tell whether that was a "yes" or a "no" but as he looked from one to the other, he knew he would get no more out of them than they were disposed to divulge.

"I still don't understand what all this has to do with me" he persisted.

At last, Caswell began to elaborate further.

"You have been translating information over the last couple of days relating to the A.I.D.S. virus – or to give it its correct name the H.I.V. Have you yet learned anything of its particular characteristics?"

Russell shook his head. "Not in any detail, no."

"Then allow me to enlighten you. It's a retro virus that attacks certain white blood cells. They're called T4 lymphocytes and are essential for the body's defences. If they are destroyed the body can fight no infection and the patient dies. The distinctive feature of a retro virus is that it can make copies of its own genetic information and inject this into the D.N.A. of any cell it invades. Are you with me so far?"

Russell nodded impatiently. He had no idea why he was being given a biology lesson but he allowed it to continue.

"The H.I.V. is unique in that it has three genes that have never been seen before. One of these is the trigger that tells the cell to start reproducing and taking over the body. That's when the patient moves from simply being H.I.V. positive to developing full-blown A.I.D.S. This trigger is the key to the whole problem. It's called a 'trans-activator' and without it the virus remains dormant and harmless. If we understood how it functions, and thereby how to stop it, the A.I.D.S. problem would be solved overnight."

Caswell took a long sip of his tea and then replaced his cup slowly and deliberately in the saucer, fixing Russell's eyes as he did so.

"You may be surprised to learn that, if our information is correct, and we have every reason to believe that it is, Professor Litvinov has not only isolated this 'trans-activator' but is only months, perhaps even weeks, away from neutralising it."

Russell's brow furrowed into a deep frown.

"You mean the old man has done it?" he asked incredulously. "Found the cure?"

"More of an immunity than a cure – but, virtually, yes."

"But I don't understand. Why are half the medical brains in Europe sitting here talking about it if he's already done it?"

"Well, that's where the good news turns rather sinister, I'm afraid."

Caswell's eyes narrowed. The confessional priest was now wholly usurped by the sentencing judge.

"There are far more unpleasant things than H.I.V. locked in laboratory vaults around the world. Possessing a gene that regulates cell reproduction means you can control them. Do you follow me?"

Russell wasn't certain that he did.

"You mean germ warfare?"

"The threat of it, to be more precise. It's long been understood that the arms race is ridiculous. It pours money down a bottomless pit to provide weapons that become obsolete before they're built and to avoid a conflict that would be mutually suicidal anyway. It saves enormous wastes of money and man-power if your deterrent is a small bottle sitting on a laboratory shelf."

"But germ warfare has been around for decades" protested Russell. "Why should this make all the difference?"

"Because this makes it suddenly totally controllable."

Russell found the whole scenario beyond belief.

"Do you mean to tell me that anyone would sit back and watch half the world go down with A.I.D.S. in order to hang on to some secret biological weapon?"

"Not necessarily. If immunity is found it might possibly be shared without revealing how it was achieved. I'm simply saying that the means of bringing it about is, in itself, an extraordinarily powerful weapon."

Suddenly, and for the first time, the calm detachment began to slip away and the Major appeared to warm to his cause.

"I'd go further. Until both sides have that information, the race to be the first is every bit as urgent and vital as the race to get the bomb was in the second world war."

"But we're not at war" Russell countered vigorously. "And we're faced with an epidemic that's killing millions of people. I can't believe that little old man is sitting on the answer and not telling the rest of us. It's obscene!"

"He tried to tell us. He's been filtering information through to us from the moment his research began. But once he realised he was getting close to an answer the K.G.B. whisked him into hiding. The Geneva conference was the first we've seen of him since."

"But the K.G.B. doesn't exist anymore" Russell complained. The Soviet Union doesn't exist any more. We're all supposed to be on the same side now, for Christ's sake."

Caswell leaned forward in his seat and it occurred to Russell that it was probably as animated as he ever allowed himself to be. None the less his voice rose with a distinct enthusiasm.

"Oh I grant you the goal posts have been moved, but we're still playing the same team Mr. Russell. The hard-line militarists haven't suddenly disappeared or miraculously reformed you know. And they're all still in place. K.G.B. or F.S.B. - it's all the same personnel. Who do you think keeps resistance at bay while Putin moves further and further to absolute power - the Moscow Boy Scouts?"

For the first time, Blair entered the conversation.

"A rose by any other name, Mr. Russell. Nothing has really changed. No nation can exist without a security service and the new Russia had no choice but to use the one it had. It was in position, it had been running efficiently for decades and was staffed by experienced professionals who are impossible to replace. It may have a new name but it is, in effect, the same K.G.B. it has always been. And in his previous incarnation, Putin was one of its star officers."

Caswell enthusiastically picked up the theme.

"The only difference is that now, like the rest of their economy, they are under severe financial pressure. Which makes the military potential of Litvinov's work all the more valuable to them."

"Eventually" said Blair, "others will duplicate Litvinov's work – but it could take a couple of years. Until then they'll hold all the cards. So they intend to keep him under lock and key."

"Then why did they allow him to attend these conferences?" Russell asked the Major.

"They had no choice. The W.H.O. asked for him and in the present climate of so-called 'co-operation' they couldn't decline. So, until the conferences are over, he's at risk. Which is precisely why the delightful Miss Petrova has been paying you such close attention and we are sitting here now at this ... 'picnic', as I believe you called it."

Suddenly Russell began to glimpse a thread of daylight in all the dark confusion that had beset him. But he didn't like some of the possibilities it was beginning to weave at the back of his mind.

"I'm still not sure I understand what any of this has to do with me" he said cautiously.

"Gurevich is a master of his profession and leaves nothing to chance. We are not yet sure of exactly who is with him but either your opposite number Pavel Golombek or, more likely, Ivan Zhukov is one of his staff. Possibly both of them. That is in addition to the charming Miss Petrova whom you have, of course, already met. Between them, Litvinov is watched every minute of the day and night. He has been told exactly what he may or may not reveal to the conference and his constant companions make it impossible for us to get information either to or from him."

"So?" said Russell tentatively.

"So if we were going to make contact with Litvinov, we'd need to get a man close to him. The interpreter, being the non-medical outsider would be the logical choice."

Daylight finally broke through and the pieces began to fall uncomfortably into place.

"You mean they think I'm working for you?" Russell asked in amazement.

"I mean they've been checking you out" came Caswell's quiet reply. He pointed to the video-player lying by the side of the television. "This little cinematic enterprise was their ammunition. It would have been used to lean on you if they needed to."

"My God" said Russell, stunned. "Well, I must have more than upset their apple-cart when I didn't play ball."

For the first time, Caswell allowed himself a smile.

"Precisely" he said evenly.

It was only one word but something in the man's tone caused an alarm bell to ring in Russell's head.

"Meaning?" he asked nervously.

"Gurevich is extremely thorough. He will have checked you out in every detail by now and found that you are exactly what you purport to be: an interpreter. Declining Miss Petrova's charms last night will have only served to confirm your admirable morals and genuine innocence. Which is exactly why you are now of such interest to me."

There was a pregnant pause. Russell looked from one to the other and realised what they were suggesting.

"Oh, now wait a minute" he began. Caswell cut him short.

"Before you say anything, let me clarify what I'm asking for. You would be required to do no more than pass a little information once the conference gets to Paris. You'd just be a messenger, that's all. And you are uniquely positioned to help and enable us to set up what must be done. The more hazardous aspects would of course not involve you and would be undertaken by those qualified to do so."

Russell was reeling under the rush of all he was trying to take on board.

"What do you mean by *what must be done?*"

The Major squared his shoulders and sat back. He was clearly reticent to explain but Russell's demanding look offered him little alternative if his attempted recruitment was to succeed. After a moment's deliberation, he reluctantly continued.

"I'm asking for your help, Mr. Russell, so I have no option but to trust you. But what you have already heard and what I am about to tell you must go no further than this room. Is that properly understood?"

"Yes, of course."

"Professor Litvinov wants to come over to us."

Russell straightened in his chair.

"You mean defect?"

"A rather outdated term for these times of détente. Let's just say we're going to help him emigrate; unofficially of course. We had originally planned for this to take place here in Cambridge but we were overtaken by events and it now has to be done in Paris. To facilitate this, we need someone to pass the contact information, that's all; nothing more."

"And you're ideally placed" interjected Blair. "You're close to Litvinov and they've checked you out and found that you don't work for us."

"I bloody well do if I say 'yes' to him now!"

"But Mr. Russell ..." protested Blair.

"Besides" said Russell cutting him off. "If this is all so important, why don't you use one of your own men? MI6 has access to linguists. Why didn't you put a man in right from the beginning?"

There was a pause. Then the response was emotionless.

"We did" said Caswell dryly.

"Then where is he now?" asked Russell in surprise.

The other two men exchanged a look before the Major spoke, as if tacitly agreeing they must break a confidence.

"Your predecessor was a man named Bentley" he said quietly.

Russell raised his eyebrows.

"*Gavin* Bentley?"

"That is correct."

"You mean Gavin Bentley works for you? He's an agent?"

"He has undertaken certain tasks for us in the past, yes" the Major told him impassively.

"Well I'm damned! I never would have dreamt it. I mean, we weren't particularly close or anything but you think you get to know someone reasonably well when you work with them over a few years." He stopped and gave Caswell a puzzled look as an obvious thought struck him. "But if Bentley is your man, what's your problem? He'll be well again by the time the conference moves to Paris."

The two men again exchanged a conspiratorial glance.

"Mr Bentley suffered a skiing accident last week" said Blair coolly.

"Was it serious?"

Blair looked down into his tea cup and paused before he raised his eyes again and replied "I'm afraid it was fatal".

"What?" said Russell, shocked. "But Gavin was an excellent skier. He skied all the time".

"So I believe" said Blair, returning his focus to his tea.

A shudder ran down Russell's spine as he realised the import of the look that had passed between the two men.

"Oh my God" he said slowly. "It wasn't an accident at all, was it? That's what you meant by *overtaken by events* right? They'd rumbled him, hadn't they?"

Caswell's tone remained as calm as ever.

"The possibility cannot be discounted. The job naturally involves an element of risk."

"An element of risk? We're talking about a man's life! He's dead, for God's sake!"

"But you would not be running those risks" insisted Caswell energetically. "Bentley did work for us. You don't and you've already been cleared. They no longer suspect you."

"I've only got your word for that, not theirs!" Russell snapped.

"But you'd be quite safe" retorted Caswell. "If there were the remotest possible chance of them suspecting you then you'd be of no use to me. As an intelligent man, surely you can see that? And it's of no exaggeration to say this is of vital importance. Perhaps to the whole of mankind."

"Look" said Russell vehemently. "I'm sorry Major Caswell, or whatever your name is, but let's get one thing clear. I'm an interpreter; a linguist. I'm Joe Schmo, the guy in the street. I don't gamble, I don't smoke and I don't drink much. Hell, I can't even cheat on my wife when I'm in a hotel room with a beautiful girl! I don't exactly fit the James Bond mould! Now you're asking me to get involved in something ... what was it? ... of *vital importance to mankind*. And what's more, you're asking me to step into the shoes of a man who was very possibly murdered for doing the same thing. Oh no, I'm sorry but you'll have to find yourself another boy."

There was a highly palpable silence. Then Blair addressed him, like a surgeon turning on his best bedside manner to put the patient at ease before a difficult operation.

"Mr. Russell you've had quite an unusual morning and it's only natural you should feel shocked by all that you've heard. Please don't make any decisions until you've had time to think it all through clearly. I assure you we would not put you to any undue risk and the matter really is of the utmost magnitude."

Russell turned to face him squarely.

"No. I'm sorry, really I am. I'd like to help but I'm just not the right man for the job. Especially if it's as important as you say it is. I'm not qualified to undertake such a responsibility and I've no intention of doing so. Nor of making my wife a widow in the process. My answer is 'no'."

Caswell's face still betrayed no emotion.

"You disappoint me, Mr. Russell. However, I obviously cannot force you to help us. If you choose to refuse there is nothing I can do."

There was a strong tone of dismissal in the Major's voice and somehow Russell felt decidedly guilty. Though he knew it was without foundation, he had a distinct sense of failure, as though he'd let the side down, not been up to scratch or worthy of the duty expected of him. He realised how easy it must have been for people like Gavin Bentley to become involved with them, to be susceptible to their persuasive line of Queen and Country. But it was not an argument to which he intended to succumb.

"I'm sorry. But I won't change my mind" he replied resolutely. "I appreciate you will want me to leave the assignment, knowing what I now know."

"On the contrary" said Caswell abruptly. "Your sudden absence would only arouse suspicion. Albeit that your innocence remains genuine, you are still of some use to us by remaining as part of the team. It makes our task all the harder of course but changing you now would only attract greater attention to your replacement. No, Mr. Russell, you must remain in post. But I need your solemn oath that not one word of this conversation will pass your lips."

"Of course. That much I can promise."

"Very well. Then, regretfully, we need detain you no longer."

Russell gave a silent nod of acknowledgement and turned to leave but the Major spoke again.

"Just one more thing. Should Miss Petrova or anyone else connected with Gurevich make contact again, perhaps you'd let us know? We like to keep tabs on these things. Here is a number where you can reach me. You don't ask for me by name. Simply say who you are and that you wish to speak to the managing director."

He handed Russell a business card on which was printed *The Albion Import and Export Company*, with an address in Poland Street in Soho. Russell pocketed the card and walked to the door that Blair was holding open for him. Then he stopped and turned again to Caswell as an unpleasant thought occurred to him.

"What about the video?" he asked somewhat apologetically.

"Don't worry. It will be destroyed" replied the Major in a matter-of-fact tone. "We have no use for it."

Russell nodded again, said a quiet "thank you" and left the room.

"That's a bit of a blow, sir" said Blair.

"Mmm. Indeed it is."

Caswell's eye fell upon a copy of yesterday's newspaper that was lying on the table next to the television set. The identikit picture of the Paris terrorist glared up at him from the folded page. He picked up the paper and continued to stare at it as he spoke.

"Blair."

"Yes, sir?"

"Order some more tea, will you?"

* * * * *

The final day of the conference was devoted to health care professionals and the problems of treating those suffering from the disease. This meant that the scientists and those concerned with research participated only in the morning's session so, happily, Russell learned that his services were only required until mid-day.

The earlier extraordinary revelations about the people with whom he was working had left him uncomfortable in their presence. He had to make a point of not looking at Gurevich for fear of staring and giving away something in his expression, and each time he heard Litvinov speak he could not clear his mind of what he now knew about the Professor. It became increasingly difficult to concentrate and he was greatly relieved when twelve o'clock arrived and his ordeal was over.

The usual mêlée gathered in the college vestibule as the various delegates thanked their international colleagues and made their farewells. Russell saw Gurevich, flanked as always by Golombek and Zhukov, move Litvinov swiftly through the handshakes and goodbyes and out of the doors to the cars that awaited them. He was pleased to see them depart. Now that he no longer had to face them he determined to try and shrug off the whole episode and put it from his mind.

He took his leave of Sir Peter Mayer and the rest of the team as quickly as he reasonably could and returned to the Posthouse to collect his bags. While he was checking out he casually asked the receptionist about Nina Petrova. She had indeed left early that morning just as Caswell had said.

It took Russell just over two hours to drive back to the cottage. The crunching sound of the tyres on the gravel drive was never more welcome as he pulled the Mondeo to a halt and switched off the engine.

Taniel had heard the car arrive and as his key turned in the lock she was already in the hall to meet him.

"I didn't expect you home so early!" she said with a delighted smile.

He adopted a look of mock indignation.

"Sorry to disappoint you. I'll go out and come back later if you prefer."

She laughed affectionately. "Idiot! Come here and give me a hug."

He put his arms around her and squeezed her tightly, never more grateful for the warmth of her, the smell of her hair and the softness of her cheek against his. For a few moments neither of them spoke and then, each with their head still over the other's shoulder, she asked:

"How was the conference? I bet it was interesting."

He nodded, glad that she couldn't see his face.

"Yes. I learned quite a bit that I didn't know before."

"Good" she said enthusiastically. "I want to hear all about it. Especially the new areas of research."

Russell pulled back his head and looked into her dark, inviting eyes.

"Well there's a fine welcome! You're not on duty now you know. Your husband's come home after three days away and all you can do is think like a doctor."

She beamed at him.

"Sorry. What does my lord and master require? A bath and a rest after his long labours? Something to eat?"

Standing there holding her close, his feelings for her were stronger than ever and he suddenly felt relaxed again and free from the unreality of the last three days. He let his forehead come to rest against hers.

"No" he whispered gently. "All that can wait. Let's go to bed."

* * * * *

If the end of the Cambridge conference was a great relief to Alan Russell, it was no less welcome to Dimitri Gurevich. While Russell was finding comfort in the arms of his wife, the Russian Colonel was settling into his seat aboard his return flight to Berlin. As flight AB8855 climbed to leave Stansted far below, like some model replica of itself, he glanced at his watch. It was 3.57pm. The plane was just two minutes behind schedule. In an hour and a half he would be landing at Tegel airport. From there he would transfer to Shönefeld and pick up the Aeroflot flight to Sheremetyevo. It would still be three hours before they touched down in Moscow with his cargo safe and sound but he was reasonably confident that the threat of any danger at this late stage was very remote.

Everything had gone according to plan and his superiors would be more than happy. But Gurevich wasn't. What continued to disturb his professional mind was the same nagging question: why was the diminutive professor so important to them? Rule number one was always to understand your enemy. Put yourself in his position. Learn how he thinks and what his problems are and you stay one step ahead. Without knowing why he was guarding Litvinov he couldn't begin to see things from the other side's point of view – and that made him vulnerable.

As the aircraft continued climbing into the clouds he noticed the spatter of rain against the window. He stared out into the grey blanket that was darkening under the coming November evening and thought about Paris and the conference in the new year. Was Melekhin right? Was it all a question of overkill? Were they baby-sitting when the baby was really in no danger at all? Logic might have said so but his instincts told him otherwise. If there was to be a threat then Paris was now where it had to be waiting. There were some six or seven weeks in which Gurevich promised himself he would do his damndest to strengthen his position. If his own side were giving nothing away then he would have to look at the opposition. Maybe their behaviour would throw up some more clues as to the importance of Litvinov and from where a threat might materialise. If necessary he would go back into the field himself. Whatever it took, he was resolved to learn more about the elderly professor who sat beside him quietly reading. He would put those weeks to good use and he would begin first thing the following morning, determined not to waste a single day.

Six

England

It wasn't until the following Friday morning that Russell realised he'd seen the car before. Even then, he might not have noticed if it hadn't been for the bend. Glancing in the rear-view mirror, he suddenly remembered seeing it in exactly the same location the previous day.

He had grown to know his usual route very well and this particular bend, in the village of Turner's Hill, wound sharply through a blind corner and then narrowed. It was something of a local black-spot and there had been innumerable accidents. Russell always slowed considerably when approaching it and checked his mirror to make sure any following vehicles were likewise decreasing their speed. As he did so, he recognised the car from the day before.

At first he attached no particular importance to what he assumed was a simple coincidence but it gradually began to dawn on him that such chance odds were excessively long. Russell never kept uniform hours and his journeys to and from London were totally without pattern. Yesterday had been a free morning so it must have been at least noon before he reached Turner's Hill. It was now 8.30am and yet here was the same yellow Nissan. He studied its reflection, framed by the large patch the heated rear window had cleared in the Mondeo's glass, frosted by the morning cold.

The events of the previous weekend had begun to be less intrusive as he had settled back into the routine of daily life but slowly, as he watched the vehicle behind follow his every turn, an uncomfortable thought began to present itself. He tried to rid himself of the idea and dismiss it as fantasy but five miles later the yellow car was still there. He considered simply driving in a circle and heading back towards Wych Cross to see if the Nissan followed suit but, if he was being shadowed, such unreasonable behaviour would let his pursuers know he was aware of them. By the time he'd reached Copthorne, a solution presented itself in the beckoning shape of a large neon Shell sign a quarter of a mile ahead.

"Alright" he said to the unhearing driver of the tailing car, "let's find out just what you're about."

He indicated left and pulled into the filling station. As he got out of his car the Nissan passed by. It wasn't easy to see the occupants clearly. All he could tell was that they were both men. He could discern that the passenger was dark-haired and wore glasses but no more. He filled his vehicle, paid the bill at the kiosk and then drove to the side of the exit slip and switched off his engine. He checked his watch and waited. Once ten minutes had elapsed he started the Mondeo again and rejoined the traffic, earnestly scanning the road and hoping that he wouldn't see the yellow car parked and waiting somewhere ahead. Five minutes later there was still no trace of it and he began to relax, chiding himself for having an overactive imagination. Then, as a red light brought the Mondeo to rest at a high-street junction, the unwelcome truth came rushing in. As he looked in the mirror, a flash of bright yellow two vehicles behind him confirmed his fears.

For a moment Russell was unsure what to do. He was angry at being followed but was very much aware that, if Caswell was right, these were not men to be treated lightly. Gavin Bentley's death was adequate testimony to that. He decided to do nothing out of the ordinary and to continue his journey. He reasoned that if he was under surveillance it was safer to give no cause for concern and to avoid arousing the suspicion of his unwanted chaperones.

An hour later he walked through the door of his Whitehall office. It was a large room where he and three other interpreters each had a p.c., a telephone on a standard issue desk, a filing cabinet and a regulation swivel chair. The four of them were seldom, if ever, in the office at the same time and he was relieved to find that the others were all elsewhere on this particular morning. Without waiting to remove his coat, he sat at his desk and dialled the number on the business card that he pulled from his wallet.

"Albion Import and Export Company" said a female voice in polite but perfunctory greeting. "How may I help you?"

"I'd like to speak to the managing director, please."

"May I ask what it's in connection with?"

He hesitated, unsure of what he should or shouldn't say.

"It's a personal matter."

"Then may I ask who's calling?" she said in a diffident manner.

"My name is Russell. Alan Russell."

"One moment, please."

The line clicked into silence as his call was put on hold. Russell heard a noise outside in the corridor and cursed himself for not using his cell phone and calling from the privacy of his car. The distorted image of the head and shoulders of one of the secretaries passed the patterned glass pane of the door and, to Russell's relief, continued by. The voice in his ear suddenly spoke again.

"I'm putting you through now, sir."

He recognised the precise tones that then addressed him.

"Good morning Mr. Russell. Is there something I can do for you?"

"You said to telephone if I was contacted again."

The voice at the other end of the line paused for a second.

"From where are you speaking?" asked Caswell, concerned.

"My office. I've just arrived."

"Then I hope you are alone?"

"Yes. Yes, of course."

"Good. Please tell me exactly what has occurred."

"I was followed. Yesterday and today. Possibly before that; I don't really know. I only realised it was happening this morning."

"Are you quite sure? It's not possible you're mistaken?"

"No. I'm certain. It was two men in a yellow Nissan. They tailed me all the way from home to the office."

"Where are they now, outside?"

"I don't think so. When I turned into the car park they drove by and seemed to continue on."

"Can you describe them at all?"

"Not really. I didn't see them clearly enough for that."

"Pity. Did you by chance get the registration number?"

"Yes I did. EK 01 CDY."

Caswell repeated it back to him slowly and deliberately, obviously writing it down.

"Well done" he said. "We'll check it out."

"But what should I do?" Russell pressed him further.

"Do?" came the surprised reply.

"Yes. What am I supposed to do?"

"There's nothing very much you *can* do, Mr. Russell. I did warn you they may still be checking up on you. Your best course of action is to do nothing at all. Provided you behave as normal, they'll eventually disappear as quietly as they came; if indeed they've not already done so."

"I suppose you're right" Russell reluctantly agreed. "It's just that it isn't very pleasant to know you're being followed."

"I can appreciate that and I sympathise with you but I assure you that to do nothing and remain calm is the best policy."

The Major's voice didn't sound in the least sympathetic.

"However, you were quite right to let me know. I doubt there will be any further developments but please telephone me again if you have any cause for concern. Thank you for calling. Good day."

The line went dead. Russell slowly replaced the receiver and sat, thoughtful, for several minutes. Like it or not, the Major was right. There was nothing to do but wait it out.

* * * * *

France

Waiting was not a favourite occupation of Henri LeBec but for the past four days he'd had no option but to do just that. He stood at the window of his fifth-floor office staring at the familiar streets that looked so strangely different under the thick snow that had fallen during the previous night. The endless stream of passers-by had forged a dark, slushy path through the white-carpeted sidewalk as they struggled to get to work. All over Paris journeys were being delayed by frozen railway points, cancelled buses and the even longer than usual traffic jams.

A wry smile broke over LeBec's face as he mused that something as natural and simple as a snow-fall could still cause chaos in a modern, sophisticated city and bring it to a virtual halt. He liked the notion. It appealed to his sense of balance and order. Mankind, in its conceit, with all its technology, and the sinister knowledge that its more perverted members used to explode bombs and wreak havoc on the streets, still couldn't get through those same streets if nature simply decided to snow and bring them to a standstill. He too had come to something of a standstill but it was nothing to do with the weather.

There was a knock at the door but sergeant Nicot entered without waiting to be asked.

"We've found the apartment" he said excitedly. "We've been checking recent lets around the Quai de Grenelle. The girl was on the level."

LeBec wasted no time in comment but snatched his coat from behind the door and marched out. The bustling sergeant was hard on his heels, completing the news.

"The whole building is owned by a property company. The letting was all done by post and the rent was paid well in advance. The two signatories are Syrian nationals."

LeBec spoke over his shoulder to Nicot, who was breathing hard and striving to keep up with his boss as he hurried down the stairs.

"How long have they actually been there?"

"The agreement was signed just over a month ago. We don't know exactly when they moved in – but they did a runner last night."

"Is forensic there yet?"

"They're on their way."

They'd reached the second-floor landing when the overweight sergeant was forced to stop and pause for air.

"Why couldn't we have waited for the lift?" he mumbled to himself as LeBec called back to him.

"Come on Paul, don't hang around. You can collapse when we're in the car."

"Thank you, Chief Inspector. Very considerate of you" said Nicot under his waning breath, and he urged his complaining bulk to a final effort.

It was a small apartment in a rather shabby, run-down block. There were just two rooms in addition to a kitchenette and a tiny bathroom. By the time LeBec arrived there were a dozen or so officers meticulously examining every centimetre of the place. Almost all the floorboards were lifted and the detective had to step carefully from rafter to rafter as he walked into the dismal room, with its long neglected décor, that was now such a hive of industry.

"Dabs all over the place. It's a gift" said a girl on the forensic team, dusting the door frame with silver powder on a small brush. "Whoever they are, they must have left in a hurry."

The Chief Inspector turned to his sergeant.

"I think our visit to the late, lamented Samir must have rattled them more than we thought. It looks as if we've got them on the run."

Suddenly there was a shout from the other room and Clémence appeared at the connecting doorway.

"Guv'nor. We've struck oil!"

LeBec and Nicot trod their way gingerly across the uprooted floor and joined the three men crouched in the adjoining room. It contained a bed, now standing on-end against the wall with its newly mutilated mattress propped next to it, and a small bedside cupboard. Its door was swung open, revealing a bare interior, and the draw at the top had been removed and emptied. A small circular rug had been dragged to one side and the boards had been lifted where the bed once stood. There, in the hollow between the rafters, was the prize Clémence had found.

LeBec took out his handkerchief and, using it to cover his hand, gently lifted one of the polythene bags. It contained Semtex plastic explosive. In the adjacent hollow was a small cardboard box that contained detonator caps. He smiled and looked at his sergeant.

"They really were in a rush to leave, weren't they?"

Further examination of the apartment showed that other floorboards had recently been lifted and replaced but no more bomb-making equipment was discovered.

"They panicked" said Nicot. "They must have forgotten the goodies in the bedroom in their hurry to get out."

LeBec nodded.

"Yes. From the look of the place and the contents of the fridge, I'd say that only one of them was actually living here – probably the quartermaster – but if it was the main store then they'd have cleared out pretty sharpish. They had no option. Once they knew we'd got to Samir and the girl, they had to assume we'd find this place. Now of course they'll run to ground."

"And out of action?" asked Nicot hopefully.

"Temporarily. They'll disperse until they think the heat's died down and then re-group. But it'll be some time before they can establish another factory to assemble the stuff so, for a while at least ... yes. I think they'll be out of action."

The sergeant grinned at him. "Maybe we're winning."

"Maybe, Paul. Maybe. In the meantime, I want a full house-to-house in the surrounding area: shops, offices, apartments; everything. And all likely personnel: postmen, street sweepers, anyone who's set foot in this neck of the woods in the last month is to be questioned; especially about the last few days. If they did do a quick removals job on the place then somebody must have noticed the comings and goings."

"I'll organise it now" said Nicot. "Where will you be if I need you?"

"I'm going to question the girl again. I don't think she knows anything she hasn't already told us but it's worth confronting her with the news about this little lot, just in case."

LeBec left the building and went back into the chilly outside air. It was snowing again and his feet left fresh prints as he made his way pensively across the road to his waiting car and told the driver to head back to his office. The discovery of the apartment had been worth waiting for. He hadn't caught the terrorists but he'd dealt them a major blow. Above all, he'd bought a little time. He desperately hoped it would be enough time to find the maniacs and stop them for good but it had certainly earned Paris a temporary respite from the indiscriminate killers in its midst.

As the Peugeot accelerated away through the slush-covered streets, LeBec felt the tension in his shoulders appreciably ease and they seemed to drop. For the first time in a week, he relaxed a little.

* * * * *

England

That Friday evening, Alan Russell was also trying to relax. He drove to meet Taniel at the hospital. Her shift finished at 8pm and marked the end of seven consecutive days on-duty, which meant she could look forward to a three-day break. It was always an added bonus when her off-duty coincided with his free time and, to celebrate the start of their weekend together, he took her to dinner at their favourite Chinese restaurant.

He had mentioned nothing to her of his experiences in Cambridge, just as he had omitted all details of it in his report to Ramsey. In Ramsey's case it was simply a question of keeping his word to Caswell but, as far as Taniel was concerned, it was more a matter of not giving her cause for concern. At least, that's what he told himself. He also knew his silence had the benefit of not having to explain to his wife what he was doing in another woman's hotel room. His conscience was appeased by the fact he had chosen to reject Nina's advance. That, he decided, was good enough reason to forgive himself.

He had seen no trace of the yellow Nissan on his return journey from Whitehall and was sure he had not been followed to the hospital. He continually checked his mirror on the way to the restaurant but knew that Taniel hadn't detected any concern in him. He hated having secrets from her but as he watched her, contented and happily chatting over the Dim Sum they had ordered for hors d'oevres, he was sure he had done the right thing. He determined to draw a line under the whole episode and put it from his mind.

The weekend passed very pleasantly. They went for walks in the forest, caught up with each other's news and daily trivia and generally enjoyed just being in one another's company. On Sunday morning they stayed in bed until mid-day, taking it in turns to go and make tea, idly browsing the Sunday papers, and twice making love. Eventually they rose for a combined breakfast and lunch before showering and strolling to the local pub. It was an idyllic, lazy and very restful couple of days. The little things, the unimportant moments, the ephemera of spending a day together; being happy just to be there and achieve nothing more than the contentment of passing time; the confirmation that, given a free choice, this was the one person you would choose to be with; that was their weekend.

By the Monday morning, as he kissed her goodbye and left Taniel curled up under the duvet, Russell was relaxed and happy. Despite the cold, the Mondeo started first time. He left the engine running while he scraped the frost from the windscreen and was about to get back inside when he was stopped by a tapping behind him. He turned to see Taniel at the window, the duvet now draped around her bare shoulders, blowing him a kiss and waving goodbye. He laughed, returned her wave and set off to face the traffic.

Driving through Turner's Hill he checked his mirror but saw nothing to alarm him. It wasn't until he reached Copthorne that the familiar car appeared again. It came from a side road and joined the stream of vehicles behind him.

"Damn you!" said Russell vehemently as he realised he once again had company. He banged the armrest in frustration, now more angry than uneasy about the presence of his pursuers. "Why the hell are you doing this? What possible bloody use can it be?"

In an effort to ignore his pursuers, he switched on the radio to listen to the news and turned up the volume.

The roads were less busy than usual for a Monday morning and Russell made good time. Within a quarter of an hour he was approaching the M23 and entering the slip road. Once on the motorway, he eased his way across to the centre lane but could not see the Nissan anywhere behind him. He slowed his speed and pulled back to the nearside lane but still saw no trace of the shadowing car. Within a couple of miles the road opened out into a long incline and, as he climbed to the top, it was possible to see across all three lanes for about a mile behind. To his great relief, there was no yellow car to be seen.

"Thank God!" he said out loud to himself. "And bloody good riddance!"

* * * * *

Later that same afternoon Russell was in Ramsey's office, being briefed for his next assignment, when the phone rang. It was 3.30pm. Ramsey answered the call and then looked across at him.

"It's for you."

Russell took the proffered receiver. "Hello, Alan Russell speaking." The voice he heard was new to him.

"Good afternoon, sir. I'm sorry to have to call you like this. My name is Denton. I'm a detective sergeant with the C.I.D."

Russell mouthed the word "police" to Ramsey and shrugged his shoulders in surprise.

"What can I do for you?" he asked.

"I'm downstairs at reception, sir. I'd like to come up and speak to you."

"Well, I'm in a meeting at the moment and ..."

He was interrupted before he could finish.

"It is rather urgent, sir. I'd like to see you straight away if you don't mind."

From the half of the conversation he could hear, Ramsey realised what was being asked and waived his consent at Russell, who nodded his appreciation and spoke again into the phone.

"Very well. Ask the girl to show you to my office, would you? I'll be there in a couple of minutes."

He handed the receiver back to Ramsey.

"I'm sorry about this. It's a C.I.D. man. He wants to see me right away."

Ramsey laughed. "Been raiding the petty cash again? I warned you they'd catch up with you."

Russell's face broadened into a wide grin.

"Well if I get arrested I'll plead insanity. Working in this place, they'd have to agree. I'll be as quick as I can."

Detective-sergeant Denton was an imposing man. Thick set and fairly tall, he seemed aptly cast in the role of burly policeman and fairly dwarfed the w.p.c. who stood quietly at his side. Russell could well imagine it would be unpleasant to be on the wrong side of him. His manner, however, belied his appearance and he spoke with a soft, sympathetic tone when Russell invited him and the female officer to sit down.

"I'm afraid I have some rather unpleasant news for you, sir."

Concerned, Russell sat up sharply.

"What is it?"

"There's been a break-in at your home."

"Oh, hell! When?"

"Sometime late this morning we think."

Russell gave an exasperated sigh.

"Damn the bastards! Did they do much damage? Make much mess?"

"A fair bit, sir, yes. They turned the place over pretty thoroughly."

"I suppose they ..." Russell broke-off in mid sentence. He suddenly remembered that Taniel was still on her off-duty and had not gone to work that morning.

"But my wife was supposed to be there today." He raised his eyes to the ceiling. "She must have gone out for something. I bet she left a window open; she's always doing it! Is that how they got in?"

For the first time, the female officer spoke to him.

"I'm afraid your wife didn't go out, sir."

For a second Russell was confused. Then, all at once, it hit him. If this was nothing more than a break-in they would simply have telephoned, and they would not have sent two officers. Panic tore into him like a knife and he went cold.

"Oh my God! Is she alright? Is she hurt? Have they harmed her?"

He looked beseechingly at the two police officers, hoping against hope that the news would not be bad but, even before Denton's softly spoken reply, he could see in their eyes that he would dread hearing what they had to tell him.

"I'm very sorry to have to tell you, sir, that your wife is dead."

Russell froze. For a full ten seconds he stared blankly at the detective, not moving a muscle, shocked beyond reaction. The w.p.c. rose from her seat, intending to put a comforting arm around his shoulder but before she could reach him he shuddered, clasped his elbows across his middle and let out a groan as the life seemed to dissolve in his spine and he fell forward, collapsing onto his desk like a puppet whose strings had been cut.

Seven

England

The next few hours were little more than a confused daze for Alan Russell. Denton and the w.p.c. drove him back to the cottage in a police car. They were met at the door by an Inspector Harris, who was in charge of the case. He was a middle-aged, stern-faced man with a detached air and hard eyes that showed he was immunised against dealing with the aftermath of violence and murder. As sympathetically as his matter-of-fact manner would allow, he asked Russell not to go inside.

"I think it would be distressing for you, sir, and it would serve no purpose to see your wife before we can move her."

In reality, his main concern was that nothing should be disturbed until his forensic team had finished its gruesome work.

"I'm afraid there will have to be an autopsy to establish the exact cause of death" he went on. "We have an ambulance standing by to take your wife's body for examination."

Within half an hour, two paramedics emerged from the front door wheeling a gurney that was covered in a grey blanket. Russell steeled himself. They brought their grim burden to where he and Harris were standing and the Inspector gently folded back the covering to reveal Taniel's face. Here eyes were closed and the ambulance team had thoughtfully turned her head to one side so as to hide the injuries while Russell made the necessary identification.

It was an immense shock to suddenly see her lifeless body. Even though he had known she was dead from the moment Denton brought him the devastating news, the only possible image of her that his mind could hold was the one that it knew; the only one it had ever seen; the vibrant, caring, bright and pretty woman who had shared his life; his lover; his wife; his closest friend. To actually confront her, cold, lifeless and inanimate, was the final confirmation that she had irretrievably gone; and it hurt almost as much as the initial shock had done. He nodded briefly to the Inspector and stepped quickly away, unable to look any longer.

Wiping away the tears, he fought to catch his breath and control himself. He was consumed with an overwhelming sense of emptiness and loss. Such a large and important part of his life had been completely erased and this sudden, irrevocable change had happened without the slightest hint of warning. It was almost too much to endure and yet, despite the magnitude of what had occurred, all that kept running through his mind was that he hadn't been able to say goodbye. It was almost as if the parting might have been bearable if only he had been able to tell her what she meant to him; to know that at least they'd had time to declare what they felt. His thoughts were disturbed by the gentle voice of the w.p.c.

"Are you alright, sir? Can I get you anything?"

It suddenly occurred to him that he didn't know her name. He wondered if she was married. If her husband worried about her job and dreaded the thought of her being injured or, worse, being told the news Russell had suffered that day.

He managed a slight smile of gratitude but simply shook his head. He felt the sadness rising up again and braced himself, determined not to break down, at least until he was alone. Despite their kindness, the police were part of the tragic events and he wanted them all to leave him to himself, to the privacy of his thoughts and his grief.

"I'm afraid I'll have to ask you to stay away from the cottage until our forensic boys have finished with it, sir" said Harris. "Do you have any friends nearby who could put you up for the night?"

Relatively new to the area, Russell had only acquaintances in the town. His friends were all in London so he reluctantly agreed to spend the night in a local hotel. The Roebuck, a small family-run concern some three or four miles away, was the nearest and Denton and the w.p.c. took him there in a police car. The detective explained the circumstances to the manager and then they went with Russell to his room to make sure he was feeling well enough to be left. Denton also thoughtfully ordered a large brandy which he handed to Russell and urged him to drink.

"It's not a good idea to be by yourself at times like this, sir" said the w.p.c. "Is there really no one we could call?"

"There are plenty of people; but I'd really rather you didn't, if you don't mind. I just need to be on my own for a while. But thanks. You've been most kind."

The w.p.c. nodded and she and Denton respectfully took their leave. For the first time since he'd received the shattering news, Russell was alone.

He sat in the armchair next to the bed and looked around him. Not twelve hours before, he'd been lying next to her. She had been warm, vital and uniquely his. Now he sat in an unfamiliar hotel room and she lay cold, naked and alone on some mortuary slab. The voices of total strangers were echoing around a stark, clinical, white-tiled room, discussing her like an object, with no solemnity, no respect for her departed soul or the tragedy of their loss. His eyes filled with tears and slowly, at last, he began to weep.

He remained in the same chair, motionless, staring at the same wall for over two hours, lost in his thoughts. He was brought sharply back to reality by the sound of the telephone.

"I apologise for bothering you, Mr. Russell" said the voice of the manager "but I wonder if we could perhaps bring you something to eat?" Forgive the intrusion but Chef will be finishing soon and, whilst I appreciate you might not feel like it, you really should eat something, sir."

Russell looked at his watch and was amazed to find it was after 9pm.

"No, thank you. You're very kind but I really couldn't eat anything."

"Very well, sir. If you should change your mind later then please let me know. We can always get you a sandwich or something."

"Yes. Thank you. I will" said Russell, and hung up the phone.

The call had broken his almost hypnotic detachment and he knew that, painful as it was, he had to get a grip on reality. He went into the bathroom and vigorously washed his face with cold water. Then, sitting on the side of the bed, he tried to take stock of all he had to accept. He carefully went over the few details the police had given him.

Taniel had been found by Mrs. Crabtree. She came two afternoons a week to the cottage to clean and do the ironing and had her own key. She had arrived, as usual, at mid-day but the police estimated that the attack had taken place somewhere between 9am and 11am. The thought of Taniel lying there while he was miles away, oblivious to what had happened, brought tears to his eyes again but he fought them back and concentrated on the rest of what little he knew.

There would be an autopsy to establish the exact cause of death but the police's theory was that person or persons unknown had forced entry to the cottage and been confronted by Taniel. It was felt there had been a struggle and, from the position of the body and the nature of her injuries, she had fallen, or been pushed, and struck her head awkwardly against the bookcase, breaking her neck.

Inspector Harris had been at great pains to point out that there was no evidence of sexual molestation and that she had almost certainly died instantly. It was of no consolation. It sickened Russell to think of her, alone and frightened, helpless against the brute force that had violated their home and snatched away her life.

In the absence of any other motive, the police were initially basing their investigation on a burglary that went tragically wrong. Russell doubted it. He was plagued by the nagging conclusion that it had to be related to his being followed. It was too much to believe it a mere coincidence that this should occur at the end of such a week. Exactly what had happened and why, he could only guess but he was certain there was a connection. He seethed with anger to think that, simply due to his job, they had become the innocent and unwitting pawns in a sordid, shadowy game that had so irrevocably swept them aside and ended her life and their future together.

Harris had said he would need to question him and that, if Russell felt up to seeing him, he would be at the hotel in the morning. Russell would be ready. He thought nothing now of his promise to remain silent. In his mind he pieced together the chain of events, ready to be accurate and concise when he related the story to Harris. Meeting Nina Petrova; the video recording; the encounter with Caswell; being followed; he could give a vague description of only one of the men but the car itself should be easy to trace ...

His train of thought jolted to a halt and he stood up. He suddenly remembered that he'd given the number of the car to Caswell three days ago. The police would have no difficulty in tracing a vehicle but identifying the occupants would take longer, whereas there was a chance they were already known to the Major.

He went quickly to his jacket, lying across the back of the chair, and fumbled through his wallet until he found the card. He checked his watch. It was 9.20pm. He didn't know if there would be any reply but, as it was evidently a bogus organisation, there was no need to presume it worked ordinary hours. He picked up the phone, pressed 9 to get an outside line and then quickly tapped out the number.

The tone sounded several times and he was about to hang up in dismay when he heard the call finally connect. The inquisitive and surprised "hello?" told him that the number was not usually called at this hour.

"I want to speak to Major Caswell" snapped Russell into the receiver.

There was a pause as the listener was clearly taken aback by the abrupt demand.

"Who is this?" came the reply somewhat aggressively.

Russell thought the indignant voice sounded like Blair.

"This is Alan Russell" he answered firmly.

"I don't know if you are aware of what time it is Mr. Russell, but I suggest you telephone again in the morning and ask to speak to our managing director." He emphasised the words to stress Russell's indiscretion in mentioning the man by name. "Perhaps he can help you tomorrow."

Russell was now certain it was Blair but he cared nothing for maintaining the charade.

"Now you listen to me" he ordered angrily. "My wife was killed this morning and I'm in no mood to be messed around playing your little games. I want to speak to Caswell and I want to speak to him tonight. If he's not there then tell me where I can get hold of him."

For a moment there was no response. Then he could hear a muffled conversation as Blair obviously covered the mouth-piece and spoke to someone else in the room. After a few seconds, Caswell's voice came on the line. His tone was guarded but there was real concern in his voice.

"Mr. Russell, I don't know if we've heard you correctly but am I to understand that something has happened to you wife?"

Despite his efforts to restrain them, the tears began to flow again as Russell answered and he gritted his teeth, fighting to keep control of his emotion.

"Yes, you understand me correctly" he said bitterly through the unnatural rise and fall of his breathing. "My wife was killed this morning by someone who broke into our home."

Caswell's voice changed abruptly and he became suddenly compassionate.

"My dear fellow, please accept my deepest condolences. I hardly know what to say."

Still catching his breath and struggling to hold himself together, Russell couldn't prevent the sarcastic tone that seeped into his reply.

"Well there's nothing much you *can* say, is there? But there is something you can do. Did you manage to trace the car that's been following me from the number I gave you?"

There was surprise in the Major's answer.

"Yes, as it happens I did."

"Good. What did you find out?"

Caswell's voice betrayed a confusion as he strove to maintain a commiserating tone.

"Mr. Russell, please understand that I fully appreciate how distraught you must be and I can only offer my deepest sympathies; but is this the time to be discussing such matters?"

Russell's anger began to break through and his volume steadily increased.

"Yes, this is the time to be discussing such matters. This is the time to discuss the fact you told me not to worry about them; that you told me they would simply go away when they knew I wasn't any kind of a threat; that I believed you and did nothing. But that they didn't go away and my wife is now dead!"

Wary of Russell's rising emotions, the Major chose his words carefully.

"Yes, I understand Mr. Russell. Of course we must look at every possibility but, if we are to catch whoever has done this terrible thing, we mustn't jump to conclusions. We must think clearly. It may be that the two events are not connected."

"Well you can think what you like. I want the information about that car and I want it now. We'll let the police find out if there's any connection or not. I don't think they'll share your doubts, do you?"

Knowing that he couldn't control the situation at a distance, and anxious that Russell should not give the police classified information, Caswell changed tack. His tone was still deliberately conciliatory.

"No. No, I'm sure they won't. You're right of course and I'll do all I can to help. Have you mentioned any of this to them so far?"

"Not yet, no. I've hardly known what day it is for the last few hours. They're coming here in the morning."

"Good. Then I'll get all the information to you by then. In fact, I'll bring it to you myself. Where are you now?"

This was something Russell had not expected.

"I'm in a hotel. But just give it to me over the phone."

"It's not that simple Mr. Russell, as I think you'll understand when I show you what we have. I'll tell you what I'll do. I'll make you a promise. I'll put all the details we have at your disposal. I'll bring them to you personally and I guarantee that you'll have them before morning. All I ask in return is that you speak to no one else before I arrive. Then you may do whatever you choose and I will support your decision. Is that acceptable to you?"

It was difficult enough for Russell to think clearly and he was unsure how to treat Caswell's sudden sympathetic generosity but it seemed that his hunch had been correct and the Major knew something about the men in the car. Eager to obtain the information, he agreed and gave Caswell the address of the hotel.

"Thank you, Mr. Russell" said the Major gratefully. "I'll be there in a couple of hours. Goodbye."

Russell put down the receiver. He wasn't certain Caswell would be able to tell him anything definite but it made him feel considerably better to think he was doing something constructive. The feeling of sheer impotence, of being helplessly at the mercy of events, had made his grief all the worse, if that were possible. Now he felt he was at least beginning to strike back.

He was glad he hadn't taken the sedative the police doctor had offered him. He wanted to be alert and awake when the Major arrived. He picked up the phone again, rang reception and spoke to the manager.

"Hello, this is Mr. Russell. I'd like a pot of hot coffee please and, if it's still on offer, I'll change my mind about that sandwich."

* * * * *

It was ten minutes to midnight when there was a knock at the door and Russell opened it to find Caswell and Blair standing in front of him. He silently motioned them into the room and they removed the overcoats they were wearing against the cold night. Blair carried a black leather briefcase that he laid across his lap as they both sat down.

Caswell began by again offering his sympathies. He seemed to be genuinely saddened by the tragic loss of Taniel but Russell kept his acceptance of the Major's condolences brief and concise. He was determined to hold himself together and remain alert and it was important to restrain his emotions if he was to do so.

"I'm grateful to you both for coming down personally like this but I'm sure you gentlemen have homes to go to, so the sooner we get down to business the sooner you can be on your way. What exactly can you tell me?"

Despite the coldness in Russell's voice, Caswell remained sympathetic.

"Very well, Mr. Russell. I'm sure we appreciate that you prefer to be alone at such a time. I'll be as brief as possible."

Blair opened the briefcase and handed some papers to him as the Major continued.

"From the registration number you gave us we were able to run a trace on the vehicle that was following you. It is in fact a hire-car that was rented from a firm in Victoria. I have the details here."

He passed Russell a photo-copy of a completed rental agreement.

"As you can see, the vehicle was taken out on Wednesday of last week and an advance rental was paid for seven days. The signature on the agreement is of a Herr Winzer. According to the sales girl who rented the car to him, Herr Winzer is a German lawyer on holiday in this country who wanted the vehicle for touring. His passport and driving licence were all in order. He was in fact accompanied by another man when he picked up the car but of course the girl had no reason to query the second man's identity."

Russell stared at the signature on the form. It was a strange and unpleasant feeling to be looking at the mark of someone who he was sure had a hand in his wife's murder.

"Did she describe the men to you?" he asked. "Have you any idea as to who they might be?"

"I can do a little better than that" replied the Major encouragingly. "You see, even though they were committing no crime in simply following you, we like to be aware of exactly what's going on, especially in our own back yard. We of course arranged to have a man standing by next Wednesday, when the car would be due back, but we also asked the girl to let us know if Herr Winzer should contact her in the interim. We received a telephone call from her this afternoon. The car had been returned prematurely to their Heathrow branch. Evidently, urgent business had caused Herr Winzer to cut short his holiday and he was returning to Berlin on the first available flight."

The hair on the back of Russell's neck began to rise and he stood up in his agitation.

"That settles it!" he declared, smacking the fist of his right hand into the palm of his left. "They must have followed me this morning until they were certain I was going all the way to London then, thinking it would be empty, they doubled back to the cottage. When Taniel surprised them and they ..." he swallowed, not able to say the actual words ... "well, they must have panicked and bolted for the nearest airport."

"Yes" said Caswell calmly. "I would agree that as a hypothesis. But there's more. We received the call at just after 1pm. We checked the passenger lists and found the name Winzer on a flight that didn't leave until 5.30. So we sent a man to Heathrow."

Russell's eyes opened wide.

"You mean you stopped them?"

"No. It was never our intention to stop them. You must remember that, at the time, we knew nothing about the events of this morning. No, we simply wanted to keep tabs on them and ascertain who they were."

"But did you find them?" Russell implored.

"We not only found them, Mr. Russell, we managed to photograph them."

Blair withdrew a couple of ten-by-eight photographs from the case and handed them to Caswell, who held them face down.

"The enlargements are not wonderful because the shots were taken at some distance" he said apologetically, "but the likeness is clear enough and the girl at the car-hire company has confirmed it is the man calling himself Winzer."

Russell reached out and nervously took the photographs. He turned them over and then, open mouthed, sat back on the bed in shock. There, staring up at him, were the unmistakeable features of Dimitri Gurevich.

Caswell and Blair sat in silence, waiting for Russell to speak. When he did so, he was strangely calm and didn't take his eyes from the photographs.

"So we've got him" he said quietly. "I take it I can keep these to show to the police?"

"You may" said Caswell evenly. "If you think that's wise."

Russell looked up.

"Wise?" he asked, astonished. "They'll need them for evidence."

For the first time since their arrival, Blair addressed him.

"I'm afraid these photographs are not evidence, Mr. Russell. They simply show a man at an airport. There is nothing whatsoever to show a link between him and the death of your wife."

"But it's Gurevich" Russell said angrily. "We know he's been checking up on me, that he used a false name to hire a car and then followed me everywhere I went. It's not exactly innocent behaviour, is it?"

Sensitive to Russell's battered emotions, Blair remained as compassionate as he could.

"In the first place, even if we could prove it was him in the car and that he was following you, that in itself is not an offence and it would all be circumstantial. In the second place, you'll never be able to prove that it was Gurevich."

"But the girl can identify him!" Russell protested. "The Major said so."

Blair continued calmly and at a measured pace.

"Mr. Russell, please try to understand. We are not dealing with an ordinary individual here. This is a high-ranking secret service officer. He was not travelling on forged documents, you know. Herr Winzer's passport would have been the genuine article. He can come and go as he pleases, with any number of identities; and each one of them holds water. There will be cast iron evidence to show that Dimitri Gurevich never set foot outside Russia after his return from Cambridge and there will be any amount of esteemed and creditable witnesses to swear to it. It would be the word of one sales girl against a cart-load of officials."

Russell could scarcely believe what he was hearing.

"Is that it then?" he asked incredulously. "Do you mean to say that a man can breeze in and out of this country as he likes, raid my home and kill my wife, and there's nothing we can do about it? Is that what you're trying to tell me?"

In contrast to Russell's charged tones, the Major's voice was cool and expressionless as he answered.

"We are simply saying that unusual circumstances require unusual provision."

Russell turned on him.

"And what's that supposed to mean?"

"It means" replied Caswell, "that we think before we act and we examine the possible consequences of all the options open to us."

He stood. It was a habit, long ingrained from his military career, to gain the natural position of authority and force his seated listener to look up at him while he put forward an argument. He then walked to the window and addressed his remarks to the black night outside, as though his words were a statement of fact and not for debate.

"Although there is no tangible evidence, let us assume for a moment that Colonel Gurevich was directly responsible for the tragic loss of your wife. Let us further assume that the police are totally convinced of this and are prepared to arrest and convict him. Let us even imagine that the Russian authorities can offer no denial of these charges. Do you seriously think they will simply hand him over? We have no extradition agreement with them Mr. Russell and no entente, no matter how cordiale, will persuade the Russian secret service to voluntarily part with one of its longest-serving and most valued senior officers."

He turned from the window and looked directly at Russell.

"In short, the effect of all this highly implausible assumption would be to permanently close the stable door behind our long-ago-bolted horse. Gurevich would simply disappear into darkest Moscow, never to be seen again."

Caswell could tell from the expression on Russell's face that his logic had found its mark. He returned to the misted window pane.

"Now let us consider an alternative. Suppose that, for the time being, we do nothing. We leave the police totally ignorant of Gurevich's existence and of your being followed. The result of this is two-fold. Firstly it leaves the police free to investigate all other avenues and I must remind you that, although I agree it's unlikely, it is not beyond the bounds of possibility that this is a ghastly coincidence and the perpetrators of this crime were not connected with Gurevich. At least, in this scenario, that possibility is thoroughly examined.

"Secondly, and most importantly, it has a direct effect upon Gurevich himself. If, as we have every reason to suspect, he is the guilty party, then he is earnestly looking to see what transpires. When he finds the police genuinely have no inkling as to his involvement, he believes he's got away with it. He continues to come and go as he pleases. Convinced he's perfectly safe, he travels freely in and out of Russia and, more to the point ..." Caswell turned and looked Russell directly in the eye. "He'll be in Paris in January."

For a moment, nobody spoke. Caswell and Blair were watching Russell, waiting to see what effect the Major's calm and clear analysis would have on his distressed and grieving emotions.

"And of course, keeping things quiet would just happen to suit your purpose too, wouldn't it?" Russell said acidly.

Caswell was calm and almost apologetic in his quiet reply.

"I don't deny it, Mr. Russell. Not for one moment. I make no pretence to you at this tragic time. For obvious reasons, I do not want the police asking you questions about highly classified information; questions you would feel bound to answer; and under the circumstances, I couldn't blame you for doing so. I merely put the facts before you, as I see them, and ask you to consider. The decision is yours. I promised you the information you requested and I've made it available to you. What you do next is entirely up to you."

Russell's mind was in overdrive. He stared at Caswell's impassive features, vainly wrestling with the pain and outrage in his heart and the cold logic that had addressed his ears.

"And if I take your advice?" he asked. "If I remain silent and

Gurevich arrives in Paris in January; what then? Are you telling me that's when we bring in the police?"

It was Blair who answered him.

All we are saying at the moment, Mr. Russell, is that Gurevich is safe in Moscow. Set up a hue-and-cry and he'll stay there. Do nothing for the moment and he'll come out again in January."

The logic was undeniable but Russell was not about to leave his desire for justice as a mere hostage to fortune.

"It's not enough" he said firmly. "I need something definite. What's to stop me telling the police everything now but explaining why nothing can be done until January? Then, when he gets off the plane in Paris, they can be there waiting for him."

"There's nothing at all to stop you" answered Blair. "But our police can't simply march into France and arrest someone. They have to liaise with the French police and set up everything in advance. The French actually have to take the man into custody and then hand him over. That poses all sorts of difficulties. In the first place the diplomatic repercussions of arresting a man in Gurevich's position, at a high profile international conference, would lead to a major political crisis. Secondly, knowing what the ramifications would be, the whole process would have to be checked and discussed in advance at many levels and it is far from easy to keep such matters quiet. If the merest whisper of trouble were to reach the wrong ears, Gurevich would never arrive."

Caswell took up the argument.

"I won't lie to you, Mr. Russell. I can guarantee you nothing and I do not deny that my main concern is, and has to be, Professor Litvinov. But I do assure you that we are highly distressed at what has befallen you and are anxious to do everything possible to bring the culprits to book. If you agree to do nothing for the present, and to wait until Gurevich goes to Paris, then I can promise you that I will do all within my power to help. I must again stress that I cannot and will not jeopardise the Litvinov operation but, within that proviso, I will make the arrest of Gurevich my next priority."

Russell gazed up at him. There was a softening of his face; probably the closest he ever got to losing his military stiff upper lip; and in his normally hard eyes, Russell thought he detected a look of generosity; a compassion. It was Blair who added the final coda to the Major's speech.

"You might also like to consider" he said carefully and deliberately, "that the clandestine arrest of Gurevich on foreign soil requires very particular talents and resources; something that, due to the general nature of our work, the Major is uniquely able to provide."

Russell put his head in his hands. He'd spent the last few hours on an emotional rack, despairing at his loss. Then he'd discovered the identity of his wife's killers and seen at least a hope of justice. Now it was slipping from his grasp. It was too much

"I can't think straight!" he moaned. "I need time!"

"Yes, of course you do" said Caswell sympathetically. He nodded to Blair that it was time to leave and the younger man stood up and gathered their coats.

Slowly, Russell's hands slid from his face and he looked up at the two men before him.

"I'm not sure about anything anymore" he said quietly. "I need to think things through and get myself together."

Caswell buttoned his coat as he spoke. His voice remained gentle.

"You know where to reach me, Mr. Russell. The phone will be manned around the clock and you may ring at any time of the day or night. I suggest you try and get some sleep. I'll leave the documents and the photographs with you. Perhaps, when you've spoken to the police, you might feel able to let me know what you decided to tell them. In the meantime, we'll bid you goodnight."

They quietly left and closed the door behind them.

Russell lay back on the bed and folded his arms across his head, wishing that somehow this would all turn out to be a nightmare and that he would wake in his own bed with Taniel sleeping silently beside him; but he knew it was all horrifically true and that, somehow, he had to face grim reality and the first of what he knew would be many long, lonely, sleepless nights.

He was eventually awoken by the sound of the telephone. He reached clumsily in his stupor and almost dropped the receiver before he heard the voice of the hotel manager telling him that Inspector Harris was downstairs and waiting to see him. He peered through heavy eyelids at his watch. It was 10.15am. He was still fully clothed and hadn't moved from the bed since the departure of Caswell and Blair. The night had been fitful and restless and, before he'd slept at all, he'd heard the dawn chorus greet the first glint of light that had edged around the drawn curtains. What little sleep he had managed had done little to relieve the tension of the last twenty-four hours. His neck felt as thought it were encased in an iron corset and he had a headache that beat merciless hammers against his painful temples.

"Tell the Inspector to come up" he murmured drowsily into the phone and eased himself upright onto the edge of the bed. Slowly he climbed to his feet and, squinting against the glare, opened the curtains. He had just enough time to dab a cold flannel over his complaining eyes and swallow a couple of aspirins before he had to answer the knock at the door and usher Inspector Harris into the room.

The policeman offered him the usual formalities of condolence and enquired as to how Russell was feeling but, within less than a minute, he was seated in a chair and addressing himself to the purpose of his visit.

"Forgive me for asking, Mr. Russell," he began, "but do you have any reason to suppose there might be someone who would wish you or your wife any harm?"

Russell said nothing. Even now he was still not sure what he should do. Harris took his silence to be confusion and elaborated further.

"It's just that there are one or two aspects of this case that bother me. They don't add up. Of course, we won't know exactly what's missing until you yourself have checked but, from what Mrs. Crabtree told us, it appears to be the usual things one might expect: d.v.d., hi-fi, drawers rifled for cash. But that doesn't quite fit the facts as I see them."

He spoke with a cold, detached, professional manner. Russell knew it was a necessary part of his job but none the less found it somewhat offensive. The "facts" were that his wife had been murdered and he couldn't see them any other way.

"You see" continued Harris, "burglary and house-breaking generally comes in three categories. There are yobs who, on the spur of the moment or the off-chance, break into a place and nick whatever they can carry; there's the professional who knows what he's doing and what he's looking for; and then of course there's the big boys: highly organised, very experienced and always after something specific; works of art, jewels, that sort of thing. But none of that seems to apply here."

As Harris delivered his explanation, Russell had the distinct impression that, rather than being informed, he was himself being watched for his reaction.

"Now a good pro wants to be in and out as quickly as possible," Harris went on. "He wants no aggravation and, above all, he doesn't want to be seen. He'll wait until he's sure a place is empty and even then he'll knock at the door first. If it's answered, he's ready with a plausible line of chat and makes his excuses and leaves. He'd rather lose doing the job than risk any trouble. If it's something he wants badly enough he can always come back another day.

"As for yobs, well it's true they might have the bravado to force their way in when they found your wife at home; but when she was obviously so seriously hurt they'd have panicked. They'd have dropped everything and run like hell. Getting rid of hot goods is one thing; getting rid of stuff connected with a murder is something else. They'd want nothing that could link them with that.

"So, we're left with the big league. Now, they are certainly ruthless enough to have done this to your wife but, with the greatest of respect, they are not generally interested in small places like yours; not unless they know there's something very special inside."

It struck Russell as odd that the policeman would apologise for demeaning the size of his home but seemed well able to discuss the murder of his wife as a matter of logic.

"There *was* something very special inside" he said firmly. "Taniel was inside."

At least Harris had the grace to look embarrassed.

"Yes, sir. Of course. Forgive me. That goes without saying. But apart from your wife, even if there was something of particular value to organised crime, they would hardly be bothered to walk off with the things that we know are missing. So you can see my problem. I've got a murder and a house-breaking that don't quite go together; and it worries me. So I must ask you again: can you think of anyone who might wish harm to you or your wife?"

As he asked the question there was the faintest hint of accusation in his eyes and Russell suddenly realised where this process of reasoning had been leading and why his own reactions had been so closely observed.

You bastard, he thought. You think I could have had something to do with it. How Harris could be insensitive to the genuine nature of his grief was beyond Russell, and the suggestion of his own complicity in such an act filled him with revulsion but, as he looked across disdainfully at the detective, he could see the suspicion was real and that Harris was not yet convinced of his innocence. At the back of his mind he could recollect having read somewhere that in ninety percent of murders the culprit is known to the victim and is often a close friend or relative. Clearly Harris was keenly aware of the same statistics.

Russell now knew there was only one course open to him. It was undoubtedly true that Gurevich, having been surprised by Taniel, had faked a burglary to try and cover his tracks but if he were to explain to Harris who Gurevich was, and why he was there, then he had to relate the whole story from the beginning. He had always known the truth would be difficult to believe and hard to substantiate but he now realised that the more implausible it was, the more the finger of suspicion would point in his own direction. Caswell's words of caution were ringing loudly in his ears and their logic was again striking home. The only way to get to Gurevich was going to be through the Major.

"No" he said calmly. "I can think of no one who would wish either my wife or myself any harm."

* * * * *

The remainder of the week was the most painful time Russell had ever known. He spent several difficult days at home, where a tearful Mrs. Crabtree helped him put the place in order. Taniel's presence was everywhere. Almost every item in the cottage held a memory of a particular day or event. He couldn't sit in a chair without remembering how they'd gone out together to choose the suite. He couldn't draw the curtains without thinking of how pleased she'd been to make them herself and how they'd celebrated with a bottle of wine the night she finished machining them. Her touch was in the vase of dried flowers she'd arranged, the medical books that sat redundantly on the shelf and the toothbrush that stood idly next to his own in the bathroom cabinet.

No longer would her smiling face appear over his shoulder in the mirror as she reached around his neck to knot his tie in the way she always did. The pillow that lay next to him, undented, would never again support her head while they lay and talked long into the night; and the dressing gown, that even now smelt of the faint trace of her favourite Samsara perfume, would hang unused on the back of the bedroom door, no more to be wrapped around her delicate, naked body.

The most difficult task was to contact Taniel's family and inform them of her death. They had never approved of their daughter's marriage and, predictably, their reaction was to hold him responsible for her fate. Their accusation that, but for him, she would be alive and well in her native country did nothing to alleviate the guilt he already felt for that very reason. Her father insisted that her body be flown back to Morocco and made it clear that Russell's presence would not be welcome.

It upset him that he couldn't convince the old man of just how much they had meant to each other and of his own enormous loss but, through a telephone line that traversed cultures and religions as well as thousands of miles, he knew the task was hopeless. He agreed to all her father's wishes and made the necessary arrangements to fly her body home.

By the Friday morning, after yet another night of erratic sleep, he knew he couldn't live in the cottage without her and telephoned the local estate agent to put it up for sale.

Harris had returned during the week to question him once again but had, as yet, made no progress with his enquiries. Throughout this time, Russell had no further contact with Caswell. He was determined that, when he did, he would be absolutely certain of what he wanted from the Major and how he could be sure of getting it.

He spent the weekend deep in thought; several times he went walking through the forest in the way he and Taniel had done so often together. It was a long and difficult two days but by the Sunday evening he'd made his decision and knew what he was going to do.

* * * * *

The address in Poland Street that was printed on the card turned out to be the most unlikely of settings for a division of MI6. A large red and white awning declaimed the name *Silvio's* above a couple of white plastic tables and chairs that vainly struggled to give a continental ambience to the outside of yet another of Soho's innumerable cafés. It wasn't until Russell was actually standing in the doorway that he noticed the grey, grime-covered plaque on the wall that stated, in letters that were almost indiscernible from the dirt, *The Albion Import and Export Company – First Floor.*

It was necessary to enter the café in order to pass through an inner door on the right hand side that opened onto a narrow staircase and it occurred to Russell that the location was well chosen. Any visitors to the Major's "office" would be indistinguishable from the day-long stream of the café's many and varied customers.

Russell was nervous. His stomach turned over as he set foot on the stairs and he had to wipe his palms against his sleeves to dry the damp that had formed there. The echo of his footsteps, as he walked up the uncarpeted wooden treads, was ample announcement of his arrival and as he pushed open the door at the top he was met by the expectant stare of a grey-haired lady in her fifties.

"Can I help you?" she asked politely.

The office was hardly an advert for a prosperous business. Gun-metal filing cabinets, that had seen better days, stood against the far wall where large shipping charts and a tatty trade-calendar for Crusader Courier Services partially hid the faded cream paintwork that was sorely in need of redecoration. Russell looked across the desk, which was probably older than the receptionist herself, to where the enquiring lady sat.

"My name is Russell. Alan Russell."

The expression on her face told him that his name was not unknown to her. She reached across to the intercom and Caswell's voice came back swiftly in reply.

"Yes?"

"Mr. Russell is here to see you."

There was a brief pause before the slightly less officious reply.

"Send him in, please."

She gestured towards the inner door and Russell made his way into the adjoining room.

The décor was only marginally improved from the outer office but the room housed two large wooden desks, behind which sat Caswell and Blair.

"I'll come straight to the point, Major" said Russell as he lowered himself into the chair they had offered him. "I haven't spoken to the police about Gurevich."

The relief on the faces of both men, and particularly Caswell, was clearly evident.

"Good. Thank you," he said gratefully. "And I'll do my best to help you in return."

"Well before you get too enthusiastic" Russell told him, "I must tell you that there are conditions for my continued silence."

Caswell and Blair exchanged apprehensive glances.

"Go on" said the Major cautiously.

"As you've so effectively explained to me, my choices are very clear. I can't go to the police. To get Gurevich out of Moscow I must keep quiet and wait for Paris. But once he's in France, I have to trust you to deliver him and frankly, Major, I'm not sure I do. You told me yourself that your priority remains Litvinov and I can see a distinct possibility that my silence now gets me nothing more than excuses and apologies later when you've acquired the Professor but Gurevich has got away scot free."

"And so?" asked Caswell warily.

"And so I'll go to Paris. I'll liaise with Litvinov, carry messages, do whatever you want me to do to help him come over. But you have to keep your promise to grab Gurevich and, when you do, I have to be present. I have to be included."

"Alan" interjected Blair in surprise, "I don't think you quite understand what you're saying …"

He was cut short by Caswell's raised hand. The Major spoke impassively.

"And if I decline?"

"Then I go straight to the police and the press and tell them everything."

Despite the implied threat, and conscious that Russell was still grieving for his loss, the Major's tone remained conciliatory.

"But that won't get you Gurevich" he said calmly.

"Maybe not. But it'll blow the lid on Professor Litvinov and your chances of getting to him."

"In short" said Caswell quietly, "you are blackmailing me."

"Let's just call it a trade. You get Litvinov - I get Gurevich. I don't care how you arrange it but, when the Professor 'disappears' in Paris, Gurevich comes with him and I have to be there to see it happen."

Wary of Russell's cold determination, Blair adopted a mollifying tone.

"Alan, you've been through a terrible ordeal and you are naturally still in shock. You're not thinking straight. Please allow yourself a little time to consider ..."

Russell turned on him sharply and stopped him in mid-sentence. His initial nervousness had gone. He felt resolute and in control and it was at that moment that he knew he'd made the right decision.

"You're right" he snapped. "I've been through a terrible ordeal - more terrible than you can ever imagine. My future is empty now. Can you understand that? It's a blank. And I will never be able to rest or try to rebuild my life if I know the man that murdered my wife is roaming around free. So nothing is possible for me - do you hear me? - *nothing* - until I get justice."

There was a moment's silence as the full import of Russell's words seemed to register. The quiet hung between them all, dark and funereal, as the pain of his wife's murder became, at least for a moment, a tangible and uncomfortable reality for the other two men. It was Blair who spoke first.

"I appreciate that," he said gently. "Truly I do. But please try to understand. You're a complete novice in all this; an innocent."

"We know you're grieving, Alan" added Caswell sympathetically. "And I understand your need to strike back at the man who killed your wife. But please don't force me to put you at risk."

It suddenly occurred to Russell that, for the first time since he had met them, they had begun to address him by his christian name. As he looked at them he was unsure if it had been used naturally, an unconscious note of genuine compassion, or deliberately to establish a persuasive intimacy. He still couldn't tell as Blair continued.

"Asking you to pass information is one thing but you can't possibly expect to be included in a full service operation."

"Why not? Russell queried defiantly. "I'm the perfect choice. Remember? They've checked me out and found I'm a legitimate interpreter." He turned to Caswell. "Isn't that right, Major?"

"You're not leaving me much choice, are you?"

"Not really, no. And there's one more thing." Russell steeled himself. "You will provide me with a gun and teach me how to use it."

Blair threw up his hands in horror.

"Alan, for God's sake!"

In contrast to his subordinate's rising frustration, Caswell's voice was quiet disbelief.

"You can't be serious?" he asked quietly.

Russell's tone was measured and steady.

"I'm perfectly serious. These are my terms for being your messenger. If you keep your word there'll be no problem. But if you don't deal with Gurevich then I will."

Caswell's eyebrows raised slightly. This stipulation was clearly something he had not expected.

"But you're not a killer, Alan. I understand your passion. In fact, I admire your courage. In your situation I'd like to think I might well make the same demands. But I repeat: you are not a killer. And you know you're not. Are you sure you're even capable of using a gun?"

"Who knows?" said Russell blithely, striving not to reveal his own doubt and fear of that very question. "If you do as you promised and arrest Gurevich the question won't arise. But if you renege on this or try to cheat me of the Colonel – maybe I'll point it at you to find out?"

Russell was unsure whether they thought the threat was serious or made in jest, but he was certain he had conveyed his determination to force the deal he wanted. He knew he held the trump card. They needed him to reach Litvinov and, he gambled, they would risk a great deal to get to the Professor. Their sympathies over Russell's loss seemed genuine and maybe they were sincere in their desire to bring Gurevich to justice; maybe the Major would pull it off and arrest the Russian as he had said he would; but, one way or the other, Russell would be there to make sure something was done. Caswell was correct; he had no idea whether he could use a gun or not. Right now it didn't matter. All that counted was that he would be in Paris and able to confront Gurevich. He would make his decisions then.

Caswell reached across his desk and flicked the intercom switch.

"Get me Grainger, will you please?" he said politely.

The secretary acknowledged the request and the Major settled back into his chair to wait for the call. His expression was a strange mixture of annoyance at Russell's demands and an almost perceptible admiration for his having made them.

"We do occasionally employ the services of, shall we say, unorthodox people" he said evenly, "though not usually in the capacity you are suggesting. If the need arises, we send them for a little instruction to one of our ... subsidiary companies."

He was interrupted by the secretary, who was putting through the call. Caswell picked up his telephone.

"Good morning, Grainger. I'm sending you another virgin to look after ... No, just a few basics, so he can avoid shooting himself in the foot."

His sarcasm wasn't lost on Russell, who found himself looking at the floor.

"Blair will explain what we need when they arrive," continued Caswell. "Yes, that's right ... His name?"

He looked up at the object of his conversation, who was sitting uncomfortably under his slightly cynical gaze.

"Let's call him ... Mr. Paris."

Eight

France

At 9.30pm, on the Thursday following Russell's visit to Poland Street, two men drove cautiously through the drizzling snow that had been falling all day on the congested Paris streets. Less than a kilometre north of the Gare du Nord, where the arrondissement Enclos St. Laurent meets the Butte Montmartre, they turned into the Rue Doudeauville. They made their way to a row of small two-storey buildings that back onto the railway line and pulled the car to a gentle halt outside number twenty-three. Despite the faded sign above the door, where the peeling letters stated Café Doudeauville, the bar was known by all its patrons as *Antoine's* after the ex-merchant seaman who owned and ran it.

Unlike *Silvio's* in bustling Soho, where Caswell's bogus company chose to hide its discrete front door, the trade in Antoine's establishment was generally slow and usually low-spending. The financial returns were in fact well insufficient to provide a profitable living but, as his main source of income was acting as a fence to most of the local petty thieves, Antoine was content to stand behind his bar and accept the meagre takings as a welcome pretence of being an honest citizen of Paris.

The nature of his real business meant that the majority of the clientele, and certainly the regulars, were usually of the criminal classes and, like thieves' kitchens of old, strangers were treated with suspicion and never encouraged to stay. So all eyes turned to the two newcomers as a gust of cold air announced their arrival and they stepped from the street into the unwelcoming atmosphere of the smoke-filled room.

One of the two, a scruffy, unshaven weasel of a man in his middle forties called Georges Peloux, was a Parisian and was known to Antoine. The other, an olive-skinned young man in his twenties wearing dark glasses and a hat pulled low across his face, was not. Had the proprietor known who he was, he would not have allowed him inside. Indeed, uncharacteristically, he would have called the police himself for, though scarcely a supporter of law and order, he was as disgusted and outraged as anyone else by the recent bombings in his home city.

Antoine had been well remunerated for the use of his back room and, as always, had asked no questions. He nodded to Peloux that all was in order and the two visitors made their way past the bar and through the door at the rear marked *Privée*.

Inside the small, dimly-lit room there were already two other men seated at a round card-table. One of them was a local "heavy" known to everyone as Le Rasoir, a brutish-looking hulk whose nickname derived from a penchant for cutting his victims. The other was a nervous mouse, olive-skinned like the man who now entered the room and also bearing a strong similarity in height and build to the new arrival. No greetings were exchanged and the newcomers silently took the two vacant seats that awaited them. Peloux turned expectantly to his companion, who removed his dark glasses and stared long and hard at the timid man sitting uneasily next to Le Rasoir.

"Well?" he asked optimistically.

The man at his side nodded. "He'll do" he said dispassionately and replaced his glasses. "What's your name?" he requested quietly of the nervous mouse.

"Siddiq. Siddiq Chaudary" was the hesitant reply.

"And are you to be trusted, Siddiq Chaudary?"

"Yes, of course" he answered eagerly.

The questioner paused and looked at his escort.

"Does he know what's involved?"

"No, not yet" said Peloux. "I couldn't say anything until you had approved the choice. But he is a reliable man and comes recommended."

His companion turned again to Chaudary.

"You have been selected for a job. You will be paid two thousand Euros; half now and half when you have satisfactorily completed your task. You will receive your instructions nearer the time. Meanwhile, you will stay out of trouble. Is that understood?"

Chaudary smiled. "No problem."

"Good."

Satisfied, his questioner rose, withdrew a wad of small denomination used notes from his pocket and threw them onto the table. He walked to the door and then turned and spoke again to Peloux.

"You know what to do?"

"Yes" said the Parisian and gestured to Le Rasoir, who got up from the table and joined the man at the door. There, for the first time, the stranger lifted his head and turned his face to the light. Le Rasoir took careful note of the scar that ran along his left cheek and nodded. With that, the other man left and firmly closed the door behind him.

"Now then, Siddiq", said Peloux as he rose and walked around the table to stand behind the clearly relieved Chaudary. "You've passed the audition and got the job. The money's all yours and there'll be another thousand later on. Couldn't be easier, could it?"

"Not really, no" said Chaudary laughing. "Thank you very much."

He leaned forward to gather the cash that lay on the table in front of him but, as he did so, Peloux reached under his shoulders and up around his neck, locking him in a half-nelson.

"One other thing I forgot to mention" he whispered sarcastically to the struggling Chaudary. "We need to help you with a little disguise; just to make sure everything goes according to plan. Now don't you worry, just sit back and relax and leave everything to Doctor Rasoir."

Chaudary stared in wide-eyed horror as he saw a glint of light reflect from the shiny steel blade that the approaching thug pulled from his pocket. Still saying not a word, the sadistic Rasoir callously thrust a hand across his victim's mouth to stifle his scream and then, forcing his head to the right, cut the terrified man across the left cheek.

Chaudary's torso stiffened against the searing pain and his outstretched legs kicked over the adjacent chair, but his muffled cry could not be heard in the bar next door. After a few seconds he went limp in Peloux's arms and the Parisian let him go.

"There we are" he said patronisingly, as if he'd just forced a spoonful of unpleasant medicine upon a child, "bet you hardly felt a thing. Here, use this."

He passed Chaudary a handkerchief which he clasped to his profusely bleeding face.

"Now you can pick up the money; that'll make you feel better. Oh, and Siddiq. Don't forget this is our little secret. You don't breathe a word of this to anyone. Otherwise Doctor Rasoir might have to perform some major surgery. And, so far, no one has survived those operations. Understand?"

Chaudary grunted a painful "yes" from behind his reddening handkerchief.

"Good" said Peloux. "Well, that's the evening's business taken care of; let's all go and have a drink."

* * * * *

England

"It's a Beretta Cougar" said Grainger as he passed the handgun across to Alan Russell. "F model. Semi-automatic. Ten rounds in the magazine. The rotating barrel reduces the recoil and gives it a high degree of accuracy for such a compact piece. It was designed for concealment, so it's small; but it'll do the job as well as anything bigger."

George Grainger was a Scot in his early seventies; a bluff, slightly overweight, ruddy-complexioned master of his own domain. He should have retired several years before but G.G., as he was known to everyone in the service, was pretty well irreplaceable and as long as he wanted to stay, which he most emphatically did, the powers that be were happy to ignore his overdue pensioning-off and let him continue to run his fiefdom. Granger's realm was an innocuous-looking unit on an Oxfordshire industrial estate that was, in reality, S.I.S.'s main ordnance and supply base.

"Have you ever fired a gun, 'Mr. Paris'?" he asked disconsolately, fairly certain of the negative reply.

Russell shook his head. "I don't think I've ever even held one before."

"Then why the bloody hell do you want to start now?" demanded the dour Scot.

"I don't really" said Russell. "But it may be necessary and, if it is, I want to be confident that I know what it's all about."

Grainger sighed resignedly. "What it's all about, laddie, is nothing to do with guns. It's all about the people who use them. Why the O.C.'s can't seem to understand that is beyond me."

"O.C.'s?" asked Russell.

The Scot laughed. "Operations Chiefs. It's who you're working for.

But don't get too excited, it's more impressive than it sounds. And you're the third bloody virgin I've been sent in eighteen months."

He stuck his hands resolutely into the pockets of the white coat that covered his tweed suit, which was also overdue for retirement, and nodded in the direction of the door.

"Well, come along with you. We may as well get down to teaching you how to shoot the thing now that you've got it. And don't worry. It's not loaded yet."

Blair, who had driven Russell to the unit and delivered him to Grainger, remained seated with a cup of coffee as the Scot led Russell out of the room and into a long corridor that ran the length of the factory-like building. Sunlight was shining powerfully through the transparent corrugated roof and illuminating the sign on the door at the end that read CAUTION: *Firing-Range*.

Russell was under strict instructions from the Major not to mention any details of who he was or why he was there but, despite the imposed distance, he warmed to the acerbic Scotsman and the down-to-earth nature of the man; something that was distinctly absent in Blair and Caswell.

"And what else do you teach here?" he asked as they walked, "besides showing novices like me how to shoot a gun, I mean?"

"Oh, various little party-pieces" said Grainger playfully. "Like the most efficient ways of killing a man with your bare hands; how to make a bomb from articles you can buy in a local supermarket; everyday things like that."

Russell's disturbed expression caused Grainger to grin at him.

"Don't worry. It's not as gruesome as it sounds. We can show you those things, it's true, but most of our work here is with new technology: cameras, recordings, bugging, that sort of stuff. If someone comes up with anything new then we try it out and, if we think it's got potential, instruct people in its use."

"But do you train agents, here?" asked Russell.

Grainger stopped walking and turned to look at him.

"Nobody really trains an agent, laddie. A good operative learns his tradecraft through experience and the right sort of instincts. He grows with the job. They're all individuals and work in slightly different ways but they've all learned it from the bottom up; learned it thoroughly and over time; a long time. That's why I get so cross when they send people like you down here."

He shrugged his shoulders and nodded at Russell as if to apologise for having caused offence.

"Oh, I know that sometimes we have to rely on outsiders and it only makes sense to teach them what little we can for their own protection; but it should only ever be in extreme circumstances. This can be a very risky business and it's never the people upstairs who lose out; it's always the poor buggers in the field who are out of their depth. So I just hope you know what you're doing, that's all."

There was real concern on the Scot's face and Russell was grateful for it.

"These *are* extreme circumstances" he said. "And I promise you that I do know what I'm doing."

"Aye, well maybe you do, maybe you don't" said Grainger with a sigh. "But either way, we've got work to do and the sooner we start the better."

* * * * *

France

Henri LeBec idly stirred his coffee and looked expectantly across the desk at his sergeant, who was about to give him a report following the much needed break the Chief Inspector had at last felt able to take.

"So how was your long weekend?" enquired Nicot.

"Heaven. But I expect you're going to bring me back to earth with a bump. What have we got?"

"Nothing much. The main problem is Madame Charnier."

LeBec grinned. "Our star witness is beginning to tire of her holiday, is she?"

"I'm afraid so. It seems that the novelty of the apartment we put her in has worn off and she wants to get back to work. What's more, the concierge is none too happy about her guest. It seems she rises at five every morning to get herself breakfast."

"What's wrong with that?" asked LeBec. "We can't expect her to change the habits of a lifetime."

"No, quite. But she apparently insists on singing at the top of her voice while she's doing it and it wakes half the block. The concierge did speak to her about it but apparently Madame's reply would have made a sailor blush!"

LeBec laughed. He could well imagine receiving the wrong end of the Charnier tongue.

"Well she and the concierge are going to have to learn to live with each other for a little longer; with or without the early morning concerts. Wherever this Kahlil may be hiding, he must know that the photo-fit was made up from Madame's description; she's the only possible source. If we let her back on the streets she's liable to end up very dead. She stays under wraps until we've got Kahlil or we're certain he's left the country."

"That brings me to the next point" said Nicot. "We had a visitor the day before yesterday asking that very question: whether or not we felt he was still in France."

"From the press, you mean?"

"No, he was from the British Embassy."

LeBec's face creased into a frown.

"Did he say why he was asking?"

"Apparently the Brits have got wind of a possible cell of the Lions of God starting up in London. They think they may be linked to our mob and wanted to compare notes."

LeBec was still puzzled.

"But we're in regular contact with London. Why should they suddenly make an approach through their embassy?"

"Well it's not the anti-terrorist squad that's asking. It's the security services. It seems they've had a sighting of someone who could be our Kahlil and got directly onto Paris and asked them to check out dates with us."

"And?"

"No go, I'm afraid. They've had this guy under surveillance for some time and when Charnier had her brush with Kahlil their suspect was definitely in England. It can't be the same man."

LeBec nodded. "I see. Did he have anything else to offer?"

"Nothing that was of any use to us. He asked quite a lot of questions, though; wanted to know everything we'd got."

"And how much did you tell him?"

The sergeant grinned at his boss knowingly.

"Not a lot. I'm all for helping out where we can but I never really trust the secret service boys; not even our own, let alone anyone else's. If the time comes when we can get some concrete results through co-operation then fair enough but, until then, I prefer to play my cards a little closer to the chest."

LeBec was pleased. He'd worked with Paul Nicot as his number two for three years and, contrary to the slightly lumbering image created by his overweight frame, the sergeant was a quick-thinking, highly efficient policeman, as thorough and as cautious as LeBec himself.

"Let me know if he calls again, Paul. In the meantime, we'd better see if we can do something to pacify Madame Charnier before she upsets the concierge so much that we lose one of our safe-houses."

* * * * *

England

The local estate agent had not yet found a prospective buyer for the cottage but Russell had already moved out, leaving what would be, for him, the painful organisation of the sale to his solicitor. He'd put his own furniture into store and moved into a small furnished flat in Queens Gardens, just a short walk from Queensway underground station.

Like most of Bayswater, the large white Regency building, which had once been a splendid town house, was now converted into as many apartments as the developer could cram into it. Russell's top-floor flat was a far cry from the peace and quiet of Ashdown forest but, for the time being at least, the bustle of London was a welcome relief from the brooding solitude of his own company. For the same reason, despite being granted three weeks compassionate leave, he had returned to work.

At Caswell's request he tried to settle back to a routine existence.

Apart from the two evenings a week when he drove to Oxfordshire to continue his firearms instruction with George Grainger, his life appeared to be all one would expect from a man trying to come to terms with the loss of his wife.

A fortnight passed with no further contact from Caswell and Russell was beginning to feel uneasy at the lack of communication when, on the morning of Tuesday the 9th of December, his office telephone rang.

"Alan, it's Blair. I wonder if you'd meet me this afternoon at around 2.30? Speaker's Corner if that's alright with you. I thought we might take a turn through the park while we chatted."

"Yes" Russell replied. "I think I can manage that".

"Good. That's splendid. Until 2.30 then."

The line went dead.

Russell was early for the rendezvous and sat himself on a bench to await the arrival of Blair. In typical style, he was exactly on time and strode casually into Speaker's Corner on the stroke of half-past two. As he reached the bench, Russell rose and fell into stride beside him and the two men strolled into Hyde Park. Blair wasted no time in idle pleasantries.

"Thank you for being prompt. The Major would like you to know that matters are progressing well but there's something we'd like you to do for us." He paused for a moment, aware that what he was about to say would be unpalatable. "We'd like you to renew your acquaintanceship with Nina Petrova."

Russell stopped in his tracks. "You have to be joking!"

"Keep walking please, Alan" commanded Blair quietly. "It draws attention to us if we stop."

Russell fell obediently back into step but his disquiet was written all over his face.

"We appreciate this may be a little distasteful to you" said Blair sympathetically. "But none the less it is essential."

"In God's name why?"

"The essence of good cover is built up over a very long time, Alan. Not just months – but often years. In your case time is a luxury we do not have. If you insist on us putting you into the field then we need back-up; which comes, in this instance, in the rather pleasing shape of Miss Petrova."

"I don't follow you."

"She's our only link to Gurevich. If we can convince her that you're nothing more than a bereaved husband with no knowledge of her or Gurevich's real identity then we convince Gurevich too – and your cover is secure. Once she feels she can trust you, then we can really take advantage and feed them all the smoke we want."

"Smoke? queried Russell. "You mean disinformation?"

"Exactly. Subtly of course; just little hints here and there but enough to let them piece together the picture we want them to see. Then, when the time comes we take them completely by surprise."

Russell's eyes closed and he shook his head disconsolately. This was a burden he had not expected to have to shoulder.

"I understand the logic of what you're saying" he moaned. "But my wife is hardly cold in her grave. Now you want me to strike up a friendship with the woman who started this whole business. I'm not sure I'm that good an actor – and if she suspects me, I'll blow the whole thing."

It was Blair's turn to stop walking. He faced Russell and looked him squarely in the eyes. Reading the pain that so clearly lay behind them, he quickly took his elbow and ushered him to an adjacent bench where they both sat down. He delivered his lecture kindly but firmly.

"Alan, Nina Petrova almost certainly had no direct part in your wife's demise. She may even be totally unaware of it. If you don't think you can convince *her*, how do you propose to deal with Gurevich? Because eventually you are going to have to face the man who killed your wife and contain your feelings until the appropriate moment. If you can't – we may as well abandon the whole operation."

It was several moments before Russell spoke. He knew that all he was hearing was true. He had wondered about little else since he had left the Poland Street office where he had made his demands. He was also only too well aware that any sign of weakness or inability to undertake his role would mean the instant cancellation of everything. He could see that very decision being weighed in the balance as he looked into the eyes of the man next to him. He could make only one reply.

"You're right of course. What do you want me to do?"

"I want you to start living the identity you are adopting. So let's look at what that is. You met a girl in Cambridge, found her attractive and formed a friendship but declined to let the relationship develop. A week later your wife was killed in a tragic accident when your home was burgled. You have now moved to London and are living alone. One day, quite by chance, you meet the girl in the street. You chat, buy her a drink and the friendship develops again from there. It's a perfectly plausible situation. But you must talk yourself into this scenario until you believe it. She's an experienced lady and she'll spot a phoney a mile away. In this case we're lucky; she'd expect you to be bitter and angry so that in itself is not a problem. What you mustn't do is to let her feel it's directed towards *her*. If you do, the game's up."

The simple, plain description made it all sound so easy. The standard fairy tale of boy meets girl, boy loses girl, boy finds girl again; but it took no account of the enormous emotional battle that Russell knew he would have to wage within himself. That would be no fairy tale; it would be cold, hard reality. Secretly, he still didn't know if it was a battle he could win; but he knew he had to conceal his doubts.

"I understand" he said as confidently as he could. "How do I bump into her?"

Blair pulled a scrap of paper from his overcoat pocket and passed it to him.

"The address of a health club in Covent Garden. She goes there Wednesday evenings and leaves around 9.30. If you're there tomorrow night you'll find her. After that it's up to you."

Blair rose to leave but he stopped, turned and looked at Russell long and hard, as if he were trying to decide whether or not he should say something. Eventually he spoke.

"Don't feel guilty about it, Alan. There's no betrayal of your wife in this. Nina Petrova can help us get to Gurevich and we must use her. Think of it as a means to an end; a form of revenge, if you like. But don't confuse it with your grief or loyalty to your wife's memory. It's a job to be done and you know it for what it is; so take solace where you can. After all, her physical charms are real enough even if her persona is false."

Russell was surprised at this sudden change of attitude.

"Careful Mr. Blair" he said, managing a smile. "For a cool, logical military man, you're beginning to sound compassionate."

Blair grunted in reluctant admission. "We'll be in touch" he said and turned on his heel and walked away across the bleak, windswept park.

Russell stared at the piece of paper in his hand, let out an audible breath of resignation and then folded it deliberately and placed it deep within his pocket.

* * * * *

Despite the more than forty years that have passed since the fruit and vegetable market plied its aromatic trade on the site, everyone still refers to it as "the market" and it remains the centre of Covent Garden both geographically and culturally. The arts and crafts shops and countless bistros and restaurants nestle closely under the huge vaulted roof, vying for the endless multitude that gathers to sample their delights and to watch the street entertainers who turn the cobbled piazza in front of St. Paul's Church into a day-long theatrical stage. The whole vivid panoply is enacted every day under the imposing shadow of the enormous Opera House. The crowds that gather last long into the evenings, when their numbers are swelled with the capacity audiences that flock to the area's many theatres and the tiny streets become as congested as anywhere in London.

On this particular Wednesday evening, the snow that had been falling on Paris for a month had finally crossed the Channel and reached London, discouraging the usual crowds and keeping those who had braved the cold night within the confines of the pubs and bars. Floral Street was therefore unusually quiet and Alan Russell wished that more people had been around to make him less conspicuous as he waited in the doorway of Bertorelli's Restaurant. From his vantage point he could see along the length of the street to the doorway of number eleven, where the large black and white sign announced *The Fitness Centre*.

Following Blair's advice, he'd thought through the scenario as though it were indeed a casual encounter. To provide himself with a "genuine" reason for being there, he'd been to the Opera House box-office earlier and bought two tickets for the following Friday's production of Die Zauberflötte. The tickets were also an insurance; he could bring their purchase into the conversation and it would give him a casual, but valid, reason to suggest seeing her again by inviting her to accompany him to the performance.

His feet were beginning to numb with the cold when, just after 9.55pm, he recognised her as she emerged from the entrance to number eleven and stepped onto the street. Wearing the same grey anorak she had worn on the morning of their first meeting, she paused to zip the collar high against her neck and then withdrew her woollen hat from the pocket and positioned it firmly on her head and over the tips of her ears.

To Russell's relief, she turned to walk in his direction rather than the opposite way. He was on edge and could feel a knot in his stomach but there was no time for nerves. Before he knew it, his feet had overtaken his thoughts and he was moving out of the doorway. He crossed to her side of the street and started towards her. He kept his pace fairly slow and his head down until she was only a few metres away then, gradually, he raised his eyes from the ground and, silently praying his feigned surprise would not appear phoney, he stopped and looked directly at her. An agonising second or so passed before she became aware of him but then she too came to a halt and the genuine shock on her face gave him hope that his own expression was probably convincing.

"Alan!" she said, unable to credit her own eyes.

"Hello, Nina" he said softly. "I could scarcely believe it when I realised it was you. How are you?"

She stood silent for a moment, still taken aback by the sudden encounter.

"I'm fine" she eventually managed. "I'm just so surprised to see you, that's all."

"Me too. What brings you to Covent Garden?"

"Oh, I've been to the gym. I work-out at a club just along the road here."

Russell had rehearsed this scene a hundred times that day but now, actually facing her, his well practised lines evaded him and there was an awkward pause while he struggled to find the words he wanted. It was Nina who broke the uneasy silence.

"Well, I must be off. It was nice to see you, Alan. Goodnight."

As she stepped away from him he reached out and gently held her elbow.

"Nina. Please wait a moment. I know it's a bit of a shock, meeting again like this, but I'm glad I've seen you. Couldn't we go for a drink or something? Just for a few minutes? There's quite a lot I'd like to say. I tried to find you that Monday morning but you'd already left."

She looked up at him. He was hoping he might see something encouraging in her face but her eyes were defiantly bright and strong and her expression was stern.

"I think we'd said enough the night before, don't you? Adding to it now would only make matters worse; so, if you'll excuse me."

He didn't let go of her arm.

"Please, Nina. Please! There are some things that I have to explain. Just a few minutes? Then you can leave. I promise!"

Whether he was acting well or his real discomfort and nerves were showing through and complementing his performance he didn't know, but her face softened and she nodded reluctantly.

"Oh, alright. But just one drink, that's all."

"Thank you" he said quietly, belying the great relief he was inwardly feeling.

He was amazed that her reactions had given away so little when she must have been considerably flustered to meet him so unexpectedly. She's good, he thought. She's bloody good. This will not be easy. But he was too concerned with his own role to dwell on how well she was playing hers.

The Nag's Head, opposite the stage-door of the Opera House, was copiously decorated with opera posters and photographs. Its piped music, in similar vein, generally drew a less boisterous crowd than the surrounding bars with their loud rock and large plasma screens showing sports or endless loops on the Mtv channel, so it was not overly crowded. Russell ordered their drinks and found a table in a quiet corner that afforded some degree of privacy.

Spending only a little time on preliminaries he soon brought the conversation to the death of his wife. Carefully studying Nina's reactions, he gave only the basic details; that there had been a burglary and Taniel had been found dead, presumably killed in a struggle with whomever had broken in.

She stared at him open-mouthed and he was sure there were tears welling in her eyes.

"Oh, Alan" she said feelingly and reached out to place a comforting hand on his arm. "Oh, Alan I don't know what to say. What a terrible thing. How dreadful it must have been for you. I'm so sorry; so very, very sorry."

It was at that moment that he knew he'd be able to go through with it. He was certain that her shock and her emotion were genuine; that could only mean Blair had been right and she hadn't known about Taniel. It was the one straw to which he'd been clinging. Now he was sure that, despite everything else, she was at least innocent of involvement in Taniel's murder and he knew he could play out whatever lay ahead.

They continued talking for half an hour and the conversation was unstrained. It was far less difficult than he had imagined and his confidence grew the more they chatted. Glancing at his watch, he decided he would try his luck a little further.

"Look" he said. "It's almost 10.30 and I don't know about you but I still haven't eaten. Would you join me for something?"

She paused for a moment and stared down into her glass, obviously reticent, and he felt a nervous quiver of tension grip his lower back as he thought perhaps he'd misjudged his progress.

"I did say just one drink" she reminded him. Then she raised her eyes and, with an almost unwilling smile added: "But I can't take food before a work-out, so I haven't eaten either." The smile broadened into a wide grin. "Nothing fancy, though!" she insisted. "I'm not dressed for it."

They made their way down Floral Street and through Broad Court, where they found *Giuseppe's* a small Italian restaurant on the corner of Drury Lane.

The evening passed pleasantly and, just as he had found during their meals together in Cambridge, she was easy to talk to and the conversation flowed freely. Sitting opposite her, chatting over a bowl of spaghetti, brought a strange normality to their being together. Russell himself found it hard to believe they weren't like any other couple in the restaurant, quietly enjoying their meal and each other's company. It was as though there had to be another reason for this rendezvous, some perfectly plausible explanation for this most ordinary of scenarios, and not the sinister motives that were its extraordinary real purpose. Despite the clandestine cat and mouse contest they were each playing, he slowly began to relax and started to feel confident that she didn't suspect him.

They left the restaurant at just after midnight and Russell hailed a cab. Had he been an experienced operative, and not so concentrated upon his companion, he would have noticed the dark green Volvo estate car that edged unobtrusively from its parking place on the corner of Long Acre to follow their taxi all the way to Chelsea. He might also have recognised the shadowy features of Blair, sitting behind the wheel.

Nina made no attempt to invite him into her basement flat but, before they parted, Russell asked her if she'd go with him to the Friday performance of Die Zauberflötte. He told her he'd bought the tickets without really knowing whom he would invite to join him; he'd just known that he didn't want to go alone because, since the loss of Taniel, he was trying hard to avoid the solitude of his own company. At first she declined but, with only a little persuasion, she finally accepted.

As the taxi headed back north towards Bayswater, Russell weighed the evening's events. It amazed him to think how well Nina could manage this pretence and, though it angered him more than a little, he realised how easy it had been to be taken in by her in Cambridge. But he was now turning the tables, playing her at her own game, and could not deny the satisfaction it gave him. He realised he was actually looking forward to Friday night.

He was pleased with what he'd achieved and hoped Blair would contact him the next day so he could report that all had gone well. He had no idea that Blair was already on his way back to Caswell with a full résumé of the whole encounter.

Inside her apartment, Nina Petrova closed the front door behind her and then leant back against it, deep in thought. She knew the odds on casually bumping into Alan Russell were long; too long perhaps for it to be by chance. Yet, if it were planned, she could not understand how he would be able to find her or why he would want to do so. After a few moments she dropped her bag where she stood and, without waiting to remove her coat, went purposefully to the telephone and made a call.

"It's Chelsea" she said as the line connected. "Would you ask 'mother' to call me, please? I'm at home." She hung up and waited. Within thirty seconds her control officer called her back on a secure line.

"I've just spent the evening with Alan Russell" she told him. "I met him on the street. How do you want me to proceed?"

* * * * *

The performance at the Opera proved an enjoyable evening and led to dinner the following Tuesday and again on the Friday. It appeared to be tacitly understood that their friendship was developing and Nina gladly accepted when Russell suggested he take her to the theatre four days later. He wondered if she would appreciate the irony when, unable to resist the temptation, he bought two tickets for the R.S.C.'s revival of *Les Liaisons Dangereuses* at the Ambassadors. If she did, it certainly didn't show in her face when he produced the tickets and, ironic or not, they greatly enjoyed the play.

They had now spent five evenings together and Russell was surprised at how easily he'd settled into being in her company. It was as if there was a level at which he could put the falsehood to one side and enjoy the relationship for its own sake, phoney or otherwise. There were other advantages too that he hadn't foreseen. The sudden death of his wife had left an enormous, unfillable void; it was not only the loss of Taniel herself but also the loss of the little things; the sharing of an evening with someone; the idle conversation and small talk; the closeness of a female and the femininity that emanates from her and suffuses all she does. These too had been snatched from him and it made the adjustment to life alone all the harder. Despite its contrived nature, his strange association with Nina had replaced many of these transient, fragile but necessary elements of his life. It had provided an alternative at a time when his feelings were too sensitive and confused to contemplate forming a new relationship, and the hours he spent with her were a welcome change from the sad and solitary isolation of his own four walls. In an odd way, this deceitful involvement, that he had so disdained when Blair proposed it, was in itself helping him, slowly, to adjust and overcome his grief.

After the play, when Russell took her back to Chelsea in his car, she invited him in. As he sat next to her on the sofa and she poured them both freshly brewed coffee from the pot she'd brought from the kitchen, he watched her and wondered what was running through her mind. Alright, she was a professional. Deception was her trade; of course she seemed relaxed and at ease with him. But there was something more to it than the naturalness of her manner. He was sure her enjoyment of their evenings was in many ways authentic and wasn't part of the act. Somehow she'd learned to play her role and at the same time take whatever pleasure it afforded. Maybe the true tradecraft of the professional wasn't acting at all, but rather the ability to inhabit two realities and move comfortably and genuinely between them?

Maybe he'd begun to master the same skill? Certainly, against his expectation, he felt no regret and no pangs of guilt spending time with Nina so soon after Taniel's passing. The fact he was doing it as part of a plan, a strategy to hit back at the man who had murdered her, was ample justification. But he needed no excuses. Whatever it was they found themselves sharing in this counterfeit relationship, it was a necessary step towards catching Gurevich; so he was content to let it follow its course. And Blair was right; Nina was charming and attractive and he may as well take solace in the game while he had to play it. That night the game made a major advance and she took him to her bed.

The sex was powerful. Russell wasn't sure if, devoid of emotional involvement, his desire was spiced by the sheer physicality of her or if he was simply purging himself of all the confused emotions of the last weeks; emotions that had begun with and seemed to revolve around the woman who lay beneath him, gently moaning with pleasure. Whatever the cause, he was strong and energetic. He wasn't making love; he was having her; using her; and each thrust was cathartic for him. And he wasn't simply taking her sexually, he was striking back; he was playing by her rules, deceiving her the way she had deceived him, setting her up for the fall just as she had tried to set him up in Cambridge. Most important of all, he was striking back at Gurevich, baiting a trap that would bring retribution and revenge for the killing of his wife. It was Nina beneath him but when he closed his eyes he saw only Taniel's face, smelt only Taniel's scent, heard only Taniel whispering his name, telling him it was alright. He knew she would understand; he knew she would forgive him this liaison and not see it as a betrayal. She would know this was his one way to justice; to find a solution, a closure that would ultimately allow him to achieve peace.

Later, with Nina sleeping beside him, these thoughts still ran repeatedly through his mind as he lay awake, staring at the dark, blank ceiling. Nina was a means to an end. Although he was sure she had known nothing of Taniel's death, and was certainly not involved, she was none the less part of the events that had caused it and must serve as a route to their resolution. Blair had been correct; she was a necessary step along the path to Gurevich and Russell would use her in whatever way he must to ensnare the Russian Colonel. Right or wrong, this was his *raison d'être*; the way he could reasonably reconcile his conscience to the extraordinary situation he was in and to his relationship with the woman whose head lay gently against his chest, rising and falling with his breathing. Eventually he heard starlings beginning their first song of the day and knew that dawn was breaking in the outside world. He closed his eyes and finally gave himself over to sleep.

Over the course of the next few days her subtle questioning of him continued whenever they met or spoke by telephone. It was never overt, never more than one casual enquiry at a time - *How was your day?* or *What are you working on?* or *How's the preparation for Paris going?* - and he never ceased to wonder at how easily she could draw a conversation around to the point where such questions were totally natural and never suspicious. He would then, equally casually, relay precisely what Blair had instructed him to include in their small talk. And so the performance continued, Russell enacting his role to perfection. Blair was pleased with his progress and encouraged to learn they had become "lovers". It was, he said, helping to build essential cover.

Cover or not, for his own part Russell's personal agenda was logic enough and sufficient justification for his "affair" with Nina. He felt secure in his task and in control. Or so he thought. It was the next Monday evening when he was caught unawares and the Achilles heel in his reasoning abruptly declared itself. It took him by surprise because it arose not, as he might have thought possible, during their sexual intimacy but in the most mundane of actions.

They had spent the evening together at her flat. She'd made them omelettes and salad and they'd eaten from trays on their laps as they watched a DVD of Polanski's new film of *Oliver Twist*. She had, so she said, an early start the next morning and he had an appointment in Whitehall first thing, so there was no plan for him to spend the night there.

"Will I see you again this week?" he asked as he stood in the hallway putting on his raincoat.

"Maybe. I'm not sure of my schedule yet but Friday might be free." All at once she smiled. "Your collar's twisted" she told him with a laugh in her voice. "Come here."

She reached and straightened the collar and stroked it down flat against his shoulder. It was a simple gesture but, inexplicably, it touched him deeply and caught him completely off-guard. Their eyes met and held. Suddenly her expression changed. She was no longer looking at him but into him, and with recognition. For a second or two, he wasn't sure if the whole pretence was exposed; that somehow she'd read the truth in his gaze; but that wasn't it. It was beyond the charade they were enacting. It was as though that simple smoothing of his collar had opened him up and drawn into his eyes an unbidden sincerity, an honesty, a confession without words: this is me; the real me; see me for the first time. Know how much I'm hurting inside; know that my world has fallen apart and I don't want games and phoney relationships, I need comfort and caring and balm for the pain. She'd seen it. And it had reached out and touched her.

"Alan ..."

She said his name softly; but that was all, just his name. Then she leaned forward and kissed him tenderly and, for a moment, it seemed to him the most natural thing in the world. It was the warmth and compassion his aching soul craved and he was almost lost in it.

The icy rush of reality came to his rescue, flooding in and hitting him like a cold shower. He pulled back and stepped away from her.

As long as he knew her for what she was, he could use her and manipulate her to his purpose. She was part of the plot, one of the foe, and their sexual liaison was nothing more than the spoils of war. But there were chinks in his armour; flaws in the cool logic of his careful disguise. He hadn't allowed for his genuine emotions; hadn't considered that the enemy might be capable of responding with real feeling; real warmth and concern for him; that a moment of simple human connection might break through the sham and disarm him totally. It would not only blow his cover, but all his emotional defences would fall; the carefully constructed walls he had built around himself and his grief would be breached through one simple defect: honesty. Such a link between the two main protagonists was not in the script; it would bring down the curtain on his two-handed drama and the show would be over.

She could read the panic in his eyes and he knew it. He opened his mouth to speak but had no words. Instinctively she raised a finger to his lips and gently shook her head.

"It's alright" she whispered. "I understand."

He nodded in silent appreciation and quickly left.

The journey home was a roller-coaster ride of doubts and fears. What had she meant by *I understand*? He prayed she had merely meant the obvious: that he was still too close to the loss of his wife; that his reaction had been his vulnerability and grief, his inability to cross emotional boundaries until the pain had eased and the wounds had started to heal. That surely had to be what she meant. If it was, his cover was intact. If it wasn't, then she'd seen through him.

He passed a mostly sleepless night and the next morning found concentrating difficult both at his early meeting and throughout the day's work. He'd even considered calling Blair and trying to explain how he may have dropped his guard but, thankfully, he didn't because that evening she telephoned and, although she didn't know it, genuinely put his mind at rest.

"I was worried about you after you left last night" she told him with apparent concern. "I just want to say it's ok. I can't begin to know how bad the past weeks must have been for you but I do understand that it's going to take time to come through it. So, if I can help then fine, and I'm here for you. But if it ever becomes too much and you need space; need to be alone for a while, then that's ok too. I just wanted you to know."

He was still on course. She had no suspicions. He was just a grieving husband. He thanked her for her thoughtfulness, reassured her that he was alright and made arrangements to meet her on the Friday as planned.

What troubled him was his own vulnerability. Maybe it was natural for a man in his position to reach out for the warmth and comfort of affection from another – but it was dangerous. It would not only unmask him but also lose him Gurevich. He had discovered he was not such an accomplished player after all. There was not long to go before the Paris conference and the conclusion, one way or another, of his ordeal. In the intervening days he would need far greater caution whenever he and Nina met.

* * * * *

France

As always, Christmas was celebrated in France in the customary and traditional way. In Paris, Henri LeBec sat at the table opposite his wife and smiled to himself. He was far from being an unsociable man but, just for once, it would have been nice to eat Christmas lunch alone with her. This year, as every year, they were joined at the table by her unmarried sister, her brother with his irritating wife and two daughters and LeBec's mother who, despite her eighty-two years, was as vociferous as the two noisy children who seemed to find an excuse for a fight and a screaming match every five minutes. Just as every other year, Monique LeBec had spent days cooking and preparing the house for the onslaught of visitors which meant that, by the time Christmas itself arrived, she was generally too tired to enjoy it.

LeBec poured himself another glass of wine and, bemused, surveyed the gathered company, all talking at once and nobody actually listening to anyone else. He wondered whether they'd even notice if he simply got up and went to sit quietly in the other room; but he didn't. This festive season more than any other, Henri LeBec had reason to give thanks and be unusually charitable. The threatened bombing campaign hadn't materialised and Paris had been able to enjoy the celebrations free from the terrorist threat. He knew that, sooner or later, they would reorganise and the danger would return but he had dealt them a hard enough blow to gain a little respite and a trouble-free Christmas. That was reason enough to be gracious and he winked across the table at his wife as he raised his glass and, through the general hubbub, mouthed "salut!"

* * * * *

England

Alan Russell felt the loss of Taniel all the more poignantly as the 25th approached. The memories of their previous Christmases together had come flooding back to him as he saw the bright shop windows, the decorated streets with their fairy lights and lanterns adorning plastic Santa Clauses and improbably smiling reindeer, and the people bustling with their bags and purchases, preparing themselves for the festival and the family parties. He had decided he would spend Christmas day alone and declined Nina's invitation to join her at her flat. She had made no protest, saying she fully understood his feelings.

Since the evening when he'd let down his guard he'd been more cautious in her company but was still able to relax sufficiently to seem natural and at ease with their conversations. The forthcoming Paris conference was a natural topic for discussion and he'd had no difficulty in raising the subject whenever, on Blair's instruction, certain fabricated information was to be included in their casual talk.

One Friday evening, over dinner, he had let slip that his boss had received an unscheduled visit from Special Branch for the checking of security clearances of anyone involved with the conference. He'd made light of the incident, claiming that Ramsey had turned it into an office joke for the rest of the day, but he was aware that her casual response continued until she had learned all the apparent details.

A week later he'd told her that he'd received an amendment to the proposed itinerary, instructing that the travel arrangements were subject to alteration and the day of return would not be confirmed until the conference was underway. Again, he was impressed by how skilful she was. Appearing to show no more than passing interest, she questioned him further, subtly gaining all the facts.

Twice every week, never missing his appointed time, Russell had returned to George Grainger and his firearms instruction. He was still unsure of how he felt when he held the Beretta in his hands and levelled it at the target. It was a man-size cut-out of a figure holding a rifle with a snarled and aggressive expression on the painted face. The body section and the head each had marked areas to indicate where a strike would be fatal.

As Grainger never ceased to remind him, aiming at an inanimate image that was replaced after every session was nothing remotely like pointing a weapon at a living, breathing target. The instructor's observation was not lost on his student and Russell constantly confronted the question of how he would feel if his sights were focussed on Gurevich. The doubt, however, did not adversely affect his progress and each week saw him steadily increasing his scores. Whether or not he had a natural aptitude for the task, as Grainger begrudgingly told him, he didn't know but, by the seventh lesson, he was able to consistently hit a moving target. When he then returned to a stationary one he was able to place every one of the ten bullets in his magazine within the tight circle of a fatal hit. That night he had read his score card with grim satisfaction.

When Christmas Eve finally arrived he realised, sitting alone in his apartment, that it was the worst possible time for anyone recently bereaved to be on their own. He hurriedly packed an overnight bag, drove to the nearest off-licence where he bought a magnum of champagne and, twenty minutes later, was ringing Nina's doorbell. The choice had been simple: the reality of solitude or the illusion of intimacy in a phoney relationship. The way he felt that first Christmas without Taniel, he needed to be occupied; needed to be thinking; needed to know he was doing something constructive and not drowning in his own sorrow. Illusion won the day.

When she opened the door they both stood there, neither of them saying anything; then she smiled and just said "I was hoping you might change your mind."

* * * * *

Russia

In Moscow, December the 25th is of significance to only a minority. The traditional Christmas celebrations are not held until January 7th because the Russian Orthodox Church has always clung to the dates of the old Julian calendar, which is thirteen days behind the Gregorian calendar that regulates the rest of the world. Also, the post-revolution ethos of atheism removed the Christmas tradition from many families and so most Muscovites view their January 7th gatherings as a party for the new year rather than holding any religious or spiritual significance. Dimitri Gurevich was no exception.

His attendance at the Paris conference would mean flying out of Moscow on the 8th of January so, with one day's grace, and for the first time in many years, he would be with his family for the celebrations. He intended to make it a memorable and full day for all of them. He sat in his high-winged armchair and watched his young son excitedly playing with a new toy truck Gurevich had bought for him. In the kitchen, his wife and sixteen-year-old daughter were preparing the family's evening meal. As he looked at the delight on the young boy's face, he hoped that his youthful innocence would last as long as possible. He hoped that, unlike his father, he would escape the entanglement of political motivation and would settle into an ordinary existence; settle to raise a family and provide Gurevich with grandchildren. Whatever else he may have done in his life, Gurevich's son and daughter were an achievement of which he was proud and he wanted them to lead normal lives; lives that were free from the sordid and secret world he had come to inhabit and that now so disillusioned him. That was the only Christmas present Dimitri Gurevich wanted; the promise that their future was safe and secure. As he opened his arms to receive a hug of gratitude from his delighted son, he swore to himself that nothing would ever threaten that promise.

Nine

France

If it's true that a major capital city reflects the real nature of its people then Paris is no exception. Where New York has its high-reaching skyscrapers, Rome its Latin flourish and London its dignified sobriety, Paris has its peculiarly French blend of the bohemian lust for life and art and a bourgeois taste for the trappings of excess. It was this distinctive mixture of temperament that had always so appealed to Alan Russell during his many trips to the capital and he never failed to feel at home there. But that same familiar atmosphere did nothing to ease his apprehension as the taxi drove him the twenty-five kilometres from Charles de Gaulle airport to his hotel in the city centre. It was just after 2.30pm on Thursday the 8th of January.

This trip would be like no previous visit and the city that he knew so well seemed to emanate a strange foreboding as his cab turned westward along Boulevard de la Chapelle towards the familiar sights of Montmartre. For the first time since he'd agreed to Caswell's request, the full magnitude of what he was involved with became tangible and ominously real. He suddenly felt very alone and his stomach turned over. He didn't want to admit to it but he knew he was scared.

He thought of Taniel and wished she was with him; wished that this was just an ordinary holiday and that she would be there waiting when he arrived at the hotel; they would go out shopping and he would show her all the special haunts that were off the tourist track, just as he had done on their last visit. Anger had been a near constant companion in the weeks since her murder and it rose in him again, knowing they would never again be able to share such trips; never again would they share any of the things that had meant so much to them. He shook himself and wound down the window, taking in a few deep breaths of the sharply cold Paris air. He wanted justice for Taniel and, frightened or not, he was going to do something about getting it.

In order to be constantly available, interpreters were usually accommodated in the same hotel as the various dignitaries to whom they were assigned. One of the benefits of the job was that such accommodation was invariably of the V.I.P. class and far above the standard usually provided for those of interpreter rank. For this particular visit, Sir Peter Mayer's party was booked into the Holiday Inn in the Place de la République which, unlike most of its modern sister hotels within the group, is an ornate, five-star Belle Époque building constructed around a large Napoleon the Third style courtyard. As the taxi pulled up in front of its large canopied entrance, Russell knew that his task had begun.

Mayer and his team were in executive rooms on the top floor and Russell's own room was one floor beneath them. As he opened the door and stepped into it, he noticed an envelope lying on the bed. His name was hand-written on the front. Inside, a sheet of the hotel's own notepaper bore the same florid penmanship. The innocuous looking message merely said *Please join us for an aperitif at 7*. It was signed simply B – 227.

Russell unpacked his case and then lay on the bed to try to get a couple of hours sleep but his attempts were no more successful than they had been during the previous restless night. After half an hour he gave up the effort, made himself a cup of coffee from the beverage tray and ran a hot bath.

Easing himself down into the welcoming warmth of the water, his tension began to ease just a little. Lying calmly with eyes closed and his head resting back against the bath, he was in two minds. Part of him wanted to lock the door and stay there hidden but the rest of him burned with bitterness, fuelled by his pain and outrage at the man who had taken Taniel's life; the man who would himself soon arrive in Paris; the man whom, in less than twenty-four hours, he would at last confront face to face.

* * * * *

As well as being a popular tourist attraction, the Tuileries Gardens, that stretch out so gracefully behind the Louvre, are also a favourite of native Parisians. The numerous benches are invariably occupied with people quietly reading, feeding the remains of their sandwich lunch to the ever-present pigeons or simply enjoying the gardens themselves. No attention is paid to anyone who sits, passes a little friendly conversation with the stranger next to him and then goes on his way; which is why Georges Peloux had arranged his rendezvous there.

The early January dusk was just beginning to draw its sombre mantle over the city when Peloux sat himself on a bench by the Orangerie and drew a packet of peanuts from the pocket of his grimy raincoat. He placed some in the palm of his hand, threw back his head to tip a few into his mouth and then, one by one, flicked the remainder to the eager birds that gathered at his feet to take their last feed of the day before flying to roost.

The man next to him continued to read his opened newspaper as he spoke. The conversation was fluent French but the stranger's accent betrayed that he was not a native speaker.

"Is everything ready?"

"Yes" replied Peloux, still keeping his attention on the busily feeding pigeons.

"Good" said the other man, casually. "No problems with our guinea pig?"

"No. He's a little unhappy but he's infinitely more frightened of displeasing us than he is of doing his job. He'll do as he's told."

"And there's no way he can be traced back to you?"

"None".

"Good. Now what about our foreign friend?"

He's satisfied with his end of things. But he won't go ahead until he has confirmation that you can deliver the goods."

"We can deliver. It's all agreed and everything is arranged."

"That will please him" said Peloux calmly. Then his voice gained in intensity. "But he's asked me to warn you that if your side of the bargain is not fulfilled the consequences will be most severe."

"Tell him he has no need to worry. When the time comes, it will only take a phone call."

"I'll tell him."

The stranger folded his paper.

"You'll be given the final details tomorrow" he said curtly and then stood and walked away.

Peloux continued to feed the birds until his packet of nuts was empty. Sure that he had allowed the other man sufficient time to be well clear of the gardens, he himself stood up to leave. As he did so, he picked up the large, plain, brown envelope that his erstwhile companion had left on the bench. Peloux placed it under his arm and walked away, not stopping to look inside. He didn't need to. He knew its contents was the same as the first such envelope he had received and the same as the third that would accompany his instructions the following day: five thousand Euros in used notes.

* * * * *

It was just after 7pm when Blair answered the knock at the door of room 227. Inside, Caswell put down his glass of sherry and looked up with a smile that welcomed but still maintained his customary air of authority.

"Good evening, Alan. Do come in and sit down."

Russell accepted the drink they offered him and sat himself in an armchair opposite the Major.

"How are you feeling?" asked Caswell.

"I'm alright" replied Russell, trying hard to sound more confident than he actually felt. "I'm a little apprehensive of course, but I'm fine."

"Well a little nervousness is to be expected. In fact, it's essential; keeps you alert and on your mettle. Only a fool would be without nerves and fools are no good to anyone; least of all in this kind of work. None the less, you'll be pleased to know that you don't have long to wait; just a few hours in fact."

"A few hours?" Russell queried, somewhat taken aback.

"Yes. Tomorrow night to be precise. Does that surprise you?"

"Well yes, a little. It's just that I suppose I'd imagined it would all happen after the conference; on Monday. I'd presumed that it would be more logical to wait until all the fuss had died down and the eyes of the world's press were turning away."

Caswell smiled knowingly.

"That's exactly what we hope Gurevich will think. The purpose of your filtering information to Miss Petrova has been to steer his concern in that direction. In fact your final act of preparation will be to phone her tomorrow morning and feed her one last snippet to confirm that idea in Gurevich's mind. In reality, however, we make our move tomorrow night. With a little bit of luck you'll be on your way back to London in just over twenty-four hours from now."

"And Gurevich?" Russell asked, unable to disguise the faint hint of suspicion evident in his tone. Even now he wasn't sure he totally trusted the Major to keep his word and half expected to be told of some hitch or problem that might yet deny him his quarry.

"All being well, Colonel Gurevich and Professor Litvinov will both be accompanying you" said Caswell confidently. "And all *will* be well, Alan." He paused. "Assuming, that is, you have no last minute doubts?"

Russell shook his head.

"Good" said the Major curtly. "Then here's to your success."

He raised his glass. The other two did likewise and all three of them drank a silent toast to the task that lay ahead. As he swallowed his sherry and put down his glass, Russell knew that his ordeal had begun. He was at first unsure if he felt exhilarated or scared but soon realised it was a mixture of both as Caswell turned and said "I suggest we begin your briefing."

Blair went to his briefcase and withdrew some photographs and a large square of paper that he unfolded and spread out on the floor in front of them. It was a large-scale, hand-drawn diagram of some road junctions. Next to it he placed a tourist's street map of the city centre.

"You are naturally aware" began Caswell "that the French Medical Association is giving an inaugural dinner tomorrow night at the hotel Georges Cinq for the various dignitaries associated with the conference. You will of course accompany Sir Peter Mayer. Cars will be sent to collect the guests at their respective hotels at around 6.15pm but they are not due at the Georges Cinq until 6.45. Plenty of time is being allowed for the short drive to take account of heavy traffic. It's during that drive we make our move. With luck, assuming everyone blames the delay on road conditions, it will be at least half an hour before anyone realises something is wrong."

Blair took up the scenario.

"Litvinov's party is staying at the Concorde La Fayette, just south of here. Their car will develop engine trouble and not arrive. The Professor is the guest of honour and cannot afford to be late, so Sir Peter's limousine will be asked to detour and pick up Litvinov. Allowing for traffic that should be around 6.35."

"And Gurevich?" asked Russell.

Caswell gave a just perceptible smile.

"That's the beauty of it. There's no way that Gurevich will let Litvinov out of his sight; so he'll leave the others to wait for a replacement car and insist on joining the Professor. That will give us just the four of you in the limousine."

"Suppose the association doesn't divert Mayer's car?" suggested Russell. "Suppose they immediately send another limousine?"

Even before the Major spoke, the condescending look on Caswell's face was enough to remind Russell he was the innocent abroad.

"The Association will have nothing to do with it, Alan" he said calmly, "*We* shall be making all the telephone calls and all the decisions."

Blair continued his narrative, dropping to his knees and leaning forward over the sketch map, indicating the various routes as he described them.

"At the Place de L'Uruguay, the car will turn left into Rue Jean Giraudoux which, as you can see, is shown on the enlarged sketch. You will be there no later than 6.40."

Russell examined the diagram. In addition to the marked out streets, there were various arrowed lines and crosses together with small shadowed squares that he took to represent vehicles.

"You will note" continued Blair "that running parallel to this street is the Rue Keppler. What isn't marked on the street map but is shown here on our diagram, is the narrow alleyway that connects them. The photographs show it in greater detail."

The glossy ten-by-eight pictures showed the alleyway from every angle.

"And what happens in Rue Jean Giraudoux?" asked Russell.

"Your car will collide with another vehicle. Nothing serious of course but enough to halt the limousine at the alleyway. The chauffeur will get out to speak to the other driver, leaving just the four of you in the car."

"The collision" interjected Caswell "will immediately put Gurevich on his guard – but he will be watching the outside and won't be expecting a threat from within. That gives you the advantage you need."

"All you have to do is get Gurevich and the Professor out of the car and into the alleyway" said Blair, taking a marker pen and making a cross on the map as he spoke. "I'll be waiting here at the other end with a van. Once we get them inside, we're home and dry."

"The whole thing should be over in less than a minute" added the Major, as he sat back contentedly in his chair and picked up his sherry glass.

"And if Gurevich refuses?" asked Russell tentatively.

The other two men looked first at each other and then back to Russell, an expression of mild surprise on their faces.

"Then you persuade him, Alan" said Caswell calmly. "It is after all for this very contingency that you have been such a willing and, I gather, very efficient student of our Mr. Grainger, is it not?"

He rose and went to the dressing table, opened the drawer and withdrew the Beretta Cougar. He handed it to Russell.

"It was your own insistence that you be present in the operation and trained in the use of this. You must surely have expected to use it, if necessary?"

"Yes. Yes, of course" Russell said meekly, taking the gun.

He held it at arm's length to see that it was loaded and that the safety-catch was on, just as Grainger had taught him, and then slipped it into the pocket of his jacket. Caswell handed him a spare magazine clip, closed the drawer and picked up the sherry bottle, topping up their three glasses as he casually continued with the details of the operation.

"As you can imagine, contact with Litvinov has been nil. He is expecting to defect in Paris but all he knows is that we are trying to arrange something at some point during his stay. He has no idea that it will be tomorrow night or that you are his liaison. He will certainly be apprehensive but you are known to him and speak his language, so we are hoping he will trust you quite readily."

The Major settled back into his chair and sipped at his drink.

"We will of course go over the details with you many times before tomorrow night but that, in essence, is the plan. Have you any questions?"

"Yes" Russell told him strongly. "What the hell is Mayer going to say when I pull a stunt like this?"

"Sir Peter will say and do nothing" replied Blair.

Russell was amazed. "You mean he knows? He's in on this?"

"Never underestimate the drive of the scientific mind, Alan" said Caswell. "Sir Peter has been the motivating force behind getting Litvinov to England from the beginning. He knows only the absolute minimum of course but he will be happy to corroborate anything we ask if it gets Litvinov out of Russia."

"And just what will he be asked to corroborate? I mean, how will you explain away what I've done?"

A smile of satisfaction broke across Caswell's face.

"*You* won't have done anything. The official story will be a kidnapping undertaken by an anti-Russian group. The Chechnyan separatists will be accorded the blame. Suddenly finding four people in the car instead of two, they snatched you as well in the confusion. After the Beslan siege, people believe them capable of anything."

"Naturally, there will be proper follow-up" added Blair. "After a suitable period, you will be returned bearing ransom notes for the Professor and Gurevich. I'm afraid you will have to be drugged and unconscious but it's necessary for authenticity. It also provides you with a valid reason for remembering nothing."

"Clever" acknowledged Russell, quietly nodding his approval. "Very clever."

"It will make headlines around the world of course" Caswell told him blithely, "and cause considerable embarrassment to the French, who will be frantically searching for the three of you all over La Belle France. Meanwhile, we will have slipped quietly back home."

"Eventually the Professor will be presumed dead" said Blair. "Murdered by the kidnappers. In reality he will be in England; with a new identity."

"Is it really that easy?" asked Russell.

"It's one of the advantages of the computer age" Caswell offered half-cynically. "Whole life histories can be eradicated or created at the touch of a key; medical records, tax files, everything from his first school report to the day he got his false teeth. All stored quite legitimately in the official listings."

"But how do we explain getting Gurevich back from the kidnappers to stand trial?" asked Russell keenly.

"Trial?" queried Caswell

"Yes, of course. For the murder of my wife"

The Major looked at him incredulously.

"We can hardly put Gurevich in the dock, Alan. He'd spill the beans on everything. There can be no question of a trial."

Russell sat up sharply.

"Now just a minute! My condition for going through with this was that we brought Gurevich to justice. You promised …"

Caswell cut him off in mid sentence.

"No *you* wait a minute, Mr. Russell" he said forcefully. "I promised to help get Gurevich and this whole mission has been meticulously planned to achieve just that. I recollect no promise about a trial. I do, however, remember telling you that nothing would be allowed to jeopardise Litvinov's defection; and that includes attracting the attention of the entire world by putting up Gurevich for public display!"

"But Gurevich must be brought to justice!" Russell protested.

The Major's tone became suddenly calm and controlled and his eyes narrowed.

"I agree" he said icily. "It would be much simpler for all of us if Gurevich's judgement was handed down to him in the limousine. No questions would be asked. It would be one more crime laid at the kidnappers' door."

Russell sat back heavily in his chair, shaking his head in disbelief.

"You're asking me to commit murder."

"No" said Caswell evenly. "Execution. But the decision is yours."

The Major fixed Russell squarely in the eye.

"I'll put Gurevich in a cell and I'll happily throw away the key. But there will be no trial. The only alternative lies in your own hands."

The room fell silent. Once again, Russell was confronted with the inevitable question. Was he or wasn't he capable of pulling the trigger? Perhaps it was what he'd really wanted from the outset; an excuse for swift and immediate justice; an eye for an eye in a personally delivered sentence of death. Was that the real motivation for his involvement? He still didn't know.

"A question" he said, his voice low and a little unsteady with the uncertainty and doubt that was besetting him. "What if it goes wrong? What if I screw up and it falls apart? What happens then?"

Caswell's voice became almost encouraging.

"Nothing will go wrong, Alan. The operation is extremely well planned and we've covered every angle. But, if there is a problem then I'm afraid you would be on your own."

The words had a cold and ominous ring to them and, for the first time, Russell realised their true meaning. It had bothered him right from the outset that it had been all too easy to persuade Caswell to his terms. He could understand why he was so well suited to the Major's purpose but it had always puzzled him that his demands about Gurevich and, in particular, learning to use a gun had been readily acceded to. Now it was all too clear why.

"You mean that if something goes wrong then I'm the perfect patsy, right?"

"I mean" replied the Major steadily "that if you fail then, just like any agent working in the field, you would bear the consequences. I would have no choice but to deny all knowledge of you and any complicity in your action."

"Yes. I can see that you would" said Russell, the sarcasm clearly evident in his voice.

"Then surely you can also see that your failure would give the Russians the excuse they need to throw a legitimate security ring around Litvinov and I would never be able to get to him. My cause would be as lost as yours. It therefore follows that I have every confidence in this operation and in your success. Otherwise I would never take such a risk."

Caswell leaned forward in his chair and, to Russell's surprise, laid a sympathetic hand on his arm.

"And perhaps you can further see that the only possible obstacle to that success is Colonel Gurevich. I would hate to see you suffer any more at the hands of this man. The decision must be yours of course, but I urge you not to put yourself at risk out of some misguided sense of morality. He showed none when he murdered your wife."

Russell knew it was true. Gurevich was the only factor that could interfere with the whole scheme. If his threat was neutralised they would all be safe. He hated Gurevich more than words could describe and the constant ache inside him for the cruel loss of his wife only served to increase that hatred as each day passed. He should have welcomed the chance he was being offered; to erase the man from the human race, to which he had forfeited all right to belong. Despite the cold logic of it, he was still haunted by what Caswell had called his "misguided sense of morality". He just didn't know if it was within him to pull a trigger and shoot another human being, even one he despised as powerfully as he despised Gurevich. The only thing of which he was certain was that there was no going back. Whatever tomorrow night may bring, he was already past the point of no return.

He looked up at the Major and met his expectant gaze.

"Take me through it again" he said quietly.

* * * * *

Dimitri Gurevich stood at the window of his room on the 22nd floor of the Concorde La Fayette and stared at the astonishing panorama of lights that is Paris by night. It spread itself beneath him like some huge sequined cloak that glistened and glittered as it enfolded the city in its undulating and ever-changing embrace. One could stand for hours and still never see all the endless patterns that kaleidoscoped across the view and teased the imagination. Gurevich, however, paid little attention to the spectacular neon pyrotechnics. His thoughts were many miles away with his family in Moscow.

The 7th of January celebrations had been special. He couldn't remember the last time his family had enjoyed such a day together and it had affected him strangely. His daughter, at sixteen, was almost a woman and yet it hardly seemed yesterday that she'd been born. He'd heard of her birth by telephone because, as usual, he'd been abroad. He could remember the call coming from his contact. The conversation had been as expected but the caller had added; "Oh and incidentally, you know mother's in hospital; well I thought you'd like to know that the gift you sent her is absolutely perfect. And pink is her favourite colour, so congratulations; you couldn't have done better."

Gurevich could remember it so clearly; the flat he was staying in, the identity he'd assumed and the two "joes" he was recruiting to be run by London station. It all seemed so close; so recent. And yet here she was, virtually grown to womanhood before he'd realised. He didn't feel that he really knew her. His enforced long absences had made him more of a visiting uncle than a father and it grieved him to think of how much he had missed. There was a charm about her; the appeal of the childish innocence that she hadn't quite lost but that now inhabited a woman's body. It made him feel protective. He wanted to shield her from the world; a world that he knew from first-hand experience could be sordid and vicious. But it was a world of which he had become a part. He'd learned the rules and, for many years, successfully played the game; a game where the lives of individuals were held cheap against the higher purpose of one's masters; a game where innocence like that of his daughter held no currency.

As he looked out over the bustling city, he thought back across the sixteen years that had passed since that telephone call. How many crimes had he committed? How many lives had he been responsible for ending? All done in the name of the cause and all done while, somehow, untouched and just one step removed from it all, his daughter had blossomed into the delicate flower that he now wanted so badly to protect.

Suddenly he felt grateful. He was thankful that his family hadn't been contaminated by the life he'd led and that he himself had survived its many dangers. He made himself a promise. This operation would be his farewell. He would resign his commission and take early retirement. The last two years behind a desk had bored him anyway and there were any number of capable men to take his place.

One couldn't simply resign from the service as one chose but he knew a doctor who'd been a little too vociferous in his political criticism of Putin and who, but for Gurevich's intercession, would have lost his licence to practise. The debt was sufficient to warrant an unfavourable medical report and an enforced retirement on the grounds of poor health. His superiors would be satisfied and, with his exemplary record of service intact, his pension would be generous and his state-granted dacha in the countryside secure.

He turned back to the room to look at his companions. The

Professor was reading quietly in an armchair. Ivan Zhukov was lying stretched out on the sofa. Doctor Radischev and Pavel Golombek, the interpreter, were in their adjacent rooms and further along the corridor, once again travelling under cover and on the authority of Gurevich alone, was Andrei Melekhin.

Just as in Cambridge, the groundwork had been thorough and had shown nothing suspicious. Zhukov was convinced it was all a false alarm and that they may as well relax and enjoy the free trip to Paris; but Gurevich didn't agree.

He still had an uneasy feeling about the whole affair and was convinced that the next four days could yet prove eventful. He turned again to the window and the neon pageant that flashed and sparkled across the sprawling city. Exactly what might be lying in wait for him there he didn't know; but if it came, he meant to overcome it. This mission would be his last and it had to be a success. Then he could retire to his family and enjoy what remained of his son's and daughter's childhood. He would allow nothing to stand in the way of that.

* * * * *

The door was unlocked and opened noisily as Siddiq Chaudary sat up and rubbed his eyes. Georges Peloux ambled into the room, placed the tray of food he was carrying on the rickety wooden table by the bed and then picked up the tooth-glass of red wine that accompanied it.

"Here, drink this" he grumbled. "Perhaps it'll wake you up a bit. Proper Rip Van Winkle you are. I never met anybody who could sleep like you."

Chaudary shrugged. "What else is there to do?" he moaned. "I've read every book and magazine in the place and there's no TV or radio. Besides, I've been here so long I've lost track of time. So I just sleep when I feel like it."

"You've been here a couple of weeks, that's all."

"No" insisted Chaudary. "It must be more than that. I remember ..."

"Well what does it matter how long you've been here!" snapped Peloux, angrily cutting him short. "Just shut up complaining and eat your food; or uncle Georges will take it away and you can go without."

Anxious not to lose his meal, the disgruntled Chaudary refrained from further comment and enthusiastically attacked his plate. Peloux was far from being a chef and the cuisine always consisted of whatever tin or packet could be most conveniently and quickly prepared. It was invariably either slightly burnt or underdone but, unappetising as it may be, Chaudary knew there was no alternative and always ate whatever arrived rather than go hungry.

"Anyway" Peloux went on, "won't be long now and it'll all be over. Besides, you agreed to stay out of trouble didn't you? So what could be better than a little holiday in your own private hotel with me to wait on you?"

The sarcasm was not appreciated but Chaudary made no comment and silently continued his make-shift meal.

"Well, like it or not, that's the way it's got to be" said Peloux. "Assuming you still want the other half of your nice fat fee that is?"

The other man looked up and nodded, still chewing a gristly piece of sausage.

"Yes, I thought so" said Peloux acerbically. "So let's have a little less moaning and a little more gratitude around here."

"But how much longer will I have to stay hidden?" Chaudary implored through a mouthful of the tasteless meat.

"As long as it takes. Now shut up and eat!"

Chaudary finished the remains of his food, snatching back the last of his bread from the tray as Peloux picked it up and stepped towards the door. Then he threw himself back onto the bed and, staring up at the cracked plaster of the ceiling, sighed heavily. The Frenchman turned in the doorway and gave a loud *tut tut* as he shook his head disapprovingly.

"Patience is a virtue, Siddiq" he said in a sing-song voice. "And remember, you're not the only one who wants to see the back of all this hanging about. Playing housemaid to you is not my idea of fun either; but we must stick it out until we're told different. So be a good boy and don't give uncle Georges any trouble, right? Right!"

With that Peloux left, slamming the door shut behind him and Chaudary was once again alone as he heard the key turned slowly and deliberately in the lock.

* * * * *

Just north of the Rue de Rivoli and next to the giant Forum shopping complex lies a large, modern apartment building called simply *Les Halles* after the surrounding area in which it stands. The block was purpose built for short lets to tourists rather than for residential occupancy and, due to its central location, quickly became a favourite with the travel companies. In January, not being an especially busy month for holiday makers, several of the apartments fall vacant and Nina Petrova had managed to secure one for the four nights she would be in Paris.

She had given the address and phone number to Alan Russell during their last evening together in London. He called her there at just after 10pm.

"Did you have a good trip?" he asked.

"Yes, I caught the 6.30 flight and got here about an hour ago. The apartment's lovely; and it's in a great spot. I ought to go out and look around really but I'm very tired so I'm going to have a hot bath and an early night. What about you?"

"Oh, I'm fine. I couldn't reach you on your cell phone though. Is it switched off?"

"No, but I think the signal's a bit erratic here. Must be the building. Have you started work yet?"

"No. Not until tomorrow morning. Although they're messing about a bit with the schedules" he added, casually bringing Caswell's prepared script into the conversation.

"Oh, why?"

"I don't know. It must be something to do with security I think because it's all supposed to be hush-hush. But they've told me I won't be going back on Monday."

"That's odd, isn't it?"

"Yes. Something about needing me to interpret – but I don't know what."

She laughed. "Well, I'm sure you won't object to an extra day in Paris."

"No. No of course not."

Inwardly, Russell marvelled at how casual she could sound when he knew her mind was working overtime and trying to piece together a scenario from the bogus fragments of information that Caswell had instructed him to provide.

"What about tomorrow night?" she asked. "Can we meet for a meal? I'd love you to see the apartment."

"No, I can't. It's the big 'do' tomorrow night. The inaugural dinner."

Oh yes, of course. I'd forgotten. Well what about Saturday?"

As he answered, he was aware that he was becoming as practised a liar as she was.

"Yes" he said warmly. "Saturday would be fine."

"Good. You can stay over at the apartment and if you're not needed first thing on Sunday we can have a lazy morning and a leisurely breakfast together. How does that sound?"

"Wonderful."

"Do you think they *will* want you to interpret on Sunday morning?"

"No" he said truthfully. "I can promise you I won't be asked to interpret on Sunday morning."

"Great. I'm looking forward to it already."

Something in her voice almost made him believe she meant it; that she really was keen to see him. But then, Nina was peerless when it came to pretence. What she didn't know was that Russell would not only miss their Saturday night rendezvous, but she would never see him again. This would be their very last conversation.

"Does eight o'clock suit you?" she asked.

"Yes. Fine" he replied, trying to emulate her casual cheerfulness but not succeeding.

"Eight o'clock it is then. You can pick me up at the apartment. And don't be late. I'm missing you already." She laughed. "Goodnight Alan. Sleep well."

"Goodnight."

The line went dead.

He stood silently for a few moments, still holding the receiver as it gave out its low, constant, disconnected signal. Then he slowly replaced it in its cradle and quietly said: "Goodbye, Nina."

Ten

France

The two Gaudry brothers, Émile and Léon, had inherited the family business from their father. He in his turn, had been handed down the ownership of Gaudry Autos at the death of his own father, old Léon, who had founded the business in 1910 with just one vintage Renault. A large sepia photograph of the old man standing beside his beloved car still adorned the office wall. Lord of all he surveyed, he watched over the daily routine of his legacy from above the desk where Émile sat finishing his paperwork at 5.45pm on Friday the 9th of January.

The firm now had seven vehicles: three brand new Espace minibuses, that worked non-stop through the tourist season, two Peugeot saloons for standard chauffeuring jobs and, the pride of the fleet, two luxurious and immaculately kept Citroën limousines. They were the personal joy of Charles, the retired railwayman whom the brothers employed to wash their vehicles. He lavished hour after hour of loving care on the sleek, black paintwork and shining chrome. As they stood in their respective bays, waiting for the coming night's work, both cars shone with their customary pristine sparkle.

The Gaudrys rented their underground garage space from the filling station that stood above it. The overall area was just sufficient to accommodate the vehicles, a service bay and the office itself, a small pre-fabricated room to the side of the main entrance-ramp that sloped down from street level. The noise of a small Fiat Uno descending the ramp in a hurry and pulling up sharply at the far end of the garage caused Émile to put down his pen with relief and move to the open door of the office.

"About time too!" he yelled to his brother, who emerged from the Fiat. "I was beginning to get worried. Everyone else has finished for the day and gone home. There'd be nobody to take your place if you hadn't arrived."

"You wouldn't feel right if you weren't worrying" joked Léon. "Anyway, my timing's perfect. We're bang on schedule."

"Well, Monsieur Perfect " quipped Émile, "we won't be if we don't leave right away. So stick this on your head and let's get these babies on the road."

He handed his brother a peaked cap, that matched the dark grey suits they were both wearing, and then a set of car keys.

"The pick-up's at 6.15 remember. So step on it! I'll meet you later at the Georges Cinq."

Émile returned to the office and put away the paperwork. He took his own cap from the corner hat stand, placing it smartly on his head, and then opened the small metal cupboard that hung on the side wall and held the vehicle keys for the entire fleet. As he took the remaining Citroën keys from their allotted hook it occurred to him that he had not heard the engine of the limousine being started.

"Now what's he waiting for!?" he moaned and started back towards the door. "Léon!" he called. "For God's sake get a move on, will you?"

As he looked across the garage floor to the Citroën's bay to see what was causing the delay, he stopped in his tracks. Léon Gaudry was lying slumped across the polished bonnet of the limousine.

Émile had only taken two hurried steps towards his prostrate brother when he was grabbed from behind and felt the sharp pain of a needle entering the back of his neck. He sensed the surge of fluid as it was injected from the syringe but his knees buckled and he slumped towards the ground before he could turn to face his assailant. He was only vaguely aware of the shadowy figure standing over him as, within seconds, his eyes closed and his senseless body fell unconscious onto the cold concrete floor.

He was oblivious to the rough hold that was taken on his neatly-pressed jacket and to being dragged back into the office and bundled into a corner. His brother's slumped body was soon unceremoniously dropped beside him. Their attacker took Émile's cap and placed it on his own head as he pulled a cell phone from the pocket of his grey suit, that was identical to those of his two victims, and made a call.

"All clear at the garage" he said calmly as the line connected. "Both down and sleeping for the next few hours. I'm on my way."

He flipped shut the cover of his cell phone and returned it to his pocket. Two minutes later, having closed and locked the office door and switched out all the premises lights, he was driving one of the shiny limousines up the exit-ramp and out into the Paris night.

* * * * *

Alan Russell stood in front of the long mirror on the wardrobe door and checked his evening dress yet again. For security, Caswell had confined him to his hotel and all day long the tension in him had slowly ratcheted up, notch by notch. He'd never been good at killing time anyway but, knowing what lay ahead of him that night, it was impossible to distract himself and think of anything else. He'd tried reading, watching television, lying in a hot bath, drinking copious cups of tea and coffee and, naturally, running through the details of the operation over and over until he could recite them like an automaton; nothing had relieved the mounting stress. Other than to the waitress in the restaurant, where he had managed only to half-eat his lunch, he had spoken to no one. Returning to his room, he had passed the loneliest and longest afternoon he'd ever known. Strangely, now that the moment had actually arrived, he felt a little easier. Having to get himself dressed and ready had provided a channel for the nervous energy and slackened the pressure. He realised the tension in his stomach had lessened and, to his surprise, felt reasonably calm and collected.

He pulled on his raincoat and picked up the Beretta. For the tenth time in the previous half an hour he checked it was loaded and that the safety catch was on. Then he took a deep breath and slowly and deliberately placed the gun in his coat pocket.

He extended the fingers of his right hand and stretched open the palm. There was no shake and, to his relief, no sweat in the centre. He checked his watch. It was 6.05pm.

He placed the hand in his pocket and cupped it around the gun so there was no discernible bulge or shape showing through the coat. Then, having checked his appearance in the mirror for the final time, he left the room and made his way down to the hotel lobby.

The limousine was already parked outside. As casually as he could manage, Russell walked out through the hotel's main entrance and nodded to the chauffeur who, having seen him approach, was politely holding open the rear door of the vehicle. He settled himself into the leather upholstery and sat back to wait for Sir Peter Mayer. After a few minutes the tall English doctor appeared, looking his usual elegant self, and

Russell could see that, beneath his overcoat, he sported the customary rose in the lapel of his white dinner-jacket.

"Sorry to delay" he said as he climbed into the car to join Russell "but there's been a slight hitch; trouble with one of the cars apparently. They've asked us to pick up the Professor." He turned to the chauffeur who was seating himself behind the wheel. "Is that alright, driver? He's at the Concorde La Fayette?"

The Chauffeur appeared to have no need for a translated explanation and, before Russell could interpret, replied in a stilted mixture of French and English.

"La Fayette?" Certainly, sir. Pas de problème."

He started the limousine's powerful engine and the car glided away to join the heavy stream of traffic in the Place de la République. Russell looked down at his watch. It was 6.18pm. His mission was underway.

The roads were fully congested and it began to look as if the journey to the Concorde La Fayette would take the full twenty minutes Blair's schedule had allowed. Mayer sat quietly going over his after-dinner speech and Russell was grateful for the excuse it provided to avoid conversation during their ride. He didn't want his nervousness to show in forced or unnatural small-talk.

Mayer's acquiescence to Caswell's plan had come as a complete surprise. It had never occurred to Russell that the distinguished doctor might condone such a daring and unorthodox plot for the defection of Litvinov. Caswell was right. To further the cause of their research, these men of science would bend whatever rules were necessary. Looking across at him, calmly reading, Russell wondered what was really going through his mind. Did he know anything of what lay ahead of them this night? Was the rehearsing of his speech merely a device so that he too could avoid showing his nerves? Russell doubted it. He was fairly sure Caswell would have told Mayer nothing more than necessary; that at some point in Paris the move would be made and it would be credited to a terrorist kidnapping which Mayer would confirm. The less he knew, the more genuine his surprise and shock would be when it occurred. Russell was tempted to say something. There was time enough before they collected their extra passengers to declare himself to Sir Peter; to let him know that he, Russell, was the contact and prepare him for the dramatic events to come. It would have been an immense comfort to share the burden of the tension and secure the confidence of an ally; but he decided against it. It would be contrary to Caswell's orders and he had been told a hundred times *follow the plan to the letter and nothing will go wrong*. The words ran repeatedly through his head like a mantra and he silently prayed they were true.

The call to the Concorde La Fayette had come at exactly 6.20pm. Colonel Dimitri Gurevich put down the receiver of the front-desk telephone and walked back across the lobby to the four members of his party, who were all in evening dress and impatiently awaiting the arrival of their limousine.

"Anything wrong?" asked Ivan Zhukov.

"I'm not sure" Gurevich told him thoughtfully. "Our car has broken down and can't get here. They don't want the Professor to be late so they've diverted the English doctor's car to pick him up. It should be here in a quarter of an hour or so."

"What about the rest of us?"

"They're organising a replacement now."

"How long will that take?"

"Too long. Organise a taxi, will you Ivan? Tell it to wait outside and follow us to the Georges Cinq."

He turned to address Golombek and Radischev.

"I'm sorry gentlemen but there's been a slight change of plan. If you would be so kind as to travel with Ivan, he will take you to the dinner in a taxi. I will go ahead with the Professor and we will meet you at the hotel. Please take a seat while you are waiting."

As his companions sat themselves down on the lobby sofas, Gurevich crossed to the water cooler on the far side of the entrance hall and began to lift the tap and fill a paper cup. As he did so, he bent forward and, without acknowledging him, spoke in quiet tones to Andrei Melekhin, who was sitting close by in an armchair, reading.

"I'll be on my own with Litvinov. Ivan will be following in a taxi with the others. Make sure you stay close."

Gurevich swallowed the cool water in one easy gulp, threw the paper cup into the adjacent waste bin, and returned to his party.

* * * * *

The chauffeur pulled the big Citroën to a halt outside the Concorde La Fayette at precisely 6.37pm. Inside the car Russell looked nervously, yet again, at his watch. They were just two minutes behind Blair's projected schedule. The knot in his stomach tightened its grip as he tried to prepare himself to face at long last the man who had haunted his thoughts and stalked his dreams for over a month.

"Ah, the La Fayette" said Sir Peter, looking up from his notes. "And there they are."

The chauffeur got out and opened the rear door. Through the opening, illuminated by the light that flooded from the foyer, Russell saw Litvinov and Gurevich come clearly into view as they descended the hotel steps and approached the waiting vehicle.

The Professor was the first into the car and sat himself next to Mayer who greeted him warmly and shook him by the hand. Gurevich, climbing in behind him, said a simple "good evening, gentlemen" and sat next to Russell.

Russell felt his fists clench inside the pocket of his raincoat and was grateful that the dark of the night and the shadowy interior of the limousine hid the grim expression on his face.

Just hang on! he said to himself, feeling his anger rising almost uncontrollably at Gurevich's sudden proximity. A few more minutes is all it will take. Just hang on!

"Alan?"

Surprised at the sound of his name, he looked up and realised that Mayer had been speaking to Litvinov and was waiting for him to interpret.

"Excuse me" he said falteringly and trying to sound natural. "I was miles away."

"I was asking the Professor if he enjoyed these occasions or whether, like me, he secretly dreads them" said Mayer. "Would you interpret, please?"

"Yes, of course. Forgive me" apologised Russell, hoping his constrained emotions weren't evident in his voice.

The small-talk between the two men of science continued and, in a way, Russell was glad of it. It forced him to concentrate on something other than his mounting tension as the car made its slow and agonising progress through the traffic. He avoided looking at Gurevich and prayed the Russian would not detect his growing anxiety.

His prayer may have been answered, for Dimitri Gurevich was totally unaware of the turmoil within the man next to him. His attention was fully occupied with the view through the rear window, where the headlights of both Ivan Zhukov's taxi and Melekhin's Renault Clio satisfied him that they were both close by.

Leaving the Arc de Triomphe, the limousine entered the Avenue de Iéna and as Russell saw the name of the road displayed on the blue street sign that passed the window, he felt the palms of his hands getting moist. His throat was becoming so dry that it seemed his tongue might stick to the roof of his mouth and he had to cough before he could continue to interpret. Out of the corner of his eye he watched the passing streets and mentally counted them down. Rue Newton, Rue Auguste Vacquerie and finally Rue Galilée. His heart was now beating so loudly that he was sure Gurevich must be able to hear it; but the Russian Colonel had a problem of his own.

The chauffeur had eased his car across the Rue Galilée junction as the fading amber light had turned to red whereas the taxi driver behind him had dutifully obeyed the signal and pulled to a halt. The space behind the limousine was now quickly filling with other vehicles as the chauffeur indicated left and turned into Rue Jean Giraudoux.

Concerned by this sudden separation, Gurevich leaned forward and spoke to the driver.

"I'm afraid we have to stop. Please pull over."

The chauffeur appeared not to understand.

"Pardon?"

"Er ... Arretez! We must wait."

"Monsieur?"

Gurevich turned agitatedly to Russell.

"Tell him we must stop. We have to wait for the taxi!"

This was the first Russell had heard of the taxi that was following them and the revelation struck him like a punch. It panicked him. If the other Russians were present as witnesses then he knew the whole operation would have to be aborted. He turned and looked anxiously through the rear window. The driver's seeming inability to understand Gurevich came to his aid. In swift French, that was way beyond the Russian's comprehension, the chauffeur explained that he couldn't pull over.

"Pardon, Monsieur mais je ne peux pas arrêter ice – c'est une zone limité. Et nous sommes déjà un peu en retard."

Gurevich hadn't understood a word but knew that his request had been denied. He grabbed Russell's arm.

"Tell him he must stop. Now!" he ordered icily.

For the first time, Russell was forced into eye contact with the Russian. He was sure his own fear must be visible in his face. Gurevich would probably have recognised it too if he had not been wholly concerned with getting the chauffeur to stop. A dozen different thoughts cascaded through Russell's mind in a frenzied kaleidoscope. Images of Taniel being stretchered into the ambulance kept cutting into a glaring picture of the face on the cardboard cut-out target at the Oxford firing range. He could see the cottage in Wych Cross and the devastation that had been the living room after the break-in; a smiling Taniel waving him goodbye for what neither of them had known would be the last time; and all the while Caswell's orders were loudly resonating in his ears: *follow the plan to the letter and nothing will go wrong.*

He was frantically trying to decide what to do or say but his panic and uncertainty were short lived. Before he could utter a word, the problem became irrelevant as the strident crash of collision shook the car and momentarily shocked them all into silence.

"Merde!" cursed the chauffeur loudly and angrily got out of the vehicle to confront the driver of a small delivery van that had driven squarely into the limousine's offside front wing.

Gurevich was as surprised as the rest of them when the sudden impact jolted them all in their seats but he recovered immediately and his field operative's reactions took over. Before the chauffeur was out of the door he had registered the situation, turned his attention away from the interlocked vehicles and begun to survey the surrounding area, making sure the incident was indeed no more than an ordinary traffic accident.

Almost before he realised it, Russell's hand went into the pocket of his raincoat. Instinctively, he released the safety-catch of the Beretta and closed his grip around the butt. The journey itself had been an unknown factor but now the well-rehearsed scene was unfolding like a familiar chapter in a book that he'd read over and over. He knew his role so well that it was as if time staggered to a form of slow motion. No more than one or two seconds passed and yet it seemed to him like an age as he took a deep breath, swallowed hard and pulled the semi-automatic from his pocket. His heart was still beating furiously but he realised his palms were suddenly dry. His voice was strangely calm and he spoke in even and measured Russian as he turned and forced the Beretta into Gurevich's ribs.

"Sit still and do exactly as I say."

Gurevich's initial amazement at the sight of Russell brandishing a gun swiftly gave way to the cold realisation of what was happening. He was far too experienced to do anything hasty in such a situation and, obeying Russell's order, slowly sat back in his seat. There was genuine surprise and real concern on the Russian's face but it was tinged with a look of curious satisfaction. He'd almost begun to doubt his instincts when, after so many weeks, no threat had materialised. Now, disadvantaged as he was, at least his professional judgement had been vindicated and he knew his intuition hadn't failed him.

"Well, well" he said calmly. "So it was you after all."

"No!" hissed Russell vehemently, "it wasn't. But it is now and if you don't do as you're told I'll shoot you where you sit like the animal you are!"

Without taking his eyes from Gurevich, Russell spoke, in Russian, as reassuringly as he could to the worried-looking Litvinov.

"It's alright, Professor, don't be frightened. It's what you've been waiting for; but we must leave quickly."

He directed himself once more to Gurevich.

"You and the Professor get out of the car. Now!"

Before the anxious Professor could move, Gurevich spoke to restrain him.

"Stay exactly where you are Professor" he ordered. "Nobody's going anywhere, Mr Russell" he said quietly. "So I suggest you put down your gun and stop being foolish."

The Russian's cool exterior belied the way his mind was furiously weighing the odds and calculating his best course of action. His own gun was holstered under his left arm but, with Russell's Beretta pushing hard against his ribs, there was no way of getting to it. Zhukov and Melekhin were not too far behind but it would probably be several minutes before they guessed the traffic hold-up might be more sinister than a mere accident. Even then, to reach him, they would have to abandon their cars and proceed on foot through the solid block of traffic that had now collected behind the incident. That would also take precious time.

What persuaded him to resist Russell's demands was the Englishman himself. Gurevich was studying him intently and his experienced eye told him that this was no professional adversary. There were several beads of sweat across Russell's upper lip and his chest was rising and falling rapidly with his high and unnatural breathing. Gurevich had faced the business end of a gun on more than one occasion and had seen the killer instinct in a man's eyes from uncomfortably close range. As he stared into Russell's eyes, he recognised no such familiar look. Knowing that if he allowed Litvinov to leave the car he would be lost for good, he gambled that Russell was no killer and that if he continued to resist his demands he could either bluff him out of them altogether or panic him into making a mistake.

The elderly Professor looked uneasily from one to the other but was sufficiently frightened to obey Gurevich's instruction and remained seated.

Vital seconds were ticking by. Russell could hear Caswell's warning: *If you fail, you're on your own*; and he knew that, having begun, there was no alternative but to see it through. He leaned towards the Russian, pushing the barrel of the Cougar harder into Gurevich's body. Almost spitting his command through clenched teeth, he yelled:

"Get out of the car. Now!"

The increasing uncertainty in Russell's eyes only confirmed to Gurevich that his opponent was not equal to murder; and moving closer with the gun was the error the Colonel had been waiting for. With a lightning-swift movement of his left hand he pushed at Russell's gun arm, simultaneously twisting his upper body to force the barrel of the

Beretta away from his ribs and into the upholstery of the seat. At the same time, with his right arm, he pushed violently at Russell's shoulder to knock the Englishman off balance, intending to wrestle the gun from his grasp as he was jolted backwards.

The force of the blow took Russell completely by surprise and he fell off his seat and onto the floor of the car; but his hold on the Beretta was the grasp of a man in fear. His knuckles were white with the pressure of his grip and, instead of coming loose in his hand, the gun held fast and pulled the struggling Gurevich onto the floor on top of him. As the weight of the Russian crashed into Russell's chest, the gun, sandwiched between them, went off.

For a few seconds neither of them stirred, maintaining the tension of their grip. Then Gurevich's face, only inches from Russell's own, contorted into a mixture of acute pain and disbelief. He gasped. A trickle of blood appeared at the corner of his mouth and then his body went suddenly limp as his eyes rolled up and his head fell forward, collapsing against Russell's cheek.

Despite the shock of the struggle, Russell's concern was still the precious passing seconds. The whole episode, from the collision to the gun going off, had taken less than a minute but his frantic mind was counting down like an alarm clock to what he knew would be the last possible moments for escape. He heaved Gurevich's profusely bleeding torso away from him and got to his knees. Mayer and Litvinov were staring in horror at the Colonel's inanimate body but, from what Russell could make of the scene outside, it appeared that no one else had heard the sound of the shot, muffled as it had been between them.

He hastily fastened a couple of the buttons of his raincoat to cover his bloodstained jacket and shoved the Beretta into the pocket. Grabbing the bewildered Litvinov by the arm, he opened the near-side door of the limousine and stepped out into the night, dragging the Professor with him.

At the front of the car a furious argument was underway between the chauffeur and the driver of the van who, as soon as he saw the rear door of the limousine opening, recognised his cue and punched the chauffeur squarely on the jaw. The attention of everyone at the scene was immediately taken by this fracas and no one saw Russell exit the vehicle.

It was no more than a few paces to the alleyway and he hooked his arm through the Professor's and hurried the old man towards it.

As Russell turned into the alleyway he could see there was a white Volkswagen van parked broadside-on at the end of it. It was less than fifty metres away and suddenly he felt a faint glimmer of hope that he was going to make it.

The side door of the Volkswagen flew open and a man dressed in a combat jacket, with a dark blue balaclava covering his face, jumped out onto the sidewalk. He carried a pistol, raised in his right hand, and he ran to the corner of the alley and flattened himself against the inner wall. A shadowy, second figure appeared within the open side of the vehicle and, despite the distance, Russell could clearly see that it was Blair. The figure waived an arm at him, beckoning him on towards the van, and Russell broke into as much of a run as the struggling Professor could manage.

"Quickly, Professor!" he urged. "We're almost there!"

The engine of the vehicle burst into life. Then, to Russell's amazement, it suddenly mounted the sidewalk and drove straight into the balaclavared man, crushing him mercilessly against the wall. Still visible within the van, that now straddled the pavement, Blair picked up something. At first, in the gloom of the vehicle's interior, Russell couldn't see clearly what it was but, as Blair raised it to his shoulder, he could make-out the distinct shape of a rifle.

A single shot rang out from the barrel of the weapon. Russell heard the sickening thud of the bullet finding its mark and the old man on his arm staggered and fell to the floor with a groan, dragging them both to a halt.

Russell stared in open-mouthed horror at the prostrate Litvinov. The elderly Professor lay still and lifeless with a small reddening hole in his left breast where the bullet had passed straight into his heart.

In stunned disbelief he turned to look back towards the van, only to see Blair raise the rifle yet again; this time his sights were levelled at Russell himself. Stupefied and frozen into inaction by what was happening around him, he could only watch helplessly as Blair took aim and tightened his finger around the trigger.

Russell heard the shot. Its shattering echo reverberated around the walls of the alley; but he felt nothing. He stared incredulously at Blair who suddenly dropped the rifle from his grasp and slumped backwards into the vehicle's interior. The driver then frantically reversed the Volkswagen off the sidewalk and, with a screech of burning rubber, the tyres spun wildly to find a grip before carrying the van off at high speed.

It was only then that Russell realised the shot had not come from within the van but from behind him. He turned to see the bent-over figure of Gurevich, propped on one knee against the alley wall. His left hand was clutching his profusely bleeding abdomen but his right held the still-smoking pistol that had just dispatched Blair.

"That was for Litvinov" he spluttered through the blood that was flowing freely from his mouth. "And this is for me!"

Struggling to hold it steady, he raised the handgun, maliciously thumbed back the hammer and aimed it straight at Russell's head; but the effort of dragging his weakening body in pursuit of Litvinov and his abductor had drained every ounce of his rapidly dwindling strength. With a final exhausted moan, his head fell forward and the gun slipped from his grasp as his crumpled body slid slowly down the cold, damp wall.

Russell was shaking. He looked at Gurevich and the Professor, both lying dead at his feet and then to the body of the balaclavared man who had been crushed against the far wall. In less than a minute he'd watched them all die at close quarters and seen Blair shot. He himself had faced the barrel of a rifle and what had seemed imminent death. Caswell's meticulously planned operation had turned into a living nightmare of disaster and he was standing among its grisly aftermath, unable to comprehend one iota of what had befallen him. He was irretrievably enmeshed in an orgy of violent and bloody catastrophe but was totally bewildered as to how or why it had happened. Despite his confusion, and the fear that gripped him like a vice, he understood that he was in great danger; yet he was unable to move. There was a leaden weight oppressing his chest, gradually squeezing the air out of him, but he could do nothing; just as in a bad dream when, desperate efforts to awaken repeatedly fail. He was rooted to the spot, trembling and feeling sick.

The sound of shouting at the end of the alleyway cut sharply and suddenly into his shocked trance like a razor, and told him that time had run out. The noise of the shooting, amplified by the echo chamber effect of the enclosed passageway, had caught the attention of passers-by and had drawn their interest away from the traffic incident.

Still rigid with fear, the basic survival instinct of a man in peril took over and rescued Russell from his stupor. Without thinking, and not knowing where he was going, he began to run. His first faltering strides were quickly fuelled by his panic into a furious pace. He bolted past the crushed body of the man in the balaclava and into the yellow lamplight of the Rue Keppler, his heart beating furiously in his breast. Through instinct, rather than decision, he turned right and headed down to the junction with Rue Bassano where he veered to the left and darted into the much larger Avenue Marceau.

Unaware of where his pounding feet were taking him, he ran furiously and blindly on, hoping for nothing more than to be swallowed up by the cold Paris night.

Eleven

France

Monique LeBec put her head around the kitchen door and called to stir her husband, who was quietly reading in an armchair.

"Henri, it's the telephone! Sergeant Nicot for you."

A little disgruntled at being disturbed so soon after returning home for what he had hoped would be an uninterrupted weekend, the policeman raised himself wearily from his chair and went begrudgingly to the phone.

"Yes Paul, what is it?" he said unenthusiastically.

"I'm sorry to bother you Chief Inspector but I think you ought to know; I've just had a call from homicide. There was a shooting in town tonight. I don't have all the details yet; just that there are three dead and one of them is some sort of V.I.P. It went down a little before seven apparently."

"Well that's their pigeon not ours. Why are they phoning us?"

"Because they think one of the other two bodies might be our boy. The description tallies with the photo-fit of Kahlil."

The news grabbed LeBec's full and immediate attention. He glanced quickly at his watch. It was a quarter to nine.

"So why the bloody hell has it taken them nigh-on two hours to let us know?" he angrily demanded of his sergeant; but he didn't wait for Nicot to reply.

"Where are you now? At the office?"

"Yes."

"Right. Get down to the scene straight away. I'll be there as soon as I can. Who's handling it from homicide, anyone we know?"

"A guy called Devaux. And he's expecting you."

"Well let's hope he's co-operative. Give me the details of where I'm going."

LeBec scribbled down the address and then abruptly hung up on his sergeant. Snatching his coat from the hall-stand he hurried into the kitchen where his wife was just putting the final garnish on the lamb chops she had prepared for their evening meal. She didn't look up as he entered the room. She already knew what she was going to hear.

"I'm sorry, darling" said LeBec hurriedly. "It's important and I have to go."

Giving her a quick peck on the cheek, he snatched two pieces of bread from the basket on the table before rushing out, adding from over his shoulder: "Don't wait up!"

Monique LeBec said nothing as she gazed despairingly at the two plates in front of her. Then, just as she had done on so many previous occasions, she placed her husband's dinner in the oven and quietly took her own into the lounge to eat yet another solitary meal in front of the television set.

The scene that greeted LeBec as he arrived at Rue Jean Giraudoux was less chaotic than he'd expected. The road had been cleared of the vehicle collision and re-opened and the traffic was now flowing freely again. The chequered tape that cordoned-off the area around the alleyway was the only indication that, not three hours since, it had been the gruesome scene of a multiple murder. He flashed his I.D. at the gendarme standing sentry and made his way inside the cordon, where Nicot was already waiting for him alongside the senior officer on the case.

Pierre Devaux was a stocky, thick-set man in his middle forties with curly, greying temples and a bushy moustache. His collar was turned up against the chilly night air and he peered out, grim faced, from under a black trilby hat as he looked up to greet the new arrival.

"What exactly do you have?" asked LeBec as he took the other man's firm handshake.

"I think it might well be a case of what do *you* have" Devaux replied. "And I'll be more than happy to pass it over. I've worked the last three weekends and tomorrow was going to be the start of four days uninterrupted golf. Now this little lot turns up and it looks as if the clubs are staying in the bag for the fourth week in a row!"

LeBec gave a knowing smile. It was a feeling he knew only too well.

"Alright" he said. "Let me have it from the top and I'll see what I can do."

Devaux needed no further encouragement and led LeBec and Nicot to the far end of the alley and the body that was lying there. He began his explanation as they walked towards the corpse.

"It wasn't until forensic arrived and one of them removed the guy's balaclava that somebody recognised the face. It was one of the medics. He said he was sure it was the bomber you're looking for. A couple of the boys agreed with him so we got in touch."

LeBec looked down at the olive-skinned face with the scar running down the cheek.

"Well it looks promising. The scar is a certain match – and the general build seems right. But I don't understand it. What the hell happened?"

"It's all a bit confused. We've got a couple of witnesses who were near this end of the alley, in the Rue Keppler. They say this guy was crushed by his own van. The driver must have panicked and thrown it into forward instead of reverse."

"Very clumsy" said LeBec dismissively. "Did they get a look at the driver or the number?"

"No. As soon as they heard shots they took flight and ran for cover. Can't say as I blame them, really."

LeBec looked back along the alleyway to the other two corpses.

"And what about these two?"

Devaux gestured towards the bodies and the three men made their way towards them, the homicide detective continuing his grisly tale as they went.

"Foreign nationals, both travelling on Russian passports. The old boy is some sort of Professor – a bit of a V.I.P. apparently. The other one is supposed to be from their Health Ministry."

"Supposed to be?" queried LeBec.

"He was carrying."

"You're kidding?"

"Nope. A shoulder-holster and a semi-automatic."

He leant down and parted Gurevich's coat to reveal the empty shoulder-holster that was fastened below his armpit.

"Since when did artillery become standard issue in the Health Ministry?" asked Nicot sardonically.

"Exactly" said Devaux.

LeBec was puzzled. "Do we have any witnesses?"

"Just one. An Englishman named Mayer. According to him they were all on their way to some reception or something at the Georges Cinq. Their car hit a van and when the accident happened Mayer's interpreter went berserk and pulled a gun."

"Was he legit?" enquired Nicot.

"Apparently so. His name's ..." he pulled his note book from his pocket and flipped to the relevant page. "Russell. Alan Russell. Mayer says he's been in the job for years; the genuine article."

"How much can Mayer tell us?" asked LeBec.

"Only what he saw. He's badly shaken up of course – we've got him down at the commissariat seeing a doctor – but he's fairly lucid and clear about what happened. It seems Russell shot this one in the car, then grabbed the old boy and hauled him up this alley. But he hadn't done a proper job on this guy and he went in after them. By the time people had decided it was safe enough to venture into the alley and take a look, both Russians were lying here dead and there was no sign of the trigger-happy Englishman."

"Have you put out an A.P.B. on him?"

"Yes, of course. We're trying to get photos sent from London but that'll take time, especially as it's the weekend. Meanwhile, we're watching all ports and airports and we've notified all border points; but I think the chances are he's gone to ground."

LeBec nodded his agreement and turned to look at the bizarre scene that surrounded him, struggling in vain to put together a picture of what had happened from the few fragments of information he'd been given. It was like attempting an enormous jig-saw puzzle with only a few strange and unrelated pieces.

"We see it as a kidnap attempt that went wrong" Devaux told him optimistically. "We figure the old boy got caught in the crossfire when this guy went in after the Englishman. But our opinion doesn't matter much – once we'd taken a look at scar-face there, we reckoned it was *your* problem. Agreed?"

LeBec was far from agreed. He had long ago learned to mistrust first impressions and had no idea whether Devaux's instant theory was right or completely off the mark. For the moment he didn't care. It seemed that the crushed and broken body at the end of the alleyway might well be Kahlil and, whatever else had occurred, he wanted to be in control to study the possibility in detail. He was not about to relinquish any authority.

"Agreed" he replied to the clearly relieved Devaux.

"Good. I'll tell forensic to report to you and notify my chief we're handing it over. And believe me, you're welcome to it!"

He turned and walked purposefully towards his car, keen to radio back to his boss that the sensitive issue of a murdered foreign V.I.P., with its attendant complications and repercussions, was no longer on his plate.

"And enjoy your golf!" LeBec called after him.

"I will, don't worry!" Devaux shouted back from over his shoulder. "And the best of luck!"

"We'll need it" said LeBec quietly to Nicot.

"Well, it may all seem a bit bizarre at the moment" his sergeant told him, "but it looks as if we've found Kahlil. So that's not such a bad start, is it?"

"Maybe so" said LeBec thoughtfully. "Let's get all three bodies to the morgue as soon as forensic gives the all-clear to move them. And arrange to have Madame Charnier brought in for a positive I.D. before the autopsy boys get to work."

"Right" said Nicot and turned on his heel to begin the night's long labours.

LeBec walked pensively back to the scar-faced corpse and looked down at the cold, still features and the eyes that stared blankly from their lifeless sockets, as if still living the shock of their final moments.

"Well, well" he said softly to himself. "Maybe we've caught our prize fish at last."

LeBec left the alleyway and returned to his waiting Peugeot. He knew an explanation of the evening's strange events would elude him for some time and that, as always, it would take days of slow, methodical police work to begin to make sense of the scenario that confronted him; but as he eased himself into the back seat and told his driver to head for his office, he was hopeful that the Lions of God had suffered yet another decisive blow.

* * * * *

Unlike Henri LeBec, Alan Russell's departure from that same alleyway almost three hours earlier had been anything but hopeful. His blind, instinctive flight had carried him three quarters of the way along Avenue Marceau before his urgent need to lessen the pace and regain his breath had finally brought him to a virtual halt outside the forbidding façade of the Cathédral Grecque. It was only then, in the act of slowing down, that his panic subsided a little and gave way to the realisation that he was far more conspicuous running than if he simply walked liked other pedestrians. Keeping his stride vigorous, but not so fast as to attract attention, he began to move at a lesser pace, gradually reducing his pounding heart-rate and evening out his breathing. At the end of the Avenue, just as his complaining body was settling and starting to recover equilibrium, he realised with horror that he was approaching the Place de l'Alma where the southern end of Avenue Georges Cinq meets the north bank of the Seine. In his desperate haste, he had actually been running towards the Georges Cinq Hotel, the one place in Paris where people who knew him and would recognise him were gathering. An icy dread began to rise again within him and he quickly turned right into Avenue de Président Wilson.

Common sense dictated that, only minutes after the event, no one around him could possibly know of the nightmare in Rue Jean Giraudoux; but he wasn't yet thinking rationally and common sense played no part in his confused and frantic thoughts. He sensed that guilt was plastered all over him in banner headlines; felt sure that anyone who saw him need only look at his face to read every detail of what had happened and know he was running for his life. He hurried past the Musée d'Art Moderne and the Palais de Tokyo, darting short, furtive glances at every face that passed, certain that among them someone must be shadowing his every move. By the time he reached Place d'Iéna, the uneasy sensation of being followed was becoming unbearable. The imagined stare of accusing eyes, stabbing relentlessly into his back, was causing his panic to surface again. The intensity of the tension in his stomach, the dryness of his throat and the pulse-beat that was drumming at his temples was reaching an intolerable pitch. It was then, just as he was beginning to feel he could go no further, that he saw it. No lighted candle in the darkest night had ever appeared more welcoming than the ornate *Metro* sign above the stone steps that led underground to I'éna station and away from the city streets.

Descending into the welcoming labyrinth of the metro system, he pulled a few coins from his pocket and hurried to the automatic machine to buy a ticket. As he went further below ground he began to feel a little easier, sheltered by this nether world as if it were another land from the Paris that bustled above it. To his great relief, a southern-bound train was pulling in as he reached the platform. He travelled one stop to Trocadéro and then, in case he'd been seen or recognised boarding the train at I'éna, changed lines and headed south again on a train bound for Nation.

Ensconced in a corner seat, with his back to the rest of the carriage, he pulled his raincoat tightly around him and raised up the collar, trying to hide himself within it. He turned his face to the window where, for the first time since his ordeal had begun, he felt a brief moment of relief. The sudden lessening of tension caused his head to fall forward and come to rest gratefully against the glass. The sound of the train wheels, beating in their regular rhythm over the rails, was a comforting reminder that every repetition took him further away from the horrific scene of Rue Jean Giraudoux; but he knew the respite was temporary and the reprieve provided by the metro would be short-lived; he had no idea where he was heading or what he would do next. He knew he should be marshalling his thoughts, trying to calm his shattered nerves and rationally assess his situation; but he could only stare blankly into the darkness of the tunnel, wishing he could lose himself in the black oblivion that raced by.

Just under half an hour later the train pulled into St. Jacques. The journey had eased Russell's agitated state a little and his mind was appreciably clearer. He still had no answers as to how or why the operation had gone so badly awry but he was thinking rationally enough to know that, whatever the cause, it was of secondary importance. His priority now was his own safety. The morning papers and news stations were certain to carry the story and it would only be a matter of hours before his name and description were all over the city. He had to adopt some cohesive plan of action, to concentrate his mind on his immediate danger, and as he tried to consider what few options might be available to him, George Grainger's warm brogue suddenly sounded in his head. He recalled a conversation they'd had during one of his firearms training sessions when the kindly Scot had seemed to sense a vulnerability in his eager student. Perhaps it was a genuine foreboding of something akin to the events that had overtaken Russell that night but, whatever it was, the older man had offered his advice: *Whatever the trouble, laddie, reduce it to its simplest elements. Always solve the problem at its basic level. You can worry about the details later.* The simplest element was that he was on the run and within hours his identity would be known to every policeman in France. The basic-level solution was therefore that he needed a new identity. Within another two stops he'd formulated the beginning of an idea. He was unsure of its viability but time was of the essence and, seeing no alternative, it was his only option.

He still considered he was safer within the metro than on the streets so at Place d'Italie he changed trains and headed north for five stops to Bastille. There he changed lines again and travelled one stop south, alighting at Gare de Lyon. He left the metro system and made his way into the mainline concourse where he carefully studied the electronic indicator board. To his relief, he found what he was looking for. At 10.35pm an overnight sleeper was due to depart from platform three for Marseille. He checked his watch against the station clock; it was just before twenty to nine.

He hurried into the street. It was not an area he knew and it took him almost twenty minutes to find a bank with an external cash machine. He withdrew the maximum amount allowed on his cash card. From the bank he set off to find the nearest late-night drug store. It took a further quarter of an hour but at least it was a large shop and looked as if it would stock all the items he needed. Picking up a wire basket at the doorway he made his way cautiously along the aisles and selected a small shaving mirror, some beige eye-shadow, an eye-liner pencil and a pair of Reactolite sun-glasses. Then, scanning the shelves of shampoo and hair-care products, he found some aerosol cans of spray-on colour. Choosing a shade of silver-grey, he took all his purchases to the checkout and asked the assistant to put them in the largest carrier-bag she had.

Russell had walked a considerable distance from Gare de Lyon and by the time he returned the station clock was reading 10.04pm. He purchased a platform ticket from the automatic machine in the concourse and then sat down on a bench opposite platform three to wait, all the time keeping a vigilant eye for signs of any police. The overnight passengers to Marseille were starting to gather and the clock was gradually ticking away the minutes to departure. Russell was beginning to give up hope of finding what he wanted when, at 10.22pm, his objective materialised.

They were a slightly comical couple. She was striding purposefully ahead, urging her companion to hurry lest they be late, and yet offering no assistance with the two tartan-coloured suitcases with which he was clearly struggling. As the unhappy husband gratefully accepted the help of a porter, Russell knew they were exactly what he had been looking for.

The porter's trolley was fully loaded with several sets of luggage and he carefully placed the additional cases on top of the pile before following the new arrivals onto the platform. Russell rose quickly from his seat and, showing his platform ticket to the collector at the gate, walked through the barrier to follow them. As he had expected, the couple went on ahead to find their compartment and couchettes while the porter paused at preceding carriages to deliver the relevant baggage.

Drawing level with the trolley, Russell surreptitiously cast an eye over the labels on the couple's luggage. His luck was still running. They were both marked with the names of LaMotte but one clearly stated Madame and the other Monsieur.

At the fifth car along the trolley stopped again and when the porter selected a bag and went inside, Russell seized his chance. He grabbed the tartan case and walked quickly across the platform to the opposite train and boarded it. As swiftly as he could, without drawing attention to himself with unnatural haste, he made his way back through the cars to the first carriage. From the doorway he could see back along the Marseille train to where the porter was still delivering his bags. It appeared he had not yet reached the LaMottes and the stolen case had yet to be missed. Russell reasoned that, having placed it on the trolley themselves, they would assume it had been inadvertently delivered to the wrong compartment and it was a fair bet that the imminent departure of the train would resolve them to look for it en route. He stepped out of the carriage and walked casually from the platform with his prize.

It was now over three and a half hours since his ordeal had begun and it was reasonable to assume that the hunt for him was well underway, but the passing of time had cleared his panic and his success in obtaining the suitcase encouraged him a little. He had seen no police presence in the station so far and, heading for the Bureau de Change, he felt sufficiently emboldened to take one small gamble that might buy him extra time.

"Excuse me, but can you help me please?" he asked the girl at the counter in English. "I have only two minutes to catch the Marseille train. Could you be quick?"

"Certainly Monsieur. How much would you like?"

"Five hundred Euros, please."

He handed her his credit card. The girl swiped it through her machine and handed him the module to type in his pin while she counted out five crisp, new one-hundred Euro notes from a wad within her drawer. Within another twenty seconds the transaction had been validated and she handed him both the money and his card. As he had hoped she would, she read the name on the credit card as she passed it across to him.

"Thank you, Mr. Russell. Enjoy your trip."

Grateful that all had gone according to plan, Russell walked back towards platform three then, as soon as he was out of sight of the girl in the Bureau, turned away and doubled back around the concourse to the men's washroom. With a quick glance about to make sure he was unseen, he pushed open the door and entered. Apart from an elderly man relieving himself at one of the stalls, it was empty. Russell waited until the old man left and then, selecting one of the lavatory cubicles, went inside and shut the door. He closed the lid of the toilet seat and placed the suitcase on it, unzipping the tartan cover to reveal its unknown contents.

He had chosen well. The case contained sufficient clothing for at least a week and Russell's estimate of the man's height and build being similar to his own had been correct. The style was conservative and of an older fashion than he would normally wear but that eminently suited his purpose. He stripped himself to his underpants and then selected and put on a pair of grey trousers, a white roll-neck sweater and a blue blazer. The general fit was a little tight but not enough to draw attention. The shoes were too small but he didn't need them, his own black evening shoes appeared natural with the clothes he had chosen. He closed the suitcase and emptied the contents of his carrier-bag onto the lid to begin the final part of his transformation.

Taking the beige eye-shadow, he rubbed a little onto his finger and, using the mirror, smoothed it gently beneath his eyes. Then, with the liner pencil, he added an extremely faint semi-circle to give the appearance of bags, smudging over the edges to blur any visible line. This completed, he traced the lightest touch to subtly emphasise the crow's-feet marks. Then, picking up the aerosol can, he sprayed the grey lacquer onto his comb and ran it lightly through his hair, taking great care to streak it sparingly and avoid any blobs of colour. He combed the grey liberally into his temples but graduated it back along the sides of his head to virtually nothing by the time it reached the back of his neck.

He was pleased with the result. The image that now stared back at him from the mirror appeared at least fifteen years older than the man looking at it, maybe even twenty. Finally, he put on the sun-glasses. He had chosen Reactolite because they have light-sensitive lenses that only darken in sunshine. In the absence of bright light the glasses remain clear and so, at this time of year, would appear only marginally darker than ordinary spectacles but enough to prevent closer inspection of the make-up, which was rendered more subtle behind their slight shading. His disguise complete, he folded his bloodstained shirt and suit and stuffed them into the now empty carrier-bag. Then he put on his coat and sat back to wait.

As the minutes ticked by, several men came in and out of the washroom to avail themselves of the facilities. Russell would ease the door open just ajar and check each and every one but it was over half an hour until he saw what he wanted. A middle-aged, tired-looking man lumbered into the empty room with a heavy case and set it down against the wall. Removing his coat and jacket, he proceeded to roll up his shirt sleeves, take off his tie and fill a basin with hot water. Russell recognised his cue. He flushed the toilet and then opened the door and walked out, carrying his case and bag. He walked to the far basin where the stranger's coat and jacket were hanging on a hook by the drying machine.

The man tilted the soap dispenser towards his palm and then rubbed his hands to a lather before lowering his head to wash his face. In the ten or so seconds he closed his eyes to the soap and water, Russell seized his chance. He pushed the button on the drier to kick it into life and, while the noise covered any sound he might make, took advantage of the stranger's momentary blindness to delve swiftly and quietly into the man's pockets. He began with the jacket, which proved fruitless, but the inside pocket of the overcoat held the wallet he was seeking. By the time the stranger had rinsed his face and opened his eyes, Russell was gone.

*****

Henri LeBec arrived at the morgue to find an enthusiastic Nicot waiting for him.

"I've been through our boy's clothing" he said animatedly, "not much to show; but look what he had in his inside pocket!"

He handed his boss a folded piece of paper. It was stained with blood along the top edge and the red mark fanned into a grim, flower-like pattern as LeBec opened out the page, but the pencilled writing was untouched and clearly visible. It was the address of the flat in the Quai de Grenelle where they had found the explosive.

"Well, well, well" said LeBec. "Now there's a turn-up for the book."

"How's that for a Christmas present?" smiled Nicot, "even if it is three weeks late!"

"Mmmm" muttered the Chief Inspector, nodding his head thoughtfully. "Though I'm not so sure I like the wrapping paper."

Before the puzzled sergeant could ask his boss to explain, they were interrupted by a firm knock at the door. It opened and Clémence stepped into the room.

"Evening, guv'nor. I've got Madame Charnier outside; alright to bring her in?"

"Yes" said LeBec. "Ask her to come through."

"Right." Clémence started to leave but then turned and grinned at the other two men. "Oh and er ... she's not exactly happy, if you know what I mean." He winked and went outside.

Madame Charnier was indeed far from happy, which was clearly apparent when she marched into the room.

"Monsieur!" she began with gusto. "I would like to know why I have been dragged here from my bed. Isn't it bad enough that you keep me locked up and away from my business? Not to mention that pompous cow of a concierge nagging at me all hours of the day and night! Now I cannot even sleep in peace. Why couldn't this wait until morning?"

LeBec walked slowly over to her, his hands clasped behind his back like a schoolmaster, and leaned down to bring his eyes level with the old woman's wrinkled face.

"I'm sorry you've been inconvenienced, Madame" he said in a quiet but firm tone. "This is important and I'm afraid it couldn't wait. But I think you may be glad you came. It may mean you can go back to your own apartment and your flowers."

"Oh" said the old woman, her manner changing abruptly. "Oh, well that's different." Tilting her head to the side, she cast her eyes coyly down to the floor like some adolescent schoolgirl. "I'll do my best to help, Monsieur, of course."

The flirtatiousness would have been overt in someone sixty years her junior and it amused LeBec to see such verve in one so old but, energetic and strong as she was, there was real concern in his voice as he prepared her for the identification.

"I'm afraid this won't be very pleasant, Madame, but I must ask you to look at a corpse."

She gazed at him in genuine surprise and gave a quiet sniff of disdain.

"You needn't worry, Monsieur. I've buried three husbands and two brothers in my time. A dead body does not frighten me. Especially if it's that little brown bastard that tried to blow us all to kingdom come. I shall be more than pleased to see *him* in a coffin and no-mistake!"

Impressed with her resilience, LeBec straightened himself and nodded.

"Very well, Madame. Then please follow me."

He led her out through the opposite door and into the adjacent room where the badly-battered body of the scar-faced man lay cold and still upon the pathologist's marble table.

* * * * *

Two streets away from Gare de Lyon a team of dustmen were working the night shift. There were numerous large commercial bins on the sidewalk awaiting collection and emptying by the approaching men and, as he passed the first of them, Alan Russell quickly lifted the lid and buried the carrier-bag, containing his bloodstained shirt and jacket, deep inside. Fifteen minutes later, his greatly altered face was staring down into a cup of strong, hot, black coffee as he sat at a quiet corner table in a small, late-night café. It was his first moment of respite; the first time since the shooting that he had begun to feel in control.

His trump card was that he was a linguist and could speak French with a near perfect accent. The police were looking for an Englishman in his late thirties and, without close scrutiny, Russell now had the appearance of a man in his middle fifties who, even to experienced ears that might detect he was not from Paris, still sounded undoubtedly French. It was time to discover just exactly who he now was. He thumbed through the contents of the stolen wallet. It held a little cash in Euro notes, a couple of letters, a book of stamps, a credit card and an identity card bearing a photograph. He read the name: *Jean Bourget*. Monsieur Bourget was also evidently a member of the S.N.E.S., the union for secondary teaching, and the wallet also held his membership card, complete with name and address but without a photo. The signature was fairly simple and, with a few practise attempts on the back of one of the envelopes, Russell could manage a passable forgery.

Ten minutes later, the new Monsieur Bourget was standing in the Avenue Ledru-Rollin, just north of the Austerlitz bridge and looking across at the Le Brun Hotel. The lateness of the hour meant there were far fewer people on the streets than there had been at the start of his flight and so anyone walking was conspicuous. Confident as he was of his altered appearance, Russell reckoned he'd already tempted providence to the limit and didn't want to push it any further. He needed a room for the night and he needed it quickly. His choice was therefore limited to whatever was close at hand. The intimacy of a small boarding house would be too dangerous and he felt sure he would be safer in a big hotel where numerous guests would preserve his anonymity and a large staff would not expect to be familiar with the occupants. The four star Le Brun was the nearest.

Russell swallowed hard and took a deep breath as he pushed the revolving door and stepped into the foyer. The reception area was deserted save for the man behind the desk, whom Russell took to be the night porter.

"Good evening" he said politely in French. "I have just arrived in Paris and I'm looking for a room for a couple of days. Do you have any vacancies?"

"Certainly Monsieur" was the welcoming reply and Russell felt he was almost home and dry.

The formalities were brief and quickly accomplished. By paying a cash deposit in advance against his bill, he avoided being asked for a credit card pin that he didn't know, and the photo-less union membership card was satisfactory identification and confirmed the details he filled out in the registration form. He ordered breakfast in his room for 8.30am together with two morning papers and declined any assistance with his case. The porter directed him to the lift and handed him his room key as he wished him a pleasant goodnight.

Four minutes later, the new Monsieur Bourget turned the key in the lock of room 310 and stepped gratefully into his hiding place. Scarcely able to believe he had managed it, he dropped his case to the floor, placed the *do not disturb* sign on the outside handle and then locked the door securely behind him. Leaning against the wall, he threw back his head and gulped deep breaths of air. The knot in his stomach eased slightly with the immense relief that was engulfing his body but the continual tension had been too much. He suddenly lurched towards the bathroom, flung open the door and vomited violently into the lavatory.

* * * * *

Sergeant Nicot delicately folded back the cloth to reveal the dead man's face. The brown of the eyes, gazing up at them in a fixed, unfocused stare, seemed strangely vivid in contrast to the pallor that had overtaken the lifeless features of the olive skin.

LeBec watched Madame Charnier for some indication of recognition but her expression was bland and showed no sign of emotion as she looked down at the corpse. After several moments' concentration, she turned to face the Chief Inspector.

"You wish to know if this is the man I saw in the Rue Scribe? The one who drove the car with the bomb?"

"Yes, Madame, I wish to know if this is the man."

"And if it is, I am free to leave that dreadful apartment and go back to selling my flowers?"

LeBec nodded silently.

She looked back down at the body and pulled the end of her nose between her thumb and stubby forefinger.

"Hmmph" she sniffed. Well I want to go back to my flowers. I will lose all my customers if this goes on much longer. And God knows I want to get away from that overblown arse of a concierge! But I've never been one for telling lies, and I'm far too old to start now. I have to say 'no'."

"But Madame! ..." protested Nicot.

LeBec raised a hand and cut short his sergeant's objection.

"Are you sure, Madame? Absolutely certain?" he asked emphatically.

Nicot had expected his boss to share his disbelief of the old woman, but the Chief Inspector's eyes, fixed on her intently, were far from dismissive of the aged flower-seller's surprising verdict.

"Of course I'm sure!" she snapped. "I may be getting on but I'm not senile and I never forget a face; especially one that tried to murder me! You can say what you like – that is not the man!"

Twelve

France

It was ten minutes to midnight by the time LeBec and his sergeant returned to their office. The Chief Inspector had been silent for most of the journey back from the morgue and was still deep in thought as Nicot wearily pushed open the door and slumped himself into a chair.

"I'll try and rustle up some coffee" he told his boss with a yawn.

"Yes, thanks" said LeBec absent-mindedly and sat down behind his desk. "And see if you can find me a sandwich or something, will you? I seem to have missed eating somewhere along the line."

Nicot looked warily across at him. He'd seen LeBec preoccupied like this on too many occasions not to recognise the prospect of a long and arduous night ahead.

"What you really need is some sleep" he suggested. "Tomorrow's going to be one hell of a day!" But he knew the hint was a forlorn hope.

"No, I'll be fine. I'll wait for the pathology and forensic reports. Anyway, Russell's personnel file should be emailed through from London in a few hours. The sooner we get to grips with it the better."

The sergeant dragged himself to his feet and set off to organise the coffee. In the doorway he stopped and turned.

"I know she's a tough old bird; and I grant you she still has all her marbles. But she *is* an old lady. Her memory can't be what it was."

"But she was so definite" LeBec insisted. "And she's far from stupid. She badly wants to get out of that apartment and back to selling her flowers – and it was all within her grasp. You'd think she'd be the first person to give herself the benefit of the doubt and say 'yes'. And yet with everything she wanted at stake, she said 'no'."

"But it *has* to be Kahlil!" complained Nicot. "How many Arabs are there in Paris with scars on their left cheek? And he had the address on him. I mean, who else could it be?"

"I know. But something about it bothers me. It doesn't ring true. I can smell it."

"Ham or cheese?"

"What?"

"The sandwich. Ham or cheese?"

"Oh, anything. It doesn't matter."

"Right. I'll see what I can find.

Nicot closed the door behind him and left his boss to his deliberations, knowing there would be no rest for either of them until LeBec had resolved his doubts. For his own part, Nicot was convinced the terrorist they had been pursuing was now lying on a slab in the morgue and would be a thorn in their side no longer. That was at least some consolation as he contemplated the sleepless night ahead.

At the end of the corridor, on his way to the little kitchen used by the night staff, he passed the duty room and was hailed from within.

"Sergeant!" called the duty officer animatedly.

Nicot put his head into the room, where the officer sat in front of several computer monitors. He was pointing to the centre screen.

"There it is. The same site as for the bombings."

"I knew it!" said Nicot with a grunt of satisfaction as he read the large headline emblazoned across the web page.

With a quick "thanks" to the duty officer he hurried back to LeBec's office and threw open the door.

"You can stop worrying about Madame's memory" he declared excitedly to his boss. "It's not what it used to be. The Lions of God just claimed responsibility for killing the two Russians. It's the same web site. It's official. And they've admitted losing one of their men in the attack. So the corpse has to be Kahlil!"

* * * * *

When he'd finished being sick, Alan Russell rinsed his mouth and then splashed more of the refreshing cold water onto his face. It smudged his carefully applied make-up and gave his eyes a strange, unearthly appearance. As he looked at his distorted image in the bathroom mirror he gave a half-smile of relief.

"Well, Monsieur Bourget" he said to the grotesque reflection, "we'll fix you up in the morning; but right now I'm too tired to breathe."

He just about managed the few paces from the bathroom to the bed before he collapsed onto it. He didn't bother to undress; nor even to pull back the covers. He simply gave in to his desperate need to release the tension that had racked his entire body for so long.

His eyes closed and behind them, just as he had for many weeks, he saw the face of Dimitri Gurevich; only this time it was distorted with pain and anguish as it lost the struggle to cling to life and slid down despairingly against the wall of the alley. Russell had never before been close to such violence. He was revolted by it; and yet he felt an unmistakeable relief that Gurevich was dead. Notwithstanding the horror and fear he had experienced, and the very real peril in which he now stood, he couldn't deny a distinct satisfaction that Taniel's murderer was no longer free. It played on his mind and disturbed him. Was it just the resolution of an ache to see justice done and punish the perpetrator of such a heinous wrong? Or was it the more sinister pleasure of finally striking back at his wife's killer? Was it simply the fulfilment of a desire for vengeance? He wanted to know; but his exhausted mind and body were too stressed and weary to contemplate it and their need for rest and recuperation quickly overcame his struggling conscience and took him swiftly into the deep sleep of an utterly exhausted man.

He was eventually awoken by a brisk knocking on the door of his room. A little startled, he sat up sharply and looked about him. Although momentarily surprised by the unaccustomed surroundings, he was off the bed in a second and thinking fast. Like all hunted animals, the survival instinct had not been submerged in sleep and it sprung to the fore to clear his mind and make him instantly alert. Hurriedly turning back the covers, he ruffled the pillow and sheets to make the bed looked slept in.

"Who is it?" he called.

"Your breakfast, Monsieur."

"One moment, please."

Not wishing to be seen with the distorted features the smudged make-up gave to his face, he hastened to the bathroom, half closing the door, and began running a tap before shouting "Entrez!"

The maid's pass-key clicked in the lock and he heard her enter the room. From the sound of her voice he assumed she was fairly young.

"I have an order for breakfast for 310 for 8.30, Monsieur. Is that correct?"

"Yes, that's correct. Just put it down will you? Thanks," he called above the noise of the running water.

The maid put down the tray as instructed and Russell heard the door close behind her. He waited another thirty seconds before turning off the tap and leaving the safe concealment of the bathroom and then went straight to the two papers that lay next to his coffee and rolls. He had hoped the events of the previous night were too late to have made the first editions but, to his dismay, it was the lead story in each paper. Both front pages showed photographs of the alleyway in Rue Jean Giraudoux with a gendarme standing guard over it's cordoned-off entrance. The headline in one read: *Multiple Murder in City Streets* and it sent a shiver down Russell's spine to see his name at the front of the accompanying article, accused of killing both Gurevich and Litvinov. He checked his watch. It read 8.29am. The maid had been a couple of minutes early with his breakfast. He dropped the newspaper onto the bed and reached for the television remote control, flicking the set to the C.N.N. news channel. He poured himself a cup of hot coffee and waited for the 8.30 news headlines. The bulletin began with the breaking story of a corruption scandal in American politics but the events of the previous night in Paris were the second-lead item. The newscaster's voice was even and unemotional, in direct contrast to Alan Russell's rising disbelief and horror as he heard what was said.

It has been verified this morning that last night's double murder in Paris was the work of the Muslim fundamentalist group known as The Lions of God. It's known that one of the terrorists involved was an Englishman named Alan Russell who was part of an official British delegation.

A photograph of Russell appeared on the screen.

He was last seen wearing a light-coloured raincoat over evening dress. Police say he is armed and dangerous and should not be approached. Protests have been lodged about Russell's inclusion in the British party, claiming he was a known fundamentalist sympathiser. Official sources in London said a statement would be issued later today but confirmed that Russell was recently the subject of investigation when his Muslim wife died under suspicious circumstances.

* * * * *

The initial priority of LeBec's investigation was speed. He knew that information gathered at the start of an enquiry, no matter how slight, was all that would sustain it during the passing weeks when leads dried-up, trails became cold and witnesses' memories faded into confusion. The anti-terrorist squad, due to the enormity of the crimes it faced, was faster than most at setting the well-oiled wheels of its organisation in motion and both the pathology and forensic reports had been at LeBec's office by 5.30am on the Saturday morning. By 2.30pm that afternoon, ten detectives had between them taken over forty statements from people who were in or around the area at the time of the incident. The Chief Inspector and his sergeant had themselves interviewed Sir Peter Mayer and by the time they arrived back at their office, a little after 3pm, Alan Russell's personnel file had been emailed through from London and was lying on LeBec's desk awaiting their return.

During his absence, the phone line to the Chief Inspector's office had been besieged by journalists wanting interviews. He left instructions with the harassed switchboard to put through no calls but when the telephonist rang to say that Chief Vollard was on the internal line, LeBec reluctantly told the girl to connect his boss.

"Henri" said the voice in his ear authoritatively, "I've got to make a statement to the media this evening and, because of the international complications, it's got to be cleared all the way up to the top. The P.M. is apparently furious about the whole business and is demanding to be kept constantly informed. His office has been on twice already this afternoon wanting to know what I'm going to say and I can't keep fobbing them off."

"I sanctioned a preliminary press release last night, sir" said LeBec. "I was told you received a copy."

"That was last night. I'm talking about now! They want a full statement and they want it to include something vaguely optimistic. I'm getting all sorts of crap about the eyes of the world watching us and the honour of France being at stake. But quite obviously the P.M. just wants something that's positive enough to save a little face and pacify international criticism."

"I'm sorry, sir, but this happened less than twenty-four hours ago. I can't work miracles."

"Nobody expects you to. But you don't have to make things more difficult than they already are! I've been told you've vetoed the release of any more information until further notice. In God's name, why?"

LeBec drew a deep breath. He knew Vollard wasn't going to like his reply.

"I'm not happy about it, sir. Having read the pathology and forensic reports, I've got a hunch it's not as straightforward as it might appear. I don't want to jump to any conclusions so I'd prefer nothing was said until I've got more of a handle on it."

"I'm not asking you to jump to conclusions; but pressures are being brought to bear and you must give me some ammunition to fight back. You're a good policeman, Henri, and I'll defend your right to handle this your own way, but for Christ's sake give me something more than a 'hunch' to keep these bloody bureaucrats off our backs!"

It was a familiar situation and LeBec knew better than to argue.

"Very well, sir. I'll prepare a brief statement and have it sent up to you."

"Good! I may tart it up a bit if I think it'll help but I'll let you see the final copy before I release it."

"Thank you, sir. I'd appreciate that."

The line went dead and LeBec looked across the desk at his sergeant, raising his eyebrows as he replaced the receiver.

"The big guns are well and truly coming out for this one."

"I'm not surprised" said Nicot. "I take it Vollard's getting it in the neck from above?"

"Yes, but that's *his* problem. We've got enough on our plate without worrying about the P.M. saving face. Right now I'm more concerned with *this* face."

He picked up the personnel file in front of him, emailed through from London, and stared at the photograph of Alan Russell attached to the cover.

"Organise some coffee, will you Paul? And we'll wade through this together. Maybe it'll throw some light into the darkness."

The bleary-eyed sergeant dutifully picked up the phone to order the coffee. He had half-hoped that, having been up all night, his boss might suggest a couple of hours sleep but, as LeBec reached into his desk drawer and pulled out his secreted bottle of Cognac, Nicot knew it was going to be a long session.

"Send up a pot of hot coffee, will you please?" he said into the receiver. And then, with a resigned smile, added: "And make it strong."

Before the coffee pot was empty, LeBec had finished the file on Alan Russell, which he had read aloud for the benefit of his sergeant. It was a full, but standard, biographical report such as is always kept on any civil servant whose work requires security clearance. It was in no way out of the ordinary and contained nothing to arouse suspicion. Only the last addition to the file was at all unusual. It was a single paragraph stating that Russell's wife, a foreign national of Moroccan birth, had been found dead last November, presumed killed by intruders to the family home. LeBec threw the file frustratedly onto the desk.

"Hardly the profile of a terrorist, is it?" he demanded.

"So the Brits thought he was clean" said Nicot. "It wouldn't be the first time they'd got it wrong."

"But it's one more piece that doesn't fit" declared LeBec, as he stood and walked to the window, his hands thrust into his pockets and his tired eyes staring through the misted glass as though he were seeking some sort of inspiration in the dull shades of the Parisian sky.

"First of all, there's Litvinov" he mused, looking out at the cold, sunless January afternoon. "Before yesterday, none of us had ever heard of him. But this man was important enough to warrant a minder; an armed bodyguard working under cover. The man was important enough for The Lions of God to mount a kidnap operation when we thought we'd got them on the run and in disarray. And it was no make-shift affair either. It took organisation, money and man-power. Now if Litvinov is so important that he's worth all this effort, how is it that nobody knew anything about him?"

"It was supposed to be hush hush?" offered Nicot.

LeBec turned from the window to face him.

"Exactly. So hush hush that none of our security services heard even a whisper. But the Lions of God heard! They knew enough about Litvinov to think he was worth going for – and they knew it well enough in advance to plan a complex operation. How?"

"A man on the inside?" suggested his sergeant half-heartedly.

"In Moscow? A Muslim fundamentalist mole?"

Nicot shrugged, knowing it was hardly a possibility.

LeBec came purposefully back to his chair. His body was fatigued but his mind was as sharp as ever and the cold, clear capacity to think analytically, that had made him such a successful policeman, was in full flight.

"But forget *how* they knew" he said animatedly. "Just look at the operation itself. Homicide's theory was that Litvinov was caught in a crossfire. How does that fit the facts? We know that Gurevich - dying from his wound remember and moving slowly - was slumped against the wall to his right. Mayer tells us that Litvinov was on Russell's left arm. So, from the gunman's point of view, Russell was centred between Gurevich and the Professor, agreed?"

Nicot nodded his silent approval and LeBec's narrative grew more spirited as he further unfolded his scenario.

"Ballistics say Litvinov was shot with an AK47 and the bullet went straight through the heart. So! If we follow the crossfire theory, we must accept that at close range, with a modern assault rifle, the killer was so far off target that he missed the slowly moving Gurevich, missed Russell and accidentally shot the Professor with a direct hit through the heart."

The Chief Inspector sat back heavily in his chair.

"It's ridiculous! Not only that - but, so far, no one has claimed to have heard more than two shots. We know Gurevich's gun had used one cartridge. So - unless all our witnesses are wrong - the only shot that The Lions of God fired was the one that killed Litvinov!"

"But if it was a straightforward assassination" complained Nicot, "why didn't Russell shoot him in the car and have done with it?"

"I don't know!" bemoaned LeBec despairingly.

"And what about Kahlil's death?" asked his sergeant.

"The whole business of Kahlil makes no sense at all. If there was shooting, how is it his gun was never fired? So what have we got? The most wanted terrorists in Paris abandon their bombing campaign, to kidnap a Professor - that nobody's heard of - and make such a cock-up that they accidentally shoot him through the heart and inadvertently run down and kill their own man - who went into the operation and never fired a shot!"

He reached forward and pounded the flat of his hand onto the desk in anger.

"The whole thing is a complete bloody farce!"

Nicot looked sympathetically at his boss.

"What you say all makes sense" he said quietly. "But if you're right, what the hell can the real explanation be?"

LeBec ran his hands back across the top of his head and clasped his skull, his frustration all the more aggravated by his obvious over-tiredness.

"I've no idea" he admitted sheepishly, knowing better than anyone that blowing holes in Devaux's theory was no use without a viable alternative.

At that moment the door burst open and sergeant Lucien hurried into the room.

"We've got a break!" he said excitedly. "Russell's been seen."

The two men sat up sharply, boosted by the news.

"Where?" asked Nicot.

"Gare de Lyon, last night. The girl at the bureau de change gave cash to an Englishman named Russell leaving on the Marseille sleeper. She heard the news report this morning and remembered the name. Description fits."

Before Lucien could explain any further, the telephone on LeBec's desk rang. He quickly picked up the receiver and barked into it.

"I thought I said 'no calls'."

"I'm sorry Chief Inspector" apologised the switchboard girl, "but it's Chief Vollard again."

"Damn!" said LeBec, raising his eyes heavenward. "I forgot the bloody press release! Alright, put him through."

As soon as he heard the call connect, and before his boss could begin to speak, LeBec forestalled him with the news.

"I'm sorry for the delay, sir, but I've held back on sending you anything while I've been awaiting confirmation. We've had a sighting of the Englishman, Russell. I thought you'd want it included in any statement."

"A sighting?" said the voice on the line with interest.

"Yes, sir. We believe Russell caught a train for Marseille last night and that the search for him should now be concentrated in that area."

"Well that is good news" said Vollard with obvious relief.

"I thought you'd be pleased, sir. It's the sweetener you need to show the bods upstairs we're not just sitting on our backsides. I'll send up one of my men with the details."

"Good. Well done, Henri. Let me know as soon as you have anything further."

The line went dead and LeBec looked up at Lucien as he replaced the receiver.

"Make sure Vollard gets all the info straight away, will you? And arrange for the girl to be brought here for interview."

"Right guv'nor" said Lucien and hastily made his exit.

"Shall I notify Marseille? asked Nicot, rising to leave.

"Yes. And find out if the train stopped en route. Tell Marseille to interview all on-board staff and as many passengers as they can trace. Email Russell's photo to them."

"Do you think he's making for a ship?"

LeBec shook his head and gave a wry smile. It was not the action of a man who had just been given a new lead.

"It's one more piece that doesn't fit" he said dryly. "If you were running from a murder, would you stop to change money – and use your real name?"

"Maybe he was desperate for cash?" offered Nicot, vainly trying to maintain a little optimism.

"And maybe he *wants* us to think he's fled to Marseille."

The tired policeman picked up Alan Russell's file and stared at it with weary eyes.

"No" he said with a sigh. "We'll check it out of course but I'd wager our mysterious Mr. Russell is still in Paris."

* * * * *

The 11th of January dawned with a further drop in temperature and the promise of more snow-falls to add to the freezing grip that already enclosed the French capital. At the Le Brun hotel, the threatening cold of the outside morning was rendered a little less forbidding by the aromas of freshly-brewed coffee and newly-baked bread that wafted from the kitchens as the early shift prepared breakfast. For the staff it was the routine beginning of a normal Sunday. For Alan Russell it was the start of his second day as a fugitive and, had his fellow residents been aware of the true identity of the occupant of room 310, it would undoubtedly have been his last.

During Saturday he had taken his meals within the safety of his room but he knew that to continue to do so would eventually arouse comment, if not suspicion. Initially, he could move to a different hotel but he was well aware that simply changing accommodation was no solution. His altered appearance was a short-term measure that would sooner or later be uncovered and he needed to take advantage of the temporary respite he had found at the Le Brun to formulate a plausible means of escape from France.

He had kept the television permanently switched to C.N.N. and had tuned in to every hourly radio news broadcast. There had been no change in the content of the bulletins and, to his relief, no apparent development in the investigation. The enforced captivity of his hotel room had at least afforded the opportunity to think and he had run through the terrifying events of Friday night over and over in his mind, vainly trying to find a feasible explanation for all that had happened. The one fact of which he was certain returned to him each time with an icy clarity: Blair had coldly intended to kill him, just as he had the Professor. The chilling terror of seeing the barrel of the rifle directed straight at him was like no other moment in the whole chaotic and horrifying incident and, no matter what confusion had reigned, Blair's purpose was plain and deliberate.

The only vague conclusion he could draw was that somehow the operation had been uncovered and Caswell's fear of exposure had driven him to ruthlessly dispose of the evidence, namely Russell and the Professor. Right or wrong, the theory didn't alter the fact that he was now a marked man and a target. He had no idea as to how the reports were now linking him to a terrorist group and could only presume it was a further smokescreen emanating from Caswell but, whatever the truth, it was of secondary importance to moving as soon as he could from the

Le Brun and making good his escape. Gradually a possible next step began to formulate in his mind. It was certainly a risk, perhaps unacceptably high, but he could see no alternative. The encouragement he needed to make his decision was eventually given by the 11am news bulletin.

The Englishman Alan Russell, wanted in connection with the murders in Rue Jean Giraudoux, was seen boarding a train for Marseille on Friday night. A police spokesman has confirmed that the search for him has now shifted to the south coast.

Heartened that his gamble with the girl in the bureau de change had paid off, and feeling that the pressure had lifted marginally, he went to the telephone and dialled the reception desk.

"This is Monsieur Bourget in 310. I will be leaving this morning. Would you please have my bill made up and ready in about half an hour. Thank you."

He went into the bathroom and carefully re-applied the make-up and hair colour exactly as he had before. Then selecting a clean white shirt and one of Monsieur LaMotte's least garish ties, a grey and blue stripe that complemented the blazer, he set them on the bed beside the suitcase and began to pack. By 11.45 he was dressed and ready. He put on the glasses, checked his appearance one final time in the dressing table mirror, and then gathered his raincoat and case and vacated the room.

The hotel lobby was reasonably busy. Several people were milling around and Russell was glad he had the spectacles to hide his face. Having paid a cash deposit in advance against his bill, only the cost of his room service meals needed totalling and deducting. All was settled without incident or query and he walked calmly out of the hotel.

After the confines of his room the cold outside air was fresh and invigorating but he still felt exposed and vulnerable being on the street. He had a strong desire to go straight to Charles de Gaulle airport and board a plane. He knew such an emotional act would be a fatal error and he wasn't even sure where he would have gone if he'd managed it, but the destination was almost irrelevant. The important thing was simply to get away, and the urge to do so was all-consuming, but he had none of the panic of the previous Friday evening and he was thinking clearly and rationally as he stopped at the first street corner and hailed a cab.

Right or wrong, he knew exactly where he was heading.

*****

Nina Petrova answered the doorbell to find Alan Russell's strangely altered face confronting her. It took her several seconds to reconcile the unfamiliar appearance with features that she recognised and, as the realisation dawned, she gasped in amazement.

Before she had a chance to speak, Russell swiftly clasped a hand over her mouth. His other hand grabbed her by the arm and he forced her back inside, kicking the door shut behind him.

"Are you alone?" he whispered urgently.

She nodded, still in shock at seeing him and being bundled back against the wall.

"Then listen!" he commanded softly. "I didn't kill Litvinov. He was shot by a man named Blair who also tried to kill me. The story that's been put out is wrong. I didn't kill him! Do you understand?"

Nina nodded gently in silent confirmation. Russell took his hand from her mouth but he was still gripping her arm.

"Maybe I'm crazy, coming to you. But you're the one person I thought might believe me. You see, I know who you are and who you work for."

Nina's eyes widened in surprise and she was genuinely taken aback. "You do?" she said quietly.

"Yes. British intelligence have known about you and Gurevich from the beginning. I was supposed to put you off the scent while we helped the Professor to get away. But that was all it was! To help him get away! Then it all went crazy. Now the French think I'm a terrorist, your people think I murdered Litvinov and I'm fairly sure the British are trying to kill me before I can tell anyone the truth."

His grasp on her arm had tightened and he suddenly realised his fingers were pressing deeply into her sleeve.

"I'm sorry" he apologised and quickly let go. "I know that coming to you is a bit like walking into the line of fire. It must seem mad. Perhaps it is. I just thought that, as we'd been so close, I'd probably stand more chance of convincing you of the truth than anyone else. I know it's a long shot; but it's all I could think of."

He leaned back heavily against the door and looked up despairingly at the ceiling.

"Maybe I am mad. I don't think I'm sure myself anymore."

Nina reached out and lightly touched his cheek with the palm of her hand.

"Oh, Alan" she said gently. "What have they done to you? What have they done?"

Russell instinctively clasped her hand and held it tight to his face. Her delicate human touch was the first moment of compassion in the whole insanity of the previous forty-eight hours and it was like soothing balm to his over-stretched nerves and battered emotions.

"I'm frightened, Nina" he confessed quietly. "Very frightened. I'm not especially brave or strong – I'm just Mr. Average. Two months ago I had a wife, a home and a job. Now suddenly I'm in a living nightmare. I've shot a man and dragged another to his death. Perhaps I'm as guilty as they say. But it doesn't matter anyway – because who the hell is going to believe me?"

Nina took his face tenderly between both her hands.

"I believe you, Alan" she said softly. "And I'll try to help you, if I can."

He looked into her eyes, full of concern, and thought that perhaps he saw her for the first time. The barrier of deceit that had hung between them during the past weeks had suddenly disappeared, like a curtain drawn aside. He reached out and pulled her tightly into his embrace.

"Thank you" he whispered into her ear and at the same time silently thanked God that he had found an ally and was no longer alone. Tears of relief began to roll slowly down his cheeks.

Over the course of the following hour or so, Russell related the whole story in detail. He told her everything from his first meeting with Caswell and Blair at the hotel in Cambridge to his refuge at the Le Brun. Nina said very little throughout, listening intently as the strange tale unfolded and showing no discernible reaction at the mention of her own participation in the extraordinary chain of events that had finally brought Russell to her apartment. As he brought his sorry narrative to a close she looked at him silently. Her eyes showed a mixture of compassion for his plight and amazement that he had survived his ordeal.

"You did well" she said, genuinely impressed. "It's the kind of resourcefulness one would only expect from an experienced operative."

"I don't know about that; but when your life is threatened you suddenly find yourself capable of things you never dreamed you could do."

"We're all capable of them Alan, if the danger is real enough. And while we're on the subject, there's something I want you to know. I'm not especially proud of some of the things I've done, but I've not yet sunk so low that I can kill innocent people. I had nothing to do with the death of your wife and I swear to you that I had no knowledge of it. I hope you can believe that."

Russell gave a grateful half-smile.

"Thank you. I didn't think you had; but it means a lot to hear it from your own lips."

She moved from the sofa where she'd been sitting and knelt beside his chair, taking his hand in her own.

"And as it's time for confessions" she said softly, "I have an admission to make. My orders during these past weeks have simply been to maintain contact. I was under no obligation to see you as often as I did; and there was absolutely no directive that I should share your bed." Her fingers closed tightly around his own. "I became your lover because I wanted to; because I developed feelings for you. The decision was mine alone."

The pressure of her hand on his was telling him more than her actual words. Over the previous weeks he had become used to the mutual deceit of their undeclared sparring and he was aware of the difference he now saw in her face; the earnest need to be believed. Her grip against his fingers tensed, willing him to accept the truth of what she was telling him. He reached out his other hand and tenderly stroked her hair.

"Then perhaps we weren't deceiving each other so much after all" he murmured gently.

The relief that she had been believed was evident in her smile.

"You know, grey hair suits you. You're going to get better looking as you get older."

He gave a half-laugh.

"At the moment, I'd settle for just getting older."

She gently took the palm that was stroking her hair, kissed it and held it against her cheek.

"Then we'd better live for the moment."

For the first time in their brief relationship he shared her bed knowing that their emotions were free and genuine, and unshackled by the veil of pretence. She was now an ally as well as a lover and he rediscovered the joy of her body in trust and without the deceit that previously had haunted their every word and every touch. It was a new and different experience and the closeness and warmth of her meant all the more to Russell after all he had been through in the previous two days. Afterwards, it was a great comfort to him to lie with her head nestled in the crook of his neck, to feel the fullness of her breasts resting against his chest and the line of her body moulded to his own. His fear and tension were temporarily exorcised and, for the moment at least, he felt safe.

Being able to relax at last, the strain and exhaustion of the previous forty-eight hours finally caught up with him and Russell fell into a deep sleep. It was past seven o'clock before he awoke to find Nina still lying beside him. The room had darkened with the coming of night but the curtains, still open as they had been in the afternoon, allowed the outside lights and street lamps to cut a shaft through the interior shadows. It threw an unnatural glow around the room and cast an eerie bluish veil across the bed, giving a strange luminescence to Nina's naked shoulders, as though she were made from fine bone china.

"Good evening" she said softly. "How are you feeling?"

"Alright" replied Russell with a yawn. "What time is it?"

"Just gone seven."

"I didn't mean to sleep so long. I must have been well away."

"Like a baby."

"Did you sleep too?"

She shook her head and gave a warm smile.

"No. But I didn't move in case I disturbed you."

"That was very kind of you" he told her, gently tapping the end of her nose. "But you shouldn't have wasted your afternoon."

She made as if to bite the tip of his finger.

"Nonsense. Spending the afternoon in bed with you can never be a waste of time. Besides, you needed the rest. It may be a few days before you get a good night's sleep."

"Meaning?"

"Meaning we have to get you out of the country and back to England. That has to be our first priority."

Russell eased himself up from the pillow, resting on his elbows.

"Can you manage that?"

"It won't be straightforward but it's not impossible. I have to make a few calls." She checked the bedside clock. "And I must start now."

"What would I do without you?" he said and leaned across and lightly kissed her forehead.

"I was the one who first drew you into this mess Alan, and I'm going to be the one to get you out of it."

She got up from the bed and walked over to where her robe hung on the back of the bedroom door. As she crossed the room, Russell was struck again by the physical beauty of her naked body. To his eye, she was the perfect shape and, as she wrapped herself into the towelling gown and pulled the cord tight around her waist, he thought how in-demand her slender and balanced body would have been as a model for the artists that had flocked to the city when Paris was the centre of the painter's art.

"It's only a local contact" she said, running a comb quickly through her hair, "but it will set the wheels in motion. I'll make the call, grab a quick shower and then fix us something to eat. How does that sound?"

"Terrific."

"All part of the service. Besides you owe me a meal together. We had a date last night and you didn't show up, remember?"

"Yes, I remember" he said, nodding his head in silent regret.

"Right. So we eat tonight. You stay there and rest and I'll be back in no time."

She turned and left the room, closing the door behind her.

Apart from the dim murmur of the traffic outside, the bedroom was quiet and peaceful. Russell lay thinking. He wished he could somehow pick up the apartment and whisk it miles away to a distant land where they would be unknown and free to forget the nightmare he was living; the nightmare that he knew all too well still awaited him on the streets below.

His reverie was interrupted by a faint clicking noise and he turned to see a small red light flashing in the semi-darkness. The base unit for the apartment's cordless telephone stood on the bedside table and the *in-use* light flickered with an audible click each time a digit was pressed on the remote handset. As the flickering continued Russell was seized by a sudden apprehension. He realised that the number Nina was calling from the other room had too many digits to be a local call. It had to be long distance.

Darting out of bed he ran to listen at the bedroom door but the muffled conversation behind it was indiscernible to his straining ears. The light on the base unit clicked off and he hurried back to the bed and settled himself against the pillows. Just as he did so, the door opened and Nina came back into the room, humming softly to herself as she walked across to the bathroom door.

"Is he far away, this contact?" he asked her casually.

"No, just across town. I told him no details; only that I needed to move someone. I'll call again in a couple of hours."

She began un-doing her robe.

"I won't be long, I promise. Are you hungry?"

"Yes, but take your time. I can wait."

She blew him a kiss and went into the bathroom and closed the door. He heard her turn on the water and waited until he could discern the sound of her under the shower, then he slipped quietly out of bed and into the lounge. The handset was lying on the coffee table where she had left it. In the bottom left hand corner was the *last number re-dial* button. He pressed it, his heart beating fast as he waited for the call to connect. What he heard at the other end of the line sent an icy shiver down his back and gripped his insides like an iron claw. A female voice said:

'The Albion Import and Export Company, can I help you?"

Receiving no response, the voice broke into his horrified silence and repeated the question. He pressed the disconnect button and slowly and disbelievingly replaced the handset onto the coffee table.

For a moment he was unsure what to do. He didn't know how long it would be before the knock on the door came. His initial instinct was to try and make a quick escape and he ran back to the bedroom and began to frantically gather his clothes. Then, suddenly, he stopped. He let go of the clothes and they dropped to the floor. To keep running seemed somehow futile. Where would he go? It would simply be prolonging the agony and trying to delay what now seemed crushingly inevitable.

He climbed slowly back into bed. He was stupefied; totally stunned by the betrayal. He couldn't believe that she had fooled him once again; that their closeness of that afternoon, or at least what he had believed was their closeness, had been yet another sham; another tissue of lies. But he had heard the evidence with his own ears.

Strangely, his fear had almost left him. The hopelessness of this new situation was so overwhelming that it had taken him beyond fear. He was now more angry than afraid. It infuriated him to think she felt able to play with him just as she chose; and it made him doubly bitter to know he was nothing more to her than a pawn in the game, to be manipulated or sacrificed as she deemed fit or expedient.

The sound of running water ceased and he could hear her quietly singing as she dried herself. He presumed she had a gun somewhere in the flat, probably close at hand in the bedroom, and, like Blair and Gurevich, she would think nothing of using it. She was probably waiting for others to arrive; or maybe she intended a moment of her own choosing, when his back was turned and one simple shot would efficiently dispatch him. He decided he wouldn't give her the opportunity. There was only one way he had ever seen Nina vulnerable and off-guard and he felt a strange poetic justice in using it to trap her.

She came back into the room, dressed in her robe and still softly singing as she rubbed a towel through her wet and unruly auburn hair.

"Dinner will be served in half an hour if that is alright with Monsieur" she announced with a broad grin.

"No. That is not alright with Monsieur" he retorted, managing to emulate her relaxed warmth and smile.

"Oh? Then what is Monsieur's preference?"

Russell threw back the covers and gestured to the bed.

"Monsieur's preference is to have dinner a little later and to have the Chef for hors d'oeuvres; right now!"

Nina laughed.

"I had no idea Monsieur had such a voracious appetite" she said, sliding her robe seductively from her shoulders.

With a deliberately exaggerated stride, playfully dragging the towelling gown behind her like a stripper on a cat-walk, she came slinking across to the bed and sidled in next to him. She began kissing his hand, slowly moving up his arm until she was nibbling at his neck. Her skin was silky smooth and spiced with the subtle fragrance of the soap with which she had just showered. She was as desirable and arousing as ever.

As she lifted her head and kissed him fully on the lips he pulled her across his body, so she was astride him as he sat upright and leaning back against the headboard. Sensing what he wanted, she slowly raised herself up on her knees and threw back her head, bringing her breasts forward and offering them to his mouth. He moved from one to the other, teasing each nipple as he rolled it under his tongue in the way he knew she liked, and then closing his mouth firmly around it and kneading against her breast.

With his lips and tongue still working at her, he slowly ran his hand along the smooth inside of her thigh and began lightly caressing between her legs. She moaned in quiet satisfaction as he gradually opened her, delicately drawing his fingers backwards and forwards while she willingly responded and moved her pelvis in rhythm with the motion. She was completely enwrapped in the tenderness of his touch. Slowly and gently he pulled downwards on her hips and eased her carefully onto his erection. As he penetrated the moist inner warmth of her, she groaned with delight and rolled her head from side to side, lost in pleasure – just as he had intended. He slid his hands around her waist and lightly drew them up along the length of her back and onto her neck, making her skin tingle as his nails ran sensitively over her flesh. The languid movement pulled their bodies closer and closer together until her armpits were caught in the crook of his elbows. Unhurriedly and sensuously he spread his fingers and brought them around under her chin, but the delicacy of his touch abruptly ceased as he suddenly and violently brought up his palms, swiftly clamping them hard against her throat.

Nina jerked as the manoeuvre forced back her head but she was caught tight and couldn't move, literally locked in his embrace. She stared at him in wide-eyed panic but, impaled upon him with her arms trapped and his hands at her neck, she was helpless and totally at his mercy.

"The Albion Import and Export Company appears to be working weekends, doesn't it?" he snarled, almost spitting the words in his wrath. "Are they waiting for a special order? One interpreter, parcelled up and ready to go?"

The rising fear within her was vivid in her panic-ridden eyes but her desperate efforts to speak were stifled in the back of her throat by his relentless grip. She could only half-groan "no" and try to shake her head as his tirade continued.

"How long have we got before they get here, Nina? A few hours? A day? Or were you going to take care of it yourself with a bullet through the back of the head over a candle-lit dinner?"

"Please, Alan! Please!" she gurgled.

"I trusted you!" he yelled loudly, consumed with pain at her callous abuse of his vulnerability.

"I promise you it's alright" she managed in a frightened whisper as her vocal chords strained against his choking grip.

"You betrayed me again!"

"No! No." she murmured frantically, still stifled by his hold. "I can explain!"

He forced his face into her own. "Oh yes, you're going to explain" he hissed, "or I'm going to snap your beautiful little neck. What did you tell Caswell?"

His grip lessened slightly, allowing her to respond.

"I told him you were in Marseille."

"Liar!" he shouted, seething with rage that even now she could think he was still gullible."

"It's true!" she persisted. "I swear to you. He's ordered me down there to look for you."

"Liar!" he yelled again, his whole body tightening against her as his anger soared. "You've shopped me! Why else would you phone him?"

"Because I had to check in. For God's sake Alan, think! If I'd wanted to shop you I'd have done it while you were sleeping. They'd have been here by now and you'd be as dead as Litvinov!"

Russell's mind was a maelstrom of pain and anguish. The betrayal was like a whirlpool, relentlessly sucking him down towards his own destruction. His last straw of hope had been snatched from his hand. There was nothing left; no one he could believe or trust; and yet, in the midst of his swirling emotions, he could sense something logical in what she said. The momentary confusion it raised in his frenzied thoughts caused his grasp on her throat to ease further and Nina, desperately aware how dangerous his battered and volatile state had become, seized her chance.

"Listen to me Alan! Yes, I work for Caswell. But I knew nothing about all this. He's been playing us both ends against the middle - telling you I was working for Gurevich and me that you needed watching. We were never going to break cover and tell each other - so it was foolproof; the perfect set-up!"

He looked at her in disbelief, unable to comprehend what he was hearing.

"Set-up?"

"Caswell never had contact with Litvinov! Can't you see? It was a plot to assassinate him from the very beginning - Gurevich was the bait and you were the patsy! And we all fell for it!"

As devastating as it was to hear, Nina's explanation was starting to make uncomfortable sense and the force of her reason began to hit home.

"And you didn't know?" he asked, almost dazed.

"No! Caswell sent me to Cambridge to get involved with you; to seduce you into helping with what he said would be Litvinov's defection. When I failed I thought that was the end of it; but they told me they'd found a new angle and that I had to keep tabs on you. I knew it had all gone wrong when I saw the news but I didn't fully understand until you turned up here. When you first said you knew who I worked for I naturally thought you meant Caswell - not the Russians!"

As the mists of confusion began slowly to clear, Russell was struck by a cold and far more sinister realisation.

"But if Caswell sent you to Cambridge" he said, reaching to fit the pieces together, "then it wasn't an approach from Gurevich."

"No! It was a set-up by MI6 to get you hooked."

"So if Gurevich wasn't keeping tabs on me, then who was tailing me?"

"It was another set-up. Think about it – nobody tails in a yellow car. You were *meant* to notice it."

Russell winced as the awful truth began to register and cut through him like a knife.

"Then Taniel's death ..." he broke off and stared at her horrified. "It can't have been Gurevich."

She slowly shook her head. "It has to have been Caswell. It was his new angle."

For a moment he was silent, unable to speak. Then he let out a low groan and began to weep, the tears rolling down his cheeks and tumbling onto Nina's naked breasts.

"I've shot and killed an innocent man" he moaned in a muted cry. His voice was racked with pain and distress, like a wounded animal caught in a trap. "All these weeks of hating him; loathing him; desperate to get revenge for my poor Taniel, and I was plotting with the very men who murdered her!"

Blinking through his tears, he looked up into Nina's face and then suddenly let go of her head, drawing back his hands in alarm.

"And I might have strangled you! Sweet Jesus! What have they done to me? What have I become?"

Nina reached out and took him in her embrace, cradling his head on her shoulder and rocking him gently to and fro as he began to sob.

"I'm sorry" she whispered softly. "I should have told you this afternoon. I wanted to – but I wasn't sure you'd believe me, or how you'd take it if I did. I was going to wait until I'd got you safely out of Paris and you knew you could trust me."

She held him tighter, willing him to believe her.

"But Alan, everything I did tell you this afternoon – about you and me – it was all true."

She lifted up his head and gently brushed away the tears from his eyes.

"This isn't how I wanted to say it – and you probably don't want to hear it – but now I *have* to tell you. I think I'm in love with you."

Thirteen

France

The promised snow materialised just as the forecasters had predicted and the Monday morning rush-hour became even more unbearable as the thousands of long-suffering commuters attempted to fight their way through yet another irritation contrived to worsen the daily Paris gauntlet of hold-ups and delays. The small café was a warm, calm oasis in the morning's cold, overcrowded insanity. Grateful for its relatively civilised tranquillity, Henri LeBec helped himself from a large pot of coffee and watched the slow progress of the traffic that crawled at a snail's pace past the window and made its laborious way along the Boulevard Saint Germain.

Bernard Gillet, bleary-eyed and totally unaccustomed to meeting anyone for breakfast at such an hour, entered the café and wearily strolled across to LeBec's table. He slumped himself into a chair and yawned a sleepy "Good Morning", struggling to make it more enthusiastic than it was.

"I hope this is important, Henri" he said, helping himself to coffee and declining the basket of freshly baked rolls that LeBec offered him. "I'm only usually up this early when I haven't been to bed the night before."

"It's a quarter to eight, Bernard" grinned LeBec. "That's not exactly early." He jerked his butter knife in the direction of the unhappy faces that stared from the motionless cars outside the window. "Most of these poor devils have been up and on the road since first light."

"All the more reason to avoid joining them and adding to the chaos" Gillet told him, gratefully swallowing the reviving coffee. "So, like I say, I hope it's important."

"It is. I need a favour."

"Always happy to oblige if I can Henri, you know that."

"I'm counting on it" said LeBec, refilling Gillet's cup. "And considering the money you must have made with that shot you sneaked of me at the Rue Scribe bombing, you can hardly refuse."

"Ah. The one with the dog" Gillet said with overt innocence. "I must confess it was somewhat lucrative. I hope you're not looking for royalties."

LeBec passed a large manila envelope across the table.

"I need a name to put to the face."

Gillet put down his coffee, opened the envelope and withdrew the photograph within. The picture was of the man who had worn the balaclava and been crushed by a van during the Rue Jean Giraudoux murders; but LeBec had deliberately had the photograph taken from the right side so that the scar on his cheek didn't show. Gillet studied the gruesome image carefully.

"Like to tell me any more?" he asked tentatively.

"Male; aged approximately twenty-nine. Of Arab origins, possibly mixed with Indian, and, as you can see, decidedly dead. There's not much else to tell."

"Background?"

"Unknown. He's not on any of our files and so far the cross-check with Interpol computers has thrown up nothing. But if I'm right, he'll turn out to be a petty villain; a low-life who happens to have a clean sheet."

"A Parisian?"

"Probably; although we can't be certain."

Gillet looked across at the Chief Inspector with curious eyes.

"And would you mind telling me why you need my meagre services when you have the considerable resources of the Paris force at your disposal?"

"Because there's something rotten in the state of Denmark and this face might smoke it out – but I want it unofficial and I want it quiet. That's a little difficult with hundreds of Paris's finest tramping around in their big heavy boots asking unsubtle questions."

"And I take it this has something to do with Friday's shooting?"

LeBec shrugged. "Ask me no questions and I'll tell you no lies."

"Be fair, Henri!" protested Gillet. "I'm a journalist. You can't dangle a juicy carrot like this under my nose and not expect me to sniff. I smell a story."

The detective downed the last of his coffee and rose to leave.

"At the moment there's nothing to tell. But put a name to that face,

Bernard, and you may have something to write about. Help yourself to breakfast. I'm off to fight my way through the traffic."

As he reached the door of the café, LeBec turned.

"Oh, and pick up the tab, will you Bernard? Let's call it royalties for the picture."

With a parting smile, he closed the door behind him and disappeared into the biting cold of the crowded street.

* * * * *

It was only a very small item on the foreign news page of *Le Figaro*, one-column width across and half-a-dozen lines in length, entitled *Suspects Go Free*. LeBec might never have noticed it but the word "Syrians" in the first sentence caught his eye and, intrigued, he glanced quickly through the article. It briefly reported that two Syrian students, held in London on suspicion of illegal arms trading, had been released from custody. The charges against them had been dropped before the case came to trial on condition they immediately leave the country. They had been escorted to Heathrow and put on a plane for Damascus.

"Look at this!" he said despairingly to sergeant Nicot and threw the paper across the desk to him. "We're breaking our backs trying to catch the bastards and London is letting them go."

Nicot picked up the article and read the first few lines.

"It says 'their behaviour was incompatible with their status' – what the hell does that mean?"

"It means the British police had them sewn up tight but the bloody politicians are too nervous about upsetting the Arab world to put them away."

LeBec had little time for politicians. In his view they were more concerned with scoring career points than counting corpses on the city streets and wouldn't recognise a terrorist supply line if it blew up in front of them. He'd had the same problem himself the previous year. He'd arrested three suspects, only needing time to make the charges stick, when pressure had come from above to deport them rather than pursue the case. The excuse given was the need to preserve international relations, which was diplomatic-speak for not upsetting the oil prices on which the national balance of payments depends. So his suspects had been spirited away, only to be replaced by as yet unknown newcomers who would pick up the trail of their predecessors; and LeBec's job would have to start again from scratch. With endless oil to finance them, and a greedy European economy ready to sell them whatever weapons they required, they would keep coming; ultimately using their arms against the very nations that supplied them.

"Sometimes I think the world is totally mad" he moaned to his sergeant.

They were interrupted by the appearance of Clémence at the door.

"Excuse me, guv'nor, but I think I may have something. I've been back to Russell's hotel, going through his things as you asked. Nothing of any use in his belongings but while I was there the girl from reception rang up to ask who was going to settle the 'extras' bill. The room had been pre-paid but he was responsible for anything additional."

He handed his boss a computer print-out of the room account.

"There are a couple of items from the mini-bar and one from the restaurant, but he also made two telephone calls between his arrival on Thursday and when the limo picked him up on the Friday evening."

"From his room?" asked LeBec incredulously, scrutinising the bill in front of him.

"Yes. One was to his head-office in London but the other was a local number."

"Have you traced it?"

"Yes. It's an apartment in Les Halles. It's currently on a short let in the name of Petrova. Nina Petrova. She booked it for a week."

"A Russian?" enquired Nicot.

"Sounds like it."

"Well, well, well" said LeBec, pleased with his officer's work. "I think perhaps we should pay Mademoiselle Petrova a little visit."

* * * * *

The sound of the telephone ringing interrupted Russell and Nina as they sat at the kitchen table, sharing breakfast. They had risen late, exhausted by the trauma of the previous evening and reluctant to leave the warm security of lying in each other's arms to face the unknown day.

Russell lowered his cup and looked up at her expectantly. The innocent sound of a phone had become as ominous as any death knell until he knew who was calling and why. Unable to enlighten him, and equally apprehensive, Nina gave a slight shrug of her shoulders and picked up the handset.

"Hello?" she said casually.

"Is that the Gas Company?" enquired a gruff male voice.

"No. This is a private address."

"Oh. Sorry to trouble you."

The caller hung up.

"Wrong number?" asked Russell.

"He wanted the Gas Company." She paused. "At least, that's what he *said* he wanted."

"What do you mean?"

"Mmm? Oh, nothing."

Preoccupied, she rose and went to the window where she intently scanned the street below.

"What's the matter?" asked Russell, concerned. "Is something wrong?"

"No. Everything's fine. It's just that sometimes you ring to check that someone is in before you ..."

The sudden sound of the door-bell caused her to break off in mid-sentence and Russell could tell from her expression that everything was far from fine.

"Are you expecting anyone?" he asked anxiously.

Nina silenced him with a finger to her lips. She crept noiselessly into the hallway and peered through the small security spy-hole in the front door. The circular image of the fish-eye lens distorted the faces outside but the stamp of the two misshapen men was unmistakable, defying even the contorting attempts of the glass to disguise it.

She went silently back to the kitchen.

"I think it's the police" she whispered.

Russell's face blanched. "How could they possibly know?"

"They don't" she replied quickly. "If they knew you were here the place would be surrounded and the street would be cordoned off. Don't panic."

In an instant, the professional in her had emerged. She was thinking on her feet and thinking fast, assessing their options and calculating her best move. She spoke with speed and with clarity.

"I'll stall them. Grab your coat and use the fire-escape. Meet me at Sacré Coeur in two hours. If I'm not there, keep checking every hour, on the hour. Now hurry!"

The door bell rang again, its insistent demand ever more threatening.

For a second he stared at her. The brief moment of silence was full of a hundred things he wanted to say but she was operating in the way she had been trained to, where survival rules and sentiment holds no credit.

"Quickly!" she ordered, breaking the spell, and Russell scurried noiselessly into the other room. He grabbed his coat and hastened to the lounge window that gave access onto the fire escape.

While he was making his hurried exit, Nina turned the kitchen tap fully on and stuck her head under the gushing water. Then, seizing a towel from beside the sink, she walked steadily to the front door as the bell sounded yet again.

"Alright, alright, I'm coming" she yelled.

She opened the door to reveal LeBec and Nicot waiting for her.

"Sorry" she said, as she rubbed the towel vigorously against her head. "I was washing my hair. What can I do for you?"

"Mam'selle Petrova?" enquired LeBec.

"Yes".

"I wonder if we might have a word with you?"

"Are you selling something?" she asked abrasively, desperately trying to buy precious seconds for Russell to put distance between himself and the apartment. "Don't tell me you've dragged me out of the bathroom to try and sell me something! I wish you people would ..."

LeBec took out his warrant card and held it open in front of her, cutting short her protests.

"No Mam'selle, we are not selling anything. May we come in?"

Nina stared at the card, still delaying them as long as she could.

"May I see that properly, please?"

Her over-zealous caution was not only gaining time for Russell but also allowing her to think, and her brain was in overdrive. Were they secret service? No, she decided; the air was definitely police. But what had brought them to her apartment and how much did they know? Stay calm, she told herself. Don't deny and don't confirm. Wait until they feed you a hint before you commit yourself.

"And you are Inspector LeBec?" she asked.

"Chief Inspector," LeBec corrected her. "Yes."

"And this gentleman is?"

"My sergeant. Don't you think it would be easier if we talked inside, Mam'selle?"

"Possibly, yes" she continued stalling. "But a girl doesn't invite just anyone into her apartment; not even policemen. Why do you wish to see me?"

"I believe you know an Englishman named Alan Russell?"

Her eyes didn't flicker. Not even the faintest trace of concern showed on her face.

"I've met him, yes."

"Then perhaps you know why I'm here?" said LeBec patiently.

Deciding that further prevarication would only arouse their suspicion and that Russell had had enough time to get clear of the building, she ushered the two policemen into the lounge and invited them to sit.

"I'm not sure I can be of much use to you, Chief Inspector" she began casually, still preoccupied with drying her hair. "What exactly do you want to know?"

"When did you last have any communication with Alan Russell?" asked LeBec.

Of course! she said silently to herself. It must be the phone call; and she cursed herself for not remembering that Russell had called her at the apartment on the day she had arrived. The police would have gone through the call records of both his cell phone and his hotel room and traced all the numbers. But if all they knew was that he had called her then she could bluff her way through their questions.

"Let me see" she said thoughtfully. "I think it must have been Thursday. Yes, that's right. He called me on Thursday evening just after I'd arrived. He wanted to know if …"

She broke off mid sentence, staring across the room, where what she saw immediately silenced her.

The two policemen turned to follow her horror-struck gaze to the window. Alan Russell, framed by the opening like a celluloid scene from a "B" movie, was standing with Clémence's gun held menacingly at his temple.

Clémence flung open the window and roughly forced Russell over the ledge and into the room.

"Just look who I found doing a runner down the fire escape!" he said with a wide grin.

Nicot quickly pulled his own gun from inside his jacket and jumped up from his seat. He grabbed Nina by the arm and pulled her towards the wall where Clémence had already forced Alan Russell to spread his arms and feet wide. Terrorist outrages had long ago taught the squad that fanaticism was no respecter of gender and Nicot was as strong as he would have been with any man as he spread Nina alongside Russell and frisked her thoroughly. She turned to face Russell and whispered to him softly.

"I'm sorry, Alan. Truly I am."

"Don't be" he said gently. The die was cast several weeks ago. It was only a matter of time. It might as well be now as later. I'm only sorry I've implicated you. I should never have come here."

Rising above the indignity of Nicot's rigorous search of her body, she managed a warm smile.

"I'm glad you did."

Clémence immediately found the Beretta in Russell's raincoat pocket. He extracted the clip and tossed the gun harmlessly onto the sofa before pulling both Russell's arms down and behind his back where he clamped handcuffs around his wrists. He then went to search the rest of the apartment as Nicot fastened handcuffs on Nina.

"They're clean" the sergeant assured LeBec. He then addressed the unhappy pair. "Alan Russell, I arrest you on a charge of murder and complicity in acts of terrorism. Nina Petrova I arrest you on a charge of aiding and abetting a felon and of complicity in acts of terrorism. You are not obliged to say anything but anything you do say may be taken down and used in evidence against you."

Clémence reappeared at the doorway.

"Rest of the place is empty" he declared. "They were alone."

Nicot roughly turned Russell and Nina around to face his boss.

"Shall I take them down to the car?" he asked.

LeBec looked up from the armchair where he had remained passive and silent since Russell's unexpected appearance. It was a few moments before he spoke. His tone was calm and unruffled.

"My sergeant is keen to get you back to headquarters" he said quietly. "But first, I have some questions. Of course I can't force you to answer them; you have a right to legal representation and should you choose to exercise that right you will be taken back now and each allowed one call to a lawyer. But if you agree to answer my questions here and now, I give you my word that you won't suffer any 'accidents' later."

"Accidents?" asked Nina cynically.

LeBec's relaxed and easy manner was of a man in total control. Their fate was now irretrievably in his hands and, like a securely hooked fish that he could net at his leisure, he casually let out a little more line, trusting that his bluff and their own fear would manoeuvre them to his objective.

"My men don't take kindly to those who bomb and murder on our streets" he said coolly. "You might find their hospitality a little 'rough'. Prisoners stumble and fall when descending stairs; trip over a chair in their cell; it happens. But if you answer my questions here and now, I promise you I will pay that little extra attention to your safety and see that no 'mishaps' occur."

The still composure of LeBec's delivery made his implied threat all the more sinister. The parameters of Alan Russell's world, already teetering from his experiences of the last three days, finally disintegrated like a house of cards blown apart in the vicious wind of reality. The so-called civilised society, that struggled for common justice, and that he had believed he inhabited, in fact had no real order, no ultimate sanction to protect the innocent and maintain right. There was only the law of the jungle, masquerading as the guardian of freedom, while it committed whatever was expedient to further its own ends.

They're all the same, he told himself. The Caswells, the Blairs, and now this cold-eyed French policeman who has arrested, tried and sentenced me before I've said a word. God help us all if these are supposed to be our protectors.

"Ask whatever you like" he said, shaking his head in despair. "You won't believe me anyway – so it may as well be now as later. It really doesn't matter."

Russell's indifferent resignation to his fate did matter to LeBec. The crime-weary policeman had questioned many villains in his time and the one thing that set a terrorist apart from the rest was his deep-rooted arrogance. No matter what their particular perverted calling, the one common bond that typified them all was their unshakeable self-righteous belief in themselves and the validity of their cause. They were united across borders, continents and oceans, blind to any justice but their own fanatical creed of violence and death. Submission was not in their make-up because they couldn't countenance defeat. Their disdainful contempt for their captors took a perverse, almost kamikaze-like pleasure in arrest as they swaggered brashly, still denying the very law that had overcome them. It was not an image that matched this self-effacing Englishman; this killer and abductor who hadn't the sense to use a public telephone booth to prevent the tracing of his calls; this weary-looking individual whose tired eyes and sad face gave him the pathetic appearance of a man in despair, not the proud defiance of an urban guerrilla.

As he indicated that Russell and Nina should sit themselves on the sofa, LeBec was struck that yet again in this affair the pattern was wrong and the pieces didn't fit. He was determined that before any of them left the apartment he would have some answers that made sense.

LeBec began his questioning and, for the second time in twenty-four hours, Russell related his story in that same room. On this occasion he omitted all reference to Nina by name and made no mention of her connection to Caswell or MI6. He spoke of her only as a reporter covering the conference whom he had got to know and to whom he had run for help, thereby keeping her cover intact and reducing her involvement to simply harbouring him. Nina didn't know if LeBec would swallow the story but she loved Russell all the more for trying.

To Russell's surprise, LeBec said very little and sat silently listening while the strange tale unfolded, interrupting only occasionally to clarify points or extract greater detail and to ensure that Paul Nicot, who was making notes, had listed all relevant dates, places and names.

At the end of his sorry tale, Russell summed up his defence, or rather the lack of it, like some losing attorney making his final plea to a jury whose verdict was a foregone conclusion.

"So it's true that I shot Gurevich" he admitted ruefully, "or rather that the gun went off while we were struggling on the floor of the car; and it's also true that I pulled the Professor out of the limousine. But it was supposed to be a defection, not a murder."

Russell looked forlornly at the floor as he added:

"Only I can't prove a thing. London will deny it totally of course and Sir Peter Mayer, whom I was led to believe was in on the plan, will swear quite honestly that I pulled a gun and took Litvinov to his death. It's the perfect set-up. They've framed me with a motive, a witness, a weapon and two corpses; and I willingly walked right into it. I virtually *demanded* to be the fall guy."

"*Three* corpses" LeBec corrected him. "There was a third body at the end of the alleyway; hit by a van."

Russell shrugged and shook his head disconsolately.

"That I know nothing about. I don't know who he was or why he was there. That part of it I just don't understand."

"No" murmured LeBec, half to himself. "But I think I'm beginning to."

Russell's story had stirred something lurking in the recesses of his memory. It was only a minor detail; nothing he had deemed worth even a second thought at the time but, as he delved back through the haze of recollection, it began to take on a possibly new and important significance and alarm bells started to ring.

LeBec rose and turned to Clémence.

"Watch them" he ordered, and then nodded to Nicot to follow him and led his sergeant into the kitchen. He spoke in hushed undertones but there was an energy in his voice as the adrenalin was beginning to flow.

"What do you think?" he asked his sergeant.

"I don't believe him" said Nicot. "Do you?"

"I'm not sure. But I'm going to play a hunch that might help us decide."

For the first time since the whole affair had begun, he sensed something tangible; a brief glimpse of daylight at the end of the tunnel. It was the first thread he could weave through the unconnected pieces that didn't come apart at the seams. It was still only guess-work, but his intuition told him it was the vital link that had been eluding him. He would have to take a gamble – and there would be hell to pay if he lost – but his every instinct said it was worth a try.

"For the time being, I want this arrest to remain off-record."

"How?" asked Nicot, genuinely taken aback by the implausibility of the order.

"I'll report that the apartment was empty and that you and Clémence are staked out here. I'll insist that telephone and radio silence is essential and that you are not to be contacted. That should buy us the time we need."

"And just how long *do* we need?" asked the sergeant, not relishing the prospect of a protracted stay in Nina's apartment.

"Two days. Three at the most. We'd never keep it quiet longer than that anyway."

Nicot shrugged in resignation.

"Ok; but I hope you know what you're doing."

"So do I" said LeBec, seriously meaning it. "Now. I want you to go out and get a camera. Also a paper; any one will do as long as it's today's. While you're gone, I'll stay here and take him through it all again."

Nicot was still puzzled, but he knew better than to query his orders when LeBec had the bit between his teeth.

"Alright. You're the boss. A camera and today's paper. Anything else you want?"

"Yes. Some information. Cast your mind back a few weeks."

* * * * *

The taxi turned left out of Rue d'Aguesseau and slowly edged its way through the heavy traffic on Rue du Faubourg Saint-Honoré to pull up outside number 35, where the shining brass name plate obtrusively announced *Embassy of The United Kingdom*.

LeBec was expected and the girl at reception asked him to go directly up to the second floor. He was met by an efficient-looking secretary whose straight pencil skirt made a faint rustling against the silk petticoat beneath as she walked purposefully in front of him and guided him along the high and imposing corridor to the room that was set aside for confidential interviews.

LeBec waited some five minutes before the door opened and James Simpson walked briskly into the room. He was a tall man in his middle forties whose angular frame didn't quite match the elegance of his beautifully tailored pinstripe. His official title was assistant commercial attaché but his actual role was that of MI6 liaison officer in Paris. He apologised for keeping LeBec waiting with typical British over-politeness and settled himself into the chair opposite the policeman where he crossed one leg rather awkwardly over the other and enquired good-naturedly as to how he could be of service to the Chief Inspector.

"You recently came to see my sergeant" LeBec began. "You were making enquiries about the terrorist known as Kahlil."

"Ah, The Lions of God man. Yes, I did. You were on a couple of days leave, I believe, but your sergeant was very co-operative."

"Would you mind telling me the reason for your interest?"

"Not at all. We were having a spot of bother ourselves and London wanted to compare notes."

"What sort of bother?"

"We had a whisper they were trying to establish a cell."

"And what happened?"

"Fortunately we nipped it in the bud before they became operational. Once they knew we were on to them they scattered like frightened mice. Of course, that's one of the few advantages of having dealt with the I.R.A. for so many years; our intelligence gathering is pretty much second to none. Can I offer you a sherry?"

LeBec shook his head. "No thank you." He replied as politely and calmly as the offer had been made but the time for etiquette had passed and he was about to ratchet-up the conversation and play his hunch.

"Would it surprise you to learn that my information shows no activity in London by the Lions of God during the last six months?"

"No, it wouldn't surprise me at all" said Simpson, totally unruffled. "As I said, we have superior intelligence gathering. Anyway, why should you expect Paris to be aware of London's problems?"

"I don't" said LeBec, equally placid. "I'm quoting Scotland Yard's own anti-terrorist squad when I phoned them earlier today."

There was a momentary pause but Simpson's expression gave nothing away and he continued his confident tone.

"The Yard were never involved" he replied nonchalantly. "I told you – we broke them up before they were operational."

Simpson's air remained unflustered but he shifted in his chair and LeBec was certain he was becoming uneasy. The thin line of his upper lip had hardened, giving a slightly sinister overtone to the smile he was managing to maintain.

"Then would it surprise you to know" continued the detective, "that, according to the press, two Syrians, who were being held for illegal arms trading, were set free yesterday and put on a plane at Heathrow?"

Simpson's brow furrowed above a slightly exaggerated and condescending smile.

"I'm sorry, old boy" he said benignly, "I don't see the connection. What exactly are you driving at?"

LeBec was about to raise the stakes. His eyes narrowed and he focussed his steely gaze unremittingly at the Englishman. When he spoke, his voice was cutting and blatantly accusatory.

"I'm driving at trading two Syrians in London for a phoney kidnap attempt in Paris – and buying a convenient death for a wanted terrorist to cover your sordid little tracks. I'm driving at the Lions of God claiming responsibility for what was, in reality, an S.I.S. plot to murder a Russian scientist. That's what I'm driving at Simpson – and I'm not stopping until I get some answers!"

Simpson rose swiftly to his feet. His anger was held in check by his diplomat's well-practised restraint but his face was flushed and the resentment in his voice, though constrained, was obvious.

"I have no idea what you're talking about Chief Inspector but frankly I find your attitude offensive. I don't think I need remind you where you are and, if I were you, I'd think very carefully before insulting me and, by implication, Her Majesty's Government with your wild and unfounded accusations. Now, I think it would be better if you leave immediately."

LeBec didn't move. Had Simpson's reaction been one of quietly amazed disbelief then he would have been forced to leave with his tail between his legs, but the Englishman's indignation, controlled as it was, was a sure sign he had struck a nerve. It was time to play the trump card.

"Oh, but these are not my accusations Mr. Simpson" he said, resuming his polite and calm tone. "These are Alan Russell's accusations."

Simpson was quick to recover but the look of shock that flashed across his face as LeBec delivered this salvo was there long enough for the detective to know his hunch had been right. He silently congratulated himself on correctly putting the final pieces of the puzzle together.

"I don't follow you" said Simpson glibly. The cracked veneer was repaired and back in place.

"I simply mean" said LeBec quietly, "that these are the accusations Alan Russell will make when we put him on trial."

Simpson sat down again and clasped his hands across his lap. His thumbs were nervously tapping against each other and, despite his efforts to appear composed, it was several moments before he spoke.

"Do you give me to understand that you have Alan Russell in custody?"

LeBec reached into the inside pocket of his jacket and withdrew a small photograph.

"Taken today" he said impassively as he handed it across to the diplomat, "as you can see by the date and headline of the newspaper he is holding."

"It's a Paris edition" observed Simpson curtly.

"Correct"

"Then I presume he is being held at your headquarters, here in Paris?"

LeBec slowly and deliberately shook his head, teasing Simpson's curiosity with his non-committal smile and the mischievous gleam that twinkled in his eyes under their raised brows.

"No" he said quietly.

"Then where is he?" demanded Simpson.

"That, I'm afraid, is classified information. In fact, apart from the two officers that are guarding him, you and I are the only two people who know he's been arrested."

Simpson was anxious and extremely concerned about this quietly confident policeman but he was an experienced man and not so flustered that he couldn't recognise bait when it was being dangled.

"And you consider this exclusivity to be significant?" he said as diffidently as he could manage.

"Oh, I consider it to be very significant. You see, I'm willing to bet you have all the men you can muster frantically looking for Alan Russell in every nook and cranny between here and Marseille. I'd also wager that a certain Major Caswell has issued top priority orders that Russell is to be shot on sight. After all, whilst it's true he can't prove anything, the revelations at his trial would cause some very awkward questions to be asked; very awkward indeed. So, if at the moment there are only four of us who are aware of Russell's arrest, I'd say it was extremely significant, wouldn't you? For you and Major Caswell, it might mean the difference between an irrevocable loss and a retrievable one."

Simpson gave a sniff of disdain and sat back in his chair. The diplomat's mask was fully restored.

"Allow me to reiterate" he began pompously, "that your allegations are of course totally unfounded and I have no knowledge of the things you mention. If, however, I can organise the resources at my disposal to help the French police in their work, it would naturally be my duty to do so."

His eyes bore full testimony to his dislike of LeBec and his voice could barely disguise the contempt he was feeling for the situation in which he found himself and the detective who had put him there. He leaned forward in his seat and asked acidly:

"Just what it is that you want?"

* * * * *

The Café Doudeauville was, as usual, not enjoying a rush of business so the few patrons who sat at the tables, casually drinking and smoking, looked up expectantly when the door opened and Bernard Gillet idled in the from the street. He met their glances with a brief nod and ambled to the bar where Antoine, the owner, was chewing a match as he wiped a none too clean cloth over the glass he was holding. The barman said nothing but raised his eyebrows in invitation to his newly arrived customer to order a drink.

"Cognac" requested Gillet carelessly and leaned an elbow on the bar as he turned to survey the room. "Not too busy, then?" he enquired.

Antoine shrugged. "It comes, it goes. Tonight's a little slow."

"Salut" Gillet wished him as he took a sip from the glass that had been set down before him. "Shame, really" he added indifferently. "I was hoping to have a word with some of your regulars."

"Oh?" asked Antoine, the immediate suspicion obvious in his eyes.

Gillet shook his head. "Nothing heavy" he reassured the barman. "I'm just trying to trace someone; thought maybe some of your customers might be able to help me."

"Why would you think that?" came the cold reply.

Gillet leaned forward conspiratorially and lowered his voice to a whisper.

"I know this guy up town; runs a couple of high-class tarts for visiting Arab oil men. He knows most of the clan who deal in, shall we say, that kind of business and thought he recognised the fella I'm trying to find; but he couldn't put a name to the face. He thought he'd seen him here though. Maybe you'd know him?"

Gillet opened the manila envelope he was carrying and withdrew the photograph LeBec had given him, laying it face up on the bar.

Antoine gave the picture a cursory glance and shook his head, still chewing on the match that was hanging from the corner of his mouth.

"Never seen him before" he said dismissively.

"Ah. That's a pity" said Gillet disconsolately as he replaced the photograph in the envelope. "Because if we can't trace him, we can't hand over the money."

"Money?" enquired Antoine, the magic word having, as usual, found its mark.

"Yes. Funny business. He was killed in a hit and run accident. He had no identity on him but he was carrying a small fortune; pockets were stuffed with notes. Must have won the lottery or something!"

Gillet took another swig of his cognac as he waited for the expected response. Antoine stopped chewing and removed the soggy match from his lips.

"Is there a reward for helping to trace him?"

"Not exactly a reward" said Gillet. "But I've been authorised to pay for certain information."

"What sort of information?"

The journalist withdraw five, new, crisp twenty-euro notes from his pocket and held them up in front of the barman.

"All I need is a name" he said casually.

"Just a name?"

"That's all" said Gillet, waving the notes slightly from side to side.

"Try Chaudary. Siddiq Chaudary."

"Thanks. I will."

Gillet dropped the banknotes onto the bar, finished his cognac with a final swig, and turned on his heel and left.

Fourteen

France

The atmosphere in the apartment was strained. Their two captors confined Russell and Nina to the one room, where they were allowed the freedom to leave their seats and move around provided they did so one at a time and avoided any physical contact. The bathroom door had been lifted from its hinges and removed, along with the entire contents of the medicine cupboard, but even so they were only allowed to answer the call of nature when accompanied by one of their guards, whose one concession to Nina was to turn their backs while she relieved herself. Every other room in the flat was strictly out of bounds. They lived, ate and slept in the lounge and were refused even temporary release from the restraining hand-cuffs, which were becoming increasingly uncomfortable as they rubbed and bruised the skin with each movement.

Forty-eight hours of such close confinement was oppressive to both the prisoners and their gaolers but, for Russell, never knowing when the phone or doorbell would announce the end of captivity and see them separated, it also provided a valuable opportunity to talk to Nina. Strangely, the permanent presence of their guards didn't inhibit him. Like a condemned man whose fate was beyond his control, he found an odd sort of calm in their remaining hours together. He told her everything about himself; the little, unimportant things, the innumerable minor details that make a person who and what they are. He needed her to know; wanted her to be sure that, despite meeting and conducting their relationship under the shadow of pretence, they could at least part in truth, certain she had come to know the real him.

The usually gradual process of discovery and nurturing a relationship was telescoped into those two days and achieved through their constant and apparently idle conversation and small-talk. They made no mention of their situation or of the tortuous path that had led them to it. They simply talked; incessantly and avidly of anything and everything; much to the bewilderment of the two French policemen who watched them, fed them their meals and thought them the strangest terrorists they had ever encountered.

By 11am on Wednesday the 14th, Clémence was becoming tired, irritable and extremely bored with his role of baby-sitter. Paul Nicot was no less discontent, although he managed to hide it more successfully from the two hostages.

"How much longer?" hissed Clémence as his sergeant offered him the cup of coffee he had brought from the kitchen. "This is driving me nuts!"

"I know" replied Nicot sympathetically. "But it can't last much longer. The boss said no more than a couple of days."

"Supposing he's hit trouble? I can't face another night of this."

"I don't think you'll have to. One way or another, he has to do something today. Time is running out."

LeBec was all too aware that time was running out but, even as his sergeant spoke, he was playing the final card in his hand.

* * * * *

The Tuileries were less crowded than usual. The cold weather discouraged most people from lingering as they crossed the gardens on that Wednesday morning so, as Georges Peloux hurriedly made his way towards the usual bench, he was a little surprised to discover that the man sitting there was not the person he was expecting to meet. Relieved that his contact had not yet arrived, and that he was not late after all, Peloux sat down next to the stranger and pulled his customary packet of nuts from his coat pocket. The telephone call had come unexpectedly and he had barely been able to make the rendezvous on time. It was unlike Simpson to be late, but a few moments respite were a welcome opportunity for Peloux to catch his breath before the Englishman arrived and explained why he had requested this impromptu meeting. As he tossed a couple of nuts to the pigeons that were gathering expectantly at his feet, he hoped the news would not bring a problem.

"Strange name – pigeon" said the man next to him idly. "Quite a pleasant bird really and yet we use the name unfairly. Like 'stool-pigeon' for instance. Why use the name of a harmless bird like this to describe something as nasty as a man who grasses on his friends? Strange, don't you think?"

Peloux merely grunted and chose not to engage with the stranger at his side, but there was something ominous in the man's tone that made him feel decidedly uneasy.

"But then names are a funny thing" continued the man beside him. Take 'Kahlil' for example. Do you know that in Arabic it means 'friend of God'? Now that's a very inappropriate name for a murdering bastard who goes around blowing up innocent people, wouldn't you say?"

Peloux froze. His stomach turned over and he felt his spine go weak. Slowly, he turned towards the man next to him and looked up into his steely eyes.

"Or take my name" the stranger continued calmly. "My name is LeBec; Chief Inspector LeBec. Which means you're in more trouble than you ever dreamed possible."

Peloux's body suddenly tensed with the instinct to run but, before he could move, LeBec gently placed a restraining hand on his forearm.

"I wouldn't Georges" he said quietly. "There's an armed man at each end of the path. They'd drop you before you got ten paces."

The colour totally drained from his face and the ashen Peloux slumped back against the bench.

"I ... I ... don't know what you're talking about" he murmured feebly.

LeBec's manner remained matter-of-fact and he gazed out in front of him across the gardens as he continued to address the horrified man beside him.

"I'm talking about murder, Georges. There are several bodies we could discuss but let's start with Siddiq Chaudary, shall we? He appears to be somewhat dead and the buck seems to stop at your door."

"But I didn't kill him!" wailed Peloux in panic.

"Probably not. But Simpson's fingered you; traded you for some information - and you're taking the fall."

"But I just found him for them. I was the fixer that's all. And he wasn't supposed to die. It was a mistake! An accident! And I had nothing to do with it. I'm just the middle-man, that's all!"

LeBec shook his head dismissively.

"Oh you're more than just the middle-man, Georges. You see, Simpson's never met Kahlil - they're both far too canny for that. But you have. And you're probably the only one who knows how to get in touch with him. So you're going to contact him. You're going to set him up just like you set up Chaudary – and we're going to nail the bastard once and for all."

"You don't know what you're asking!" moaned Peloux as though in pain. "I'd be a marked man – and they never give up. It'd be like signing my own death warrant for Christ's sake!"

LeBec's unruffled manner didn't falter.

"Let me explain something to you, Georges" he said in an almost avuncular tone. "You're a nasty, cowardly, miserable excuse for a human being and you're keeping me from a man who's been killing and maiming innocent people."

He turned and stared the whining Peloux directly in the eyes and his tone suddenly became ominously threatening.

"You may well be scared of Kahlil and his friends. But if you don't co-operate, I'm going to lock you in a cell – where no one will hear you scream – and personally beat the shit out of you until you talk. So what's it to be – them or me?"

Terrified, Peloux sank lower into the bench, visibly crushed by the inevitability of his fate.

"It's all done by cards" he burbled miserably. "I put an ad in the personal columns of a couple of the dailies; always the same wording. The next day a postcard arrives with a time and a call box where I have to be. He calls and tells me when and where we meet."

LeBec nodded with satisfaction and glanced down at his watch.

"Good" he said calmly. "We've still got time to make the second editions."

The detective stood and beckoned to the two men at either end of the path, who began to make their way towards the bench.

"Stand up, Georges" he commanded the hapless Peloux. "You're nicked."

* * * * *

LeBec was back at the apartment by 1.30pm, much to the relief of the waiting policemen.

"Is everything ok?" enquired his sergeant.

LeBec nodded. "Yes. Everything's fine; and by tomorrow we should have what we want."

"You don't mean we're here for another day?" grumbled Clémence.

"No. We're finished here."

"Great!" He jerked a thumb towards Nina and Russell. "Shall I take them back and book them?"

"No. They're staying."

LeBec's two officers exchanged a look of quiet disbelief; but they knew better than to argue.

"You're the boss" said Nicot with a shrug. "So what do we do now?"

"You can take it easy for the rest of the day" the Chief Inspector told a delighted Clémence. "I'll call you when you're wanted." He turned to Nicot. "Paul, I'm afraid I need you just a little longer."

Determined to make his escape before his boss changed his mind, Clémence gathered his jacket and, with a sympathetic smile to Nicot, hurried out of the door.

LeBec handed his sergeant a piece of paper.

"My car's outside. I want you to go to this address and pick up the guy who's waiting there. No conversation; no questions, no answers. Just bring him straight here. Ok?"

Nicot nodded. "Got it." And with a silent smile of bewilderment he set off to do his boss's strange bidding. LeBec sat himself in an armchair and looked across at the two hand-cuffed prisoners.

"It would seem that your story, at least in part, was true Mr. Russell" he began. "I am satisfied that you are not in league with any terrorist organisation."

Russell fell back against the sofa in relief and exhaled loudly as the tension in him released.

"Thank God! Then you know I've been framed; that I'm innocent" he urged.

"Hardly that" countered LeBec, unmoved. "On your own admission you were directly involved in the killing of three men and, according to your own testimony, were responsible for shooting Dimitri Gurevich, accidentally or otherwise. Leaving aside the charge of attempted abduction, there is still a prima facie case of murder, or at the very least manslaughter, to be answered. Make no mistake, Mr. Russell, I have little sympathy for anyone who comes to the streets of this city, armed, and causes the kind of mayhem you were involved with, no matter what the motive. In my book, you are far from innocent."

Russell's momentary optimism sank without trace. Not so much due to LeBec's attitude but more because he knew that all the policeman had said was perfectly true.

"However" LeBec went on, "the extent of your guilt has become somewhat academic. In order to establish the validity of what you told me I was forced into a trade. So I shall be handing you over to a Mr. Simpson of the British Embassy. My sergeant has gone to pick him up."

The name was unknown to Russell but he could tell from Nina's reaction that this was far from good news.

"But they'll kill him!" she cried. "You know they will!"

"I believe that is probably their intention, yes" said the Frenchman calmly.

He rose and led Russell to the table, where he sat him down in one of the dining chairs and began to refasten his hand-cuffs behind him and around one of the struts of the chair-back.

"And you're going to hand him over? Just like that?" exclaimed Nina in disbelief. "He won't stand a chance. Not a hope in hell!"

"That all depends" said LeBec, clamping the hand-cuffs shut.

"On what? Caswell's forgiving nature?"

"No. On you."

Nina frowned and looked quizzically at the detective.

"I don't understand" she said, lowering her voice a little. "What are you saying?"

"I'm saying I can hardly arrest you for harbouring a man I 'officially' haven't found. Consequently you are free to go."

To the great relief of her aching wrists, LeBec released her hand-cuffs.

"I suggest you leave by the fire-escape" he continued in an even and measured tone. "I believe there's a Citroën parked at the back in which someone has carelessly left the keys."

She looked at him, reassessing her opinion of this French policeman; but she was unable to accept the lifeline he was throwing her.

"I can't leave without Alan" she told him quietly.

She thought she could detect the faint hint of a knowing smile behind the detective's eyes and his face softened slightly.

"I didn't think you would" said LeBec. "So, if you're staying, I'd better return this."

He reached into his coat pocket and withdrew Russell's Beretta.

"As Mr. Russell hasn't been here, I can only presume this belongs to you."

He handed the gun to Nina and then turned to face them both.

"Simpson will be alone - I insisted on that - although I doubt that others will be far behind him. Once I've given him the key to these handcuffs, my side of the bargain is complete. What happens then is not my concern. But I warn you both that this is not a licence for more killing. If I find Simpson's corpse in here I'll haul you both in for first degree murder. Understood?"

They had no doubt he meant it. LeBec was clearly not a man who made idle threats. Yet, despite his stern stamp of authority, he was bending the rules and allowing them an avenue of escape. Neither Nina nor Russell could quite believe the chance they were being offered and they looked at him in stunned silence. It was Russell who eventually spoke.

"Thank you, LeBec. I know you're going out on a limb and I appreciate it."

The detective looked down at him dispassionately.

"I have no intention of handing you to Simpson like a lamb to the slaughter, Mr. Russell. But you're a wanted man in this country and nothing I can do will help you if you are caught. Don't forget it."

It was less than half an hour later that Simpson arrived. He climbed the stairs to the apartment, accompanied by sergeant Nicot, and was met by LeBec outside the front door.

"Is he inside?" the tall Englishman asked off-handedly.

LeBec nodded silently and gave him the keys to the hand-cuffs, but as Simpson made to enter the apartment the detective placed a preventive hand upon his shoulder.

"No rough stuff, Simpson" he said firmly. "Not while he's on French soil. If I find him floating in the Seine, you'll answer to me personally. Understood?"

The diplomat looked at LeBec with all the contempt and derision he could muster as he forced himself to answer with a quiet "understood". He stepped forward towards the door but LeBec held him back a second time.

"One more thing" said the detective icily. "I don't like you, or your kind Simpson; and I like what you tried to pull here on my patch even less. So I'm warning you now. You step out of line just once - even so much as a parking ticket - and diplomatic cover or not, I'll nail your arse to the wall so fast you won't have time to breathe. Got it?"

The Englishman gave a sniff of disdain and walked into the apartment, closing the door quietly behind him.

"Were you followed?" LeBec asked his sergeant.

Nicot shrugged. "Nothing close up; but he's sure to have set up a tail of some sort."

He raised his eyebrows and looked at the Chief Inspector, genuinely unsure of where the day's strange events were leading.

"Now what do we do?"

His boss looked him squarely in the eye.

"Pray I've done the right thing."

Simpson appeared at the doorway to the lounge and stopped to savour the sight of Alan Russell hand-cuffed securely to his chair.

"Well. Mr. Russell, I presume" he said with a sneer. "My, but you've caused me a headache or two these last few days. What a pleasure it is to meet you at last."

"I'm afraid the feeling isn't mutual" snapped Russell.

"Tut, tut, Mr. Russell. Such ingratitude. A great many people have gone to a good deal of trouble to bring you back to the family fold. I really think you could show a little more enthusiasm for your reunion."

"I have a feeling the reception will not be all that warm" replied Russell acidly. "So you'll excuse me if I decline the invitation."

"Oh, I'm sorry Mr. Russell" said Simpson, as he pulled a gun from inside his jacket and levelled it menacingly at Russell's chest. "But I'm afraid you have no choice. A car will be arriving for you shortly, so perhaps you'd be kind enough to accompany me downstairs."

He crossed to where Russell was sitting and used the keys LeBec had given him to release one of the captive's hands and disengage him from the chair, but before he could refasten the cuff around Russell's wrist he heard a voice behind him speak evenly and clearly.

"Don't turn around Simpson, or I'll shoot you where you stand. Just put down your gun - slowly - and then release the other cuff."

Simpson froze; unsure of what to do. But as he heard Nina click back the hammer of the automatic and coldly command "Now!" he needed no further prompting and obediently did as he was bidden.

Once released, Russell sprang to his feet. He forced the tall, angular man into the chair and cuffed him to it.

"You won't get half a mile" sneered Simpson.

"That's as maybe" Russell told him. "But I'll take my chances; and I like the odds a lot better than the ride you were planning."

Taking a handkerchief from his pocket, Russell stuffed it into his captive's mouth and then secured it with Simpson's own scarf, which he stretched across his face and knotted tightly behind his neck. He then took the belts from Simpson's trousers and raincoat and tied each of his legs to the chair so that he could neither walk nor bang on the floor with his feet.

Less than a minute later, Nina and Russell had descended the fire-escape and found the Citroën. The keys were in the ignition, just as LeBec had told them. They had no idea when Simpson's men would arrive but they knew it would not take long before they sensed something was wrong and entered the apartment.

"Where are we heading?" asked Russell anxiously as he climbed into the passenger seat and Nina hurriedly sat herself behind the wheel.

"North, towards the motorway - and fast. Simpson's men can only be minutes behind us."

She gunned the engine into life and raced the car away to put as much distance as possible between them and the apartment before their flight was discovered and the inevitable pursuit began.

As the Citroën sped to the corner of the street, it passed LeBec's parked Peugeot. Inside, as they watched the couple's flight, sergeant Nicot turned to his boss.

"Do you think he'll make it?"

LeBec shook his head. "I doubt it."

"Well at least you've given him a chance."

"For what?" said the detective despondently. "A life on the run?"

"It's better than what Simpson had in mind" offered his sergeant encouragingly.

"Maybe. But it's out of our hands now. From here on, Alan Russell is on his own."

Nicot started the car and the two men headed back to their office.

It was 4.15pm and the Citroën had reached Rouen before Nina felt it was safe enough to stop for the first time. On the outskirts of the town she drove into the car park of a small roadside café. She bought much-needed coffee and sandwiches and took them back to the car.

"Thanks" said Russell as he gratefully accepted the hot paper cup. "I needed this."

"Me too" she sighed and for a few moments they remained silent, enjoying the respite and the reviving coffee.

Nina had spent most of the journey mentally evaluating their options. She knew her choices were limited and that time was against them, so she would have to make decisions and make them fast. But before she could settle on their best course of action, she had one overriding concern. She turned to share her thoughts with Russell.

"Alan, to get you out of this mess we're going to need help. There are people I can contact - but we have to be careful. We don't yet know how high up this goes."

"Meaning?"

"Meaning, I'm fairly sure this whole rogue operation has been Caswell's personal madness and if I can go over his head and reach a higher authority we can get help. But if he was acting under orders then I might be leading us right into the Devil's lair."

"How do we find out?"

"I need to get back and speak to people I can trust. In the meantime, you have to go to ground."

"Here in France?" he asked uneasily, not wanting to contemplate that they part company and he go into hiding while she returned to England without him.

"No. You're too hot," she told him resolutely. "Even with your gift for languages it would only be a matter of time before they pick you up.

We have to get you back to England where I know I can keep you hidden."

He was glad to hear it. "So do we head for the coast?"

"You do. I don't. We have to split up."

Her decisive words cut his short-lived relief at a stroke and his spirits fell.

"No. I don't want to leave you" he complained.

She looked at him and smiled warmly as she reached out and gently ran her forefinger down his cheek.

"I know. I don't want to leave you either. But I can buy you the time you need."

"How?" he asked her anxiously. "I don't understand."

"I'll make a couple of calls on my cell phone. By now they're sure to be tracing the number. Once they've got a fix they'll think they've located us both and they'll pour everything into the area. It should take the heat off long enough for you to get away elsewhere."

"No!" he protested. "Absolutely not. It'll draw them right to you."

"Don't worry, I know exactly what I'm doing. This is my sort of game, remember?"

She took his hand and kissed the back of it reassuringly. Her eyes were full of quiet confidence; but it didn't make him any less concerned. He had to believe she was right; she was the professional; cool, calm and thinking clearly. If she proposed parting company then he was in no position to argue; her experience and knowledge were all they had to protect them. But the logic and validity of the suggestion didn't alter the anxious feeling that gnawed at his insides.

"We'll drive into Rouen and hire another car" she told him. It was a simple statement of fact and not up for discussion.

"I still don't want to leave you" he said quietly.

"Stop worrying. I'll be fine."

"I know" he whispered. "It's not that. It's just that we don't know what's out there. If something goes wrong and I'm caught, we might never see each other again."

She leaned across and took his head between both her hands and kissed him gently.

"We'll see each other again, Alan; I promise you. You're going to make it – don't doubt it; not for a second."

"Ok" he said softly. "You're the boss."

"Good. Now – we don't have much time. How much money do you have?"

He took out his wallet and emptied his pockets. Nina produced her own cash and they counted it all out on the centre console between them and then divided it into two.

"Do we have enough?" he asked her doubtfully.

"Yes, it should be plenty. But do you also have a cash card?"

Russell withdrew the card from his wallet and placed it alongside the meagre pile of his total resources.

Thirty-five minutes later Russell was sitting alone in the Citroën, parked in a quiet Rouen side street, as a Renault Clio, driven by Nina, pulled up in front of him. He got out to meet her as she too stepped from her vehicle.

"Documents are in the car, and there's a full tank of petrol" she told him, business-like, as she handed him the keys.

"Right."

"Make good time, but don't speed. The last thing you want is to get hauled in for a traffic offence."

She handed him a plain, black baseball cap.

"And I bought you this. Together with the glasses it will help hide your face without looking too conspicuous."

"Right."

She then gave him a slip of paper.

"This is a safe number. You can reach me there once I get back; but it may take me a couple of days so keep trying until I answer. Alright?"

He nodded. For a moment they stood silently looking at each other, then he pulled her into his embrace and squeezed her tightly.

"Take care" he whispered closely into her ear.

"You too."

He let her go, climbed swiftly into the Renault and drove away. As she watched the car disappearing into the dusk she quietly added:

"And for God's sake be careful, Alan."

Once Russell was gone from sight, she addressed herself to the business in hand. She took out her cell phone and navigated through the menu options until she found the profile setting she was looking for. She moved the cursor and selected *Auto Answer – On*. Looking about her to make sure no one was in view and could observe her actions, she crossed to a waste bin on the other side of the street. She found a paper bag near the top and secreted the cell phone inside. Then she carefully pushed it down through the rubbish and buried it deep at the base of the bin.

After an hour and a half's driving, Nina had put a considerable distance between herself and the waste bin. At the next roadside call box she saw, she pulled the Citroën to a halt and got out to make a call. She dialled the number of her cell phone and after three rings she heard the line connect. She allowed a few seconds to pass and then replaced the receiver in the cradle.

As sergeant Nicot had suspected, Simpson's men had tailed his car from a discrete distance and stopped outside the Les Halles apartment when they saw it parked in the street. Having waited in vain for Simpson to emerge, they knew something was wrong but had no way of knowing which apartment he had entered. They were forced to make a flat-to-flat search before they found him, a full half-hour after Nina and Russell had fled.

The furious and implacable Simpson was convinced that LeBec had set him up but knew he could make no official protest without exposing their "trade-off". So, determined to get even with the detective at a later date, he confined himself to gathering every operative that Paris station could put into the field. He contacted London to keep Caswell regularly informed of the situation but it was not until 6.45pm that he was able to report some progress.

"We've got a fix, sir. There was a call to the girl's cell phone about a quarter of an hour ago. It looks as if she's in Rouen."

"Good" said Caswell with relief. "Have you sent someone after them?"

"No, sir" replied Simpson quickly, "because there's something else. Russell's not with her. They must have split up."

"What makes you think that?" demanded Caswell curtly.

"He's withdrawn some cash in Cherbourg. The numbers are being run by the French service. I gave them the account details and they've been monitoring the computers of the clearing banks since earlier this afternoon. It flagged up a short while ago and they've just called me."

"Are the police aware of this?"

"Not yet, sir, no. My connections with the French service are good and they've promised me a one-hour 'heads-up' before passing the information on to the police."

"Good" Caswell told him with evident satisfaction. "Let's keep it that way."

"I've diverted the nearest available men, sir" added Simpson urgently, "but I'd lay odds he's aiming for the seven o'clock ferry to Poole. I doubt they'll be there in time."

"What time does it dock this end?"

"It's a four and a half hour run, sir, so it should be in around 10.30 your time."

"Right" said Caswell decisively. "We'll be there to meet it. Alright, Simpson; after this afternoon's fiasco, you may have redeemed yourself a few points – but not many. So make sure you stay in touch."

The line clicked into silence as Caswell hung up on his troubled subordinate. He then immediately tapped another number into the telephone handset. As the call connected he barked into the receiver.

"I want a team sent to Poole to meet the Cherbourg ferry. Now!

Glad of the cover of darkness, Russell brought the hired Renault to a halt in a quiet side-street about a kilometre from the docks. He got out of the car, turned up the collar of his raincoat, put on his glasses and donned the baseball cap Nina had given him, pulling the brim low over his forehead. He then went to the rear of the vehicle and opened the boot where he found the Renault's tool-kit and opened it. Relieved to discover what he needed, he withdrew a screwdriver and dropped it into the poacher's pocket of his raincoat. He then locked the car and resolutely set off on foot

The freezing night air, biting and abrasive as it rolled in from the sea, cut into his clothing and stung his cheeks like small, icy needles peppering the skin. But he gave little thought to the cold. He was concentrating hard on his surroundings and watching avidly for any police presence or what might be a sign of Simpson's men. He was very conscious of the weight of the Beretta in his coat pocket, half afraid of it and half grateful that it was loaded and ready, his only ally in whatever might lie ahead.

As he rounded the corner of the main road into the ferry terminal his hopes began to rise a little. There was only one gendarme by the main gate and he seemed to be more concerned with checking cars and their occupants than paying attention to the foot-passengers who, several metres away, were passing through a small gate in the tall wire-mesh fence that surrounded the yard. The pedestrians were all making their way to the check-in. There were a number of back-packers in their late teens or early twenties but there were also enough ordinary looking people of various ages and types for Russell to avoid looking conspicuous.

He slowed his pace a little, wanting to seize the right moment, and then saw a party of a dozen or so passengers, laden with shopping-bags, noisily chatting and laughing as they approached the entrance. Russell lowered his head and started towards the group.

He slipped in amongst them and walked through the entrance alongside a portly couple who were struggling a little with their carrier bags and too busy talking to each other to pay him any attention. Once inside the gate his eyes began scanning the vehicles that were queuing to board the ferry. Cars were lined up to his right and coaches and lorries were assembled to his left. The yard was floodlit from high above by lights on tall pylons that radiated a cold and fierce white glow across the scene, but they mostly illuminated the areas around the ticket office and the boarding points, which left much of the vehicle park in semi-darkness. He knew there would be police and passport checks as the foot passengers went through the final gate to board the ferry and so as the group continued on towards the check-in he began to hang back.

He saw the type of coach he was looking for three from the front of the queue. Silently he gave thanks for the more mundane aspects of his profession – that he so often disdained and found boring – but that on this occasion were providing his salvation. As his pace continued to slow he finally found himself at the back of the group and he stole away to his left and passed between two large container lorries and into the shadows. Weaving his way through the stationary vehicles he moved stealthily to the coach. It was left-hand drive, with English plates, and was a luxury tourer designed for long-distance travel. That meant there would be a sleeping compartment for the relief driver on the near side and Russell knew it would be empty.

He knew because two years previously he'd spent a tedious couple of days working on an E.U. update of the licensing rules for cross-channel ferry operators. After the Zeebrugge disaster of 1987 new laws had been drafted and were subject to review every five years. Russell had translated the latest edition. From inception, the legislation had stressed that no personnel were allowed onto freight decks during crossings so, once boarded, all vehicles had to be empty. Russell swore to God he would never again complain about the endless regulations generated by European bureaucracy.

Shielded from the light by the height of the coach, he was able to sidle up to it unseen and on the blind side of the driver until he drew level with the rectangular door in the vehicle's lower-body section. He inserted the screwdriver between the door and the frame at a point just above the lock. Then he waited.

His cue came when the driver began revving the engine in preparation to move forward in the queue. As the noise rose and the coach began slowly to advance a few metres, Russell jerked down hard on the handle of the screwdriver. The lock gave way at the first attempt and the loud snapping sound was easily masked by the strident growl of the engine. The vehicle settled one place further forward in the line and, as it came to a halt, Russell slipped inside and closed the door behind him.

The outskirts of Cherbourg had grown used to the steady flow of traffic that wound its way through its narrow streets, and to the lorries and coaches that rumbled by and shook the houses and sidewalk shops that were built in a quieter, more sedate age and never intended to withstand the deafening vibrations set up by the noisy, throbbing diesel engines that strained past them. They were not so accustomed to the screech of brakes and burning rubber that aroused the neighbourhood as a black Renault Laguna drove through a red light and cornered at high speed into the main road that led to the docks. Inside, one of Simpson's two men checked his watch, hoping that the 7pm departure of the Cherbourg ferry might just be delayed enough for them to reach it before it sailed.

Russell was in total darkness. Eventually, working by feel, he made out the shape of an internal light and switched it on. The compartment was small, with a ceiling height of only a metre or so, but it was wide enough to accommodate a moulded ledge that served as a bed and on which rested a mattress and a pillow. There was a blanket on the floor, alongside a couple of out-of-date newspapers and some old orange peel, but otherwise the place was bare. He knew he had to get organised quickly in case a spot-check was made before the coach boarded the ferry so he removed the mattress, wrapped the blanket around himself and climbed onto the bed. He then leaned out and switched off the light before reaching into the darkness for the mattress and hauling it up onto its side. He wedged it between the bed and the low ceiling so he was cocooned in the space behind, like some hibernating animal. As he did so he felt the coach move forward again. This time it travelled some distance and the clatter of the wheels told him it was climbing the entrance-ramp and boarding the ferry.

The black Laguna sped past a small road-sign that showed a silhouette of a ship with a hollow interior containing the black outline of a car, the international symbol for roll-on roll-off ferries. Beneath the image, in peeling lettering that needed re-painting, was written: *Ferry – 2 Kilometres*. As the car swung around the next bend it topped the hill that took the road directly down into the docks, which were now fully visible below. The ferry was still there. The anxious passenger again checked his watch and then turned to the driver.
"We might make it yet. Step on it."
His companion pushed the accelerator harder to the floor.

From where he was lying, Alan Russell couldn't hear the metallic grinding of the chain mechanism or the dull thud that registered the bow doors drawing closed. But he could hear the feet of the noisily chatting passengers just centimetres overhead as they made their way from the interior of the coach to climb the gangways to the lounges on the ferry's upper deck, leaving their vehicle empty save for the hidden extra cargo that was now secreted just above its chassis.

The Laguna screeched to a halt and its two occupants darted out. They ran swiftly though the courtyard and into the empty vehicle park. Finally gaining the quayside, the sight that greeted them pulled them to a sudden stop. The 7pm ferry was tantalisingly close – just some hundred metres or so out to sea – but it was underway and, without alerting the authorities as to why they were there, there was nothing the two men could do to stop it. Cursing loudly, the senior of the two men pulled a cell phone from his pocket and called to tell Simpson the unwelcome news that, by a few minutes, their quarry had eluded them.

In the quiet darkness of his hideaway, Russell had sensed the motion of the ship as it had slipped its mooring and put to sea. So far so good. He was off French soil and on his way back to England. With great relief he rested his head on the pillow and settled down to wait out the journey home.

*****

England

A little over four hours after Simpson's cohorts had so narrowly missed intercepting the ferry, a group of three men stood by a Range Rover that was parked alongside the harbour wall on the quayside at Poole. One of them, taller than his companions and with an unspoken air of authority, carried a pair of night-vision binoculars and was focusing out to sea. As he did so, a Jaguar saloon drew up and Major Caswell, accompanied by the dour-looking, thick-set driver, stepped out of the vehicle and walked over to the group.

"That's the Cherbourg ferry now, sir" said the man with the binoculars, indicating a cluster of bright lights hovering out across the water.

"How long before it docks?" asked the Major, clutching his coat around him as the on-shore wind sliced through his clothing.

"Fifteen ... maybe twenty minutes."

"Good." Caswell turned to the other three men. "Gentlemen."

His erstwhile chauffeur, a man named Carver who had served in Caswell's department for seven years, reached inside his coat and under his arm and pulled out a Smith and Wesson semi-automatic, which he began methodically to check over. The other two walked to the rear door of the Range Rover and one of them opened it. He withdrew a sniper's rifle, complete with telescopic sight, which he handed to his companion. He then picked up two magazine clips and a silencer to attach to the Browning pistol that was already holstered at his side.

Caswell turned back to face the ever approaching lights of the ferry. He gave a narrow smile and murmured quietly to himself:

"Welcome home, Mr. Russell"

A constant, strong wind that night had thrown up a large swell on the icy January sea and the switchback ride it provided as the ferry made its tortuous way across the English Channel had made it a far from pleasant voyage. The passengers had nursed their queasiness and whiled away the time within the warmth of the upper lounges but on the freight deck, with no engine running to power the heating system, Russell had become colder and colder as the unpleasant crossing churned his stomach and seemed to drag on eternally. Eventually, to his immense relief, he heard the noise of people re-boarding the coach and knew that the ship must be close to docking.

The man with the sniper rifle remained on the quayside. The cover provided by the Range Rover hid him from view as he knelt on one knee, resting his elbow on the other, and trained his telescopic site onto the gangway that was being rolled into position for foot-passengers to disembark. As he brought it into focus and scanned the arc of his possible shot he saw his colleague standing at the foot of the gangway. He knew that the right hand that was thrust into his coat pocket was holding the Browning pistol with the silencer now affixed.

Accompanied by the other two men, Major Caswell walked down to the vehicle exit and flashed his I.D. at the customs officials who were just beginning to man the check point in readiness for the docking ferry.

The taller of his two subordinates stood to his left and Carver moved forward to his right. They formed a triangle around the customs gate through which all disembarking vehicles would have to pass.

Caswell told the customs officials he was looking for a fugitive and had received word he was on the ferry. Three excise men were detailed to filter all lorries into the sheds and check their cargo doors for forced entry and their cabs and documentation for anyone other than the prescribed driver. The Major and his men would check the occupants of all cars, which was how Caswell expected Russell to be travelling, and the remaining two customs men were to open all vehicle boots.

If Russell had abandoned his transport and opted to travel as a foot passenger then the man at the gangway would arrest him as he came off the ship. Whichever way he was travelling, if Russell should try to run and make an escape there was the marksman on the harbour wall to anonymously and efficiently dispatch him and solve the Major's problem at a stroke.

Inside the darkness of his lair, Russell couldn't see his watch to check the time but estimated it was around fifteen to twenty minutes after the passengers had re-boarded the coach before the engines kicked into life and the vehicle rolled slowly forward. The heaters were evidently in use again and he began to thaw a little as the warm air penetrated the small compartment. Eventually the vibrations of the wheels trundling down the exit-ramp told him he had left the ferry and he became fully occupied with trying to monitor the coach's progress through its engine speed and movement.

To the complaints of many drivers, who wanted to know why they were being delayed and having their vehicles searched, the Major and his team had checked over thirty cars before they saw the first coach come rolling off the ferry. The tall man to his left stepped smartly up to the door and indicated to the driver he should open it. Before the pneumatic swish had finished sounding and the door had glided fully back he was onto the steps and inside the coach. He politely, but firmly, instructed the driver to get out and unlock the luggage bay for his colleague. He himself walked down the centre aisle to the rear of the coach silently checking the faces of the puzzled and inquisitive passengers and declining to respond to their several questions. The luggage bay was tightly packed and full. Satisfied, Carver bade the driver close it again as the tall man stepped down from the coach and shook his head at the Major.

It was as the driver put the vehicle into first gear and let out the clutch to drive off that Caswell spotted it. Further along from the luggage bay was the rectangular door of the sleeping compartment and it was flapping slightly and clearly not fully shut.

"Carver!" he yelled and immediately held out his arm, pointing to the unlocked door. In response to his command, his grim-faced subordinate banged hard on the side of the coach and the mystified driver hurriedly hit the brakes.

As the vehicle halted Russell was nervous. He waited apprehensively for what he assumed was the inevitable customs check. Lying in the darkness he was unsure of what was happening. He thought he could hear rain beating down quite heavily outside, then he suddenly became aware of footsteps immediately outside the door.

"Over here!" yelled Carver to his companion and the tall man came around the front of the coach to join him. They both moved down the side of the coach to the compartment door. Realising that anyone inside would be cornered and might start shooting, Carver withdrew the Smith and Wesson from under his arm.

"Yours?" said the taller man to him.

"Mine" said Carver as he spread his feet evenly and took a stance, arms half-stretched in front of him and both hands on his pistol, training it on the compartment door.

"Right" he said quietly and nodded as the taller man stood with his back flat against the side of the coach and reached out for the compartment door handle and prepared to fling it open.

Russell thought he heard a snatch of conversation between two men but was unable to make out anything clearly. As he strained his ears, trying to distinguish every sound, a sudden gust of cold air blew in as the door was jerked open. A powerful torch beam danced around the interior of the compartment and Russell froze, hardly daring to breathe.

The tension bit into Carver's neck and shoulders as the door was flung back and he faced the unknown interior. The pressure lasted only for a second as, in the white glare of the check-point's neon lights, he could instantly see it was empty. Nothing. Just the cold aluminium plating of the floor and the plastic moulded cubby hole where a mattress and pillow were supposed to be laid but that lay starkly bare in front of him.

Russell could not see the two men but he could now hear every syllable of their conversation, which was far too close for comfort.

"I thought you said it was locked?"

"It was. Bloody thing must be broken."

"I should get it looked at, if I were you. You don't want anybody getting a free ride."

The gruff cackle of low-pitched laughter cut through the noise of the driving rain and the wind.

"How was the crossing from Calais?" asked one of the voices. "It must have been rough on a foul night like this."

"You're telling me! People were throwing up left, right and centre. Glad I'm not clearing it up."

Both men laughed again. But the weather was far too severe for idle conversation.

"Alright. Off you go. And take it easy, I should. The road'll be treacherous in this wet."

"I will. Cheers!"

The door closed again with a slam and the noise suddenly died like a tuning fork thrust into a cushion. Russell let out an audible sigh of relief. He guessed, correctly although he didn't know it, it had been the driver and a customs man checking out the compartment. A few seconds later the engine roared and he felt the coach lurch forward as the driver took his vehicle out of the port gates. The teaming rain began falling even more heavily as the coach drove past a large sign that said "Welcome to Dover" and turned left and headed for the M20 motorway.

Alan Russell was back in England.

One hundred and thirty miles to the west of Dover, on the quayside at Poole – where it was not raining – Carver shook his head at Caswell and then gave two short taps of his palm on the side of the coach to tell the driver he was cleared to proceed. The Major and his team, and the customs officers inspecting lorries, continued checking until all the vehicles had disembarked and been cleared. The man at the foot of the pedestrian gangway waited until the last passenger had departed and then waived an arm above his head to signal the man with the sniper rifle behind the harbour wall to stand down.

Caswell then sent all four of his men and three of the customs team onto the ferry itself.

Half an hour later they returned empty handed.

Caswell took out his cell phone and dialled Paris, where Simpson had been anxiously awaiting news of Russell's final apprehension.

"Nothing" snapped the Major into the receiver. He wasn't on the ferry."

"But he must have been aiming for the ferry" protested Simpson in vain. "He withdrew cash in Cherbourg. I can prove it! Why else would he be there?"

"You fouled up again Simpson" Caswell told him with a cold finality. "This is becoming a bad habit."

The Major angrily flipped his phone closed and walked back to his Jaguar where Carver was waiting patiently behind the wheel to drive him back to London.

* * * * *

France

In the port of Cherbourg, overlooking the harbour, stands a small all-night café keeping its lonely, twenty-four hour vigil whether the dock below is a hive of activity or falls silently to sleep. As most of the customers are those arriving or departing on ferries, the trade varies from hectic to almost nothing dependent upon the times of sailings. It was gone midnight and, apart from the pale girl behind the counter who was reading a magazine as she settled into the lazy routine of the late shift, there were only two customers sitting quietly at separate tables. One was a taxi driver who was on his break and enjoying a coffee and the last strand of a Gauloise before returning to work. The other was Nina Petrova.

Several hours before, from her parked Citroën, she'd watched Simpson's men arrive in their black Laguna and dash too late onto the quayside in pursuit of the ferry in which, they believed, Alan Russell was escaping from France. Their frantic arrival told her that her earlier ploy had worked. It had been a close run thing but the timing couldn't have worked out better. The fact they had missed the ferry and been unable to board it assured her that Caswell's men would be arranging to meet it on the other side of the Channel. They would not be looking for Alan Russell at the ferry ports to the East where, she hoped, he had by now managed to arrive.

She took out Russell's cash card and looked down at it, moving it delicately from side to side between the two outstretched second fingers of each hand. She had known Simpson would be monitoring the computers of the French clearing banks, so she and Russell had exchanged cards. She had driven into Cherbourg and found the cash point that was closest to the ferry dock and withdrawn money from Russell's account.

She silently read the name on the card between her fingers and wondered where he was and what he was doing. She trusted he was now out of harm's way and could remain hidden until she could join him and get him to a safe-house.

She had spent the evening in a small bed and breakfast pension, deciding it was best to remain out of sight for several hours in case Simpson's men were still in the area. Now it was time to leave Cherbourg. The longer she could convince Caswell that Russell was still in France, the safer he would be in England so, before she crossed the Channel herself, she would once again put the cash card to use. Simpson would be suspicious of a second location but he'd have to check it out. She would drive through the night across country and find a bank close to the border in Lille or Roubaix where, early the next morning, she would make one final withdrawal, making it look as if Russell was heading inland to Belgium. Then she would double back and take a ferry from Boulogne. Within twelve hours or so, she too would be in England. It would take her a day, possibly two, to reach people she knew she could trust and ascertain the true picture of Caswell's operation and just who was involved. Then, with luck, she could finally set in motion the help she needed to bring down the curtain on the Major and free Alan Russell from the nightmare he was living.

She slipped the card back into her pocket, downed the last of her coffee and quietly walked from the café to begin her long drive.

* * * * *

England

It was just under two hours before the coach stopped again. The movement of feet above Russell's head and the opening of the luggage bay next to him were ample evidence that the driver had reached his destination and was setting down his passengers. The vehicle emptied quickly and the snatches of conversation and laughter from outside showed that people were more concerned with getting out of the pouring rain than with long goodbyes, so in less than ten minutes the coach was underway again.

Three-quarters of an hour later, the shunting motion of the vehicle told Russell the driver had returned to his depot. Eventually the engine was switched off and all was quiet outside but he waited and let what he estimated to be a further twenty minutes pass before deciding it was safe to risk making a move. His body was stiff from the confined position he had held for so long and he took a few moments to massage and stretch his aching limbs before subjecting them to movement. Then, as noiselessly as he could manage, he opened the compartment door and ventured quietly outside.

His first priority was to establish where he was. The place was in darkness but there was enough light from the moon to make-out four coaches, parked alongside each other, looking pale and ghostly in the ice-blue light and cemetery-like silence of the yard. They were of different sizes but their livery was identical and each back panel bore the company's name and logo above its address and telephone number. Russell was evidently in Collier Row in Essex in the yard of a firm called *Lawrence Travel*.

He checked his watch. It was 1.05am, local time. He was cold, tired and hungry. He hadn't slept properly in three days. The heavy rainfall had faded to a thin, misty drizzle but the freezing night air was, if anything, colder than when he had left France and he knew he had to find shelter quickly. His wallet still held over a hundred euros but he had only a few pounds in sterling. If he could find a cash machine he could use Nina's bank card but he had no idea as to which road he should take and a mistake might mean walking for hours in the wrong direction. At the entrance to the yard he decided the road to the right looked residential, so he opted to turn left and stepped out at a brisk pace. He had neither showered nor shaved since his captivity had begun three days before and he was becoming more bedraggled by the minute with the continual drizzle that was now beginning to wet him through. At that hour of the morning, alone and lost, he cut a pathetic figure as he walked the deserted streets, praying there would be no police patrols to stop and question the dishevelled individual who was hiding a semi-automatic in his coat pocket.

After twenty minutes he found himself at the junction of a dual carriageway and his hopes picked up a little. The large sign in the central reservation declared it to be the *Eastern Avenue* and, recognising the name, Russell realised he was closer to London than he had thought. Several cars were travelling the road and he tried thumbing a lift, but to no avail. He didn't blame the drivers. He himself would not have picked up a stranger at that time of morning, let alone a tramp-like figure of Russell's unkempt appearance. He was just beginning to think he would be walking until daybreak when his heart leapt; in the distance he saw the familiar, yellow *for hire* sign glowing atop an approaching black cab. He ran into the road, frantically waving both his arms above his head. The driver slowed the cab, pulled over to where Russell was standing and wound down his window.

"I'm on me way 'ome, mate. I can only help you if you're goin' my way."

"I need a cash machine and then a hotel for the night" Russell told him earnestly. "And I'll pay you double the meter if it's out of your way."

The driver had no desire to travel anywhere but towards his own home but the offer of twice the ordinary fare was a tempting proposition. He gave a sniff.

"I s'pose Romford centre's your best bet; and it's kinda on me way. Oh, alright. 'Op in."

With enormous relief, Russell climbed into the warmth of the cab's interior and slumped onto the grey vinyl of the back seat. Thirty minutes later he was in his room at the Mawney Hotel and running a hot bath.

He was still a wanted man but, as far as he knew, the search for him was concentrated on the other side of the channel. He had shelter and enough cash to see him through the next few days and, most importantly, he had time. Time to rest; time to think; time to plan his next move. He didn't yet know what that move would be but he was certain that a life on the run was not an option. One way or another, he was going to force a conclusion.

Fifteen

France

On the morning of Thursday the 15th January, a wretched Georges Peloux sat nervously in the offices of the French anti-terrorist squad. Before him was a telephone but, unlike conventional units, this one trailed additional wires leading across the table to a hard-disc recorder that flashed a row of small L.E.D. lights at the hapless Peloux.

LeBec, Nicot and Clémence stood around him, each wearing a monitoring head-set, and sergeant Lucien hovered in the doorway to the adjacent room, where a sophisticated bank of digital tracers was set-up and ready to respond to any incoming call. LeBec checked his watch and turned to Lucien.

"Everything ok?"

"All set."

The Chief Inspector bent down to the hunched Peloux.

"The call box he gave you has been routed through to here. One false word that lets him know you're not in that box – and your life won't be worth living. Understand?"

A reluctant nod was his only reply.

Exactly on time, the receiver rang to signal the incoming call.

"Please!" said Peloux pathetically. "I ... I ...

"Answer it!" commanded LeBec.

The abject prisoner did as he was bidden, picked-up the handset and clicked the receive button. He was frozen with fear and couldn't speak.

"Hello?" said the voice on the line.

LeBec raised a threatening hand and Peloux jump-started into speech.

"It's me. I got your postcard."

"The gardens of the Palais de Chaillot by the Pont de l'éna. Second bench along, opposite Plaçe de Varsovie. Got it?"

"Yes. Got it. When?"

"Tomorrow morning. Eleven-thirty."

The line clicked and went dead. LeBec immediately looked across at Lucien.

"Well?"

"A call box in the Gard du Nord. He'll be long gone."

The unhappy Peloux bent his head and shook it slowly from side to side.

"They'll kill me" he moaned. "If it takes them ten years – they'll find me and they'll kill me."

"I shouldn't worry, Georges" LeBec told him as he patted his shoulder. "With luck, the judge will put you away for a lot longer than that."

He turned to the assembled crew.

"So, gentlemen. It's the gardens of the Palais de Chaillot – and we've got less than twenty-four hours. Let's go to work!"

* * * * *

England

That same Thursday morning Alan Russell had not risen until past 10am. The much needed sleep had been worth missing breakfast but he was now nagged by pangs of hunger and ordered coffee and sandwiches from room service. Although still a fugitive, there was something about being back in England, in his own country, that he found settling. His mind was clearer than it had been for the past few days and, as he ate his food, he became certain that there was really only one course of action open to him. By the time he had showered and shaved, he knew exactly what he intended to do.

He no longer had the make-up and hair-colour he had worn as Monsieur Bourget but he felt it would be safe to risk walking into the town if he wore the baseball cap and his glasses. The shopping-centre was crowded and he was able to buy the various items he needed without mishap or incident. He had to consult a local telephone directory to find the address of the nearest car-hire company but by 2pm he had rented a vehicle and was on the road.

It was gone midnight before he returned and parked the hired Ford Fiesta in front of the Mawney hotel. He then passed most of the night in writing out his story in full on the sheets of a notepad he had purchased earlier in the day. It took him several hours but he related every detail, citing names, places and dates. He then wrote a brief last will and testament. His final act was to write a personal letter to Nina, explaining all he proposed to do and asking her to deal with the relevant documents if she failed to hear from him again. He signed it simply "with gratitude and love – Alan". He placed all three items in a large brown envelope and addressed it to Nina at her flat in Chelsea.

The first light of morning was breaking as he finally settled back on his bed and tried to take a few hours sleep before facing the trials of the day that lay ahead of him.

* * * * *

France

In Paris, Friday the 16th of January dawned with a clear, bright sky. It brought a lightness and a smile to the grey winter streets as the sun reflected from the rooftops and sparkled on the morning frost that lay thick upon the parks and gardens. The weather reports had described the day as "bracing" but to Clémence, dressed again in the guise of a street cleaner, it was simply a morning that was far too cold to be standing around waiting.

The gardens of the Palais de Chaillot are always a tourist attraction, even at that time of year, because they stand next to the Seine and immediately opposite the Eiffel Tower which rises majestically on the other bank, just across the Pont de l'éna. It's a favourite spot for photographs so even at eleven-thirty on a cold January morning there were several groups and tour parties, all armed with their video and stills cameras, happily posing for each other in front of the backdrop of the city's best-known icon. Their noise and general laughter were in marked contrast to the silent and miserable Georges Peloux, who sat, literally shivering with fright, on a bench opposite the Plaçe de Varsovie. He glanced continually at his watch, anxiously counting down each second to the rendezvous as though it were his last.

LeBec sat facing him on a bench across the path. Kahlil's chosen well, the detective thought to himself. He'll be guaranteed a crowd and there are pathways leading in seven directions if he needs to make a run for it. Open spaces and yet dozens of people for cover; he's no fool, and this will not be easy. LeBec didn't like the situation, especially the implied risk to passers-by, but he consoled himself with the fact that he had spread his team well. There were three men and two women taking it in turns to stroll by, which meant the same face didn't repeat for twenty minutes; Clémence was performing his street cleaning act just a few metres away and Lucien was sitting reading a paper one bench further along from Peloux. Two support vehicles were in attendance in the adjacent roads and Nicot, seated in the Peugeot and with sight-lines to Peloux, was co-ordinating the whole operation by radio. In addition, LeBec had two plain-clothes officers mingling with the tourists at the entrance to the bridge and two at each corner of the square. Theoretically, he'd covered all the options. Now, just as always, it came down to a simple matter of waiting.

It was LeBec who saw him first. He was standing with a tourist group. He was on the periphery but close enough to appear to be part of them. He wore a dark-blue corduroy cap and a tan-coloured sheepskin jacket, with the collar turned up, and a scarf high around his neck as though it were meant to keep his ears warm but which in reality hid the scar on his cheek.

How long he'd been there LeBec wasn't sure but he knew without doubt that it was him. It was a strange recognition. A man he had thought about constantly for so many weeks but had never met; a face he had studied in photo-fit pictures and artists' impressions until it had consumed his days and haunted his nights, but that he had never actually confronted; a man who had lived in the same city, perhaps even passed by in the street, but had remained elusive, unseen and unheard, until he surfaced to wreak his havoc of death and destruction; always one step ahead; always just out of reach. Now, at last, he was within sight and LeBec knew him instantly. He recognised him with as much certainty as if it were his own mother.

Turning his eyes away, for fear his expression might convey the recognition, he pulled a handkerchief from his pocket and blew his nose, which was the pre-arranged signal from any of them that the target had been sighted.

In the parked Peugeot, Paul Nicot flicked his handset into life and barked into the mouthpiece.

"All units. The guv'nor thinks he's seen him. Repeat – we think we have contact."

As his words echoed in the earpieces of all the officers around the link, each one of them tried unobtrusively to scan the surrounding crowds and locate the suspect. It was Nicot who spotted him.

"All units. The guy in the sheepskin and the cap. Repeat – the guy in the sheepskin and the cap."

One by one, the waiting police men and women sighted their objective. The rate of heartbeats rose, necks tensed and hands went into pockets and closed around the butts of handguns, each officer manoeuvring to a spot to give him or her maximum visibility of target and greatest distance from any bystanders.

For a further two minutes, Kahlil didn't move from his position alongside the tourists. He's not sure, LeBec told himself, keeping the Syrian just within his peripheral vision. He's nervous about this unexpected request to meet and he's not going to commit until he's convinced it's safe. Come on you bastard, just a few steps; that's all we need, just a few steps.

As though in response to LeBec's silent plea, Kahlil shoved his hands into his jacket pockets and began walking slowly towards the appointed bench.

"He's off!" Nicot hollered into his mouthpiece. "It's going down!"

Still looking carefully about him, the Syrian gradually came closer. He passed Clémence, who was idly sweeping leaves from the path. The distance shortened. Ten metres; eight; five; even LeBec's battle-weary constitution was finding it a strain and his stomach knotted with the increasing tension. Four metres; three; and it was then that Peloux caught sight of the man approaching him. He looked up, his eyes wide with fright, and the terror on his face stopped Kahlil in his tracks. Peloux's mouth opened as he struggled for the words that wouldn't come but explanations were unnecessary. The Arab didn't need telling he'd been betrayed.

"They made me!" Peloux finally blurted out. "I couldn't do anything else." His voice rose to a near scream. "They made me do it! They made me!"

LeBec stood. Clémence and Lucien, seeing their boss rise, both drew their guns and trained them on Kahlil, Lucien down on one knee and Clémence with his legs evenly spread and his arms outstretched. The sight of the weapons brought a scream from someone in the crowd. Other anxious voices sounded as some focused on the unfolding scene and others, although unaware of its cause, became alarmed by the panic that was breaking out around them. Nicot yelled "Go!" into the radio and the entire team began running from their various positions to close the net.

In marked contrast, Kahlil hardly moved. He turned slowly and stared at LeBec, as though he knew who he was. There was an unnatural calm about him; a stillness that was all the stranger amid the chaos that was surfacing around him. He exhibited an almost mystical air as he seemed to accept the inevitability of his fate without the least attempt to fight it. He smiled at the Chief Inspector; a benign, knowing smile that quite unnerved LeBec. It was as though his very complacency was taunting the policeman, telling him that to resist was beneath Kahlil's dignity and that his capture, even his death, was but nothing in comparison to what he represented or to those who would come after him. Then, equally slowly and deliberately, he turned back to face Peloux.

"You fool" he said quietly but with utter contempt. "You pathetic little fool!"

There was no change in the Syrian's expression; not one scintilla of movement in his facial muscles as, in one swiftly flowing movement, his hand suddenly emerged from his jacket pocket holding a gun and he fired.

He put two bullets into Peloux as, almost simultaneously, Clémence and Lucien's shots burst into his body and he fell to the ground. Within seconds Clémence was at his side and had his gun barrel pressed hard against Kahlil's temple; but it was unnecessary.

LeBec looked down into the olive-skinned face. The scarf had fallen away to clearly reveal the scar on the left cheek but it was now tinged with red from the trickle of blood that was running from his mouth.

Kahlil gazed up at the detective, his eyes bright and intense, giving no quarter, even in death. Then he let out a short breath, that was half sigh and half contemptuous laugh, before his eyes rolled upward and he slipped quietly away from the world to learn if all that his particular God had promised him would be delivered.

"Peloux?" LeBec asked Lucien.

"He's had it."

The Chief Inspector nodded in unwelcome resignation.

"Alright" he said wearily. "Let's get them out of here."

He started back towards his car and was met by Nicot hurrying towards him.

"Dead?" the sergeant asked.

"Both of them" LeBec told him gloomily.

"Oh." Nicot could clearly see the despondency on his boss's face. "But no one else was hurt" he said encouragingly. "It was a textbook operation. And we finally got our boy; the big fish. This will end their campaign. You can't ask for much more than that."

LeBec knew he was right. There would be congratulations all round, plaudits from above, slaps on the back and commendations to add to his record. LeBec has done it again, they would be saying, the streets are free from bombs and Parisians can sleep safely in their beds. Good old Henri has got his man, just as he always does. But none of it felt relevant or gave him cause to lift his spirits.

"Don't look so down" Nicot urged. "You've won."

"Have I?" LeBec asked him, hunching his shoulders against the cold wind. "Then why does it always feel so empty?"

Nicot had no answer. Nor did LeBec.

The detective turned away, dejected, and walked pensively back to his car.

* * * * *

England

The evening of that same Friday found Alan Russell sitting in his hired Ford Fiesta, parked in a tree-lined avenue in Hampstead, watching the house across the street. By 8.30pm he decided that the road was quiet enough for his purpose. From the back seat he grabbed a bag containing his purchases of the previous afternoon and, closing the door gently, left the car and cautiously made his way to number 36.

It was a cold, dry, moonless night and no one saw him as he walked up the short driveway to the front door. As a precaution, he rang the doorbell but he knew from his long vigil that no one was at home. With a last look around to check that the avenue was deserted and no neighbours were about, he walked quickly and quietly to the rear of the house.

The windows were of the old sash-cord type and the one he selected was in bad need of attention to its cracked and flaking paintwork. He took a pencil torch from his pocket and slowly ran it around the edge to look for contact plates or window locks that might link to an alarm. Satisfied there were none, he withdrew a gardening glove and a small tube of super-glue from his bag. He squeezed a little of the glue onto the palm of the glove and held it against the upper pane just above where the two halves of the window met. It set firm in less than a minute. Then, with a glass-cutting wheel, he inscribed a square around the glove and scored it until it was almost cut. Inserting his left hand into the glove, he then tapped it firmly with his right and the glass gave way. Carefully he withdrew his hand, with the square of glass from the pane attached to it, and took off the glove. Then, reaching through the hole, he released the centre catch and raised the window.

Once inside, he closed the curtain behind him and used a larger torch to take his bearings. It was a small laundry room with a butler sink and a washing machine and an open door that led into a kitchen. Treading carefully, and checking the corners for sensor alarms, Russell made his way very slowly through the kitchen and out into the main hallway. The doors were large and panelled in rich, deep mahogany and stood under ornate plaster covings. The first led into a dining room but the second yielded what Russell was looking for and he stepped inside.

Again, there appeared to be no sensors but he avoided stepping on anything but the edges of the central carpet for fear there might be alarm pads underneath. It was a spacious room, expensively furnished and with two, thick Chinese rugs on the floor. There was a large Victorian desk in the window bay, a bulky three-piece suite arranged opposite the fireplace and a full drinks trolley in the far corner. The walls were hung with several small prints, mostly English landscape scenes, and a large Stubbs horse adorned the space above the mantelpiece. The air smelled strongly of furniture polish and the atmosphere was all tidiness and order. There was a loud ticking from the grandfather clock that stood against the left wall and its regular beat echoed like thunder through the silence of the darkened room. Next to the clock stood a single high-backed dining chair. Russell moved it to behind the door and sat. How long he would have to wait he didn't know but time, for once, was on his side.

The grandfather clock had just finished striking the third quarter after midnight when the flash of a headlight beam across the window bay and the sound of a car pulling to a halt outside made Russell sit up and listen intently. The slamming of a car door and the sound of footsteps on gravel all caused the tension in him to surge. Finally he heard the release of a mortise lock and the metallic turn of a latch key. Russell's heart was beating fast but he was thinking clearly and in control. The hall light was turned on, followed by the sound of a slight cough and someone entering another room, which Russell presumed was the kitchen. Then, moments later, the heavy fall of a man's tread across the hall was followed by the light in the room being switched on as the newcomer entered through the door. Crossing to the fireplace, he reached down and ignited the gas fire before moving to the drinks trolley where he began pouring a whisky from a large cut-glass decanter.

Slowly and silently, Russell eased back the door until he was revealed, the Beretta in his hand and pointing directly at the back of the man at the trolley.

"Good evening, Major" he said evenly.

The intense shock of suddenly hearing a voice behind him jolted Caswell into dropping the decanter and his glass. He spun around in disbelief to confront the intruder. When he recognised Russell he was stunned into a silence that was only broken by the drum roll of the whisky that was cascading from the trolley onto the carpet.

"It's quite a blow, isn't it, to find your home has been broken into?" said Russell acidly, the Beretta trained on Caswell's chest. "But believe me, it's nothing to the shock of finding your wife beaten to death. Although I suppose you wouldn't know about that, would you? I dare say you employ others to carry out the messier side of your squalid escapades."

Caswell quickly recovered a little of his bearing and the military man began to re-emerge.

"How did you get in?" he snapped.

"Oh that was fairly easy. Surprising really; for a man whose job is supposed to be security, your own leaves a great deal to be desired."

"And how did you find me?"

"That too was easy. I followed you home from Poland Street last night. Although, I must confess you nearly gave me the slip when you jumped that light at St. John's Wood. I nearly collided with a lorry when I went across after you. It was quite a close shave."

The Major raised his chin with a confident air.

"You won't get away with it, you know" he said glibly. "The others will be home soon. They're only minutes behind me."

Russell shook his head.

"Tut, tut, Major. You'll have to do better than that. You live alone. At least, according to the lady next door you do. She was most helpful when I knocked there this afternoon. When she heard we were old friends and how sorry I was not to have found you at home, we had a long chat about you. It was quite a detailed account, really; very neighbourly of her."

Caswell gave a derisory sniff.

"Well, well" he said cynically, "you've done your homework too." His composure was now almost restored. "I congratulate you, Mr. Russell. Here we are hunting high and low for you on the other side of the Channel and you not only elude us all but turn up under my nose; a veritable Daniel in the lions' den. Although just what good you think it will do you, I can't imagine. Would you like a drink?"

He pointedly turned his back on Russell and began to pour himself another whisky.

"Don't patronise me, you bastard" Russell warned him icily. "You're in no position to play God any more."

The Major took a relaxed and deliberate sip from his glass and then slowly rounded to face his opponent.

"And just what *is* my position, exactly?"

"You're finished, Caswell. I'm going to see to that. But first I want to know why?"

"Litvinov of course" the Major replied indifferently. "He had to be eliminated."

"Why? If his work is as advanced as you say he might have saved hundreds of thousands of lives; maybe millions."

Caswell eyed him with total disdain.

"His work can be duplicated. Eighteen months – two years at the outside – and we'll have the solution. But until then he gave his totalitarian masters an advantage that no one could match. What price the lives of a few against the security of this nation; maybe the whole of Europe? Answer me that, Mr. self-righteous Russell."

Russell stared at him in amazement and disgust.

"In God's name, man, we're talking about people! You can't treat them like statistics in some bloody equation!"

"Typical!" sneered the Major. "Really Mr. Russell, I'd expected more from a man of your intelligence. But you're all the same, you bleeding-heart liberals. You're the first to cry 'foul' and spout about freedom and justice, but by whose efforts do you have the right to speak? Who guarantees you the freedom to stand up and say what you want? Who maintains the precious law and order you're always quoting? Who keeps this country free from the gulags, the concentration camps, the political prisons? We do! Me and those like me. And remember this: every soldier who ever picks up a gun and goes to war, kills and gets killed on behalf of all those who are sitting at home – including all those who enjoy his protection while they belly-ache about pacifism and peace! Well, this is still war, my outraged friend. An undeclared, clandestine war perhaps, but war none the less; and thank God some of us are still fighting it; fighting for you and all the whining, left-wing subversives like you who keep stabbing us in the back. And if I had to, I'd kill a dozen Litvinovs to keep you and your kind from bringing this country to its knees!"

Russell slowly shook his head, scarcely able to believe the rhetoric that was assailing his ears.

"If you were plain, ordinary insane, Caswell, there might be some excuse. But yours is a special kind of madness. It's evil. You know exactly what you're doing and exactly whom you're hurting and you don't give a damn. This was cold-blooded murder from the outset. Litvinov was the victim, I was the patsy and my wife was the bait; my poor Taniel, whose only crime was to be a Muslim and married to me – which gave you the perfect cover to set me up. But you slipped up Caswell. I didn't die. Thanks to Colonel Gurevich whom, to my undying shame, I sent to an early grave, Blair got shot instead of me. And I've come back, Caswell. I've come back for you."

There was steel in Russell's eyes and they narrowed when he mentioned Taniel. It unnerved Caswell, though he fought to conceal it. Raw emotion was volatile, unpredictable; there was no logic in it and his military mind knew of no strategy for contending with it.

"The matter of your wife was most regrettable" he muttered uncomfortably. "Most regrettable."

Russell was almost speechless. He could feel the anger and rage that was rising in his chest and the pain of losing his wife swept over him afresh, as though it had only just happened. His finger tightened around the trigger.

"Regrettable?!" he managed to utter in disbelief. "You callous bastard. You mad, callous bastard."

"Yes!" barked Caswell vehemently, ever unrepentant. "I can be callous if I have to be. I'm a soldier and I do what has to be done. I don't live in your sanitised little universe. I live in the real world where hard decisions have to be made. It's life! It's being a man! And we have to understand that if we're going to survive. But then, I was forgetting; that's your problem, isn't it? Because if you'd behaved like a man in the first place and taken Nina Petrova when I offered her to you in Cambridge, maybe your wife would be alive today. But I don't suppose your high moral standards allow for anything as animal, as fundamentally human, as *having* a beautiful woman, do they?"

Russell's hatred and contempt for Caswell boiled over with every word of the Major's extraordinary sermon. The volcano of his battered and bruised emotions erupted within him and finally burst free. He let out a cry and rushed across the room. It was a low, deep-throated wail that exploded in a crescendo as his whole body resonated with the anguish and pain of the recent weeks. His loss, his fear, his hurt, and his rage at the destruction of the man he had been and the life he had known, all came together in one voice, one yell that was the lamentation of his very soul.

The full force of the blow struck Caswell across the temple and sent him tumbling backwards into the drinks trolley and onto the floor. The butt of the Beretta had torn a six-centimetre gash along the left side of his head and the blood from the wound was flowing freely down the Major's cheek and onto the Chinese rug, where it streamed into the broken glass and river of spirits in which he was lying.

Kneeling at the side of him, Russell thumbed back the hammer of the Beretta and forced the barrel hard against Caswell's head.

"You see, Russell! You see!" the Major taunted him, blinking through the blood that was clouding his left eye. "You're animal after all – just like the rest of us! You want to pull the trigger, don't you? Only you can't! Because, unlike me, you haven't got the backbone to do what has to be done."

Russell grabbed him viciously by the shirt-collar and lifted his shoulders from the floor. Caswell's head, suspended by Russell's vice-like grip at his throat, fell back like a child's doll with a broken neck. Russell drew him so close that their faces were only separated by the width of the Beretta's barrel. The smell of sweat, tinged with the strange odour of newly flowing blood and the faint scent of hair cream, filled his nostrils.

"Don't kid yourself, Caswell he hissed vehemently. "The only thing that stops me putting a bullet through you right now is that I haven't finished with you yet. Now get up!"

He hauled the Major to his feet and marched him across the room to the desk, where he forced him to sit.

"Pick up a pen" he commanded, taking a sheet of paper from his pocket and thrusting it in front of Caswell. "And sign this!"

"What is it?" the Major asked, vainly mopping his face with a handkerchief and trying to stem the flow of blood from his temple.

"It's a confession; an admission of your guilt. It lists everything; from the convenient skiing accident you arranged for Gavin Bentley and the strings you pulled to get me onto Mayer's team, right up to the assassination of Litvinov. Most of all it's a confession of responsibility for the brutal murder of my wife."

"You're crazy" Caswell scoffed. "Even if I did sign it, who do you think would accept a confession forced at gunpoint? Who would they believe – a high-ranking officer in Her Majesty's security service or a criminal wanted for abduction and murder?"

"They may not believe me, Caswell; not at first. But there will be a trial. And questions will be asked – awkward, uncomfortable questions. I'll make such a noise that the echoes will ring around Whitehall for years. And the suspicion alone will be enough to ensure you never surface again."

Caswell burned with scorn and derision.

"And if you're right – what difference would it make? I told you – this is war. It's not me that's important; it's the work that has to be done. If I go, there will be another to replace me, and another and another."

"The same as you?"

"Yes!" Caswell exclaimed acidly, vindication shining in his eyes.

"They'd murder Litvinov?"

"Yes!" he repeated passionately.

"And murder my wife?"

"Yes, yes!" the Major shouted, lifting his head in arrogant triumph. "And if you think otherwise, you're insane!"

Russell drew a deep breath. A look of relief spread across his face and he nodded slowly.

"I may be insane, Major" he said softly, "but I haven't yet lost all reason. Which is why there's a small recorder on the mantelshelf – and it's just taken your proud confession."

Caswell shot an anxious glance across the room. There above the fireplace, it's tiny red light glowing, was a pocket-sized recorder.

"Damn you, Russell" he cursed almost under his breath. "Damn you to hell!"

"You're too late, Major" Russell told him quietly. "I've already been there."

He turned away and walked across to the mantle to retrieve the recorder.

It was only a slight noise; the rustle of paper perhaps or the faint scraping of the desk drawer as it was opened. Maybe it was an undue creaking of the chair as Caswell leaned forward. Whatever it was, there was something Russell heard that triggered an instinct within him and he turned to look behind. He was just in time to see Caswell level the Browning at him and hammer it back. As the noise of the shot exploded in Russell's ears he was already flinging himself sideways and crashing into the sofa. The bullet tore a hole through his coat as it flapped in the air beside him but missed his body and smashed into the far wall. Before the Major could fire a second time, the Beretta in Russell's hand barked. Caswell toppled sideways and fell onto his desk, where he lay slumped and silent.

For a few moments, all was quiet. There was no movement and no sound. The stillness was only broken by the sweet smell of cordite that wafted through the room and the relentless ticking of the grandfather clock. Russell sat motionless on the floor, leaning against the sofa, and staring at the figure sprawled over the desk top. He felt nothing; neither pleasure nor pain; no elation, no regret; just a numbness. There was no satisfaction, no sense of justice or revenge; just a cold, unemotional indifference.

The silence was interrupted by a careful and deliberate knocking at the door. Russell looked up to see it open slowly and three men appear. The first two carried guns and moved cautiously into the room. Pausing only briefly to take in the scene, one crossed immediately to Caswell's lifeless body and checked in vain for a pulse, the other walked slowly to Russell and reached down to relieve him of the Beretta. The third, an older man dressed elegantly in a camel-hair coat, remained in the doorway.

"Mr. Russell?" he enquired gently.

Russell nodded.

"I wonder if you'd mind stepping into the other room? My colleagues will attend to matters in here."

As Russell sat himself on a chair in the kitchen, the elegant stranger filled a glass with water from the tap and passed it to him.

"Here, drink this" he told him. "You look as though you could do with it."

Russell sipped from the glass in silence.

"I've spoken to Miss Petrova by phone" the other man went on. "She finally managed to get through to me a couple of hours ago. We don't know all the specific details yet, but she's given us a pretty fair idea of what's been going on."

"Us?" Russell queried.

"The service. I know it's of small consolation Mr. Russell, but I was really quite appalled at what Miss Petrova had to say. I will naturally do all I can to help you and to see that you are properly compensated. Not that anything can compensate you for the loss of your wife of course, that goes without saying. I can only offer you my deepest sympathies and, for what it's worth, the sincerest regrets and apologies of the service and Her Majesty's Government."

"And who might *you* be?" Russell asked indifferently.

"I'm known as 'C'."

Russell lowered his chin in affectation of being impressed.

"The head man" he quipped sardonically. "What's the matter Mr. 'C', scared that heads will now roll and yours might be the first?"

"I'm just trying to help, Mr. Russell."

"You're a little late. And I've got all the help I need in here." He held up the small recorder. "This is going to light a bonfire under your whole perverted organisation."

"Don't judge us all by Caswell, Mr. Russell. One rotten apple doesn't mean the whole barrel is bad."

"Oh, excuse me. Am I jumping to conclusions? Correct me if I'm wrong but I was under the impression that the men who murdered my wife and were trying to kill me were working for you."

"I sympathise with your attitude, Mr. Russell" said the other man patiently. "And I appreciate your distress; but please try to understand. Our work is carried out, of necessity, in secret; on the 'need to know' principle. It cannot be explained all the way down the line. Sadly, that means that bad orders are carried out without question just as good orders are. Caswell had gone 'rogue' and, unfortunately, was able to do considerable harm before, thanks to Miss Petrova, we became aware of it. We came here tonight to arrest him."

"So that let's you off the hook, does it?" Russell asked him coldly.

"No. You were quite right. It is my organisation and ultimately I carry the can for the actions of those within it. There will be an internal enquiry and heads may well roll. If they do, then mine will probably be the first to go. If that gives you any satisfaction then, under the circumstances, I can hardly blame you. But I do assure you that I am not seeking to pacify you or trying to protect my own position. I'd sincerely like to help."

Russell looked at him long and hard. He wasn't sure if he believed him or not and wasn't certain that he cared either way.

"Where is Nina now?" he asked eventually.

"She's waiting at a number for you to call her and tell her where you are. None of us guessed you'd turn up here."

"And Simpson?"

"On his way back from France; under escort."

"Will he stand trial?"

"C" pulled up a chair and sat opposite Russell at the table.

"In your own interests, Mr. Russell, we have to avoid a trial at all costs. You were instrumental in the murder of two men. The Russians are creating merry hell over it and the French are screaming for your blood. No amount of recorded confessions can change that. My whole department could resign tomorrow but it won't alter what you did. Even under the quite extraordinary mitigating circumstances, you would be found guilty."

Russell stared down into the glass he was holding, rolling it from side to side as though he were searching for some kind of solution at the bottom of the water.

"I'm not sure I care" he said softly. "I killed Gurevich; an innocent man. I *am* guilty. Nothing that can change that."

"That may be true for Alan Russell. But identities can change. These things can be arranged."

"Yes. At the touch of a computer key. Caswell told me."

"Then won't you let me help you?" asked "C" earnestly.

Russell slowly shook his head.

"You might be able to change my official face, Mr. 'C'. But I have to look at the real one every morning when I shave. It doesn't matter what you call him; it's the same man; the same life."

"Then it's the same life that was once worth something" countered

"C". "The same life that your wife wouldn't want to see thrown away needlessly."

Russell closed his eyes and let his chin fall forward to his chest.

"Maybe you're right" he sighed wearily. "I don't know if I care anymore. I'm too numb. I need time."

"Yes, of course you do. And we can give you that time. I have a car outside. We can take you to a safe-house. You'll find we look after our own."

Russell was taken aback.

"Your own? Oh no, Mr. 'C'. I'm not one of yours. I think I'd rather take my chances with the French than join your kind of brotherhood."

"C" didn't react to the insult.

"We're not all villains, you know" he said calmly. "Caswell was an exception. Some of us genuinely believe there's a job to be done and a good reason for doing it."

"Funny" said Russell cynically. "But I seem to have heard something similar already this evening."

He swallowed the last of his water and put the glass down on the table.

"And what about him?" he asked, nodding in the direction of the room across the hall. "What about Caswell - or whatever his bloody name really was?"

"His time is over, Mr. Russell. You've seen to that."

Russell shook his head. "No. I mean what about the fact that I just shot him?"

The other man shrugged. "People get careless cleaning guns. Accidents happen."

"My intention was to bring him to trial, you know - not to kill him" Russell told him dryly, not expecting to be believed. "And it *was* self-defence."

"I have no doubt of it. And I certainly don't intend pursuing the matter."

Russell's face registered genuine surprise. "Then am I free to go?"

"If you insist. But *where* will you go?"

It was a simple question, but one to which Russell had no answer. For the first time, he was struck by the awesome reality of his situation.

Until that moment, his one preoccupation had been to force a confrontation with Caswell, regardless of the consequences. But that was done and Caswell was no more. Now there was nothing; just a void. He knew in his heart that, as Alan Russell, it could only be a matter of time before he was arrested, extradited and convicted and, contrary to what he had said, he *did* care. Despite all he had undergone, the survival instinct had not been totally extinguished. But he was tired; desperately tired. He wanted rest. He wanted peace.

He looked across at the man opposite. The man who represented everything that had ruined his life and yet who now seemed to be offering the only possible route to safety and a new one. It was too much to take in.

"I need air" he said quietly. "I'd like to leave."

The other man nodded, pulled a card from his pocket and passed it across to Russell.

"Get in touch with me as soon as you feel able to" he said sympathetically. "And you will have to Mr. Russell. There's no other choice. Please don't leave it too late."

Russell rose and made his way out of the kitchen. As he stepped into the hall he stopped and turned.

"One question. How long were you waiting outside the room?"

"Long enough" came the calm reply.

"But it could have gone either way. He might have shot me.

"But he didn't."

Russell stared at him.

"And you'd have had one less problem to deal with either way, wouldn't you?"

"C" made no attempt to respond. Russell walked silently out of the house.

The air was cold and clammy as it drifted off the heath and was redolent with the fragrance of damp foliage and grass. Russell walked slowly down the driveway, the echo of his footsteps the only sound in the empty silence of the night. He stopped by the dustbin that stood next to the front gate. He pulled the card "C" had given him from his pocket and, lifting the lid of the bin, was about to throw it inside when he stopped. For a few moments he stared at it, pale in the orange reflection of the sodium street lamps. Then, quietly, he replaced the lid of the dustbin and slipped the card back into his pocket. He turned up the collar of his coat, and walked silently into the dark of the night to find a phone and call Nina.

End